THE EIGHTH CHANT SERIES

ÉLAN MARCHÉ
CHRISTOPHER WARMAN

This is a work of fiction. Names, characters, places, and incidents either are the product of the author's imagination or are used fictitiously. Any resemblance to actual persons, living or dead, events, or locales is entirely coincidental.

Copyright © 2025 by Christopher Warman & Élan Marché

All rights reserved.

The moral rights of the author have been asserted.

First paperback edition June 2025

Cover art by Ömer Burak Önal

Map art by Dewi Hargreaves

Vizen art by Coldwitch

ISBN 979-8-218-67012-2

ACKNOWLEDGEMENTS

There are too many people to thank and not enough words to thank them properly. But we will do our best.

This book would not have been possible without the support of our families and friends. And it would not be nearly as aesthetic without the contributions of talented artists like Ömer, who took our vision (and Élan's incredibly crappy pencil drawing) and brought it to life, Clara, who gave shape to the Royal Palace of Vizen (the setting to much of this book), and Dewi, who gave our audience (and ourselves) amazing maps to reference.

A huge shout out to Clara, Jay, Alex, and Rid for reading our words even when they were abysmal. If this book is in any way compelling, it is mostly thanks to them.

And thank YOU, our readers and community, who support us through thick or thin. Thank you for reading our words and finding meaning in them. We wouldn't be here without your support.

Sincerely,

Élan and Chris

Contents

PROLOGUE 1
I. An Exchange of Gifts 8
II. Cabbage Green 23
III. Pevine 28
IV. A Better Way to Live 48
V. Discernment 63
VI. Legacy 78
VII. Purpose 87
VIII. Spare Boots and Journeycakes 99
IX. Chanter's Cove 117
X. The Womb of the World 130
XI. Yulma 143
XII. Petar the Just 155
XIII. A Jar of Dirt and Maggots 173
XIV. Bunch of Scoundrels 181
XV. The Funeral Feast 203
XVI. The Door 211
XVII. The Red Road 218
XVIII. A Change in the Winds 232
XIX. Passed the City Gates 244
XX. A Sparring Partner 257
XXI. On the House 274
XXII. The Hearth Beneath the Palace 283
XXIII. The Appointment 294
XXIV. No Children Here 311

XXV.	A Chant of Life	325
XXVI.	Cloth, Dishes, Cutlery...	338
XXVII.	Ser Knott	349
XXVIII.	A Rescue in Vizen	360
XXIX.	Infiltrators	392
XXX.	A Toast	405
XXXI.	Free	425
XXXII.	A Dead Woman	438
XXXIII.	Searin	447
XXXIV.	Mother and Daughter	463
XXXV.	Vision	479
XXXVI.	The Stranger	488

EPILOGUE 501

PROLOGUE

    We made anchor four days ago, but only now have I found the time and fortitude to set upon parchment all that has transpired since our arrival in this new land. Most of what I had previously recorded was destroyed by sea water when we took on an unexpected squall toward the end of our two-month-long journey, so I will attempt to be concise in surmising what we have undergone and found since landing in this strange, unexplored, world.

    We left behind us, in Oderlen, a desolation so profound. It made our venturing out into treacherous seas to seek lands that were thought only myth seem like something not only sane but reasonable. That is how desperate my people had become. United in our escape were our brothers and sisters from northern Ummit, as well as our cousins from the Spellor Isles, though it is with great heartache that I must record that no one from the Isles has survived the voyage. There are rumors that the Sassars and the Yokes have undergone a similar journey, though we never spied any of their traitorous ships.

    Because my lineage placed me closest to the old gods, the other noble families tasked me with leading our fleet of twelve ships in this fool's errand—this suicidal escape attempt. For weeks, my hands shook for I have never led so many people. Can blood alone ever make one ready for such a thing? "You were born for this," they assured me. Even now, our quest answered, I am not so certain. But I kept up the appearance that I knew what I was doing, and I managed to see us safely to the other side of the world.

Prior to setting sail, I studied at length the logs of captains and explorers who had set out across the ocean before us. The longest of these voyages lasted one month, with the only sight of land being an occasional rocky island: black sharp stones jutting out of the water with no fertile soil to be found.

I prayed endlessly to Inla, the Sun, father to us all, that he would guide us and provide what we needed, for we carried only what we could. But I had already started feeling in my very soul that our gods had forsaken us. Our prayers had gone unanswered for years as we watched our people die, and our lands crumble beneath our feet. I prayed, and my words echoed off the ceiling of my cabin back at me as I imagined that the swaying of the ship upon the waves was the rocking of my mother's arms. I still miss her terribly.

The silence of our gods lasted countless sleepless nights as the days became weeks, and the weeks resolved into a month. One morning, we received a message from the Azurefyre, one of the ships in our fleet, that they were diverting north. The Tuska and the Swiftbelle planned to join it. On what they based this diversion, I did not know. But *they asked that I support them and order the rest of the ships to follow.*

It was my most critical test as a leader. Should I hear them out, or remain firm in my command and treat them as mutinous? I asked them to provide me with the basis for their plan. The message I received in return stated simply, "Inla and Umla will it so." I could not accept such an answer. In my anger, I burned the message and never returned a reply.

The next morning, the Azurefyre, the Tuska, and the Swiftbelle diverted from the fleet and headed north. The Sevar joined with them at the last moment, trailing behind the three larger ships. I commanded the remaining seven ships to stay the course eastward.

That mutiny was only the beginning of our tribulations. My biggest fear had been fights breaking out on the ships. Instead, I witnessed something worse: my people's spirits breaking. Sailors took their orders and labored with the passiveness of work mules. Passengers sat about silently, waiting for the provisions to run out. Hunger and hopelessness had taken hold of the fleet entirely. Where I once feared mutiny, I instead grew to fear that I may never see my people smile or laugh again.

And then death found us, thirty-four days into our voyage. It started with Myka. We don't know if it was hunger or illness that claimed her. All we could do was throw her body overboard and pray that no one else would contract what ailed her. Next was Stoll, two days later. The sailor fell off the mast and broke his neck, too weak to keep his grip as we were pelted by a sudden storm.

A fortnight after that, the Gimora vanished. It's unclear to me how an entire ship could disappear overnight in such a way. I had performed my usual checks before sunset after we had anchored for the evening, but when I awoke just before dawn, it was to a company of six ships rather than seven. The only clue as to the fate of the Gimora and the poor souls upon it were reports from the ship that had been closest to it of strange sounds in the night like the sudden cracking of wood and sightings of a few personal items floating in the dark waves.

I reached out to the remaining ships in our fleet to gauge their morale. Hunger, illness, and disillusionment were rampant. Speculation of what had occurred to the Gimora ranged from the reasonable (it was theorized that they too had decided to venture off along their own route or even that they had turned back) all the way to the outlandish, with whispered talk of sea monsters.

My thoughts traveled often to the four ships that had headed north. Had I made a mistake by not following them? Had I doomed my people to die of starvation? I prayed. Not to Inla, Umla, or any of the lesser gods. I prayed to the very people I was tasked to lead that they forgive me.

We cut our pittance of a ration in half and then in half once more. Those who could find leather boiled it or gnawed upon it wetly in a half-delirium. We lost several more to hunger, but, even for those of us who endured, starvation made ghosts of us all.

I knew that our true terror would be in running out of fresh water and I watched in powerless horror each day as our supply grew lower and lower. My ribs grew sharper and sharper beneath my graying skin. This time I prayed to no one, having neither the strength nor faith remaining to do so.

I cannot tell how much time passed between then and the morning when a sailor called out "land!" I am still in disbelief as I scribe this now. I stared out at the horizon with my spyglass, and I saw it: a sliver of green promise, a vision of life.

For the first time in many weeks, the passengers stood on the railing, chittering amongst themselves, their hunger soothed somewhat by hope. Salvation was but a day's journey away, and what a day it was! Many of the passengers remained on deck, as if the land would vanish if they looked away. I, too, found myself staring in the distance at the approaching phantom of a shore.

Soon, the silhouette of a great tower appeared through the ocean spray. An immense city greeted us as we neared land. I feared suddenly that we would be attacked or turned away. Surely the occupants of this city might take issue with the sudden arrival of seven... no six, boats of starving strangers from a distant land with no intention of leaving. It would not be strange.

What is strange, however... No, more than strange, utterly eerie, is that there doesn't seem to be anyone here.

The docks are deserted but for a few strangely built ships covered in moss and barnacles as if they haven't seen use in a lifetime.

After we docked, I sent out an exploratory party within the port city. A few hours later the party returned and confirmed that the city was indeed abandoned. Uncertainties and questions filled my mind (what caused the people here to abandon such a place? Was there illness?) but the passengers were growing unruly, eager to leave this ship for good and hungry to tear through each empty structure to plunder for any scraps that might be edible.

So, we disembarked into these mysterious ruins, seeking food and shelter.

The city is full of overgrown gardens that drip with fat, brightly colored fruits and gourds the likes of which none of us have ever seen. They appear as if they are edible although it will require more observation to make a full determination of such. We found the occasional goat, deer, and rabbit wandering about. Those who knew how, set out to trap them while others built cookfires. That's how our first two days in this new strange land were spent.

We ate our fill and rested. It felt miraculous to have warm meat in my belly. It was all I could ask for; it was all I could ever want. Though we do not have wine or ale, my people raised a toast to me for delivering them from our ruined world and into this one. They call me Claud, the Chosen by the gods. I do not have the heart to tell them that our gods have not followed us here. Our gods died in the old world.

Today, I lead a group to explore. They were most interested in claiming clothing and artifacts left in the empty habitations, but I found the state of those structures too disturbing. The artifacts inside were articles of daily life of the sort we all had left behind in order to journey here. Foreign, and yet immediately familiar at the same time. And they were lying about the way one might arrange a still life, the effect of which only deepened the impression that the original owners of these... homes... have simply vanished into thin air.

I had instead set my eye on the enormous tower at the center of it all. The tower is taller than any structure I have ever seen, taller than anything we had ever built in Oderlen, and much stranger, like a twisting vine aimed for the heavens. My escort followed me inside, but they were reluctant to climb the spire.

This was all right with me. Some things are best done alone.

I.

AN EXCHANGE OF GIFTS

It was an hour or so before daybreak and every soul in the Royal Palace of Vizen was asleep—all but Searin. She had been restless as of late, choosing to spend most nights and early mornings in the second courtyard of the palace, where the palace guard sparred and ran drills. She was the only one out there at this lonely hour. She wore her light armor of polished steel, the green sparrow crest of her family—the Royal Talessi—embossed upon its chest. Black wispy clouds floated about in the bruised sky. The morning air was brisk and rejuvenating, a pleasant contrast from this year's punishingly long rainy season.

Searin raised the lid from a large wooden crate tucked away at the back of the canopied armory. Inside was a wooden dummy in the shape of a man roughly her height with a chain tied around its neck. Several battle scars adorned its chest, limbs, and formless visage.

She hooked the chain to a pole and hoisted the practice dummy like a limp flag. The gentle breeze swayed it to and fro—the metal links clanked softly like atonal chimes. Searin stretched her arms and back and stared intensely at the featureless wooden soldier. Her instructors had told her to project onto the dummy the face of anyone who had wronged her, or anyone she disliked, perhaps to encourage her to be more ruthless. She had never needed the help, preferring the blankness. When her time came to command on the battlefield, it would make killing easier to picture blank wooden faces upon her enemies' heads. She would be the woodsman, and they her sea of lumber.

Searin unsheathed her sword, Vow, and cut the air to warm up her wrist and arm. The sword had been a gift from her uncle Clavio for her twelfth birthday. He had asked what her greatest wish was, and she had answered honestly: "*To be the high captain of the King's Guard.*" Clavio had looked at her disapproving father, King Petar, with a devious smile. Three days later, he had presented her with Vow, a beautiful longsword with a large blue-green opal crowning its pommel.

"*With this,*" her uncle had said, "*You vow to protect your family, forever and always.*"

Searin could barely lift the weapon when she had first received it, so she had begun her lessons with wooden practice swords, always keeping Vow in sight to remind herself of her ultimate goal. By age fifteen she could swing Vow as easily as any wooden sword, and now, at eighteen, she was as good a swordswoman as any knight in the palace, if not better.

She wasn't sentimental by any means, but her uncle Clavio held a special place in her heart for setting her down this path. It wasn't the destiny her family had wished for her—the eldest daughter of the king renouncing her inheritance in favor of knighthood—but the alternative was to become a queen. She shuddered at the thought.

Whoosh! The sword sliced the air. Searin lunged at the dummy, striking swiftly at its vital points. Had the dummy been of flesh and blood, it would have been dead before it could so much as gasp. Searin caught her breath and approached her victim, examining the points of impact. The slashes were neat and clean, as if they had been done with a scalpel rather than a longsword. She nodded in approval and even cracked a rare smile. She could have easily sliced through the dummy, but a sword was more than a tool for hacking off limbs. Why lop off an arm when an artery could be elegantly severed?

She practiced a few more forms before returning the dummy to its crate. The sun was starting to crest the palace walls, and the yard had begun to populate with guards. Many eyed her strangely, but that was nothing new. Like everyone else, they too expected her to be something she wasn't. She knew they all judged her for abdicating her throne to her younger sister, Arisa.

No one would understand her reasons, and she owed no one an explanation. Searin kept her chin raised as she walked back to the palace.

Servants scattered out of Searin's path as she climbed the stairs to her chambers where she could change into something appropriate for the breakfast table. Her mother wanted everyone to look 'nice and regal' for all shared meals, and she could not stand the sight of Searin in armor.

As she walked up the stairs, the muffled sound of voices reached her, followed by quiet giggling. Arriving at the second floor, she turned the corner and noticed a door there she had never used before. She wasn't sure where it led or if it was just some closet. Searin placed her ear against it. A sound came from within—a man and a woman speaking.

"It's not as if anyone will find out," the woman inside whispered. "And no one ever checks in here, anyway."

"Maybe I want them to find out," the man said, playfully raising his voice.

"Stop it! I don't like it when you speak that way." Searin recognized her sister Arisa's coy tone.

"Then why are you smiling?"

A quiet wet smacking was the only audible noise beyond the door. Kissing, Searin cringed. She halted her breathing—she knew she should leave, but curiosity kept her feet stamped to the floor.

"I don't think you understand the risk we run," Arisa cooed.

"But I do. If we are caught, I will be executed. And you... you will still be queen."

The door opened suddenly. Searin backed away before it could smack her on the side of the head. She watched in astonishment as her sister stormed out of the small coat closet, followed by Ser Dregor, the youngest of the King's Guards. The two stared at her wide-eyed for a few moments. Dregor, suddenly recalling his station, bowed slightly. "Princess Searin," he greeted. His long red curls reflected the fire from the wall sconces.

Searin sized up the knight, then coughed uncomfortably upon seeing his pants were unfastened. Dregor turned around quickly to rescue what was left of his dignity. "What were you doing in there?" Searin probed.

Arisa stepped in front of Dregor and smirked condescendingly.

"I should tell Father," Searin said unsurely. "This is no way for the future queen to behave. Especially not with an anointed knight of the King's Guard!" Dregor lowered his gaze to the floor. He seemed utterly terrified—Searin could end his life if she wished to.

"And to what end?" Arisa asked.

"The King's Guard is supposed to protect the queen-to-be, not let themselves be groped by her."

Arisa shook her head with a smile. Was this all some sort of joke to her? "Sweet Sister, I didn't take you for pious. Are you sure you wouldn't rather join the House of the Gods than the King's Guard?"

Searin furrowed her brow in that way her mother said made her look ugly. "Since you'll allow your knights to fondle you, perhaps when I'm high captain, you'll allow me to wring your neck."

Arisa sighed. "Come, Sister. Let's have a chat in my chambers." She turned to Dregor and dismissed him with, "As you were, Ser Dregor." To the man's credit, he bowed deeply and properly to them both, then calmly retreated down the stairs. How could her sister be so blind to the consequences of her actions? Dregor was mostly right—had they been caught, he would have been executed, while Arisa would remain unpunished, though her reign would be irreparably marred by scandal.

They reached Arisa's solar at the top of the western wing of the palace. Woven tapestries adorned each wall, showing scenes from histories and myths. A scene from the First Arrival was most prominent across the bed—their ancestor, Claud the Chosen, stepping foot onto the continent for the first time. Ursa and greatwolf pelts cushioned nearly every inch of the floor. Arisa removed her shoes before stepping in. Searin kept her boots on and did her best to avoid the pelts. Arisa walked to a small table next to a large shelf bursting with books and poured herself a cup of wine from a silver pitcher.

"A bit early to start drinking," Searin observed cooly.

"Never too early to sample a new vintage from Pallew," Arisa said, taking a pleased sip. "The vines there aren't as old as the ones in Sol Forne but it's a promising substitute considering the poor harvests being reported across the rest of Hovardom. Would you like a cup?"

"You're acting like a fool by flirting with one of Father's sworn knights. It's scandalous!"

A dark look poisoned Arisa's eyes. "But it was never scandalous when father spent most of our childhood fucking his way through the kingdom."

"Father is the king!"

"And I am to succeed him," Arisa raised her tone. "What makes you think you have any say in how I choose to conduct myself?"

Searin tried to steel herself, but something about her sister's tone always made venomous words spill out of her. "A king can hide a bastard far more easily than a queen can hide her swollen belly."

"Of course, I know that!"

"A queen must marry well in order to sire a lineage."

She expected Arisa to burst into flames and scream in her face—as she often did when broaching this topic. Instead, Arisa lowered her eyes and sat on a chair facing the northern windows. A cold breeze sent the curtains fluttering. "I've wrestled with who I must be since you left me this golden hand-me-down of a position. I've come to terms with my destiny and what I must do to achieve it."

Searin's lungs deflated. "Sister, I—"

"Don't worry. Our agreement still stands. When I am queen, you shall be high captain of my guard. I know I can trust you with my life... and my secrets." Arisa smiled as if she had won a game of cards. "Now, unless you're planning on sharing a drink with me, I would prefer to be left alone before breakfast."

Searin nodded. "Promise me you'll be careful."

Arisa sipped her wine and smiled brightly. "Aren't I always?"

Those words would have been convincing to anyone who didn't know Arisa. She had always been overly confident in herself. Where Searin's strength lay in her skill with the sword, Arisa's was in her charm and wit. She always knew what to say and when to say it. Even as children, it had felt like Arisa was always several steps ahead of everyone around her. That was how Searin knew her sister would make a better ruler for Hovardom than herself. The kingdom didn't need a queen that could only swing a sword. It needed a leader knowledgeable in histories, who had a knack for strategy and governance. It needed Arisa.

Tucked away at the opposite end of the palace was Searin's room. Anyone who wasn't aware of who this room belonged to would have mistaken it for a guard's meager dwelling. It was devoid of any tapestries or plaques. No rugs or pelts covered the cold stone floor. The only adornment to be found was a small painting of their family that her brother Hovard had made a few years ago. Searin didn't care much for art, but that messy, blotchy piece held a special place in her heart. It reminded her of simpler days before her personality had begun to chafe against the expectations of being a royal.

She removed her armor and replaced it with a plain yellow tunic and dark leggings. A newly filled washbasin had been placed near the window moments before, as it was still steaming. Searin did not enjoy having servants in her space but understood the necessity—even so, they had been instructed to wait until she was away to tidy her room or replace her water. She rinsed her face, dried it on a clean lavender-scented towel, and called it good. She didn't pay much attention to her looks these days. No matter how much or how little effort she took, her mother always seemed to find a fault—so why try at all?

Lately, however, the queen had become consumed by an obsessive interest in her young brother Hovard, who had turned eight last autumn. It was the same age Searin had started learning the ways of royalty. Unlike her younger siblings, Searin had failed spectacularly at every lesson, and soon her mother had surrendered all hope. As the youngest heir, Hovard would eventually become either a thane, a minister, or a knight. Searin had taken the latter path already—to her mother's chagrin—so Hovard was condemned to a life of politics.

"Good morning," Hovard greeted when Searin reached the breakfast room. The boy was draped in a scarlet-tinted fur cape, his hair intricately adorned with gold and diamond beads. The boy had the same pitch-black hair as Searin and Arisa—just like their father—though his was wavy instead of straight, like their mother's. He was posed near the hearth, as a painter rendered his likeness on an enormous canvas. As always, the boy was barefoot, though the painter had sketched him a fetching pair of red velvet boots.

The windows were open and the curtains drawn. Cold breezes sliced into the room that the roaring hearth could not dispel. Last week, the royal chemist had recommended morning air to ward off evil humors, and their mother seemed to have taken his words to the extreme.

"Good morning, Brother. Good morning, Mother," Searin greeted, taking her seat at the table across from Queen Altima. The woman seemed tired, as if she had not gotten a good night's sleep, but that wasn't something Searin would ever dare to mention.

The long breakfast table was covered in bowls of fresh grapes, plates of steaming sausages, and sliced boiled goose eggs. A basket of sweet bread was the table's centerpiece. A carafe of wine sat next to a warm teapot. As custom dictated, nothing was to be touched until the king joined the table, no matter how small or intimate the meal was.

"You look tired," the queen told Searin, not even sparing her a glance. The woman's attention was on the painter like a hawk on a mouse.

"Good morning everyone," Arisa chirped, entering the room with a confident swagger.

"Good morning Arisa!" Hovard replied, excitedly.

"Oh my! Stand still, little brother," Arisa said with feigned concern. She walked towards Hovard and slowly reached for his hair as if plucking a dangerous insect.

"What is it?" Hovard asked, wide-eyed and horrified.

"There's a... There's a..."

"A what?!"

"A... *me*!" Arisa yelled, messing up Hovard's neat hair.

"Stop it, Arisa!" the boy complained. "I'm trying to look princely."

Searin chuckled under her breath.

"Leave your brother alone!" their mother admonished sternly. "And must you be so loud at such an early hour?"

"Why shouldn't I be? Everyone is up and about already, it seems," Arisa said.

"Everyone besides Father," Searin corrected. "Where is he, anyway?"

"Right," Arisa agreed. "Where is the old man? I am famished."

"He was finishing his morning bath when I last saw him," the queen answered, distractedly. She stood and walked over to the painter. Tilting her head, the queen examined the work. The painter stood aside and lowered his gaze. "Does his forehead look too large?"

"I don't think so," Searin said.

"It's definitely taller than it ought to be," the queen nodded. "Fix it," she barked sternly to the painter.

"Of course, my queen," the painter replied, bowing deeply.

"Your uncle is at the palace," Queen Altima announced as she turned her attention to the table at last. Hovard followed her on tiptoes. "Uncle Clavio is here?" he exclaimed giddily, eyes bright with excitement.

"That's rather unexpected," Searin observed.

"Unexpected," the queen grumbled in agreement. "He arrived at dawn. What made him appear as such a spectral hour, uninvited and unannounced, is beyond me. But he is here, so we must entertain him." She picked a chalice from the table and reached for the wine carafe. Searin rose and grabbed the carafe first, pouring the light breakfast wine for her mother. *Looks like we're no longer waiting for Father*, Searin noted.

"I hope he brought presents," Hovard yelped.

"Uncle always brings us something good," Arisa agreed. The princess followed their mother's lead and picked up a chalice, holding it up for Searin to fill. Searin set the carafe on the table and took a seat. Arisa snorted at her sister's small act of protest as she filled her own cup.

"That man is such a showoff!" The queen shook her head and sipped her wine. "There's no end to his hubris, I tell you."

"Is that how my brother's wife speaks of me?"

Every head turned towards the doorway where Thane Clavio Talessi stood in his neat riding clothes, grinning like a fool. His long golden hair was neatly collected in a tail that reached the middle of his back. The only thing about him that stood out as unorderly was the shadow of a morning beard blemishing his complexion.

"Uncle Clavio!" Hovard exclaimed, running up to the man. Clavio wrapped his arms around the boy and scooped him up. "Hovard? Is that you? You are so big!" he marveled.

Searin stood and waited for Clavio to sit at the table before reassuming her seat. Arisa and the queen remained seated. "Searin, my dear!" Clavio called out. "What happened to your..." The man pointed at her head.

"She chopped it," the queen interjected. "Haven't you heard? She abdicated the throne, and now she lives her life as a man. Can you blame her? Men get to fight and travel the world, while we women stay put and warm their beds."

Searin's face flushed with anger and embarrassment. Every time she thought they had moved past their differences, the queen was there to remind her otherwise.

"Must we talk about such things at the breakfast table?" Arisa groaned.

"And a good morning to you, as well, niece," Clavio greeted with an appropriate bow.

"And to you, Uncle," Arisa nodded.

"And where might my brother be?" Clavio asked. "Still in bed, I presume?"

"Taking his morning bath, Mother was just saying," Arisa replied.

"What did you bring me, Uncle Clavio?" Hovard begged shamelessly.

Clavio set the boy down and rubbed his chin thoughtfully. "What did I bring you? Isn't my presence enough of a treat? Well, how about you go see for yourself? In my usual chambers, in the blue velvet sack on the bed. Go on."

Prince Hovard glanced at his mother for approval. The queen waved the boy away with a lazy hand. Hovard hugged their uncle, then sprinted out of the room, his bare feet pitter-pattering on the marble floor.

"And don't you two worry, I brought gifts for you as well. You'll find yours in the stables," Clavio directed at Arisa. "His name is Wick, and he's from an excellent line. A bit rowdy, and not yet saddle-trained, but he'll make a fine horse. And yours," he said to Searin, "is being placed in your chambers as we speak."

Searin grimaced at the thought of servants entering her space, but she donned a smile and nodded thankfully.

"Painter," Altima called out. "You are excused for the day."

The painter bowed deeply and thanked the queen. He quickly cleaned his brushes and set them away before leaving the room.

"Don't worry, Sister-queen," Clavio said, taking a seat at the table next to Arisa—where the king would have sat. "I haven't forgotten about you. I brought you a bottle of that northern scent you like."

"And Oma? Did she travel with you?"

"I'm afraid my wife has business to oversee at the estate. But she sends her love."

The queen grimaced. "A pity. She's my favorite thing about you. So, what is this visit really about, Clavio?" the she probed, all pretense dissipating from her voice.

"Am I not allowed to visit my family?"

"You've vanished from court for over two years, and now you appear unannounced? Don't blame me for finding this behavior unusual, even by your standards."

Clavio poured himself some wine from the carafe. He swirled the bright liquid in his chalice and then took a sip. "I would love to visit more often, but things in Perimat have been rather chaotic these past few years."

"We've heard about the rebellions," Arisa said.

"They're not a pretty thing to behold, but they are finally quelled thanks to the Blue Scarabs' intervention."

"Best not speak of the Scarabs around Father, unless you want a lecture on the importance of a unified royal militia, and whatnot," Arisa cautioned.

"He's still on that, I see." Clavio shook his head.

"I wonder how many rebellions one city must suffer before its leader is deposed," Queen Altima threatened.

Clavio smirked. "You wound me, my queen."

"That was the intent. So. You've quelled your little rebellion, *again*, but you still haven't answered my question. Why are you here? You don't expect me to believe you missed your brother."

"I have urgent matters to discuss with the king." Clavio faced Arisa, then added, "And my queen-to-be."

"But not me?" Altima arched an eyebrow.

Clavio curled his lips in a strained smile—he seemed to tire of Altima's line of questioning. "The King has called a meeting with the Azurats of Pallew that I am to participate in. Thanes Ronnan and Priscenda are unfortunately unable to attend due to illness, but they've sent their son in their stead. He is a two-day journey from Vizen as we speak."

"And you thought your queen was simply too dull headed to participate in these talks?"

"Never, I—"

"Mother, I'm sure Uncle Clavio didn't mean anything by it." Searin regretted her words instantly. Her mother's dark eyes skewered her.

"Even my children are against me."

"Altima, don't let a slip of my tongue ruin your morning," Clavio pleaded.

"*Altima?*" the woman fumed. "I am your queen, and you will address me as such!"

"I apologize, my queen." Clavio lowered his head and said nothing more, knowing that any word spoken would be used as fuel for the hearth of the queen's foul mood.

A scream from within the palace broke through their discomfort and made the hairs on Searin's neck rise. She stood and instinctively reached to her hip for the sword she had left in her room. Clavio rose abruptly and ran to investigate. The queen began to speak but Searin did not wait to hear what she might have said. She followed her uncle up the stairs and down the hall, toward the source of the commotion. A small crowd of servants had gathered around the large doors that led into the royal chambers. Two men carried out the limp body of a servant girl.

"What happened to her?" Clavio asked a pallid servant woman.

"Oh, Thane Clavio, what a tragedy!" the woman cried.

"Is she dead?" Searin asked.

The woman shook her head. "Lyza only passed out at the sight of all the—Oh, gods!" The woman's sobs became unbearable. Searin pushed ahead of the crowd and entered her father's chambers. Whatever was inside, she would see for herself.

The antechamber was strangely still. Searin could not remember the last time she had set foot here. Small changes had been made to the decor—new curtains and chairs—but for the most part, it was still the room she recalled from her childhood. As she walked towards the open door that led to the main chamber, something cracked beneath her foot. Shards of colored porcelain were scattered about. She picked up a shard, recognizing the likeness of a sparrow's head painted upon it.

"That was my gift for your brother," Clavio said. His eyes were wide, and his face paled in something resembling fear. "Perhaps it's best if you remain outside."

Searin set the porcelain bird head back on the floor, then continued forward. She pushed the door open further and walked inside. A copper tub occupied the middle of the room. Within its cold waters was a man with skin as pale as milk. Red blood spilled from his wrists into the dark water of the tub. A bloody dagger was lying on the floor. Searin did not immediately recognize her father.

King Petar's dull eyes stared ahead as if seeing something that wasn't there—a face as blank as her practice dummy's.

"Stay there, child." Clavio's voice reached her as if from a dream. Searin sat on the floor as the room spun around her. The king was dead. Her father was dead. It was impossible. It had happened.

Searin gave no resistance as she was helped to her feet and escorted out of the room. Somehow, she found herself back at the breakfast table, though her mother and sister were no longer there. The untouched spread had grown cold and congealed. Hunger felt foreign to her—who could feel hungry at a time like this? Searin needed something else, something familiar.

Though it was fully morning, the courtyard was empty besides the guards up on the ramparts. The news of her father's death had traveled fast throughout the palace. Searin retrieved the practice dummy from the chest and hung it. She hit it again and again with a practice sword, tears and sweat mingling across her face.

Yes, this felt right. This felt real.

II.

Cabbage Green

The woman placed a copper piece in Lyr's hand, then picked a head of cabbage from the stall. She held it for a moment, contemplating its weight and ripeness against the few remaining in the crate. They were each pathetic, shrunken, things. The woman finally settled on the one she had selected, nodding in thanks and proceeding to the next stall. Lyr leaned forward and adjusted the remaining cabbages in a feeble attempt to replicate plenty. Yenn, the stall's owner, always said that it made for a more attractive display if the crates looked full—the best produce at the top of the pile, of course. It was a piece of business advice that had been near-impossible to adhere to as of late.

Lyr had worked odd jobs at this market since she was a child, from tending stalls to sweeping the courtyard, and even alerting for pickpockets. Today she was working the cabbage stand. Yenn had business with some farmers in Urstway, the outer forecity. The shrewd woman had promised Lyr one copper for each ten she earned from selling the produce. It wouldn't be much, especially considering how slow the market was that morning and the lacking state of her wares, but it would be enough to pay for a hot meal for her and her mother.

Lyr sighed, banishing thoughts of her mother, focusing instead on putting on a cheery disposition to attract potential customers.

While the market was hardly a showy affair, little more than a disorganized maze of rickety wooden shacks and carts, it somehow felt like a home to Lyr. To the left of the cabbage stall was Dego, the spindly carrot and potato peddler, wearing a perennial disdain for his produce on his face. He was a sweet man otherwise and always paid well when Lyr tended his cart. Across from her were Shizem and Tyra, the always-tinkering husband and wife, busy showing off a new cast iron pan to an interested mother of three.

And next to them was Tommes' turnip cart, tended today by his sons Del and Saul. She had always thought Saul handsome, even when he was a gangly sprig of a boy running with her through the city streets. But the sudden maturity he wore with such ease at nineteen made Lyr's heart thrum at the sight of him. The broad young man caught her eyeing him and flashed a grin. Lyr couldn't help but smile back. Saul was wide-shouldered and tall like his father and brothers, but his features held his mother's Perimatese softness. The scruff of a dark beard did its best to conceal those features. Even so, the beard looked good on him, Lyr decided.

Saul touched his brother Del's shoulder and whispered something to him. Del turned to Lyr with a smirk, and she instantly felt her face flush. She quickly turned her attention to the cabbages, needlessly shifting them about as to look busy. In a few moments, Saul reached her and leaned forward across the stall.

"Cabbage-green doesn't suit you," he said coyly.

Lyr narrowed her eyes. "I didn't realize we were supposed to coordinate with the produce. Is that why your head looks like a turnip?"

Saul laughed and it was his turn to blush. He leaned forward and suddenly Lyr felt her lungs seize up. Saul whispered, "You've been granted passage."

"What?" Lyr asked, momentarily blindsided by the change of subject.

"The Free Kings."

The name alone was enough to choke any remaining air out of Lyr's chest. The existence of the mysterious group was a topic of much speculation in Vizen. Most people denied its existence while secretly wishing it was real. But Lyr didn't need to wish. A passing comment she had made to Saul a few weeks prior had led him to reveal that he knew where the Free Kings held their secret meetings. The moment she had learned of the group's definite existence, little more had occupied her mind.

"I spoke to their leaders, and they agreed to allow you to attend one of their meetings. Tonight."

"Tonight," Lyr repeated stupidly. "That's so soon."

"It is," Saul agreed. "But you may not get another opportunity."

This was so sudden. She needed time to think. The decision to associate with an organization whose rumored goals included the dismantling of the nobility and its enforcers could not be taken lightly. "Can I think about it?" she asked.

The question seemed to take Saul aback, but he agreed. "Come to me with your answer by the end of the market day." With that, Saul headed back to his family's turnip cart.

Lyr masked the turmoil within herself with a pleasant smile. This offer was a peach pit her curiosity was bound to choke on. But what harm could there be in attending only one meeting?

Amid her pondering, she almost didn't notice the man standing in front of her stall. Her smile instantly vanished at the sight of the city guard before her. The middle-aged man picked up a sad cabbage from the crate and examined it with disappointment. He placed his plunder in a sack, then moved on to the next stall.

Each stall, in turn, had a member of the city guard confiscating produce without paying for it. No one protested. Everyone knew better. It was something they were all used to. 'City guard tax,' was its unofficial name. Denying a guard would earn you a beating or, worse, an arrest for some infraction invented on the spot. This was just part of the daily routine now.

The guards had done much worse. She and Saul had both witnessed a haunting incident about a year before. A caravan of carriages was crossing the market from the southern gate. It had been unclear who occupied the carriages—for all Lyr knew, they were empty. A woman with a young girl in tow spilled a sack of potatoes and, while trying to quickly collect them, her daughter ran into the street after the few that had rolled into the path of the approaching convoy. The child froze, and the carriage at the front trampled unflinchingly over her little body. Lyr had never seen something so horrible. The procession carried on, each carriage running over the child, one after the other, rendering her body an unrecognizable mess.

The woman ran to the retinue of city guards flanking the procession. Lyr could not hear what was being said over the gasps and cries of the people nearby, but the woman's voice had been loud and strained, fully mad with grief. The guards had carried on, ignoring her pleas.

Lyr had stepped towards the scene, but Saul held her in place. It had angered her at the time but likely saved her life. That, she had recently come to learn, had been a tipping point for Saul—the moment he had actively sought out the Free Kings and joined them.

For Lyr, it had been the moment her discontent crossed irrevocably into a need for action.

By the time the fourth guard had robbed her stall, only one bruised head of cabbage remained. Yenn would expect Lyr to make up the cost of the stolen goods. She would be lucky if she made any coppers at all.

As the guards left the market, Lyr looked over at the turnip cart, and somehow Saul's eyes were already on her. She nodded at him, her decision made, and he nodded back, sealing her fate.

III.

PEVINE

Pevine—the place the True One forgot. Across the kingdom of Hovardom, almost all had heard of the Tragedy of Albadone, as it was now known. It had been seven years since those raging fires, yet Pevine had not returned to even a shadow of its former self. The smell of wood rot choked the air like a permanent curse. The buildings that lined its main circular street were a quilt of overlapping temporary repairs that had clearly endured for longer than practical. Even the brief offerings of sunlight interrupting the incessant rain and gusts of wind served only to accentuate the gloom of the surroundings by garish contrast.

And yet, the desperate inhabitants worked to salvage this wreckage with a hope that even the torrential rains couldn't quell.

Wooden posts sunken into the perennial mud that pooled on the streets alerted the locals of where the sludge was more than ankle-deep. Yona, the man who had taken charge of these repairs, led volunteers in demolishing damaged structures, salvaging anything that could be recycled for materials to build anew. But progress was slow, hindered by the need to split labor between the rebuilding efforts and tending flooded fields that refused to grow much of anything.

It hadn't always been like this—at least that's what the townsfolk often recounted in the one remaining nameless tavern over melancholy pints of ale or stale cider. Pevine used to be somewhere, a place where townsfolk and woodsfolk mingled in the sun-dappled morning market. It was no center of culture, like Rondhill or Sol Forne, but it had possessed a charm. There had been laughter here once, spilling through the night from its taverns. There had been celebrations, good-paying work, and thriving families then. Now, all that remained was Pevine—and Pevine was nothing short of a shithole.

And that made it the perfect place to be.

Weathered boards shifted precariously under Rovan's weight. It was best not to think of how fragile this section of roof was—what Rovan needed now was a dose of courage, not a reminder that he could crash beneath the rotted wooden planks if he wasn't attentive. None of them had any carpentry experience to speak of, but with the guidance of Yona and a few knowledgeable locals, Rovan and his companions had been slowly fixing some of the town's more dilapidated habitations. His friends had initially been reluctant at the prospect of repairing homes, but they had eventually convinced themselves that this was the best use of their time and able bodies.

"Head!"

The warning arrived a moment too late, and a wooden plank whacked Rovan on the back of the skull. "Watch it!" he exclaimed, rubbing his hand over the sting.

Iseo stood behind Rovan, looking abashed. The boy apologized and gingerly set the plank down. Iseo was nearly fifteen—old enough to be more aware of his surroundings. As quickly as the sting vanished, it was replaced by a pang of embarrassment as Rovan was reminded of his own carelessness at that age.

"Just be more careful," Rovan cautioned. Iseo nodded and returned to his work.

For the past few years, Rovan had been collecting strays. Not intentionally, mind you. They just seemed to insist on following him. There were four of them now—although Iseo, the boy whose house they were currently working to repair, seemed adamant about making himself a temporary fifth. Rovan couldn't fault the kid. There were few youths left in Pevine for the boy to spend time with, let alone ones his own age.

Fellen was the youngest of the group at thirteen, followed by nineteen-year-old Tieg. The twins, Terreck and Scintilla were twenty, only one year younger than Rovan.

It had been six years since Rovan left his home in Sol Forne, and yet, no amount of time or travel could put enough distance between the entitled, naive, brat he had been back then and who he was now. The best he could do was focus on the next good deed, to let it consume him for as long as possible. And, when that was completed, to focus wholly on locating the next.

This was why Pevine was so perfect. It offered a constant supply of need for Rovan to lose himself in. From the outside, he knew that this must look like the exact sort of noble heroism he had once aspired to. Perhaps that was what had enticed his 'strays' to follow him so adamantly. He dreaded the day when they would wake from their delusions about him and see him for what he really was—more haunted than hero, a wandering man trying desperately to pay the debts of his selfish boyhood.

They'll see through me eventually. The thought dogged Rovan and, though he would never admit it, it frightened him too.

His first two years alone had been grueling ones. One of the principles Rovan had established for himself early on was to neither request nor expect any form of compensation for the help he gave to others. "*The reward is the deed itself,*" he had grumbled to himself over the sounds of his aching stomach and a stale heel of scavenged bread, or, just as often, no food at all. That said, Rovan had been pleased to discover that, for the majority of people he aided, coin, food, or housing did typically follow gratitude.

When the twins started trailing him, Rovan had hoped the harshness of the lifestyle would be enough to dissuade them of their notion that he had anything to offer them. On hungry nights, although secretly grateful for the company, Rovan would remind them that stable homes, good-paying work, and reliable food were only a town away; that if they wanted to leave him, they'd likely be better off for it. For reasons Rovan still couldn't parse, this argument never took off with the members of his slowly growing party.

While he still thought of them as 'strays,' the word that came to him more often now was 'friends.' And that made the worry that they would eventually uncover his true nature a knife inching towards his heart.

Although Pevine stood only ten or so miles east of the kingdom's capital, Vizen, news, much like travelers, performers, and merchants, seemed to skip it entirely. No one here had heard of the recent fall of Sourrock, or even that the war in the Red Coast had been called to an end.

The Order of the Blue Scarab, whose presence had festered into a proper militia force, had formed limited outposts along the Red Road on the outskirts of the town, setting foot into Pevine very rarely. This was preferable—Rovan had no love for the Blue Scarabs or any other fringe group that imposed its will across the kingdom. "*Their justice is not my justice,*" someone had once told him.

Rovan became aware of the approaching sound of boots stomping through the mud towards the front of the house. He looked below to find Scintilla stopped just beneath the roof where he sat, her hands to her hips. Her thick hair was a black storm cloud above her soured face. "When were you going to tell me?" she fumed.

"Tell you what?" Rovan replied, though he knew exactly what she referred to.

"Don't play games with me."

Rovan sighed. "I didn't think it was my information to relay."

"And you're allowing this?" The young woman sounded on the verge of angry tears.

Rovan felt affronted that she would even ask such a question. "I know you still see Tieg as the boy we picked up in Rondhill three years ago, but he's at the cusp of manhood, and must be allowed to make up his own mind about his life."

Scintilla grunted—Rovan braced for her impenetrable stubbornness. "And where is he going?"

"You can ask him that yourself."

"If I come close to him, it'll be to smack him."

"Scintilla! You need to cool off," Rovan reprimanded. Scintilla spat and stomped away. Rovan shook his head. He had expected a negative reaction to the news but for her to act like Rovan should be holding the boy hostage wasn't like Scintilla at all. Rovan had always been clear that they were free to leave whenever. He'd even been pushy about it at times. But as much as he tried to convince himself they were a burden he would like to be free from, he knew this was exactly what he had been dreading.

Tieg had revealed to Rovan his intention to leave them nearly two months ago, just prior to their arrival in Pevine. But despite Rovan's probing, Tieg had refused to divulge his reasons for leaving or his destination and had made Rovan promise not to mention it to the group.

"Tieg's leaving? Where is he going?" Iseo asked.

Rovan let out a sigh. "Let's take a break. Would you mind taking a message to Tieg and Terreck?"

Iseo nodded, happy to be included.

"Tell them to meet at the tavern as soon as they can."

Rovan descended from the roof, then brushed his shaggy curls from his eyes. Iseo followed, then ran off to summon Tieg and Terreck, who were helping other townsfolk drain the mud from a particularly clogged alleyway near the town square.

Fellen would be napping at their 'base'—a rickety abandoned home that wavered loudly beneath each gust of wind. The teenager had injured his foot after crashing through the rotten floorboards of a home and into its basement cellar, so Rovan thought it best that Fellen stayed put to convalesce for a while. The boy had protested this suggestion, as all boys that age would have, but eventually acquiesced. Rovan entered the musty structure and called out, "Fellen!" There was no response. Maybe he was still sleeping. Rovan reached the small back room Fellen shared with Tieg.

A foot was visible through the slightly open door. The hairs on Rovan's neck raised in a cold panic. He pushed the door further, revealing Fellen spread out on the wooden floorboards. The stink of grog wafted insipidly through the small room emanating from the empty bottle that sat in the corner.

Rovan kicked Fellen's foot several times before the youngster stirred. "What?" Fellen asked, still dazed by sleep and drink.

"You're drunk," Rovan observed.

"So?"

Rovan let the slurred question hang in the air. Fellen rubbed his eyes. "It's not like there's anything else for me to do, is there? You've condemned me to rest. Ow! My head!" Fellen pressed onto his forehead with the palm of his hands.

Rovan should have known better than to leave Fellen to his own devices. Though the teenager was cheerful and eager to lend a hand, he also had an obsessive side. He could dive into his work as if the world around him ceased to exist. Often, Fellen ignored his friends' calls for supper, working, trance-like, deep into the night. Rovan suspected this behavior was adopted from childhood. The youngster didn't speak at all of the days before he had joined the group. What crumbs he let slip hinted that he had been laboring since he was little more than a toddler. Work was all he knew, and it should have been obvious to Rovan that ordering the boy to rest would feel like an unjust punishment.

Rovan rebuked himself for once again lacking as a leader and resolved to find Fellen a task that could be performed while sitting down. "We're calling a meeting," Rovan announced.

"Is this about Tieg leaving?"

Of course, Fellen knew already. The two shared this room, so it was obvious that they would have spoken on the matter. "Can you pretend you don't know about it? I don't want Scintilla to get more incensed than she already is."

"Scintilla doesn't know?" Fellen's hungover eyes widened in surprise.

"It seems like Tieg waited until today to tell her."

Fellen shook his head, then reached a hand out towards Rovan. Once on his feet, the boy grimaced. "Pained head, pained foot, pained life."

"One of those was self-inflicted," Rovan remarked. Fellen laughed through his aches.

The two slowly sloshed their way to the nameless tavern that crowned the town square, Fellen clinging to Rovan's shoulder for support the whole way. The tavern must have had a name at some point, but whatever it was had been erased by the fires, and the man that ran it—not its original owner—either out of respect or indifference, hadn't seen the need to supply it a new one. It had become a place for the remaining folk to gather and commiserate, a true temple to daily miseries which rendered its namelessness all the more appropriate. It was nothing like the Sol Fornian taverns Rovan remembered frequenting in his younger years—and for that, he was thankful. He enjoyed the lack of pretension here. These folk were honest and simple, albeit morose, making the tavern the perfect place to gather and plan.

When Rovan and Fellen entered, the others were already wading deeply through an argument. Terreck sat with his feet kicked up on a stool, consuming more space than he ought for such a scrawny build. His tabby, Trinket, sat on his lap purring softly. Like his cat, Terreck's eyes were lidded, as if he intended to escape from the meeting and into his dreams.

Iseo stood apart from the rest, staring at the floor before him. He nodded upon seeing Rovan, seemingly awaiting dismissal now that he had completed his task of gathering everyone. Rovan gestured instead to an empty chair. If the boy wanted to, he was free to stay. Iseo accepted sheepishly.

Tieg stood, arms folded at his chest, feigning a casual air though his tensed muscles told another story.

Scintilla paced before them all, her face darkened further by her mood. "—and your plan is what? To just wander around by yourself?" she demanded loudly.

"You couldn't wait for us?" Fellen asked, limping over to the stool and shoving Terreck's legs off of it before taking the seat. Trinket gazed needles at Fellen, angry at having his nap disturbed.

"Tieg is leaving!" Scintilla informed Fellen, still campaigning for her side.

"What!? That's terrible!" Fellen's feigned surprise was accented by his slight drunkenness.

"You all knew," Scintilla paused, "and didn't tell me?" Scintilla aimed this last angry question straight at Rovan.

"Everyone sit down," Rovan said, calmly.

Scintilla looked on the verge of tears. "This isn't right—"

"Sit down!" Rovan exclaimed, a bit too loudly. The few tavern patrons turned to look at him. Silence landed in the space like a brick. "Please," he added, more gently.

Tieg grunted and took a seat first. Scintilla kept her eyes on Rovan, but she did not budge. Rovan nodded encouragingly towards an empty chair, which she hesitantly accepted. "You all know how we do things. We will each have a chance to speak while everyone else remains seated. And we don't start a discussion until we're all present."

"Apparently everyone's already been having this discussion without me," Scintilla spat venomously.

"Scintilla!" Rovan admonished—but he regretted it immediately. "You're right and I'm sorry for that. But now we will all have a chance to speak, and that includes you." He paused. "Before I met any of you I was looking for purpose. I know each of you have your own reasons why you decided to join me in my wandering and help me at this, often thankless, sort of work—even if, I'll be honest, I can hardly imagine what they could be. We all share this bond now though, and I'm sure you all feel it too. You all are my home. I don't say this enough, but I love and care for each of you deeply, as if you were my kin."

Rovan watched their eyes. All of them, even Terreck's, were on him intently.

"A home we may be, but we are not a prison. Any of us may leave at any time, for whatever reason. Whether it's to find a greater purpose, or simply because you're bored by this way of living. We've supported each other all this time—I hope we can continue to do so, even in this." Rovan sipped in a slow breath, then slowly took a seat. He had said his piece, now it was time for one of the others to state their minds.

Tieg stood. "I am returning to my family home."

It was the one thing none of them had been prepared to hear.

It had taken weeks for the bruise on Tieg's swollen cheek to disappear when they had rescued him from his family three years before. No, 'family' was too kind a word for those monsters. Rovan was certain that back there was not where Tieg belonged.

Whatever insane reasons Tieg had for making this decision, Rovan would hear him out. But before he could say a word, Scintilla shot to her feet.

Oh, no.

"This is shit!" Scintilla shouted.

"Scintilla, please—" Rovan attempted, but Scintilla had become an unstoppable force.

"This doesn't make any sense!" she lamented. "What could ever make you want to return to those people? Who gave you this stupid idea?"

"This is my idea, Sin," Tieg said. "And if you'd just listen—"

"Well, then you're stupider than I could have ever imagined."

Rovan grimaced. These were his people—shouldn't he have seen this coming? Tieg had seemed happy with them, like he was finally moving on from the abuse of his past, not back to it. And Scintilla was stubborn but never this unreasonable.

Did he even know his friends at all? He really was a rotten excuse for a leader.

Rovan stood, but it was Terreck who spoke first. "Enough!" he shouted, his voice booming in the tavern. Trinket bounded from his lap with a chirp and sauntered across the hall. Rovan realized that the tavern patrons were staring at them. His ears burned, but it was not the time to show his embarrassment.

"Haven't you heard a single word Rovan said?" Terreck continued. "This is not how we handle things. Now, everyone settle down, and let's give Tieg a chance to explain himself."

Tieg crossed his arms and waited for Scintilla to take her seat. But Scintilla remained standing, challenging her twin brother with an arrow-pointed stare. Terreck returned it with a darkness that chilled Rovan. The siblings each had tempers, but where Scintilla's came as easily as lighting a torch, Terreck's burned slow and steady like a hearth. Scintilla grunted and left the tavern.

"Well," Tieg said, watching Scintilla leave, "that's that."

"We'll still hear you out if you've got anything you need to say," Terreck assured.

"I don't see the point. My mind is made up." With that, Tieg left the tavern too.

The rest sat in uncomfortable silence. Rovan shook his head, more at himself than anyone else. A real leader would have known what to do. But he was just a clueless young man who had stumbled into the role. Instead, he sat there, ruminating over his shortcomings until he felt a meek tap on his shoulder. He turned to find the lanky barkeep standing behind him, fidgeting with a damp rag.

Rovan summoned an apologetic smile. "Sorry for all the noise, Keith. We'll take our meeting elsewhere next time."

"It's not that," Keith said in a voice as thin as his dark hair. "The noise is rather welcome. Reminds me of the days when I tended my inn." His eyes glowed with reminiscence as a smile cracked through the wall of his gloom. Keith had owned the busiest inn in Pevine back in the town's heyday. It had, like much else of the town's spirit, burned to the ground during the riots. He had assumed ownership of this tavern only after its previous owners had failed to return a year after the fires.

"There's someone here that would like to speak with you," Keith said, waving the dripping rag towards a table at the other side of the tavern occupied by two women.

"This may not be the best time," Rovan replied.

"They've traveled quite a ways," Keith explained. "From Rondhill, they say. They require help with a rather sensitive task, and I thought of you."

"Me?"

"You and your friends, you're not from here. They need the assistance of someone more well-traveled than, well... any of us here."

Rovan glanced at the women. One of them met his gaze with intensity, while the other's head sagged in exhaustion. "I—" he began before Terreck placed his hand on Rovan's shoulder.

"Don't worry about Scintilla and Tieg," Terreck said. "Give them some time. We can resume our conversation later."

"Very well. Iseo, would you tell Yona I'll return to help with the roofing later?" Rovan instructed. Iseo nodded and headed to complete the task.

"And what should I do?" Fellen asked.

A very good question. Fellen needed a firm hand now more than ever. "You stay with me and Terreck as we see what these women want."

"Can I get a drink first?" Fellen grinned.

"Only if that drink is tea or water." Fellen did not like that answer, but someone had to rein him in. "Come." Rovan made his way across the room. Terreck helped Fellen up from his seat, and the two hobbled behind Rovan until they reached the bench across from the two women.

"A loud bunch aren't you?" the fairer woman admonished—the one that was gazing at Rovan moments earlier. More of a glare, Rovan now realized.

"We're not always so loud. Only when we're disagreeing." Rovan had hoped to ease the tension, but it seemed to have an adverse effect.

"This was a mistake," the woman said. "Come, Ashe."

As the two women got up, Rovan quickly stood with them and widened his arms apologetically. "We've had a long, hard week, and our manners seem to have run out the door. My name is Rovan, and these are Terreck and Fellen. The barkeep said you needed assistance with something. I can't guarantee we can help but we will at least hear you out and offer what we can."

The two women looked at one another for quite some time. Something passed between them, an unspoken decision, and eventually, they resumed their seats. Rovan sat after them, feeling some of the tension ease. "My name is Alanda, and this is Ashe," the woman introduced her olive-skinned companion.

"It's nice to meet you," Rovan nodded. "I heard you came all the way from Rondhill."

"Not an easy journey given the flooding we encountered. My father would have called our safe arrival here a blessing." Alanda smiled thoughtfully. The other woman, Ashe, took her hand and held it tenderly. Alanda seemed to gain some strength from that. "We are both from here, originally. Six, no seven, years ago—my, has it already been that long?—we fled after the riots broke out in the wake of the great fire. Pevine was a horrible place to be, and we were more than lucky to escape it with our lives. We started a new life in Rondhill, us, my sister, and Father. I never would have thought I'd see this place again, let alone still operating."

"You mean this tavern?" Fellen asked.

Alanda nodded morosely. "*The Rat's Nest*, it was called back then."

"Strange name for a tavern," Terreck interjected.

Alanda's smile reached her gray-blue eyes. "It was my mother's joke. She had originally purchased the place from a notorious crook. *'This place is nothing but a rat's nest'* my mother complained when faced with the tavern's slimy clientele. And the name stuck. We worked hard to change this place's reputation from a den of thieves to a respectable gathering place for townsfolk and woodsfolk alike." She let out a pained sigh. "I'm glad someone has been taking care of it, despite all that has befallen Pevine."

"Keith is a good man," Rovan said, glancing over at the barkeep, who was busy pouring some dark ale for himself.

"But we haven't come to reminisce. We are here for her," Alanda said, nodding towards the other woman. "Around the same time we had to flee Pevine, Ashe was forced to surrender her baby daughter, Sesha."

"Forced?" Terreck asked, sitting just slightly more upright. "What do you mean?"

Ashe lowered her head. Alanda's grip on the woman's hand grew firmer. "Her baby was dying after suffering terrible burns in the fires. Ashe had to leave Sesha behind with an enchantress in order to heal her."

"But why wait so long to come back?" Terreck interjected. "Why not return for your baby after she was healed by the enchantress?"

Alanda's thumb drew slow calming circles on the back of Ashe's trembling hand. "Leaving the baby was the cost of the healing. I'm not sure how much you know about enchanting, but costs can't be negotiated. There was nothing she could have done."

Rovan stiffened. "I know enough to understand that."

"So, you want us to find this baby?" Terreck asked.

"Not a baby. A child of six or seven now," Fellen corrected.

Ashe nodded her head, then raised her eyes to meet Rovan's. "Please," she said in the thinnest trickle of a voice—the sound of two silver pieces rubbing against each other.

Rovan folded his arms and held the silence between them all. Terreck and Fellen kept their eyes on him. "How do we know where to find her?" he asked. "Seven years is a long time."

Ashe reached into her pocket, then set a cracked gray stone on the table. It took but a glance for Rovan to recognize it as a spent runestone. "A runestone of *Guidance*?" he asked. Ashe nodded.

"We used it to find our way," Alanda explained. "Ashe held an image of her child all the way here until the runestone cracked. It's safe to assume the child is nearby."

"But you came from Rondhill. That could mean she's anywhere north of here, right?" Fellen said brusquely.

"More like north-west of here," Terreck corrected.

"Fellen does raise a good point," Rovan said. "That's a lot of ground to cover between here and the sea."

"And if she's in Vizen, forget about it!" Fellen exclaimed, swatting his hand. "I hear that place is a mess. Streets built upon streets, built upon dungeons, built upon grimy sewers..."

Ashe shook her head fervently. Alanda was her voice, "We know where she is. Right where she was left. At the Womb of the World."

The weight of the entire mountain was suddenly hovering over Rovan's head. A quick glance at his friends showed that they felt similarly, their eyes wide with unspoken fear. As the people in the area told it—mostly the woodsfolk who had been forced to abandon their homes in the forest—the Albadonian fires were a curse brought upon them by an evil enchantress. It was unclear why or how this woman supposedly had done such a thing, but as the story went, she now lived at the Womb of the World. The more superstitious woodsfolk avoided any place at the foot of the mountain where the evil black earth could be found.

So, this woman hadn't left her baby with just any enchantress but the crazy one that had delivered doom to an entire region. Just his luck.

"I ain't going nowhere near that cursed mountain," Fellen said as if a decision had already been made.

"Why would you take your baby to such a place?" Terreck asked, pragmatic as always.

"At the time, all other healers had been forcibly removed from every town surrounding Albadone and taken to Vizen. The city was then locked down. To this day I wonder what made the royals do such a thing, but it left Ashe with very few options. It was either leave Sesha up there with the enchantress, Mother Adriel, or watch the baby die."

Ashe sighed deeply but held Rovan's gaze as if challenging him to judge her decision. "Mother Adriel," Fellen said. "That's her, ain't it? The one what caused the fires?"

The women both turned to Fellen in confusion. "No," Alanda said. "The fires were caused by all the digging in the forest. I would know, I served many of those workers at this very tavern. Mother Adriel is just an enchantress."

Fellen squinted as if that story didn't quite add up. Rovan, however, was more inclined to believe this woman's firsthand account. He had seen the brutal power of enchantments gone wrong, but he wasn't convinced that burning an ancient forest was an aim any enchantress would reasonably have.

"If it was part of the cost or whatever, won't you be going against your word by finding her?" Terreck asked.

Alanda and Ashe exchanged an uncomfortable glance. "Ashe felt now was the right time."

"How?" Rovan prodded.

"She just... does. It's hard to explain."

Rovan looked at Ashe and, this time, the woman didn't shrink from his gaze.

"Paid... enough now. I know." That same thin voice was barely a whisper, but it did not falter.

"We don't have much coin—" Alanda began to say before Rovan interrupted her with a raised hand. "We are currently having some trouble in our group, as you may have overheard," Rovan explained. "Added to the fact that we're already quite busy helping rebuild this town."

Ashe sighed in defeat. "I see. We'll just have to find her on our own, then," Alanda said.

"I didn't say we wouldn't do it." Rovan backtracked. While compelling, the women's request was not an easy one. "We just need some time to think about it," he said, pushing his shaggy hair behind his ears.

"We wouldn't ask you to rush into anything," Alanda said.

"Very well." Rovan stood. "If you need a place to stay, just speak to Keith at the bar. He will find room for you.

"Must be strange for you, since this was your tavern," Terreck deadpanned.

Alanda smiled softly. "Quite strange," she replied.

Rovan smiled politely. "We will return to you once we've made up our minds."

The two women remained seated. There was a subtle defeat behind their eyes, as if they expected Rovan to refuse their request. In truth, Rovan was full of reservations. He did not feel the timing was right, with Tieg leaving the group soon. Also, there was Fellen's injury and the fact that some of them seemed to have been swept up by the rumors of a powerful, evil enchantress living on the great mountain. This quest would be a hard sell. But then he caught a glimpse of the two women quietly comforting each other as he walked out of the tavern and the sight left a chink in the armor of his resolve.

Could he really bring himself to deny this request? He would think about it, though part of him knew his mind was already made up.

IV.

A Better Way to Live

Their squalor was all his fault—her father, the coward.

Lyr kept thoughts of her father from sinking their claws too deeply into her mind, though they were always there, waiting to toy with the last strands of hope Lyr desperately clung to. Hope was all she had—hope for a better life, not just for herself and her mother, but for all inhabitants of Vizen, this blasted capital of Hovardom. Tonight, that hope would be her compass.

Cold night air invaded the small home through the cracks in the wooden slatted walls. Lyr pulled her wool blanket up to her chin. Even wearing her day shift and boots under the blanket, it was too cold in the shabby, single-room structure. A quivering sigh from the other side of the space indicated that Elga, Lyr's mother, felt the same. This spring had been a continuation of winter rather than a season of respite, and their shabby dwelling was hardly up to the task.

Lyr slowed her breathing to better hear the sounds of the outside street. At this time of night, the Pleasants—the ironic name of the shanty town she inhabited—would be bereft of people beyond the occasional city guard patrol, stumbling drunkard, or those up to no good. And what would that make her when she crept from her home into the streets tonight...

Up to no good, of course.

The sound was feeble, but she had been listening for it: two pulsing whistles, followed by a third longer one—just as Saul had described. The three whistles repeated, and now she was certain that this was the signal. Slowly, she removed the blanket from her body and rose from her cot. Like all the neighboring structures, their tiny home had been built over the wobbly cobblestone street, so there were no creaky floorboards to give her away like there had been in her childhood home.

Lyr spared a glance at her still-sleeping mother. The shivering woman's hair was a tangled mess that seemed to have taken root in her secondhand bedding. Lyr placed her blanket gently over her mother before leaving.

The cold outside matched the cold inside exactly. It was dangerous to light a fire within such a small dwelling, and even more dangerous to keep such a fire lit overnight. Last year, her friend Kalli had been swallowed by a roaring blaze along with the rest of her home and family—a grim reminder of the reason for their abundance of care. It had taken almost all of the inhabitants of the Pleasants working together to ensure the fire did not spread further. Two other homes had been destroyed, but only Kalli and her family were killed.

There was a certain irony to the situation since the royals claimed they had brought these very people to Vizen to keep them safe after the Albadonian fires. The Pleasants had another, perhaps more apt, name—the Healers. The inhabitants of the neighborhood were, in great part, healers and chemists who had been forcibly removed from the neighboring towns and villages of Albadone in the wake of the fires and subsequent riots. The official order stated that the king had collected them here to keep them safe until the period of unrest was settled. Then he would disperse them back to their respective towns.

Six years had come and gone, and they were all still detained here—for what reason or for how much longer, nobody truly knew. Stranger yet was the fact that the inhabitants of the city didn't seem to care or even remember that there had been fires at all.

"Are you ready?" Saul's voice startled her, returning her to the frigid present. Lyr turned to face the tall young man.

"In all honesty, not really," Lyr admitted, pulling her cloak over her head to match Saul's concealment.

"It's all right," Saul said with a grin. "You'll fit right in."

"That's not what worries me. I..." Lyr trailed off for a moment, scanning through the list of concerns that suddenly flooded her mind. "I've never done anything like this. If my mother finds out—"

"She doesn't have to. Not yet at least." Saul's calloused worker's hand gently grabbed hold of hers. Lyr thanked the darkness of the street for concealing the redness that bloomed on her cheeks. "Do you trust me?" he asked.

What a question to thrust upon her. It didn't take much reaching to find that she did trust Saul. More than most people in her life. Truth be told, besides her mother and him, she didn't have anyone else.

She nodded, and he smiled. "Let's be on our way, then," he said. "We're already late."

Saul led her through the quiet streets of Vizen. At first, Lyr struggled to keep up with his wide gait, but she soon matched his step. The cold night air numbed her cheeks, but the quick pace helped keep her warm. She had never been out this late before. Besides their muffled steps on the uneven cobblestones, the city was silent. In the distance, one could barely make out the sounds of a cat in heat meowing wildly and a few barking dogs.

Saul hooked an abrupt left into an area Lyr did not immediately recognize. The maze-like streets snaked inwardly like entrails, the tall habitations looming overhead, leering at them with dark, judging, window-eyes. The street seemed to stretch on for an eternity until it unexpectedly widened into an internal courtyard. At the far side of the yard, a candle-lit shrine glowed ominously.

A small mound near the shrine shifted, revealing itself to be a person cocooned in dark robes. They faced Lyr with eyes that sparkled beneath their hood in the candlelight.

Saul grabbed Lyr's hand and pulled her into an alleyway.

"Ignore the Marked," Saul whispered. "They're bad luck."

Lyr shot a pointed glare at him before he caught himself. "Sorry, I didn't mean—"

She put a hand up to stop him. They were in a hurry.

"We're almost there," he said, quickening his pace.

They eventually reached a nearly pitch-black dead end. Several wooden crates lined the wall in front of them. "Grab the other side," Saul whispered, as he moved to one end of the largest crate. Lyr obeyed, helping Saul drag the crate away from the wall. From the preciseness of it, one would have easily believed Lyr had done this before, all the while her heart was threatening to frog-leap out of her throat.

Removing the crate revealed a small hole in the wall. *He doesn't expect me to crawl in there, does he?*

"In there," Saul pointed.

Great. Lyr sighed and did as she was told, crouching and shoving her legs into the small opening. To her surprise, the space opened up and stretched further down into the earth. How much further, though?

Sensing her apprehension, Saul added, "Don't worry. It's only a small drop."

Lyr took a deep breath, as if she was readying herself to dive underwater, and plunged into the hole. As Saul had said, the drop was only a couple of feet, though the enveloping blackness of the space she found herself in made it feel much steeper. Saul landed behind her and tugged on a rope that was affixed to the crate above, concealing the opening. The bit of light from the moon and stars that had been trickling into the space was now completely dissolved.

Lyr felt Saul grab her hand. "Hold onto me. I know the way."

They trudged through the impenetrable blackness until the steady voice of a man broke through the silence. Orange candlelight spilled through cracks in the slatted walls. Saul led her into a dimly lit room packed with dozens of men and women. It was a larger group than Lyr had expected to see. Everyone's hood was down to reveal their faces. Lyr scanned the crowd, recognizing a few of them as neighbors or acquaintances from the market, while others she had never seen before. She stiffened upon realizing that a large man standing towards the back was a member of the city guard. Saul must have felt her tension through her hand. He looked to the man and gave her hand a gentle squeeze to reassure her everything was fine.

A man in his later years with a shiny bald head and a white beard like a cluster of summer clouds stood atop a squat wooden box in the middle of the room. He was listening intently to an exchange between members of the audience.

"Well, what is stopping us from breaking into the shuttered bakery and using their ovens?" someone suggested. "Horace says the ovens are built into the place. The only thing blocking the way are a few planks of wood and some nails. We could all pitch in to buy flour—"

"The only reason we've been able to accomplish anything at all is because we only operate in secret," a woman said. "Breaking into a place and setting up shop there would be begging for the city guard to finally confirm the Free Kings exist."

"This is a transportation problem, then. The nearest bakery is in the Azlaid District. We need to find a way to get bread to the Pleasants on a daily basis. Those of us who have the time and the carts to do so should take on that responsibility."

"It makes no sense! Why would my rent have gone up?" a man, who could have only been the displaced baker, sobbed. "The Pleasants keep getting shittier, and gods know there hadn't been any improvements made to the building in decades, at least none that I hadn't done myself."

"Soon, there won't be any businesses left in the district at all," someone sympathized.

"That's exactly what the royals want!"

There was a blood-thirsty edge to the crowd now. "Peace, neighbors!" the old man on the makeshift stage called out. "We can work ourselves up into a panic, imagining that the royals want to clear every business out of the Pleasants. But what they definitely want is for us to be at each other's throat like this, feeling desperate and hopeless. Now is the time for us to come together as neighbors and keep people fed while we find a more permanent solution."

The words appeared to have a soothing effect on everyone but the baker, who remained visibly distraught. The conversation steered itself back to the logistics of transporting carts of bread from Azlaid to the Pleasants despite the stagnant construction that choked the only connecting road between the two.

"I thought you'd never make it," someone behind Lyr whispered.

"But we're here now," Saul replied quietly.

"*We?*" The red-headed young man noticed Lyr standing silently next to Saul. "Who is this?"

"Hush!" Saul admonished. "After."

The two returned their attention to the speaker, though Lyr felt dread slowly creeping into her chest. Had Saul not informed his companions of her attendance at their secret meeting? Would they think her unworthy of their group or, worse, suspect her of being a spy? If they did suspect her, it was plausible that she wouldn't be leaving this meeting alive. Suddenly, Lyr was greatly aware of how easy it would be for them to make her disappear. Nobody but Saul knew she was there.

When the transportation of bread to the Pleasants had been arranged, the speaker concluded the meeting with,

"We outnumber the nobles one thousand to one. Let the hands that toil this land also control it."

"This is our land," the crowd repeated in unison.

The air was imbued with electricity. The man descended from his makeshift stage and the audience began retrieving loose produce and baked goods from pockets, skirts, and sacks and passing them to the front of the stage. It didn't take long to fill a pair of crates with the stuff.

"What is all of this?" Lyr asked wide-eyed. She hadn't seen that much food in quite some time.

"After each meeting, those with the means donate what they can spare, and those in need take what they require to sustain themselves until the next meeting." Saul smiled. "It's beautiful, really. Sometimes you're the giver, and sometimes you're the taker. But between us all, we usually have enough to keep everyone fed. Even considering how scarce food is nowadays."

The crowd dispersed soon after, back into the dark hallways of this strange, dilapidated tunnel system. The crates at the front of the room were empty besides a small loaf of bread and three small red potatoes. "Take them," Saul suggested.

"I couldn't." It didn't feel right to take from strangers who knew nothing about her.

"Really," Saul insisted. "If you don't take them, I will."

Lyr's empty stomach was a growling reminder of her scant pay that day. She reached into the crate and took the meager bounty.

"Brother Atrew!" Saul greeted.

The man who had addressed the crowd earlier approached them. "Brother Saul!"

"A great discussion as always," Saul said.

Atrew nodded and smiled. "You would have enjoyed it more had you been here for all of it. We started off with a stimulating debate on theories of taxation. How do I find you tonight?"

"Tired. It was a long day at the market."

"Good man. I hope your father has been well." Though Atrew kept the pleasantries going, he had directed his attention to Lyr, who was suddenly very aware of the produce she still held in her hands.

"This is Lyr," Saul introduced, sensing the unspoken question.

"Lyr?" Atrew moved in closer to get a better look at her. "That's a woodsfolk name. Albadonian?"

"Yes, sir," Lyr replied. "Though, my family is from Pevine."

Atrew smiled congenially. "Of course. Lyr. The True One blesses us with neighbors no matter where life takes us." Lyr found herself smiling at the old man's words. It had been a long time since she had heard that particular woodsfolk saying. "I am Atrew, originally from the northern woods, though I have not been back in quite some time. A lifetime ago, I worked as an errant priest, a neighbor to all, spreading the True One's goodwill across the world."

Lyr had fond memories of visiting the True One's temple in Pevine as a child. She remembered how High Priest Yvan used to give her and all the other children honeycomb slices after temple visits. She had never heard of such a thing as an errant priest.

The man continued, "After many years spent spreading the True One's kindness as far north as Yiwwe, in Tuskisk,

I returned to Hovardom because I observed in my travels a better way to live and run a kingdom. A way that does not involve royals. A way that brings back the order that the True One intended: where every man and woman owns every aspect of their work."

Lyr found herself grinning. It was strange to hear her heart's desire spoken so plainly. "So, you started the Free Kings?"

"With much help from others that saw the world as I do." Recognition flitted over Atrew's eyes. "Lyr?" He pondered as he squinted his eyes. "I think I knew your father. The chemist."

Lyr took an involuntary step back, recoiling from that word—*father*.

A tall, hooded figure neared them. A long sword bulged beneath the newcomer's robe. "Time to go," they said in a hushed voice.

"It is getting quite late." Atrew bowed. "We'll have to pick this up some other time. I hope to see you at another of our meetings, Sister Lyr. Punctually, if you can." That last, Atrew directed at Saul.

Lyr smiled uncomfortably and returned the bow.

The tall figure took Atrew's arm and escorted him into the darkness. Lyr pocketed her bread and potatoes, realizing that only she and Saul still lingered in the space. Only one candle remained lit, which Saul quickly blew out. He did not lead her back the same way they had come. Instead, he took her down an opposite path, through a labyrinth of twisting and turning cinder-black hallways and stairways. Light returned as they exited into a torch-lit cemetery. Saul raised his hood over his head. Lyr did the same.

Lyr's mind was abuzz with what she had witnessed. The Free Kings were no longer just a rumor spoken about in hushed tones around a crude tavern's hearth. They were a reality, and she had just attended one of their meetings—and met their leader. She had seen firsthand how the royals could strip families of their livelihoods, but she had never seen peasants come together to provide for each other like this. Until now. Saul was right—it *was* beautiful. And she had been invited to return, but would that be wise? She had much to consider, though she had not yet shaken off the strangeness of the experience—the strangeness of Atrew mentioning her father.

"Are you going to tell me who the girl is?" A hooded man sat on a cracked tombstone with his arms crossed. This was the same person that had approached them during the meeting, Lyr gathered.

"She's right here," Saul replied. "Why don't you ask her yourself?"

"Very well." The man hopped off the tombstone. "Who are you, and who are you spying for?"

"My name is Lyr, and you're very rude."

"Happy now, Rob?" Saul asked.

"Happy? Must I remind you of the risk we're taking? You can't just involve some unvetted girl on a whim. I hear the royals train all sorts of people to be their spies, even girls. Reveal yourself, before I do it for you!"

"Oh, shut it!" Saul snapped. "Lyr lives in the Pleasants, near the market. We've been friends since before I even met you."

"And what is she doing here?" Rob rebutted.

"I was invited," Lyr deadpanned. "Has asking people if they're spies actually helped you catch any? Seems a bit unsubtle."

Rob huffed. Saul turned to Lyr and said, "Forgive his lack of manners. We have to be cautious of people we don't know."

"It's all right," Lyr replied. A part of her still wondered how far they'd take such caution if they truly suspected her.

"Shhh!" Rob shushed loudly, lifting his hand. Lyr and Saul quieted and listened to the surrounding night. The clicking of boots reverberated across the empty streets. "City guard!" Rob bolted on feathered feet.

Saul gripped Lyr's arm. "We have to go!" They took the long way, careful to avoid the main streets. Lyr was entirely lost, but she trusted that Saul could find the way back to her home. Abruptly, Saul pulled her into a dark alleyway and held a finger to his mouth signaling for her to remain silent. Two men's voices echoed in the night.

"Told ya so!" one said.

"No, you didn't!" the other spat onto the ground. "You said she had four nipples, but she only has three."

"You just didn't look well enough."

"I looked plenty good. You're just inventing stories again. Didn't think I'd actually find her and bed her, eh?"

The two guards passed the alleyway, unaware of their presence within its darkness. Lyr and Saul shared an amused glance, holding in their laughter.

"I'm telling you," the man continued. "You just didn't—hey!"

A *thud* echoed through the street. Saul and Lyr peeked their heads out of the alleyway. A man lay on the ground, rubbing his smarting back. His body was covered in rags that at some point must have been a cloak or coat. The two guards towered over him.

"Watch where you're going, you wretch!" one of the guards called out, landing a kick to the man's side.

The man covered his head with his bony hands. "Sorry, so sorry," he uttered.

"I think he did it on purpose," the other guard said giddily.

"Did he, now?" the other replied. "If that's the case..." The guard stomped on the man's side. The other guard joined in, raining kicks and stomps on their poor, yelping, victim.

Lyr stared at the appalling scene in frozen awe. She only noticed Saul approaching the guards when it was too late. He hit one on the back of the head with a large plank of wood he had picked up from somewhere on the street. The guard fell to the ground like a limp ham. The other guard turned to face Saul, only to receive a swing of the plank to the face. The man's nose cracked wetly, and blood ran down his chin. He gargled a sob, then received a smack of the plank to the side of the head. He landed in a pitiful display atop his companion.

Saul held out his hand and helped the poor man to his feet. "Thank you," the man said, catching his breath.

"They patrol here often. You should stay out of this area for a while," Saul said. The man nodded and limped away into the night.

Saul returned to Lyr. "Come on," he urged, resuming their speedy walk home. Lyr eyed his back. She had heard him tell stories of scuffs with the city guard. Witnessing it was more intense than she had imagined. The reality of the people she was choosing to associate with was setting in. But the city guard was just another means the royals used to keep people like her in their place. And she wouldn't resign herself to a life of submission.

"Will you be back?" Saul asked, perhaps fearing he had scared her away.

"I think so," Lyr replied.

"Good. I would love to see you again."

"You see me almost every day."

Beneath his shifting hood, Lyr could tell Saul was smiling.

Soon, Lyr began to recognize her surroundings. Her modest home looked like a muddy chunk of stone tossed around in hay. Before she could reach the door, to her surprise, Saul hugged her tightly. Lyr hugged him back—the wonderful smells of the market were an indelible part of him. "Come to my booth tomorrow," he whispered. "I'll try to save you something good."

She smiled and released the hug. "I will."

Lyr quietly pulled open the wooden door of her home and removed her boots, carefully setting them on the stone floor. After setting the loaf and potatoes on their small table, she slid into her frigid bed and exhaled deeply, too tired to disrobe. Daylight was only a couple of hours away—she knew she should get some sleep, but memories of the night's events kept her awake and abuzz. But it wasn't the illegal meeting she had attended that flooded her thoughts: it was Saul. The wide-shouldered, handsome, young man had not hesitated to act when he saw a stranger being abused. She couldn't help the warmth spreading across her chest.

"If you know what's best for you, you'll stay away from that boy." Her mother's words deflated Lyr's fancies. Lyr turned to face the bed at the other side of the room, but all she could see was darkness. "Promise me, Lyr. Promise me you won't go back there."

"Go back where?" She feared that her mother was about to lecture her on the risks of sneaking around at night with boys.

"Those people are nothing but trouble. They want to start a war between us and the royals. How do you imagine that would go? More a slaughter than a war. Please, promise me you will have no part of it."

Lyr was stunned. Her mind filtered through a selection of denials she could offer but, after taking too long to pick one, "How did you know?" was all that came out.

No answer came from the darkness.

V.

Discernment

A sudden downpour had made continuing their work on the roofs impossible. Rovan softened a small heel of stale bread in a bowl of thin broth. Iseo and Fellen sat across from him, each with their own steaming bowl in hand. Normally, the two younger boys joked and teased one another, but today there was none of that. With no work to occupy them, dwelling on the fight between Scintilla and Tieg was all they had to fill the void of time. But the conversation between the two had taken a path Rovan felt he needed to interrupt.

"I hope you two understand that I would never force any of you to do anything against your will or prevent you from doing something you wished."

The two boys looked up at him as if they hadn't realized he was there. "I'd kick your backside before I'd let you boss me around," Fellen said, seemingly unaffected by Rovan's words. Iseo chuckled.

"It doesn't make me happy to see Tieg leave," Rovan continued. "But he has made up his mind. There's nothing I can do."

"We know that," Fellen said. "It's just..."

Iseo gently touched the boy's shoulder—this was the first time Rovan had ever seen such a tender action from him—then said, "I hope you don't think this is too bold of me, but from what I've heard—".

"Go on," Rovan invited.

"Tieg's family gave him plenty of reasons to never return. You say you won't use force but... But there's really nothing else you could try?" By the time Iseo finished, his face was flushed. It was the most Rovan had heard him speak. The local boy seemed perpetually nervous around him, no doubt resulting from a combination of their age difference and Rovan's role within the group.

Rovan looked at his hands. Perhaps there was a way he could make his thoughts clear to Tieg, but this was an issue of family. What could he possibly know about family? His sister had done her best to support him on her own and he had made her life miserable for it. Fellen wouldn't understand either. The boy's parents were still alive, Rovan assumed, although from what he knew, they hadn't been a part of his life. Scintilla and Terreck had grown up in an orphanage that was later attacked by a *reaverlord*—they were the sole survivors of that slaughter. No, family wasn't a subject any of their group had much right to lecture on.

In contrast with the others, Tieg reminisced often about the past, although his recollections were seldom positive—the way his parents forced him and his brother to work their decrepit strip of land, all while berating and tormenting them as if they were lower than dirt.

Rovan did not understand Tieg's urge to return to those people. Part of him wanted to call Tieg a fool—a desperate child. Didn't he have it good here? Weren't they enough for him? But ultimately, it was not his choice to make. The importance of respecting choice was a lesson Rovan had learned at a great cost and one that he often imparted to his friends.

He tilted the bowl into his mouth. The broth wasn't flavorful, but it was at least warm. He heard the sound of footsteps approaching the main hall of the tavern. Ashe and Alanda entered through the door next to the bar. He did not wish to face the two women until his mind was fully settled, so he stood and bid farewell to the two younger boys. "I'm going to see if there's any work that needs doing that doesn't require me to sit out in the rain."

"Are you sure?" Fellen asked. "You could use a wash."

Rovan chuckled and exited the tavern. The rain had slowed to a gentle pitter-patter on the muddy streets. He sloshed aimlessly through the town, glancing up at the dilapidated buildings. Once, there had been many people here—perhaps, one day, there would be again.

Abruptly, he came to a halt. He stood in front of the first structure their group had helped repair: a local healer's home. Of course, Leila wasn't a trained healer—those had all been taken to Vizen years ago. She was just an older woman with a keen eye for observation and a strong memory trying to do her best for her neighbors. It had made sense to Rovan that an untrained healer would accept a bunch of untrained carpenters to help repair her place. The crisp blonde wood of their repairs stood in stark contrast with the remaining bits of the original building. The sight of it filled him with pride. This was the purpose of his work.

His mind traveled back to the tavern, to Ashe and Alanda. The two women had been here during the Tragedy of Albadone. He thought of Ashe surrendering her baby in order to save it. While Alanda was adamant that a mother did not regret such things, Rovan found that difficult to fully believe. Everyone carried bundles of regret on their backs whether they acknowledged it or not.

Overhead, the sky rumbled, and the air thickened with more rain. Rovan ducked into the old, crooked barn where Blot, the only remaining work mule in Pevine, was housed. The animal was resting calmly in the depths of the barn, enjoying its dryness. The smell of hay and manure was musty in the humidity.

To Rovan's surprise, Scintilla was standing beside the beast with her bow raised, an arrow perched lightly between her ring and middle fingers prepared to take flight. *Thunk.* The arrow buried itself into a makeshift target nailed to the wall a few feet from his head. It was a greeting, and not a welcoming one.

Rovan raised his hands in mock surrender before turning to retrieve the arrow. He walked to Scintilla and placed it into her hand. He could see now that she had been crying.

"I know we can't force Tieg to stay," Scintilla broke the silence. "It just doesn't make sense to me why he would leave us to return to his... his..."

"His actual family?" Rovan suggested.

Scintilla shot him a pained expression. "They hate him. You don't know the worst of what they've done—what he has confided with me. Why would he willingly go back to that?"

Rovan took a seat next to Scintilla and breathed in deeply, the smell of fresh manure stinging his eyes. "I've been pondering that myself, but really the only one who can answer that question is Tieg. You didn't really give him that chance."

"I know," she sighed, releasing tension from her shoulders. "I'll apologize to him for that. But I won't apologize for being honest."

"Fair enough. All we can do is respect his choice and be there for him in the event that he needs a place to return to."

Scintilla seemed to ponder his words. "That's not all we can do. Respecting his choice doesn't mean we have to hide our concerns." She might as well have notched another arrow and hit him with it. Rovan *was* holding back his concerns from Tieg, but only because he didn't want to overstep.

"You all put too much weight on what I think."

Scintilla smirked. "More than you seem to at least."

Rovan blinked.

"Terreck told me about those women," Scintilla shifted topics. "The ones looking for their baby."

Rovan wished she had brought up anything else. "Not a baby anymore," he corrected. "A seven-year-old child."

"Are we taking the job?"

"I don't know."

Scintilla stretched her shooting arm. "You always talk about the importance of choice. But yours are so painfully predictable."

"I really haven't decided yet," Rovan retorted.

"A choice between helping a mother find her missing child and doing nothing? Do you want me to feign surprise when you tell us or..?"

Rovan smiled. Leave it to Scintilla to always clear his mind of doubt. She was right. Rovan had no intention of turning the women down, even though it was terrible timing to split the group apart right as a member was leaving.

"Who would you take with you?" she asked.

Rovan shook his head. "I don't know. I haven't thought that far ahead."

"You definitely can't bring Fellen. The kid can barely stand upright."

"Of course not," Rovan laughed.

Scintilla smirked. "I think it's time that you make your choice known."

"I think you're right."

"Then maybe your next choice can be about what to do with that hair of yours."

Rovan reached for his soaked curls, flattened by the rain. "That bad?"

"I don't know about bad, but it's definitely not good." Scintilla placed her bow into its leather holster and made for the door.

"It's still raining," Rovan warned.

"I wasn't in here to hide from the rain," Scintilla said as she left the barn.

Rovan smiled, regretting that his first thought upon seeing Scintilla was that she would badger him about Tieg's leaving. She seemed to have had time to think things through. He had to remind himself that she was not the same Scintilla he had first met several years before—that

Scintilla would have bullied him into having it her way. People did change.

Maybe even he had changed, though it was hard to know for sure. He thought of his sister, Ensa. What would she think of him if she saw him now?

The rain did not seem to have any intention of stopping or even slowing down. Rovan gently patted the mule's back, then returned outside. He was drenched the instant he stepped past the door. The small house he inhabited was on the other side of town, so he opted to return to the tavern instead. Fellen and Iseo still sat at the table talking animatedly, a steaming cup of tea in front of each of them. A few damp locals sat quietly at tables while puffing on their pipes. Most of the townsfolk had chosen to stay within their humble abodes today—the image of rain invading those homes through leaky roofs pestered him.

Among those seated at the tables, Rovan spotted Ashe and Alanda. A knot formed in his throat, though he was now certain of what he must do. He moved aside the wet hair that clung to his face and sat across from the two women. Water pooled onto the floor around him.

"Rovan," Alanda greeted unsurely.

"What was Pevine like when you lived here?" Rovan asked them.

For a moment Alanda seemed taken aback by such a question. Slowly, her face came alight. "It was lively. The morning market especially. Every day, I could see merchants setting up right outside that window." Rovan looked over at the rain-streaked front window, trying to conjure the scene Alanda was describing.

The woman continued, "I would sweep the porch listening to the music of it all. Then, in the afternoons, my sister Neverene would prepare a roast like you've never tasted before. The smell, oh, that smell! It would drive people in like nothing else. In the evening, woodworkers returned to town from the woods. Their excited voices carried all the way here, and I knew I better start pouring or I would never keep up."

A shadow of grief passed across her face. Ashe grabbed the woman's hand and pressed her forehead against her cheek. Alanda smiled sadly. "It's hard to see that it has all been erased as if it had never happened."

Rovan glanced at the missing fingers of his right hand and thought back on his life in Sol Forne—it too no longer seemed real, as if it was never his. "And you?" Rovan asked Ashe.

The woman shook her head. "She's from the northeastern edge of Albadone," Alanda answered. "She was forced to come here after the fires. That's how we met."

Rovan cleared his throat—he wanted to make sure his words were clear and forthright. "I will do as you request. I will help you search for your daughter."

Alanda was the first to break their shock by smiling and hugging the other woman. Ashe, on the other hand, sat stunned as tears began to well in her eyes. She suddenly cupped Rovan's hands and kissed them.

"No need for that," Rovan said, reddening, and gently pulling his hands away. "There are preparations which must be made. Though the Womb of the World is reachable in a day, I do not want to go there unprepared, especially since this storm doesn't seem to be letting up, and I've never been there before."

"We'll guide you," Alanda said as Ashe nodded in assent.

"I don't think that's such a good idea," Rovan said.

Ashe frowned.

"I know it's your daughter that I am seeking, but you both seem travel-worn and, quite frankly, exhausted. I won't ask you to venture out for what may be news your daughter is somewhere else entirely. Besides, I can be ready to depart by tomorrow if it's just myself."

"Are you certain?" Alanda asked. "The mountain can be quite perilous to those inexperienced."

"I will find a way," Rovan said, resolutely.

"I will take you." Rovan turned to find Tieg standing behind him. The young man stood with his hands behind his back. He wore a strangely determined expression. "I've been there before," Tieg added. "My family's farm is a few miles northwest of it. My brother took me there once before he died."

"And you think you still remember how to get around?" Rovan asked.

Tieg's face grew serious. "It took the whole day to reach the canyon. When we did, it was night. The stars were so close, it looked like you could catch and hold them in your palm. How could I forget? It was the best day of my life." Tieg had recounted this story to the group many times before, but never with such affection.

Rovan nodded. "Very well." He faced the women and added, "Allow us the rest of the day to gather supplies. We will leave first thing in the morning. In the meanwhile, if you can think of any information that may aid our search, please do not hesitate to share it."

The women nodded. "You are doing the True One's work," Alanda said. "Know that you will be repaid with a full and bountiful life."

Rovan smiled. "I will content myself with actually finding this child. Tieg," he called. "Follow me out." Rovan bid farewell to the women, then left the tavern. Tieg followed closely behind.

They headed for the northern side of town, towards the small house the townsfolk had allowed them to occupy. Though Tieg walked next to him, Rovan could not find any words to offer the young man. What Iseo and Scintilla had said bothered him. He did have concerns he wanted to share with Tieg, and he was suddenly certain that his reticence to confront the young man came as much from a lack of confidence as a lack of courage. If Rovan actually got the nerve up to ask Tieg why he wanted to leave them, could he handle it if the answer was due to his lacking as a leader? Or as a friend?

Rovan pushed open the unlocked door of the small home and let Tieg in first. He quickly closed the door, barring entry to the rain. The musty smell of the interior was only accentuated by the several leaks that had sprung in the haphazardly mended roof. Their drip-drop sounded strangely soothing, the outside rain like a restful gray hum as it hit the roof and surrounding muddy earth.

Rovan picked a small iron firestarter from the wobbly table Terreck had assembled for him and gripped it in his left hand. He grabbed a handful of dry hay from a basket and placed it gently below the blackened wood within the small hearth. With a squeeze, the firestarter's teeth ground against each other, causing sparks to fly into the hay. It took three tries for the hay to hold a spark and begin smoldering. Meticulously, Rovan blew onto the hay until a timid flame rose. Tieg fed a few thin sticks and some more hay to the flame, encouraging its spread to the larger logs.

"Thank you," Rovan said.

"I remember how bad you used to be at starting fires when we first met," Tieg teased.

"Not just about the fire." Rovan sat on the floor watching the flame grow, its welcome heat lapping at the side of his cheek. "Thank you for offering to come with me."

Tieg shrugged and sat next to Rovan. "It's on the way to my family's farm. Figured I'd catch two fish with the same bait."

"Do you miss them?"

"It's not really about missing them," Tieg said. He sounded irritated by the topic. "They're my family."

"Yes, they are," Rovan agreed reluctantly. "But so are we."

Tieg glanced at Rovan blankly. "You never talk about your family. Do you have anyone?"

Rovan suppressed the pang of guilt and regret the question summoned. He looked into the flame, remembering a much bigger hearth—the ever-diminishing recollection of his parents' touch. "I have a sister," he said. "In Sol Forne."

"And do you never wish to see her again?" Tieg pried.

Rovan realized his hand was balled in a fist. "She's a colorist for a noble. You know what a colorist does? It's very fascinating work. They study pigment and find novel ways to dye fabric. Ensa took care of me, but I was terrible to her. She is doing much better without me, I'm sure."

"Wouldn't you want her to give you a chance to show that you've changed?"

"Is that what you want?" Rovan asked. "To know if your family has changed?"

"Everyone deserves that chance, even them."

Rovan wanted to tell Tieg he was making a mistake and that they all wanted him to stay more than anything. Instead, Rovan choked down his earnestness and said only, "I hope they welcome you back."

"They're my family," Tieg said, as if that was a good enough answer.

They sat by the fire in silence for some time. The rains continued to pound on the roof overhead, but Rovan knew the time had come to inform the rest of the group about his decision. He left Tieg in charge of preparing their travel provisions and headed out in search of his friends.

He found Terreck squatting in the vacant town square, smoking his pipe. Trinket zigzagged fluidly around him. Both were absolutely drenched from head to toe. While Terreck was wise about many things for someone his age, other things—like common sense or decorum—seemed to elude him entirely. And Trinket, the cat they had found as a kitten in an abandoned barn, was just as senseless. The only thing keeping Terreck's pipe from going out was the old, ugly, wide-brimmed hat he insisted on wearing, to their group's chagrin.

Terreck looked up and blew a ring of smoke toward Rovan, who waved it away. Unlike his friend, Rovan did not enjoy the feel of smoke in his lungs. "So," Terreck began, "you accepted the job."

Trinket rubbed his face against Rovan's leg. "Am I really so predictable?" Rovan asked.

Terreck stood and lightly punched Rovan on the shoulder. "Finding a missing child? That has your stamp all over it. It makes me curious to know, though, at what point will you find a job you're going to refuse?"

Rovan kneeled to pet Trinket. The cat purred in delight under his touch. "I've refused jobs before."

Terreck swatted at him with his pipe. "Sure. Sure. But those were bad jobs. Things like stealing, looking for a runaway thief, or other unlawful nonsense. The heroic-sounding jobs you never refuse."

Rovan felt his cheeks redden.

Terreck continued, "But seeing as you never ask for payment, will there ever be a *heroic* job you refuse? Surely some things are too dangerous, even for you. And not all strangers can be trusted, even I know that."

"I believe them," Rovan stated firmly.

"Oh, I do too," Terreck said. "Their story is too strange to be false. But the fact that you're willing to do what they ask is... is..."

"Foolish?" Rovan asked.

"Definitely. But also, admirable."

Rovan stood and turned away from Terreck to conceal his reddening ears and neck, then coughed loudly to give himself a reason to be doing so.

Trinket plopped down and then rolled in the mud. Terreck chuckled at the sight as he pulled from his pipe. He blew out three perfect rings which were immediately dissolved by the rain. "You act like you have something to prove. I'm just afraid that one day you'll take on something you can't handle."

Rovan turned back to his friend. Worry marred Terreck's boyish face. "You have nothing to prove to us, Rovan. Can you promise me one thing?" Terreck asked.

"What?"

"Promise me that—that you'll walk away if something is too much."

Terreck's concern cut Rovan like a knife. How long had the young man harbored these misgivings? Rovan had to admit that he had used very little discernment in selecting jobs in the past, particularly when he had been on his own.

Discernment was a good thing. Fixing Pevine was a difficult task, but Rovan was convinced it was possible—and beyond that, it was the right thing to do. These people needed help reclaiming their home. They needed to feel safe—to feel pride in their abodes. Finding this child, on the other hand, could ultimately prove impossible. But Terreck was right: Rovan could never refuse such a request.

"I'll be leaving in the morning. Tieg is coming with me," Rovan said. "Then, he will carry on past the Womb of the World to his family's home."

Terreck nodded. "That makes sense."

"He's gathering provisions for us. I just wanted to make sure everyone was aware of the plan. Think you and Scintilla can continue the repairs while we're gone?" Rovan asked.

"Of course," Terreck replied.

Rovan smiled and slapped Terreck's shoulder amicably, then turned to leave.

Terreck stopped him by grabbing his arm. "You didn't promise," he said gravely.

Rovan raised his eyebrows. "Promise what?"

"I need to hear you promise that you will walk away when things get too dangerous to handle."

Rovan stared into Terreck's eyes, perhaps trying to find an ulterior motive for his request. When he found nothing there but a friend's care, he replied, "Of course. I promise."

Terreck slowly released Rovan's arm, then resumed a squat. Trinket stood and rubbed the mud from his back onto Terreck's leg. "I hope the rain never stops," Terreck yearned.

VI.

LEGACY

The delicate crunch of porcelain beneath her boot interrupts the stillness around her. She lifts her foot to find the powdery remains of the red sparrow's body. Her eyes carry forward to another type of red—deeper, darker, as smooth and glassy as a mirror. A ripple forms as a ruby droplet joins the pool, slipping easily from the ghostly white finger of the corpse resting in the tub. Its pale eyes stare forward without focus or recognition. Searin can see her own horror reflected back at her, eyes wide and mouth open as if to scream out. A haunting royal portrait on the canvas of her father's blood—

"Do you wish to read the missives and announcements before they are sent off?" Searin realized with a jolt that the question had been posed to the group at large. She sat at one end of the table, surrounded by the queen, her sister Arisa, and her uncle Clavio. The late king's seat, taller and gilded, remained empty. Across from them was a small congregation of ministers: Lord Fare Koren, Lord Kell Trett, Steward Ibessa, and Lord Julius Arvington—the ever-silent Minister of Diplomacy.

High Captain Knott completed their party. His neatly trimmed white beard was disrupted by a large dueling scar on his left cheek. The golden armor and red cape of the King's Guard were the most handsome things about him.

"Messages for the criers have also been drafted," Lord Koren, the Minister of Information, continued when no response came from the table. The queen, now the highest-ranking person in the kingdom and default head of this meeting, seemed every bit as distracted from the discussion at hand as Searin was. It was unusual to see her mother so befuddled. The woman was well renowned for possessing an unshakable grace and royal bearing even in times of great tension. It seemed her father's blade had ripped through that demeanor as easily as it had his wrists.

A brief assessment of her side of the table revealed this to be true for all of them. Clavio and Arisa looked as if they were off-axis in their own ways. Clavio's eyes were red and swollen from crying. Arisa's had the darting, panicked, quality of a cornered animal. Her anointment would now be only a matter of days away. Searin felt sharp guilt at having placed her sister in such a position but stopped short of regret.

"Messengers will reach the nearest noble houses in..." The queen trailed off.

"In this weather? Three days, at the least, to reach Perimat. Four for Rondhill," Lord Trett, the Minister of Coin, informed.

"The criers can be dispatched as soon as you command," Lord Koren continued, in a voice as thin as his build. "I've placed the servants who witnessed the scene under lock to ensure not a word of what they've seen gets out. As far as anyone in the kingdom will know, King Petar—gods rest him—passed peacefully in his sleep during the night."

"Locking them up is quite unnecessary," Steward Ibessa, the Palace Steward, interjected. "The servants have already been warned that any rumor spreading within and without the palace shall be met with severe punishment."

"At the point punishment becomes necessary, the rumor will already have legs and be strolling through the city streets. An abundance of caution is warranted here, I'm sure you'll agree, my queen." Lord Koren bowed his liver-spotted head when he finished. He was laying it on a bit thick for Searin's taste, but the queen didn't seem to mind.

The queen nodded. "If you need to bring in additional people to make up for the ones being held then see to it. In a month, they can be released. The kingdom will be too absorbed in scrutinizing its new ruler to bother with any gossip they might let slip by then." Arisa cleared her throat nervously. "Hold off on sending the criers and birds until tomorrow. The mourning bells will sound at first light." Queen Altima paused thoughtfully before adding, "The message for the city criers... Have it amended to include a week of mourning for the late king. Every marketplace is to be shuttered during that time."

The ministers exchanged nervous glances. "My queen, a period of mourning is a fine idea but to shut down the markets for seven days would be—"

"And at every drinking hall, there shall be a toast raised in King Petar's honor and a second to the future Queen Arisa." The queen stared down the other side of the table as if daring them to raise a rebuttal. The smile on Lord Trett's face would have been convincing had Searin not spotted the pulsing vein at the large man's temple.

"My queen, the rains have caused much damage in Urstway and our surrounding lands," Trett began. "While the palace is still well stocked, I fear the people of our city are in a delicate state. I do not want this period of mourning to feel..." the man's eyes flitted between the queen, Arisa, Clavio, and Searin trying to find a sympathetic place to perch, "like a scarcity of resources. We don't want to make the peasants hungry." He laughed nervously.

Arisa sighed. "Seven days is rather long, Mother." The queen eyed her daughter with distaste. Arisa challenged that look with one of her own—they were suddenly very much merely mother and daughter.

Lord Koren interrupted the tension. "I'm afraid I have to agree with Lord Trett on this. A week of closed markets will seed a good deal of ill will amongst the people."

"And?" Queen Altima looked almost bored. "Why should their will matter more than my own?" Searin was slightly embarrassed to see her mother behaving so flippantly. The queen had never been one to involve herself in such logistical affairs, and Searin was beginning to understand why.

Lord Koren, to his credit, was unshaken by her dismissiveness. "My queen, may I share a story with you that I once told to King Petar—gods rest him?"

"Go on."

"Several years ago, there was a nest of aspiring revolutionaries that grew large enough to pose a threat to the palace. The king asked me how I thought he should handle them. I told him that one summer, when I was just a young boy, lightning struck a large oak outside the walls of my family's estate—burned it entirely to the ground. We all thought that was the end of it, until, months later, fires started popping up in our fields several miles away from where the tree had turned to ash. One of our oldest laborers came to my father, claiming to have seen something similar before. He said that what we were experiencing was the result of a root fire. The oak tree that had ignited was still burning beneath the soil, the fire running along its root system, reaching the roots of other trees, and igniting them in turn. The only way to put it out was to dig up the root system and flood it with water. It took weeks and most of our field hands to accomplish the task."

"And what was my husband's response to this story of yours?"

Koren shook his head, "Sadly, King Petar decided that the best course of action was to have the group's leaders killed quietly. He said that making the executions public would lend the group legitimacy. I see how that might have been true, but..."

"You fear my brother left space underground for the flames to continue spreading?" It was the first thing Clavio had said since sitting down.

Lord Koren met Clavio's gaze with his bloodshot eyes and replied, "We have protections in place for you all, of course. We will discuss digging up the root system in the near future, but, for the short term, let us at least not bring the fires to the surface if we can help it."

"My husband must be mourned."

Arisa placed a hand on the queen's arm. Her mother glared at it but did not shy away from the touch, "May we find a compromise?" Arisa insisted.

"Three days?" Lord Trett suggested reluctantly.

The queen shook her head. "This is repugnant."

"That is reasonable," Arisa countered.

Her mother folded her arms but nodded.

"Very well, my queen," Lord Trett agreed with a bow. "Three days of city-wide mourning."

"Is there anything else that we must go over?" Arisa asked.

"Just one thing," Clavio said. "It's the matter of your anointment."

"Ah, of course." From Arisa's tone, the upcoming funeral might as well have been for herself.

"Customarily, an anointment is to be held within one week of the previous ruler's funeral. And that means that we have very little time to address your need for a husband."

"No need to worry on that front," the queen assured the table. "I had already begun considering that issue before my husband's," she paused, "*accident*. I have a list prepared of potential consorts for Arisa to choose from."

Clavio looked at Arisa with sympathy. "A topic for us to revisit in a future meeting then. We are decided that three days of mourning are to be announced tomorrow, with the funeral ceremony to be held within the week. Will five days after that be a suitable amount of time to prepare for the wedding?"

Every member of the group mumbled their assent. All matters discussed, the meeting had reached a natural end. Searin wiped at her face and found it damp with sweat. The windowless room somehow managed to be humid and sweltering even this time of year.

She closed her eyes and there it was again, interrupting her thoughts—that redness oozing from her father's arms, that knife on the floor. There had been a knife, hadn't there? Searin was nearly certain, though she hadn't taken a good look at it. Had anyone even noticed the weapon? Was it her father's? Who had it belonged to? Suddenly, that object seemed to be the most important thing in the world. She resolved to ask about it.

When she opened her eyes, she found that everyone else had already vacated the hall leaving her alone. Gods, she hadn't slept in too long. Searin retired to her chambers. She lay on her sturdy bed and stared up at the ceiling.

King Petar had never been a good father. He had ruled his household with the same fickle ruthlessness he had applied to the rest of the kingdom. But he had always stressed the importance of legacy. It was the one thing Searin had known him to care about. He had been so proud of the Talessi blood that flowed through his veins to the point of using it as a weapon against her and her siblings in countless arguments. He'd made them each feel small and trapped under the weight of it. And then, in a moment she'd never understand, he had betrayed all of that by giving up his legacy and all of that royal blood as if it was no more valuable than the bath water he soaked in. He had died like any other man might have. A pathetic end for a king.

Suppertime came and went. Searin opted to remain in her room, attempting to rest and sort her thoughts. She decided she would head for High Captain Knott's chambers, determined to ask about the dagger that had ended her father's life. She stood from her bed and opened her wardrobe, hoping to change into something clean. Within, she was surprised to find a brand-new set of armor—the gift her uncle had mentioned the other morning. Unlike her old armor, which was engraved with her family's crest, the Talessi Sparrow, the breastplate of this one was smooth, unmarked, and polished to a mirror finish. A red plume jutted out from the finely crafted helmet like a fountain of blood.

She slammed the wardrobe door shut and caught her breath.

Besides the occasional servant, the halls were rather deserted, something that would change in a few days' time as nobles flooded in from near and far to pay their respects. The pitter-patter of tiny bare feet made Searin duck behind a corner. Her brother Hovard had seen their father's corpse too. Searin hated thinking the poor boy might be haunted by visions similar to the ones she was having. She did not have it in her to confront him now and confirm that to be true.

She waited a few moments more, then resumed her ascent towards Knott's chambers. Searin knocked on the unguarded door, and it opened slowly. She peeked into the room and called out, "High Captain? Are you in there?"

"Come in," Knott called out in a wavering voice. Searin entered the room and closed the door behind her. She had never been inside the high captain's palace chambers. She realized with a shock of excitement that this room would soon become her own. The space was clean and smelled of fresh jasmine and sea dew, though the decor was out of fashion by several years.

Knott entered the room from a side chamber. His eyes were puffy and red, and Searin realized he had been crying. "I can return at a better time," she said, uncomfortably.

"Apologies for my... disheveled look. I just..."

"It's all right," Searin comforted awkwardly. Knott and her father had been as close as brothers, closer, perhaps, than even Clavio and her father had been.

Knott wiped his face on his sleeve, then asked, "To what do I owe this visit?"

Searin looked away, unsure of how to broach the subject. "The weapon my father used to..." She steadied herself before saying, "Kill himself."

Knott understood instantly. "It was an old knife. Mostly decorative, not really a weapon."

"I'd like to see it," Searin insisted.

"I had it disposed of," Knott said. "In truth, I didn't know what I should do with it. Destroy it? Bury it?" After a brief pause, Knott continued, "I chose to give it to our palace smith. It will be melted down and thrown into the Cleo so that nobody can ever find the thing."

"That's good," Searin said, hiding her disappointment.

"Was there anything else, my princess?"

Searin shook her head and left the room. She haunted the dim halls, unsure of where to settle. Her chambers felt too small to encompass the scale of her complicated feelings. The image of her father still came to her unbidden when she closed her eyes. She still could not conjure a single tear for the man despite this. High Captain Knott was shedding tears for her father that his own daughter couldn't summon for him. She should have felt guilty. Instead, she remembered that she had skipped supper and decided to head for the dining room to see what had been left over.

VII.

Purpose

The bells of the Hall of Gods bellowed in Lyr's head like a hollow drum, though their sound came from the other side of the city. Whatever had happened, must it be announced in such an obnoxious way? Her mother still slept—or, rather, refused to accept that morning had come—so Lyr pulled back the frayed curtains to peek out. The light of the morning sun was just draining the last of the purple from the sky. It was clear by the crowd gathered outside that something tremendous had happened.

Lyr dressed quickly in a simple brown shift cinched at her waist by a faded rope belt and made for the door. As she pushed it open, a thin shaft of sunlight swelled into the little abode. Her mother shifted in her bed.

"Where are you going?" the woman asked.

Lyr closed the door, restoring the home to its usual darkness. "Something's happened. I want to see what the commotion is about," Lyr replied.

Her mother lifted her head curiously, as if hearing the bells for the first time. "Will those cursed royals never leave us be?" With that question, the woman retreated into her bedding. Lyr waited for her mother to settle back into what they both pretended was sleep before leaving the home. The warming sun kissed Lyr's olive skin. Even after her mother had been marked, she had remained positive that they would someday leave Vizen. But since her father's suicide, the sun had become an unwelcome houseguest as far as her mother was concerned. Lyr's heart ached to see her like this. Her mother's grief had transformed their shabby house into a sepulcher in which she lay, shrouded in darkness, as if she, too, had died.

The crowd outside embodied a range of emotions, from somber and outright crying, to passive or even gleeful. The chatter was too loud for Lyr to make out what was being discussed. The shouts of the city criers competed with the bells as they carried their news onward. Lyr approached Catrice, one of her neighbors who worked at the launders. The middle-aged woman stood by her door dabbing at her tear-soaked cheeks with her sleeve.

"Excuse me, Catrice, what's all this about?" Lyr asked. The woman briefly looked up at her with red eyes, then returned to her sobbing. Though it had been before Lyr was even born, the woman had been a weepy mess ever since her son had died in the war on the Red Coast.

Lyr patted the woman amicably on the shoulder, then turned to seek information from anyone else. At the far end of the street, Lyr spotted Tommes dragging his turnip cart back home—very strange. The tall, broad, man sported his usual gruff expression, though today it was rendered even more indignant by the crowd that stood in his path. "Make way!" he demanded, entirely unheeded.

Next to him was Saul, wearing a handsome frown. If anyone knew what was going on it would be him. Lyr battled the thick crowd to make her way towards the young man. It took a considerable amount of effort, though thankfully the cart had not progressed much from where she had first seen it.

"Saul!" she called out.

The young man's face brightened at the sound of her voice. "Good morning, Lyr," he intoned.

"Where are you going?" Lyr asked.

"The market's closed today. We're headed back home."

"Move outta the way Gregon, you oaf!" Tommes barked. The dopey man loitering in front of the cart scooted absentmindedly aside, and Tommes pushed forward. "Put your weight into it, boy!" Tommes complained to Saul, who quickly joined his father in pushing the cart.

"Walk with us," Saul suggested to Lyr.

"Why is the market closed?" Lyr asked.

Tommes answered before his son could. "Because those royals don't care whether we make a livin' or not. All they care about is that we pretend to give a shit about their traditions. Gods damn them all!"

Saul rolled his eyes. "The royals are in mourning, so by extension, we're all in mourning as well. Apparently, people in mourning don't buy things."

"Mourning?" Lyr asked. "Mourning who?"

"You really haven't heard? The king is dead." Saul looked absolutely elated at being able to speak those words. Lyr, on the other hand, stopped in her tracks as the cart continued past her. The king was dead.

Lyr caught up with the cart. "The king—"

Saul leaned in close to her face. Lyr could feel his warm breath on her cheek. "The royals are going to be so busy arranging the funeral rites and trying to find a suitable mate for the princess-heir, that they won't even notice our activities."

Lyr gave a start, from both his words and his proximity. Saul smiled mischievously.

"Boy!" Tommes exclaimed. "Don't make me call for you again!"

"Yeah, yeah," Saul replied, returning his attention to the cart. He then nodded for Lyr to come closer to him. "We're holding a special meeting tonight. You should be there."

"I... I don't know about that." Her mother's warning had prevented her from getting much sleep the previous night. The danger of returning to the Free Kings' hideout was even greater now that the king was gone. Lyr felt the sting of curiosity, but for now, caution was a balm.

"Things are just starting to get exciting," Saul said. "Please. Just once more. You know you want to," he taunted.

He was right. Lyr wanted to be there. As much as she didn't wish to worry her mother, Atrew's words the previous night had awakened something within her—something she hadn't known she needed to feel. Lyr found herself nodding back at Saul, whose smile broadened. "I'll come get you. Same time as last night," he said. "But we'll have to run if we're to make it on time."

Saul then reached towards his cart and plucked a bundle of turnips, handing them to her with a wink. Lyr watched the cart slowly vanish into the crowd. The bells continued to ring incessantly, their sound a constant reminder of what she had just agreed to do. She returned home and sat on the street just outside her door, watching as neighbors slowly trickled back to their respective abodes. Since the market was closed, there was not much left for them to do other than sit around and wait for the day to be over. People busied themselves with domestic tasks. Neighbors bartered amongst themselves for ingredients to make the meals they had planned.

One bundle of turnips, a loaf of bread, and three small potatoes. That was all the food she and her mother had for the day. It wouldn't have been enough for one person, let alone two. And what about tomorrow? Or the next day? Just how long would this forced mourning last? How could the royals be so selfish as to make the city come to a halt to pay respects to a man none of them had ever met? Lyr had never even glimpsed the king from afar. She had only seen his likeness rendered crudely on the wall of a tavern she had once swept for coin. If that drawing was anything to go by, then the king must have been quite fond of eating feces.

Lyr realized that returning to the Free Kings' hideout was a necessity if only to collect more food to help her and her mother get by. She also wanted to hear more from Atrew and the others about this new idea of running the kingdom without royals.

The royals were nothing but vultures picking off the bones of those they ruled. Without them, she would be living peacefully in Pevine, where her mother could use her skills as a healer and lead her life with some dignity. Perhaps then her father wouldn't have abandoned them by killing himself.

Her stomach growled. Lyr stood and walked back home to boil the turnip and potatoes for her and her mother. The bells still rang. Night could not come soon enough.

※ ※ ※ ※

The air within the Free Kings' hideout was palpably different from that of the previous night. This time, it was Atrew who was late, though the crowd seemed to anticipate this. One by one, speakers took the small stage. A woman read a translation of an Efrayan text detailing their system of tax-funded houses of learning, where people of any age could go and learn to read and figure. Afterward, a trio harmonized the ballad of a rebellion Lyr had never heard of. She would be humming its infectious melody the rest of the week.

"She has returned," Rob snarked as he approached Lyr and Saul.

"Atrew already met with her," Saul replied, puffing his chest slightly. "She has his approval."

Rob shook his head. "We better not come to regret this." Turning to Lyr, he added, "Otherwise, I will make you regret ever pretending to be one of us."

Saul placed his hand on Rob's chest and lightly shoved him back. "Go," he said firmly. The man shot daggers at Lyr, then grumbled away into the crowd.

Though she understood why he would be hostile towards newcomers, the man's suspicions felt oddly personal. Saul placed a gentle hand on her shoulder. "Don't worry about him. He'll come around after he learns how important you are."

Before Lyr could ask what he meant by that, Atrew hurried into the room. "I am truly sorry for my tardiness, everyone," he apologized. Atrew's armed escort towered next to him. Unlike the prior night, his lowered hood revealed his hardened face. He was handsome in spite of the hole that was where his right ear should have been. Lyr would have to ask Saul about him later.

The place grew silent. Atrew scanned each and every one of them with his inquisitive eyes. "I'm sure that by now, you all have heard the news. Either that or you're very good at ignoring those blasted bells." The crowd chuckled softly. "The king is dead. And before you ask, no, it was not our doing." The murmur that passed through the crowd revealed that at least a few of the members present had held this as a possibility. "Nor anyone else's, it would seem. It appears King Petar decided to off himself."

A darker murmur filled the crowd. Atrew raised his hand, waiting for silence to return before continuing. "Obviously, this greatly accelerates our plans." Atrew licked his lips and took a deep breath. "After her impending wedding day, Princess Arisa shall be anointed as queen. The date is yet to be determined, but we suspect it will be within the fortnight. There is to be a funeral ceremony in three days at the House of the Gods. As most of the nobles and the palace guard will be away to attend it, this gives us the perfect cover to infiltrate the palace." Another round of soft murmurs swished through the crowd. Lyr found herself breathing heavily.

"Did we ever decide which of us will be involved?" someone asked.

Atrew once again raised a placating hand to silence the buzzing crowd. "To protect the families of the infiltrators, that will have to remain between those directly involved. While that phase of our plan is underway, we each will have our own set of tasks to complete, as we've already discussed."

"When will we know if we've been selected?" a nearby woman asked.

"Only a handful of those who can pass as palace servants and possess the necessary skills will be offered a role," a tall and skeletal man replied. By the way the crowd regarded him, he must have been someone important within the group. "I have asked Brother Saul to inform the candidates after tonight's meeting."

Saul shifted and stood a bit taller after hearing his name. Sudden anxiety descended upon Lyr. Up to this moment, she had thought Saul to be just another of the many casual members of the Free Kings. To be handed such an important task... *How involved is he, exactly?* Lyr wondered.

"Thank you, Brother Erven," Saul said. "And it was with great honor that I accepted this job. If I come to you, and this is something you cannot do, you are welcome to refuse. Though, why be a part of the Free Kings at all if you're not willing to act for the cause?" With those words, Saul placed his hand on Lyr's shoulder. The gesture made her want to vanish entirely.

The crowd nodded emphatically. "Well said," Atrew smiled.

For the rest of the meeting, all Lyr could focus on was Saul's hand, which remained on her as if he intended to hold her in place. Earlier this evening, she would have enjoyed this unexpected intimacy. For some reason, it now filled her with dread. The way he touched her after saying those words... Could he mean to include her in this infiltration plan? That was ridiculous!

And yet, when the crowd finally scattered, Saul began, "So. What do you think?"

"What do I think about what?" Lyr asked. The implication petrified her.

"Of us infiltrating the palace."

Lyr bit her lip. "It's ambitious. Dangerous."

"*Very* dangerous. Don't you think you would be perfect for it?" The words did not immediately land in Lyr's ears. She stared Saul down as if daring him to take the offer back, but he only smiled.

"No," she replied.

"No?" he repeated. Lyr turned away from him and headed for the now-familiar exit. Saul grabbed her arm. "Lyr, please listen..."

"Are you joking?" Lyr snapped. "You want me to participate in an infiltration of the Royal Palace? You cannot be serious!"

"Of course I am, Lyr," Saul said, earnestness brightening his eyes. "And you would be perfect for this. You're so... You—"

"Fit the part of a palace servant?" Lyr suggested. "Is that it?"

"In part."

Lyr narrowed her eyes and shoved out of Saul's grip. She could not believe what she was hearing. Her face had grown hot, her eyes threatening tears.

"But that's not all of it," Saul continued, following behind. "For years now I've been watching you in the market. There isn't a single job you haven't done there and done well. If anyone has the skills to pick up palace work and blend in like they've been doing it for years, it's you. But, more importantly, I want you to join me in this because I trust you, Lyr." Lyr stopped. "Sure, we're all united under the same cause, but I know you. I've known you for longer than anyone else here." Lowering his voice, he added, "I know you won't betray us. I..."

Lyr looked into Saul's deep gray-green eyes.

"I need you," he finally said.

Those words washed over her. She calmed herself with several steady breaths. "I don't even know what the plan is. Infiltrate the palace, to do what, exactly?"

"I can't really..." Saul stopped himself short, perhaps noticing the deep frown lining Lyr's face. "The whole operation won't be long. Just a couple of days spent impersonating servants, and then we'll be out of there. I'll be there too, so you'll have nothing to fear."

"And the purpose?" Lyr pried once more.

"We've received credible reports that the royals are planning to restart the war on the Red Coast."

"Why would they do that?" Lyr asked.

"A last desperate attempt to regain ground? Who knows? But we have it on good authority that the Minister of Warcraft has orders drafted and ready to be sent out. We need to steal those plans and make them public. The people have shed enough blood for a war the royals are never going to win. The King's death may have bought us some precious time."

After a long silence, Lyr whispered, "All right," trying to convince herself that she really meant it. Saul smiled and hugged her, as delighted as if she had agreed wholeheartedly. She closed her eyes taking in everything about him—his smell, the gentleness of his calloused hands on her back, the firmness of his shoulders. It was almost enough to make her forget what she had just agreed to do.

Was there truly no one else Saul trusted amongst the Free Kings? What did that say about the group?

Saul accompanied her home. Neither spoke, a deep solemnity erecting itself between them. As if sensing it, Saul reached over and grabbed her hand. What was she to him?

Simply another hopeful member of an aspiring group of revolutionaries, helping him to fulfill an end? Or more? "*I need you,*" he had said. How far did that need reach?

"I need time," she said suddenly.

"Time for what?" Saul asked.

"Time to think."

"You're not backing out already, are you?" Saul asked, releasing her hand.

"I didn't say that." Lyr shook her head. "I need to speak to my mother. I need to tell her."

"No," Saul said firmly. "You must not mention this to anyone."

"Mother wouldn't tell anyone," Lyr protested. "She barely leaves the house as it is."

Saul halted, a worried cast dimming his eyes. "Lyr, listen to me carefully. What we are planning is so deeply criminal that, if we are caught, your mother will be imprisoned simply for knowing you. Or worse, executed. Do you think I've told my father about any of this? At least this way he and my family can sincerely plead ignorance if the worst comes. Spare your mother the worry and the added risk. That is how you can protect her."

Lyr could not stand to look in his eyes anymore. "And you don't think I should be protected too?"

"Lyr, I need you."

"Stop saying that!" She almost yelled it but caught herself—the dark streets did not need to hear. "Is this about you needing me or is this about me being right for the task?"

For the first time, Saul looked genuinely off balance.

"I'm sorry." Lyr was not sure why she had apologized. She had done nothing wrong. "I won't say a word to my mother. But you must give me time to think."

Saul nodded, defeated, as if she had already denied his request. "I understand," he said, then carried on towards her home. Their hands did not touch again that night.

Embarrassment washed over Lyr as she lay in bed later. Her stomach growled and she was suddenly reminded that one of the reasons she had attended the meeting was to pick up provisions. She had been so shocked by Saul's request that even her hunger had been forgotten.

She must have seemed like such a shallow idiot to Saul, saying one thing and then immediately changing her mind. No doubt, Saul was already rethinking offering her a place in this infiltration. Another thought darted out from behind the first: would the Free Kings trust her with the information she now possessed if she refused this job? She knew they were preparing to invade the Royal Palace. She had seen their faces. Saul trusted her, but the others had every reason to be wary of a stranger in their midst.

She shook her head to dispel the paranoid thoughts. Lyr turned over, facing her mother's cot. The woman slept—it was all she did as of late. The royals had taken everything from her, including any semblance of a purpose. Could Lyr risk leaving the woman with no one? Who would tend to her then?

If I do this, Lyr thought, *it will not be for Saul. It will be for her.*

It would also be for herself and for everyone who was suffering at the hands of the royals. She had felt stuck in the life she had been thrust into for too long. Perhaps it was time to change things. To take this risk. To find purpose.

VIII.

Spare Boots and Journeycakes

Rovan's shoulder joint popped under the weight of the rucksack. As always, Tieg had overpacked. The journey to the Womb was only one full day, so there was no need to bring along a week's worth of hard cheese and journeycakes. The rope was good thinking on Tieg's part, though the extra set of boots was a bit much. Rovan deposited the excess weight onto the tavern table under Tieg's disapproving eye.

"And what if the boots you're wearing burst at the sides?" Tieg asked.

Rovan laughed. "I don't expect my foot to grow in a day."

"And the cheese? What if you get hungry?"

"It's only a two-day trek—there and back. I'll be fine with two days of provisions. And if I'm truly famished, I can always forage for berries or hunt for a rabbit. But I don't predict that will be the case."

Tieg shook his head, unconvinced. "Don't go asking me for anything when the time comes. I won't be sharing any of my supplies, no sir."

It had been like this all morning. Tieg had begun his overthinking and overpreparing when the sun had barely tinted the sky. It was only normal for him to feel some nervousness—the journey he was embarking on would take him away from them and back to a family that, for all Rovan knew, did not want him. Rovan had not pressed him, hoping to bring a calm and jovial air to the trek, though, in truth, he felt incredible apprehension at the task at hand. Finding Ashe's child without any sort of description to go by would be impossible. His best chance would be to find this Mother Adriel instead.

If he reached the Womb and found no one there, would he return empty-handed or carry on blindly? *Discernment.* The word had become a chant to him since the previous day.

"Hey idiot," Terreck greeted.

"What did I do this time?" Rovan asked. He was passing a block of milky beeswax over the outside surface of his pack to keep the worst of the rain from seeping inside.

Terreck shrugged. "It's good to be reminded. Keeps your feet on the ground."

Rovan smiled and pulled his hair back behind his ears, tying it into a tail with some twine. He then raised his, now, much lighter sack over his shoulder. "Make sure Pevine doesn't burn down again," Rovan teased.

"In this rain? It'd really have to be trying."

The rain had not stopped since the previous day. At times, it slowed to a teasing trickle but then would resume abruptly at full strength. The prospect of sloshing through mud all day was not enticing. Perhaps Tieg had a good point about bringing an extra set of boots, though Rovan would not admit to it now.

Tieg was busy saying his goodbyes to the rest of the crew. He hugged Iseo, then Fellen, who feigned indifference though it was obvious that he was quite distraught by the farewell. Tieg placed a hand on Fellen's cheek and smiled sorrowfully. "Be good," he said.

"Whatever," Fellen snarked, swiping a tear from his cheek.

"Don't go causing too much trouble, now," Terreck playfully reprimanded. He held out his arm, hand open.

"I don't plan on it," Tieg replied with a smirk, gripping Terreck's palm tightly. When they released the handshake, Tieg crouched and scratched Trinket's chin. As always, the cat was adept at making each social interaction about himself. Scanning the rest of the tavern, Tieg frowned. "Where's Scintilla?" he asked.

Terreck shrugged. "I haven't seen her all morning. You know how it is when she doesn't want to be found..."

Tieg nodded in disappointment.

"We can wait for her, then leave after you say goodbye," Rovan suggested.

Tieg shook his head. "If she wanted to say goodbye, she'd be here. Are you ready to go?"

"Wait!"

They turned towards the voice. The excitement that creased Tieg's forehead vanished when they saw the two women, Ashe and Alanda. Ashe held out something lumpy and gray. "For you," she mouthed to Rovan.

Rovan took the gray cracked stone from the woman. "Your spent runestone?"

"The one that *Guided* us here," Alanda explained. "Ashe wants you to have it. It's the only thing she possesses that connects her to Sesha."

"And what am I supposed to do with it if it's spent?" Rovan asked.

"In truth, I don't know," Alanda admitted. Then, holding Ashe's hand, she added, "But Ashe believes it will aid you in some way. I cannot explain."

The voiceless woman held Rovan's gaze. She placed a hand on her chest, then placed it upon the runestone. From the gesture, Rovan gathered that the woman meant some part of her heart was within that stone. Rovan did not have it in him to turn down the strange offering and dropped the useless stone into his pocket. "Very well," he said. "If I can't find your daughter, I will hopefully return with news of her."

The woman nodded, accepting his terms.

"Ready?" Rovan asked Tieg.

Tieg looked at his friends solemnly, one by one. The young man turned to exit the tavern as a means to hide his tears. The pelting rain outside assisted further. Rovan pulled his hood over his head as he followed behind, but that did a poor job of keeping him dry. It took only a few steps through the streets of Pevine before his boots were caked in slick mud. Tieg glanced back at Rovan's feet, smirking, his tears briefly forgotten.

"I know, I know," Rovan dismissed.

The trip ahead of them wasn't particularly arduous, but the weather promised to make it unpleasant enough.

Then there was the matter of the girl he was tasked to find. Sesha would have someone caring for her—an enchantress, if the two women were to be believed. And not just any enchantress: Mother Adriel, the villain the townsfolk of Pevine blamed for the fires. How would this enchantress react to two men demanding the surrender of the child she had been raising all these years?

No, Ashe and Alanda had only asked him to *find* this child, not to retrieve her. Rovan had learned years ago that the way a request was worded was as important as the task itself. He resolved that there was almost no chance of him returning with the child. Rather, his focus would be gathering as much information as possible about the child's whereabouts for the two women. He struggled to convince himself that was enough.

The clearest route from Pevine to the Womb of the World was to travel north along the Red Road, then turn south using one of the many footpaths that cut through the sparser woodland on the outskirts of Albadone. It seemed like a roundabout way, but Rovan did not want to chance getting lost on the wooded foothills that surrounded the mountain.

An hour up the Red Road from Pevine, they spotted the first Blue Scarab outpost. These outposts now punctuated the Red Road every few miles all the way south to Sol Forne and beyond. Rovan's experiences with the group had been both more unpleasant and frequent than he would have liked. He had almost been successfully recruited by them when he was younger and had even met their leader, Master Eggar o'Tamiar. Word was that Eggar had perished during the Portos revolt—Rovan wondered who commanded the Scarabs now.

Besides the fact that he would have had to shave his head to join the group—eyebrows and all—he also had moral reservations about the way the Scarabs operated. They fancied themselves the unifiers of the Kingdom of Hovardom, but Rovan had seen what their version of unity and justice looked like. Choice was an important part of what made a person free, Rovan believed. But the only way the Blue Scarabs saw to make progress towards their goals was to remove choice entirely.

Rovan knew the consequences of forcing his will upon another. However noble the supposed intentions of the Scarabs, their methods inevitably caused more harm than good.

A pair of blue-armored soldiers eyeballed Rovan and Tieg as they approached the tented outpost. Rovan did all he could to avoid interacting with the Blue Scarabs, but it had become just about unavoidable when traveling the Red Road. "Halt!" one of the two called out. "Declare yourselves."

"Rovan and Tieg, of Pevine," Rovan replied.

"Relation?" the Scarab asked, penning something in a ledger splayed across a rickety table under the tent.

Rovan glanced over at the fidgeting Tieg. "Brothers," Rovan stated.

"And where are you headed?"

"To the Womb of the World," Rovan answered.

The Scarabs looked at them in confusion, Rovan assumed—it was hard to tell without the eyebrows. "Why would you ever want to go there?"

Rovan shrugged. "Is that Blue Scarab business?" He should have known better than to say it, but sometimes words spilled out of Rovan's mouth before he could catch them—a bad habit he had carried with him since youth.

The two Blue Scarabs exchanged looks, affronted at having had their authority questioned. "By word of King Petar, we have jurisdiction over the entirety of the Red Road," the soldier explained. "Without us, anyone could use this road freely, as they see fit."

"Isn't that the point of a road?" Tieg teased.

"Yes, but—" The soldier floundered, flustered.

The other soldier stepped in front of his companion. "You can get to the Womb through the woods," he said, nodding towards the denser foliage across the way.

"You must be joking," Tieg protested.

"Let's not waste any more time with these bald bootwarmers," Rovan said. He took a few steps up the Red Road, deciding to test the resolve of the soldiers. In unison, the two Scarabs unsheathed their swords and blocked his path.

"You do not have our leave to walk the Red Road," one soldier declared.

"This is ridiculous!" Tieg exclaimed.

Rovan sighed. His experiences with the Blue Scarabs had taught him that there was no point in arguing with them. He grabbed Tieg's arm and pulled him away. "We'll take the long way then," he acquiesced.

Tieg shook his head in disbelief. "Is this how you *serve* your countrymen? Bullocks, the lot of you!"

"Say that here to my face!" the soldier yelled, stomping towards the two young men with his sword raised.

Rovan and Tieg bolted into the woods as the Scarab barked insults at their backs, only stopping when the shouts became inaudible. Rovan's boot slipped in the mud, sliding him firmly into a rough tree trunk. Tieg reached a hand out to him. The two laughed giddily—though they were now forced to take the long way, at least they were in one piece.

The Albadonian fires had barely grazed this area of the woods, and even still their effects were immediately apparent. The surrounding trees stood spindly and barren, contrasting greatly with the lush green grass at their feet. Cracked, charred, bark peeled back in surrender exposing the bleached bone-like heartwood underneath. The previous year, they had briefly traveled north of Pevine, where the worst of the fires had devoured the forest. There, the desolation gave the woods the impression of a graveyard.

Bit by bit, things were getting better, if the townsfolk were to be believed. Some had observed trees making miraculous recoveries, from charred to verdant in the span of less than a year. Woodland critters, such as birds, squirrels, and the occasional greatwolf, had repopulated the area. It all still looked quite grim to Rovan, but why spit where people found hope?

With no lush canopy to conceal it, the great mountain was already visible ahead of them, dark and looming. Stories of all shapes surrounded the legendary Womb. It was where the *life energy* that filled the world and all living creatures was said to have originated long ago. It was where *dragons* had lived until a great disaster forced them to flee to the icy north. It was where witches and shadowfolk took naughty boys and girls to gobble them up. The only story he could trust, as it was the most corroborated, was that Mother Adriel resided there.

As he had heard it, the young enchantress had been the apprentice to one of the most renowned enchantresses in the kingdom, some even argued the world. The Albadonian woodsfolk regarded enchantresses very highly—as other places did with chemists, blacksmiths, and village elders. This contrasted greatly with the southern parts of the kingdom, where Rovan was brought up. In Sol Forne, enchantresses were thought of as 'witches' who defied the laws of nature for their own nefarious purposes. He had certainly met one like that. He had also met enchantresses in his travels who revealed themselves to be nothing more than glorified runestone peddlers.

This Mother Adriel held a very strange place in the imaginations of the residents of Pevine and the few who remained in the surrounding woods. The woodsfolk there no longer saw her as their elder, but rather as a betrayer. She had abandoned her home in the forest for the Womb of the World just before the fires came without warning anyone of their onslaught. Some went as far as accusing her of starting the fires herself. Why she would do that was a matter of great contention. Some theorized it was punishment for their digging into the forest and extracting its lifeblood. Others were more fantastical, claiming she was simply a merciless fiend possessed by evil gods. A few claimed the young woman had gone mad after the death of her mentor. Whatever the truth was, Rovan would soon find out.

He placed his hand on Tieg's shoulder, halting him.

"What is it?" Tieg asked.

Rovan quietly shushed his friend with a finger to the mouth. They stood still, only the constant droning of rain surrounding them. And something else. Rovan placed his left hand on the pommel of his hunting dagger. Tieg did the same, readying himself for a possible fight.

"Someone has been following us for the better part of an hour," Rovan whispered.

"The Blue Scarabs?" Tieg asked.

"I don't know. We need to move."

Rovan resumed the trek, though at an accelerated pace. Tieg remained at his side while keeping an eye behind them. "Stop doing that," Rovan said. "We can't seem like we know we're being followed."

"Then what?" Tieg asked. "We just let them catch us?"

"Keep moving," was all Rovan said. His mind was mulling over a plan. Tieg was right, they could not be caught, but they needed to proceed cautiously. Whoever was behind them was less covert than they thought they were. The infrequent wet rustling of leaves, like a slithering snake, bled through the hiss of the rain. The sound moved away, towards the right, then got closer, encircling them—a trap was being set.

"Keep straight," Rovan said, unsheathing his dagger and dashing right.

Upon seeing the blade, Scintilla raised her arms. "Stop!" she exclaimed in a panic.

"Scintilla?" Rovan called out incredulously. "What are you doing here?"

"I'm... following you," she replied.

"I can see that, but why?" Rovan asked.

Tieg finally reached them. He glanced between Rovan and Scintilla in disbelief. "What's going on?" he asked.

"I'm coming with you," Scintilla declared, lowering her arms. Her tone was resolved and left no room for debate. The hood that barely contained her thick hair was drenched. The only thing that remained dry was the hunting bow at her back, which was enshrined in a bulky leather case.

"Why didn't you ask to come in the first place?" Rovan asked.

"I didn't want you to say no," she replied.

"Why would we refuse you?"

"Because..." Scintilla glanced at the wet mud around her feet. "I'm coming with you," she said, finally raising her eyes to leer at Tieg. "To your home."

"What? Why?" Tieg asked in astonishment.

"I have my reasons," she said.

Tieg wiped the rain and bewilderment from his face. Rovan remained silent, hoping that the two would work out their differences without interference. "We're all free to make our choices, even when they make no sense," Tieg said coolly.

"We are in agreement on that," Scintilla uttered.

Tieg narrowed his eyes and then faced the distant mountain. "Now that that's settled, can we get on with it?"

Rovan sipped in a breath. It wasn't the sort of resolution he had hoped for, more of a stalemate really, but at least they hadn't jumped at each other's throats like they had back in Pevine. Rovan couldn't help but relate to Scintilla's motives for following Tieg to his family home. She wanted to protect him from what they all worried was waiting for him there. But could Rovan trust the two to be alone on their journey beyond the Womb? He wasn't entirely certain.

A few hours passed without so much as a word from any of them. The droning rain was partly to blame. "I think this is a good time to eat something," Rovan said as soon as the rain showed signs of slowing.

Tieg produced a journeycake and a piece of hard cheese from his sack. He sliced the cheese with his knife and sandwiched the slice between the savory cake before voraciously biting into it. Rovan only nibbled on half a journeycake, while Scintilla, to their surprise, retrieved a full wineskin from her bag.

"What?" she asked in response to their questioning eyes. "I'm soaked to the bone. This will help." Scintilla took a swig from the wineskin then handed it to Tieg, who eyed it suspiciously. "I'll save you the worry: it's poisoned," Scintilla mocked.

Tieg's face lightened and he took the wineskin. When it was Rovan's turn to drink, he did so happily. The cider within was heavily spiced and still warm. He would have preferred a mulled wine, but this did the trick.

Wiping his mouth and handing the skin back to Scintilla, Rovan announced, "We're not making the best of time, but that was expected. Approaching it from this side, the Womb is surrounded by foothills. Had those Scarabs not diverted us, we would have been further along."

"What happened back there?" Scintilla asked.

"Scarabs..." Tieg cursed. "Who put them in charge anyways?"

"Royals," Rovan answered.

"That's right," Scintilla recalled. "You used to be part of the Blue Scarab lodge in Sol Forne."

"No," Rovan corrected. "I visited their lodge. I met their leader, but I never joined them."

Scintilla smiled deviously. "Is that why you're intent on keeping your head so terribly shaggy? To stick it to the baldies?"

Though it was a funny joke, Rovan could not bring himself to laugh.

"I'm sorry, Rovan," Scintilla said. "I forgot..." She trailed off.

They were all aware of Rovan's distaste for discussing his past. "It's all right," Rovan appeased. "I'm just not proud of the person I was back then. Lately, I've been thinking I should stop feeling this way. It's not like I can change what I did in the past, and refusing to talk about it only feels like denial. Instead, I should try to learn from what I've done, the bad and the good, and carry on with my life. But it's easier said than done." Rovan smiled tentatively and restored the unfinished half of his journeycake to his pack.

"At times I too feel as if I cannot move past who I was," Tieg said, unprompted. "What if I am stuck and unable to learn anything?"

Rovan opened his mouth to speak but Scintilla was faster. "Going backward is worse than being stuck. It's like admitting defeat."

That was obviously not what Tieg wished to hear. The young man returned his unfinished food to his sack. "Shall we carry on?"

Rovan nodded. "I think that's a good idea. The rain is starting back again anyway. Nothing worse than eating soggy food." *If I leave these two alone, they might kill each other,* Rovan thought. But the prospect of accompanying them all the way to Tieg's home was less than appealing.

Rovan felt the wetness of his feet within his muddy boots, regretting that he had left the extra pair behind. It was not a pleasant thing to trek in the rain. Rovan had assumed that eventually, he would become accustomed to the misery of it. In truth, it had only become more pestering as the hours passed. A mile or so later, the woodland grew denser, finally looking like a proper forest and shielding them from the heavier rain. Tieg removed his hood and shook the wetness from his unkempt hair.

A scent of death seeped through the wetness and assaulted Rovan's nose. His companions seemed to notice as well. Tieg stepped ahead of them. "Look," he said, pointing at a nearby mound of dark wet fur and red gore. Rovan circled the carcass marveling at the immense size of the dead stag. The beast's side had been torn open, its shiny entrails spilling across the earth.

"What could have done such a thing?" Tieg wondered.

Rovan ungloved his hand and held it out, feeling the heat emanating from the carcass. "This was recent. Maybe a greatwolf?" But it wasn't just heat that Rovan felt—a dark anxiety began to build within his chest. His vision doubled and blurred at the edges. His breathing quickened.

A scream like something out of a nightmare shattered the forest.

"No. No. No..." Scintilla repeated, quietly panicked.

"What? What is it?" Tieg asked.

Rovan wiped his eyes, his vision steadying. He only had to glance at Scintilla's paling face and wide eyes to understand her fear: the scream was a *reaverlord's* call. Rovan had heard of such creatures before—he had even met an errant knight once who claimed his crew had slain one, though that could have been merely a tall tale. No one knew exactly where the creatures originated from, only that they were powerful, bloodthirsty, and nearly unkillable. They roamed the countryside aimlessly, seeming only to target villages, caravans, and traveling merchants. A *reaverlord's* destruction was so brutal and effective that they were often tailed by groups of opportunistic brigands, known as a *reaverlord's* band, who pounced on the loot left over in the aftermath.

Scintilla and her brother Terreck were the only ones in their group to have had a direct experience with one—when the orphanage they were brought up in had been massacred. Scintilla backed away from the direction of the scream, then bolted. Rovan and Tieg exchanged a panicked glance before following behind her.

"Where are you going?" Rovan called out. Scintilla gave no reply. Another scream sounded, loud and piercing, this time further away. Scintilla did not stop running. She was taking them off-course. "I think it's moving away," Rovan yelled. "Scintilla!"

Scintilla was only yards away now, but she was still running blindly at full speed. In a few more paces, Rovan would be close enough to reach out and grab her arm, and then he could—

Suddenly, Scintilla vanished.

Rovan came to a stop just as the earth did. He was standing on the lip of a steep cliff. "Scintilla!" he cried out again. Dropping to his knees with his hands clutching the edge, Rovan scanned the deep crack in the earth. He spotted a dark mass on a narrow ledge several feet below. It was breathing.

Rovan barely had time to let out a sigh of relief before he was joined by a frantic Tieg who he had to stop from nearly tumbling over the edge as well.

"Sin!" Tieg was crying so much that Rovan realized he could not see she was down there.

"She's okay, Tieg. I can see her on a ledge below. It looks like she's coming to."

Below them, Scintilla was slowly sitting up, her breath coming in quick jerky motions. She was still panicking.

"Scintilla, please calm down," Rovan begged. Scintilla inched away from the ledge until her back was pressed into the cliff. It was as if she couldn't hear them calling to her at all.

"What do we do?" Tieg asked him.

"I don't know." This was exactly why he shouldn't be their leader—when something actually bad happened, he was just as lost as anyone else. Yet he was the one burdened with responsibility.

Another scream came from even further away, headed east. The *reaverlord* was too far to reach them. Their most pressing issue now was getting Scintilla back up without slipping down themselves.

"It's all right, Sin," Rovan called down. "I'm here with you. You don't have to worry. No one is going to hurt you."

Scintilla did not look up at him. Rovan had only heard brief stories of the *reaverlord* attack she and Terreck had witnessed, but now the scars of that terror were manifested physically. This was not something he could fix. So, what could he do?

"I need you to lower me down."

"What?" said Tieg in alarm.

Rovan reached into his rucksack and pulled out the rope Tieg had packed that morning. "We have to move quickly. She's stunned from the fall for now, but I don't think that will last. I need to calm her down before she hurts herself."

Rovan secured one end of the rope to the closest tree, a spindly little thing that hardly looked up to the job, and tied the other end around his waist. Tieg grabbed the rope length and nodded to Rovan, an indication that he was braced for Rovan to descend.

All things considered, the descent took no time. Once at the ledge, Rovan knelt carefully beside Scintilla. Her cheeks were tear-stained, and her entire body shook as if seizing. Her inhalations and exhalations were interrupting each other with how fast they came. Her eyes were white and unblinking.

Rovan hesitantly touched the sides of Scintilla's face, gently holding up her head. "What's my name?" he asked, hoping that the simple recollection of who he was would be enough to snap her out of her daze.

Scintilla mouthed a "dor" sound, unable to form the word.

Rovan slowly lifted her head, until their eyes met. "Do..." he helped her. She repeated the sound. "Do...ro...van," they sounded out together.

"And your brother's name?" Rovan asked. Scintilla chuckled mirthlessly and shook her head. "Who is your brother, Scintilla?" he repeated.

"Terreck," she finally answered.

"And his name?" Rovan asked, pointing up toward Tieg.

"Tieg," Scintilla replied, seeming to only now realize fully where she was.

"And who else is there, in our family?"

"Fellen." Her trembling was starting to subside. Somehow, this was working.

"And your name?

"Scintilla."

"And my name?" he asked again.

Scintilla took in a strained breath and wiped her face. She pressed her cool forehead against Rovan's. "Rovan."

"Who else is in our family?" Rovan asked once more.

"Terreck. Tieg. Fellen."

"Good. Good," Rovan said, brushing the back of her head. "Now, I'm going to tie this rope around you and then Tieg will pull you up. How does that sound?"

Scintilla nodded as Rovan completed the knot. By the time they were both hoisted up, Tieg was a panting mess. He approached Scintilla reluctantly, then embraced her tightly.

Rovan felt spent. "I think we should make camp," he told Tieg. Though they had not budgeted enough supplies for an extra day, Tieg did not protest. He set his large bag on the ground and began to rummage through it.

"We can't stop here," Scintilla whimpered.

"It's going to be all right. Nothing can hurt you. Would you like to help us?"

Scintilla nodded.

The camp was a small, oiled tarp tied to nearby trees. It wouldn't retain heat through the night, but it would be enough to shield them from the rain. Tieg had even cared to cover the wet ground with thick wool blankets. How he had fit all of that in his bag, Rovan had no clue. They sat beneath their dreary abode as evening descended upon the forest. The mountain was suddenly imperceptible. *So close, yet still a ways to go,* Rovan huffed.

From his bag, Tieg produced a journeycake, which he broke into thirds and shared with the others. These were the moments Rovan couldn't help but crave—the times he spent eating, doing busywork, or sitting in companionable silence with the members of the group. His friends. In these moments, they felt like a proper family.

"Rest up," he told the two once they had eaten. "I will keep the first watch." To Tieg, he added, "I will wake you in a few hours to take over, and then you do the same with Scintilla. We move at first light." Though, if they would move forward to the Womb, or back to Pevine, Rovan was not sure yet. Perhaps the night would reveal that to him.

IX.

Chanter's Cove

Lyr had one more day to rethink Saul's invitation. It was entirely too much time. Already her resolve was giving way to further anxiety. She had only just joined the Free Kings. Or had she? There had been no initiation or ceremony, and now Saul was trusting her to be part of something so important. So dangerous.

Lyr watched through the window as rain soaked the streets. The market would have been closed due to the weather if it wasn't already shuttered in forced mourning. Lyr sighed—she would have appreciated the distraction.

What answer would she give Saul? If she accepted a role in the infiltration, who would take care of her mother?

As if in reply, Lyr heard Elga's thin voice calling out to her from across the home. Lyr turned and saw a silvery trickle of water running steadily from the roof and down the far wall into a quickly growing puddle.

"Not again," Lyr grunted. "I thought that man fixed it last year."

"Not well enough," Elga replied from her bedding, the edge of which had sponged up a good deal of the water.

"We have to get you to someplace dry," Lyr resolved.

The woman looked at her flatly. "I suppose you're right."

Lyr was relieved. Despite her melancholy, Elga still knew when to take care of herself, though her face betrayed consternation at the prospect of leaving her usual space. Lyr gathered the wet bedding. "We can take these to *Chanter's Cove* and dry them by the hearth."

Elga nodded slowly and stood from her cot. Lyr helped her mother up, quietly aghast at the woman's skeletal frame. It was the sort of thing she used to cry about, but Lyr had learned that such outward showcases of concern towards her mother only made the woman recede further inwards. Once Elga was on her feet, Lyr reached the old chest at the far end of the room and produced a fresh shift for her mother. As Elga dressed, Lyr placed their bedding into a thick cloth sack, tying its mouth with a rope.

"Are you ready?" Lyr asked.

Elga nodded, and the two made their way out into the rain.

Chanter's Cove was a nearby tavern and inn run by Amya, a childhood friend of her mother's from back in Pevine. It wasn't fancy, but it made a good gathering place for the humble citizens of the Pleasants. Like them, Amya and her husband Filli had been displaced following the fires and subsequent riots. Unlike Lyr's parents, who were immediately marked for being healers, the couple had been well connected in Vizen and were able to open an establishment of their own. Even as restrictions on the Marked had grown, they had continued to offer Lyr's parents employment in the back kitchen of the inn, where they could stay out of sight. But after Lyr's father died, and her mother confined herself to the house, it was up to Lyr to support them.

Lyr opened the inn's door and let her mother inside. The heat within greeted her wet face. Two old men sat in front of the fireplace, hands stretched towards it.

"Come, come in," a voice greeted. Amya approached them, then stopped short with an astonished expression. "Elga. It's been so long."

Elga nodded, then lowered her face, overwhelmed. "Ah, yes... I..."

"Hello Amya," Lyr pulled the attention away from her mother.

"Lyr," Amya replied. Her tone sounded strange, as if Lyr was supposed to infer something from it. "Well, come sit by the fire. Let me get you both some tea. That'll warm you just right." With that, the woman paced to a door leading into the kitchen.

Lyr raised her sack and deposited it in front of the fireplace. She unfastened the rope and released the bedding, setting it at the foot of the fire. When she turned, she noticed her mother was still dripping by the door. "What's wrong?" Lyr asked her.

"Perhaps this isn't such a good idea," Elga said. The woman tugged on her sleeve, covering her branded hand. "I should go back home."

"Momma, no," Lyr said sternly. "It's warm here. Sit down and make yourself comfortable. We'll get the bedding dry, warm ourselves with some tea, and we'll head right back."

Elga grumbled, then walked over towards the fire. Lyr grabbed two stools from the bar and placed them within range of the heat. Moments later, Amya returned to the main hall with two steaming cups of spiced tea. Lyr thanked the woman and blew on her cup.

"It's a pleasure to see you both here," Amya said. "What brings you in?"

Lyr waited a moment to allow her mother to answer. When Elga didn't offer anything, Lyr explained, "The man that fixed our roof last year did a terrible job. Momma woke up to a flood in the house."

"Oh, my!" Amya exclaimed. "You know, Filli is quite the handyman. He and his friends could fix it up at no cost!"

"That's very kind of you," Lyr answered, bowing her head.

"Anything for an old friend." Amya directed that at Elga, but the woman barely registered the words.

"Why is the *Cove* so empty today?" Lyr changed the subject.

The old man nearest the fireplace snorted and said, "By royal decree, each drink served must be accompanied by a toast for the dead king and then another for Princess Arisa's health."

Amya scowled. "Most of my patrons aren't so eager when it comes to that sort of thing, so they've decided to forgo the drinks altogether."

After a few silent moments, Amya asked, "Don't get me wrong, it's a pleasure to see you both. But it's been, oh, what? Three years? I started wondering if you no longer cared to keep my company."

Elga kept her eyes on the full, steaming, cup in her lap. "I'm sorry," she said.

Lyr met Amya's eyes with an imploring cast. "Well, I'm happy you're here now," Amya said. "Are you hungry?"

"Momma?" Lyr asked, touching Elga's shoulder.

"Sure," the woman said.

Amya smiled tentatively. "I've got sour turnip soup simmering in the back. Just like our mothers used to make. Better, even, if I say so myself! I'll get you some. Do you mind helping me with it, Lyr?"

Lyr's mouth tightened, but she didn't question the woman. She stood and set her tea on the empty stool, then followed Amya to the tavern kitchen. The rich earthy smell of sour turnip soup immediately returned her to her childhood in Pevine.

Amya quickly closed the door to the main hall, then approached Lyr with a serious expression. "I saw you there," the woman said.

Lyr did not need to hear more to understand what the woman meant. Dread squeezed the air out of her lungs. "Please don't tell my mother. Please. It would kill her."

"Oh, child, I'm not going to tell her." Amya kindly held Lyr's shoulders. "We Free Kings must remain united. It's the only way our goal will ever come to fruition."

Lyr let out a sigh of relief.

"Though the cause is noble, you must be careful being part of such a group," the woman continued.

"You do not trust them?" Lyr asked.

"I do trust them—most of them, with my fate. But you, Lyr, are young and have a whole life ahead of you. Are you sure you want to dedicate yourself to such a dangerous cause?"

Though Lyr's mind had been plagued with doubt about accepting Saul's request, she couldn't stop thinking about the generosity she had witnessed amongst the members that first night. What could Vizen look like without rule by the royals? Was there a way for the people to use their own voices in how the city—the kingdom—ran?

"Doing nothing seems more dangerous," Lyr said.

Amya's eyes narrowed. "Then I must ask," she continued. "Are you going to do it?"

"Do what?" Lyr asked.

"The infiltration. I know you've been asked to participate."

"How do you know that?" Lyr asked. "Saul and I were alone when he asked me."

Amya put a comforting hand on Lyr's shoulder. "Filli and I have our own parts to play in the mission. You'll soon find out more... should you choose to join, that is."

"I'm still considering," Lyr answered.

"There should be no room for doubt when deciding whether to undertake such a task. And with so little time to decide... I do not envy you, girl. Whatever you choose, I won't fault you."

Lyr looked into the woman's kind honey-colored eyes. "It's not that I do not wish to do it. It's just that... Momma isn't well. She doesn't ever leave her bed. She barely eats, bathes, or takes care of herself in any way. If it hadn't been for our roof leaking, today would have been just another day of her wasting away. I'm afraid that, if I leave too long for any reason, she will simply..."

Amya rubbed Lyr's shoulder, then turned towards the cauldron hanging over a small hearth. She scooped the soup into two bowls with a wooden ladle then added a bit more broth on top for good measure. She handed Lyr a bowl, then returned to the main hall of the tavern.

The two men who had occupied the seats in front of the fireplace had moved to the bar—they were comfortable enough to pour drinks for themselves. In a mocking voice, one raised a glass and said, "The king is dead," before taking a drink.

"That he is," the other man added, lifting his cup in the air, and then to his lips.

Lyr sat on the more comfortable seat that was now open. Elga remained on the stool, her impassive eyes fixed on the fire in front of her. The heat had returned some color to her pallid gauntness.

"Here you are," Amya said, handing Elga the bowl of steaming soup.

Elga nodded in thanks, gave the bowl a cursory glance, then returned her gaze to the fire in front of her.

"I hear the oracles say the rains are supposed to last for some time," Amya said. "The inn is quite empty at the moment, so I have spare rooms. How about you stay here until the storm passes?"

"We don't have any coin for that," Elga replied.

"I would never charge a friend in need," Amya said. "Stay here, where it's dry."

Lyr touched her mother's arm. "Doesn't that sound like a good idea, Momma?"

"If you truly wish to pay me," Amya resumed her pitch, "you can pick up a broom and give the storage room a good sweep every now and then. But it's wholly unnecessary. Please stay, Elga. At least until your roof is repaired."

Elga nodded. "If you're both so insistent..."

Amya smiled brightly. "I will prepare a room for you." Before leaving, she shot Lyr a knowing glance. Had the woman intentionally cleared the way for Lyr to join the Free Kings' infiltration? Now that her mother would have a solid roof over her head, daily meals, and people who cared enough to ensure her wellbeing, nothing was preventing Lyr from participating.

"I may be spent, but I'm not dull-witted," Elga suddenly uttered under her breath. The woman lifted her glassy eyes to meet Lyr's. "I know what this is about."

Guilt stabbed at Lyr. "Momma, I—"

Elga lifted a bony hand. "I will remain here until the rains die down. Then I will return home. But know that if you choose to pursue whatever this foolish errand is that they've roped you into, you will no longer be welcome back."

Lyr's eyes widened. "But why? Am I not free to pursue what I wish?"

"Aye. Free. But so am I. Free to kick you out of my life."

Lyr's heart sank. "Don't say that. Why would you say that? You're all I have."

"You'll end up just like your father."

Lyr stared at her mother dumbfounded. "What are you talking about?"

Elga shook her head. She picked up her spoon and pretended to be interested in the bowl of soup before her.

"Momma. Tell me," Lyr begged.

"He was one of them," Elga said after a long pause. "A Free King. He ranked highly in that little band of criminals. He always spouted about wanting to change the world." Elga's lip quivered, though no tears escaped. "They had planned some sort of mission to infiltrate the city guard. Then, one day, I found him... hanging from the rafters."

"Father killed himself," Lyr said, a knot forming in her throat.

"That's what we told everyone. His friends were always so worried about being arrested and publicly executed for their involvement. But they forgot that there are other ways for the royals to make a problem disappear. Quieter ways."

Lyr gripped the side of the chair as if to stop herself from falling off. She could feel the blood draining from her face—felt no heat reach her despite the fireplace. "How do you know he was killed?"

"Because I know my husband."

Lyr searched the woman's face for any signs that this was some final ploy to convince her to cease her involvement with the Free Kings but instead, she found only sincerity—sincerity and guilt for having kept this truth hidden so long and allowing her daughter's grief to run to hate.

Her father had been a Free King. Her father had been murdered for it.

The weight of the infiltration mission felt suddenly unbearable. It was no longer just a dangerous job she had been requested to assist in: it was the same sort of dangerous job that had killed her father. Was fate having a laugh at her expense when Saul asked *her*, of all people, to join?

Anger, blood red and far hotter than the nearby fire, spilled over. Her mother had suspected her husband was murdered and, instead of doing anything to get justice for him, she had laid down and pretended not to exist. Even worse, she had turned him into a coward in death. The idea of sharing the same fate as her father seemed less daunting now, appropriate even. It was never her father she needed to fear taking after—it was her mother.

Lyr released her grip from the chair and looked into her mother's placid face, unsure if the woman had asked her a question or said anything more. Lyr found herself breathing out some of the heat that had begun to boil over within her—somehow, she couldn't hate the woman, even now. She looked down at the bowl of soup in her hand—it no longer steamed, but the bowl was still warm—and picked up the spoon. She took a bite and relished the earthiness and familiarity of its taste. "It's good," she said.

Elga looked at the fire, picked up her spoon, and sipped the broth. "It is," she said. "It's very good."

The rest of the meal proceeded in silence. Though it was more than Lyr had seen her mother eat in weeks, it was still not enough. Normally, Lyr would have encouraged Elga to take a few more bites, but she didn't have it in her to push the woman any further. Amya retrieved the bowls and led them to the room she had cleared for them. It was about the same size as their small home, though it was far more inviting—misery and dread did not stain the walls and thicken the air here. The rain hit the small window softly like a baby's rattle.

"It's very nice," Lyr complimented.

"I'll replace the bedding with the one you brought once it's dry," Amya offered. "That'll make it feel more like home."

Elga reluctantly stepped into the room and touched the wool blanket—it was much nicer than those they possessed. "If you don't mind," Elga ventured, "I'd like to rest for a while."

"Of course," Amya agreed. "If you get hungry, feel free to come into the kitchen and grab anything you want. If you need a bath, we can warm some water. If you become bored, let me know and I'll put you to work. It's good to see you again, old friend." Amya stilled, seemingly hoping for a reaction from Elga. When she received none, the innkeeper turned and left the two alone.

Elga sat on the bed cautiously, perhaps afraid to ruin it.

"I'll go see if Amya needs help with anything," Lyr said. Her mother did not respond. Lyr left the room and softly closed the door behind her.

The tavern was now empty, save for Amya who stood behind the bar scratching notes into an overstuffed journal. "Has she been that way long?" she asked.

Lyr sat at the bar and nodded. "Ever since Father... *died*, she's been different. But the past year, it's as if she no longer makes any attempt to be alive."

Amya looked up from the journal. "It's hard, losing your partner. Gods know, she'd lost so much already when she came here."

Lyr nodded. "I will do it."

Amya's eyes met hers. The woman cautiously nodded and added no comment, as if saying anything would change Lyr's mind. She reached beneath the bar and produced a bottle containing a brown liquid, the same the two patrons had drunk from. She poured two small cups and handed one to Lyr. "My husband's mead. For courage," she said, raising her cup. Lyr half expected the woman to raise a toast to the king, but instead, all she said was, "To the cause," before downing the drink.

Lyr mimicked the woman. Warmth immediately filled her throat and chest. The drink did not make her forget the weight of what she was agreeing to do, but it did momentarily raise her spirits.

"I better find Saul and let him know," Lyr said.

"Do so. And, please, be careful," Amya cautioned.

Lyr exited the warmth of the tavern into the cold wetness of the city streets. The wind tunneled between the buildings, pelting her face with a wet chill. Lyr clenched her hood and pulled it closer to her face. Since the market was still closed,

Lyr would most likely find Saul at home. She headed westward, just outside of the Pleasants.

The three stories of Saul's family home were occupied by his parents, two brothers, grandparents on his mother's side, and his uncle. It was a tight fit and they were naturally loud people, so Lyr could gauge her proximity to the house using sound alone. She knocked loudly on the wooden door, and quickly Tommes came to meet her. "What?" the man blurted. "Oh, it's you." Saul's father's wide frame blocked any view Lyr might have had inside the home.

Tommes threw his head back and bellowed out Saul's name. Lyr had every sympathy for their neighbors.

After a few moments, Tommes was elbowed out of the way by a grinning Saul. "Lyr! I wasn't expecting to see you until tomorrow. Come inside, out of the rain."

"Actually, I was wondering if we could talk. Just the two of us. Somewhere quieter." As she said this, there was a loud crashing sound from somewhere on the floor above.

Saul's face fell. "Of course. Let me just grab my cloak."

They walked in silence for several paces. Lyr knew Saul was waiting for her to speak first. "I'm going to do it." Lyr expected another of Saul's broad, infectious, smiles, but instead, he stood still, blinking at her.

"You're sure?" The seriousness of his question made the air feel colder.

"I am," Lyr confirmed. Suddenly, she was being hugged. As quickly as it began, it was over, and she was face to face again with a blinking Saul.

"I'll be by tomorrow with information on your role," he said. "We'll all need to pass as palace servants, so you'll need to memorize as much as you can about your schedule, tasks, and the layout of the palace before then. The first two days of the mission will be focused on blending in. On the third day, you'll be summoned for a meeting. The details of the plan will be revealed then."

Lyr frowned. "Why not tell me the rest now? You don't expect me to go in blind, do you?"

Saul nodded. "I understand your concern. But it must be this way for the security of everyone involved. We cannot afford any of us being caught and questioned. The less you know now, while we're only just beginning, the better. I promise the secrecy is only about keeping you safe." Saul said the last part quietly while leaning in close as if anyone else was around to overhear.

Lyr felt her heart flutter. Saul seemed to believe that keeping the latter part of their plan from her would offer some protection, but she knew full well that, if caught, no amount of feigning ignorance would change the outcome. But she wasn't afraid any longer. She felt eerily calm. It was like resolve had eclipsed every other emotion. Had her father felt this way about his mission?

She and Saul walked back to his house in silence and parted with a final hug. Afterward, Lyr was so lost in thought that she didn't notice she had walked back to her home instead of the inn. The inside was dark, and the trickle of leaking water still gurgled down the far wall into what was now a quite impressive puddle. She turned to leave but not before wondering with a chilling calm if, should she meet her father's fate, the rafters above would be able to support her weight.

X.

The Womb of the World

The mountain loomed ahead of them like a great beast. As they neared the Womb of the World in the late morning, the muddy earth beneath their feet melted from reddish-brown to black. The black earth here was said to have special properties and could be used in both healing and enchanting. To Rovan, however, the thick slop of it was nothing but an added inconvenience. Rain had continued the entire way there with no sign that it intended to end. Rovan was soaked to the bone, and, from his companions' tense silence, he knew they too were suffering from the wetness.

"We need to be very careful," Tieg warned as they began their ascent. "The mountain is covered in black earth. If the stuff down here is slick and sludgy, it will likely get worse the higher we climb." A dark, unwelcoming path snaked up the side of the mountain. It was wide enough to be traversed by no more than a single small wagon at a time. Even then, the mere inches separating a wagon from the nearly sheer drop would be enough to challenge even the bravest of cart drivers.

As they climbed, Tieg's words proved true. The path was slick, chunks of loose sediment skittering unsteadily beneath their boots. Instead of congealing into mud, the wet black earth became like a slime. The smell of it, too, had amplified in the rain, staining the air with a sour, eye-stinging, haze. Rovan wiped the rain from his eyes, losing his footing in the process. Scintilla and Tieg both caught him, holding him up by each of his arms. Rovan thanked them and embarrassedly steadied himself.

The higher they climbed, the harder the rain pelted them. Tieg retained the lead. Rovan wasn't sure how handy his previous experience on the mountain would actually be on the treacherous path but was glad to defer his default leadership for a change.

After a half hour, they reached a sort of plateau that led inwards into a cavern. The opening widened further into what Rovan could only describe as a collection of habitations—or, rather, a tiny village. The blue and purple light of lanterns stuffed with glowing *dreadhall* mushrooms lent the space a peaceful, albeit frigid, air. The small buildings were made of wood and were constructed favoring the cave walls' natural slopes and indentations. A wide decorated tent lined the space as well, containing a long table with chairs occupied by supping folk. Many of them paused their meals and stared at the three in startlement. They were clearly not used to visitors.

An elderly man and woman stood and approached them at the entrance, cautious, however, to not step beyond the safety of their cave. Rovan, Tieg, and Scintilla greeted them with polite nods.

"Who are you?" the approaching old woman asked. She wore her hair in a thick white braid that snaked around her neck, an old fashion followed by a few of the matronly townsfolk in Pevine. The hand of the man standing next to her hovered over a large hunting knife at his belt.

Tieg surrendered the leadership of the group back to Rovan with a quick, panicked, glance. *Very well.* Rovan took a step ahead of his two companions. "My name is Rovan. These are my friends, Tieg and Scintilla. We've been hired to find someone we think might be here. A child."

At those words, several adults at the tables drew their children in close, perhaps in fear that his group was there to snatch them. Rovan needed to diffuse the unintended tension. "Her name is Sesha. Her mother is searching for her."

The woman and the man looked at each other worriedly.

Scintilla stepped beside Rovan. "May we discuss this inside the cave? We're very wet and we would prefer to not be."

"Of course, of course," the woman said apprehensively. "We've lived up here so long, we seem to have misplaced our manners." The woman waved them through the mouth of the cave and they gladly obliged. The elderly man whispered something in the woman's ear and then entered a nearby home. He emerged moments later wearing a heavy hooded coat. He passed the three and left the cave through the curtain of rain, headed further up the mountain path.

"Is there a bonfire anywhere?" Tieg asked between chattering teeth.

The woman shook her head. "Black earth is highly combustible, so our fires are confined within our homes."

"I see," Tieg replied in disappointment.

"We'll get you some warm blankets," the woman said. She directed this to a younger woman, who scurried away to retrieve said blankets.

"So," Scintilla resumed. "About the child?"

"Ah, yes," the woman said. "My husband went to fetch, well... the girl's mother. I'm sure you'll have some questions for each other."

Rovan shared a knowing glance with Tieg and Scintilla. They were about to meet the enchantress.

The young woman returned and handed them thick wool blankets, which they graciously accepted. Most of the other cave inhabitants had returned to their seats at the long table. "Would you care for something to eat?" the old woman asked, motioning towards the food.

"Please!" Tieg replied enthusiastically. "I'm close to famished." They were led to the table where Tieg and Scintilla took their seats. They were offered bowls of cold porridge peppered with small chunks of something meat-like. Tieg plucked out a piece and promptly deposited it beside his bowl upon realizing it was a lizard's tail. Rovan politely declined and remained standing. Even if it had looked appetizing, Rovan would still not have accepted it. He felt a pit of worry in his stomach—a precursor of something bad to come. "What's it like living in such a place?" Rovan asked the woman.

"We make do," she answered. "It's more scarce than living in a town or the woods, but we've tried to make the space our own."

"Where did you come from?"

"Most of us are from Pevine. We came here before the fires to be close to Mother Adriel."

"The enchantress?" Rovan asked.

"During a disaster, there's no better company to keep than someone with such a special connection to nature."

Rovan crossed his arms. "Even when the disaster is a fire and the person is on a highly flammable mountain?"

The woman smirked. "Our faith in her was clearly not misplaced. The intersection of the rivers Cleo and Ellot kept the fires from ever reaching this place."

These people's opinions of the enchantress differed greatly from those back in Pevine. Why had the enchantress saved these few people from the fires while leaving so many behind to perish?

"This Mother Adriel," Rovan began, "She's who your husband is bringing here."

The woman looked at him oddly. "Who are you really?"

"I already told you," Rovan said. "My name is Rovan. We were hired by the girl's mother to ensure she's all right."

The woman considered for a few moments before resolutely saying, "I think it's best if you sit down and wait for her." Rovan nodded in agreement and took his place at the table next to Tieg.

A flash of lightning briefly silhouetted two figures at the mouth of the cave. The rolling thunder that followed sounded like an ancient creature stirring within the earth's core. The elderly man re-entered the cave followed by a young woman—Mother Adriel, Rovan presumed. Though the man held his coat over her head to keep her dry, the enchantress did not seem at all bothered by the rain. Her nest of hair was wild and unkept, jutting in every which way and adorned only by several bird feathers. The hooded cloak she wore was dingy and in disrepair, several patches as the only embellishment. Her hand was gripped around a gnarled wooden staff, which she used to support herself as she limped forward, her face stern and impassable.

"That's them," the man said, pointing towards Rovan, Tieg, and Scintilla.

The enchantress nodded and approached them. Rovan stood and took an instinctive step back. He wasn't quite sure why he did it, but something about this woman commanded the sort of reverence he was not comfortable giving out. Tieg and Scintilla stood slowly and in unison, leaving their spoons in their unfinished bowls of porridge. Those who occupied the tables, too, stood and bowed, before resuming their seats.

"I hear you're looking for someone," the enchantress said.

"Yes, mistress," Rovan replied formally. "We were hired by a woman to search for her long-lost daughter. Sesha." At the child's name, the woman's nostrils flared. "Do you know anything about this child's whereabouts?" Rovan asked the question as a test.

"How is that woman?" Mother Adriel asked. "Still without a voice?"

Rovan nodded.

"A pity it never returned. That one survived so much tragedy: death, destruction, and having to surrender her child."

"So, you do know where the girl is!" Tieg exclaimed. The woman shot him an admonishing glance. Tieg folded under it like a blade of grass in the wind.

Returning her attention to Rovan, Mother Adriel continued, "The child was entrusted to me as part of the cost for a very powerful enchantment."

"To heal her burns, right?" Rovan asked.

"More than just her own," Mother Adriel elaborated. "The girl's and the forest of Albadone's fates are *Sealed* to one another. Do you understand?"

"I know something about *Sealing*," Rovan admitted, thinking back on Vaelin, his past mentor, whose fate had also been *Sealed* to an object. Was this something similar?

"Tell me, child," Mother Adriel said, "Do you ever hear nature calling to you?"

"What?" Rovan asked, taken aback by the sudden change of topic. "I don't think so."

"But I see it so clearly! *Life energy* surrounds you like a cloak. It's as if you've been touched by the Cycle. How can that be?" The woman traced through the air around Rovan's head with her hand.

So much had happened to Rovan six years before in Sol Forne. His fate had become temporarily entangled with that of a djinn—a being of pure *life energy*. Could this enchantress be seeing the residue of such a powerful *life energy* clinging to him? "I don't know what you mean," Rovan replied, hoping to leave it at that.

The enchantress sized him up skeptically, then shook her head. "You may deny it, but you are of great importance to the Cycle. As is my Sesha."

"Speaking of," Scintilla interrupted, "where is the girl?"

The enchantress looked away from Rovan as if exiting a daze. "I'm afraid I do not know."

"What do you mean?" Rovan asked.

The enchantress took a seat at the table, lowering herself with great strain. She wiped her skirt and made herself plenty comfortable before speaking again. "Sesha is my apprentice. I moved us briefly to the bog lands in the south. We remained there a year until one day Sesha ran away."

"If she's in the bog lands, then why did you come back here?" Scintilla asked.

The enchantress narrowed her eyes. "I am her Mother. I can more or less sense where she is. I followed her all the way here, assuming she had returned to our first home. But instead, she's gone further north, past the mountain. Towards that cursed city."

"Vizen?" Tieg asked.

The enchantress glared at him and nodded.

"Why would a child go all the way to Vizen?" Rovan asked.

"I haven't the faintest," Mother Adriel replied. "The girl was raised wild and free, as all apprentice enchantresses ought to be. But she has never seen a proper town, let alone a city. I fear she is in grave danger, and I am too weak from an injury to travel that distance on my own."

"So, her real mother was right," Tieg said.

"I am the only mother that child has ever known," she hissed. "But if even the woman who birthed her can sense the child is in need of being found, then it must be true. My poor Sesha... In Vizen..." The woman shook her head.

Rovan sighed deeply. To his chagrin, he found his lips moving, "I will go there and find her."

"You will?" Tieg, and Scintilla asked in unison.

"I promised the girl's mother—Ashe—to find her daughter and ensure her safety. I will continue to Vizen and find the girl."

The enchantress smiled. "Then you will escort me there." The demand seemed calculated, as if the entire conversation had been steered towards it.

The woman made Rovan uneasy. He didn't know where he would begin searching for Sesha in the vast capital of the kingdom. But bringing the enchantress along could only be beneficial—the woman did say she could sense Sesha's location. That was, at least, something.

"Very well," Rovan resigned.

The woman looked impassive, as if Rovan's permission was not something she required. "We leave in the morning. Tonja!" the enchantress called out. The cave village matron joined them. "Yes, Mother?" she asked.

"Treat these three as our guests," Mother Adriel commanded. "They are to be warmed and fed. Find them a place to stay the night and restore their supplies for the journey."

Tonja bowed her head and agreed. Overhearing the command, a few others had already sprang into action. A younger couple took Tieg, Scintilla, and Rovan's cloaks and brought them within a home to be warmed in front of the oven fires. Tonja pointed at a small structure. "That's where you'll stay tonight," she said. "We use it for storage, but it will fit three mats quite nicely, as long as you don't mind the close quarters."

Rovan glanced at his friends to get their quiet consent. After each nodded, Rovan replied, "That will work splendidly."

Tonja immediately headed for the building. Others joined her, removing crates and sacks from within and stacking them under the dining tent.

"I will retire now," Mother Adriel said. "I will meet you back here at first light." The enchantress stood with help from a young woman, then limped out of the cavern. Rovan frowned—her slow pace would add an extra day at least to the journey.

The three friends were led back to the dinner table where Scintilla and Tieg finished their cold lizard porridge. "Are you sure you don't want any?" a woman asked Rovan. Once again, he politely declined. The mucousy meal did not seem appealing to him in the slightest. The rest of the afternoon within the large dwelling was spent packing. The cave folk brought a variety of supplies for them: belts, ropes, shoes, cloth, onions, cheese... asking Rovan if each was needed. Rovan waved most of their suggestions away gratefully, growing steadily annoyed by their exuberant benevolence.

Scintilla and Tieg both packed as well. Tieg much more than either of them, naturally. "So, you will be carrying on, I suppose?" Rovan asked them.

The two stared at Rovan with a mix of offense and confusion. "What are you talking about?" Scintilla asked. "We still have a job to do."

"I said I'd help you with this task before going home," Tieg said, shaking his head. "We're not done yet."

Rovan smiled. He had been apprehensive at the thought of journeying to Vizen with only the enchantress for company—the woman made him more uneasy than he cared to admit. His relief was apparent enough that Scintilla rolled her eyes with a smile. They returned their attention to packing, every once in a while asking one another if they needed this or that.

When evening came, they retired to the small shack that had been set up for them. The space was cramped, the pallets hard beneath their backs, and the air inside was musty and stagnant. But at least they were dry. The glow from the *dreadhall* lanterns crept within the shack, giving their quarters an eerie cast.

"Not the most uncomfortable place I've ever slept in," Tieg volunteered.

"What would you say was the worst one?" Rovan asked.

"The campsite in that little prairie," Tieg said. "Where was that, again?"

"The one with all the berry bugs?" Scintilla offered.

"Yes! That's the one," Tieg replied.

"Oh, I was finding those little fuckers on my legs for weeks," Scintilla grimaced.

"More like months," Tieg gagged.

"For me it was Yorne," Scintilla said.

"Really? Yorne wasn't too bad," Rovan said.

"Oh, the inn was fine, don't get me wrong. It was the folk there that were awful. Do you remember how they would slam their fists on our doors and then run away in the middle of the night?"

Rovan chuckled. "I don't think I've told you this, but I went to empty the chamber pot in the ditch before dawn and met an old woman there. I said, 'Good morning.' What a mistake! She gave me the evil eye and then flung her chamber pot at me. Thank the gods I was fast enough to dodge her shit."

The two laughed. "What made everyone there so awful?" Tieg asked.

Rovan shook his head. "As far as I'm aware, that's how things have always been."

"I heard they don't even pay taxes," Scintilla said. "I don't understand how they manage to still be part of the kingdom."

"What about you, Ro?" Tieg asked. "Worst place you've ever stayed the night?"

"It's hard to say. I've enjoyed all the places I've gotten to share with you all," Rovan dodged.

Scintilla tossed her pillow at his head as Tieg booed loudly. Rovan laughed, returning the pillow to her. "Fine. The worst place I've ever slept was in Lornaros, the first night after I left Sol Forne. I had no idea how to fend for myself. Or what I was doing, really. I was hungry and broke. I simply walked up the Red Road until I reached the next town. It was swarming with Blue Scarabs. I said something to one of them—my temper ran hotter at the time—and I ended up getting beaten and tossed in a cell. But it wasn't my bruises, empty stomach, the cold stone floor, or even the absolutely massive rats that made that the worst night of sleep I've ever had. It was the loneliness."

The heavy silence in the room was interrupted by Scintilla. "We've all had nights like those."

"Yeah," Rovan said, looking at Tieg. "What I said before—it sounds stupid but it's true. Thanks to you two, and the others, no matter where we sleep—whether it's in a town that hates our guts, or in a field crawling with berry bugs—I at least don't have to do it alone."

"The berry bugs are a close second, though," Rovan added, as a way to alleviate the weight of his words. His companions laughed and soon, silence and tiredness descended upon them. As he often did at bedtime, Tieg broke into song, softly crooning an old lullaby from his hometown. It was a bit morbid for Rovan's taste—a song about a baby dangling over the wide mouth of rabid wolves—but Tieg's voice always seemed to lull him into a state of comfort.

Even then, Rovan found sleep elusive. Something the enchantress had said was echoing in his mind. "*You may deny it, but you are of great importance to the Cycle.*"

Him, of all people. He had almost caused unspeakable damage to the Cycle by imposing his will upon a being made of pure *life energy*. Mother Adriel must have been mistaken. But then again, why did the words chill him so, as if they were true? Rovan could not say. He squeezed his eyes shut to dispel the ghostly blue glow spilling within the shack, and tried, unsuccessfully, to conjure sleep.

XI.

Yulma

The next two days were a blur of preparation. By day, Lyr did what she could to help Amya around the inn, and by night, she read and reread the small scroll that contained her new identity as well as a map of the inner palace. The servants' quarters and a few secret alcoves they would use as meeting points once inside were marked in red. Lyr stared at the sketch in the dim candlelight committing it to memory. She felt her mother shift beside her. The two had hardly traded any words since Elga's revelation about Lyr's father. Lyr preferred that. It made it easier to not think of the risk she was taking.

Lyr glanced at the sketch of the palace one last time, as if she could impress it into her eyes. Night had already descended, and soon she would have to leave for her task. She looked over at her mother's sleeping form. Lyr could not bring herself to bid the woman farewell. She was afraid that by doing so she would be closing this chapter of her life forever—that she would be burying Lyr, the girl who lived in the Pleasants with her mother, and replacing her with Yulma, the kitchen hand.

Once downstairs, Amya placed a steaming mug of spiced tea in front of Lyr at the bar. She took a sip, tasting the bittersweet notes from the mead Amya had spiked it with.

"You'll need all the courage you can muster," the woman said.

Lyr knew that the time had come. She placed her now empty mug on the bar and donned her hooded cloak. Amya placed her hands on Lyr's shoulders. "Whatever happens, I will take care of your mother. Be strong. And thank you."

Whatever happens, Lyr thought. *She means, if I die.*

Before leaving *Chanter's Cove*, Lyr dropped the scroll and map she had committed to memory into the fireplace. The wisps of parchment were gone in seconds.

The streets of Vizen had never felt so unwelcoming. It was as if each towering building screamed for her to turn back. The rain was her only companion on her solitary walk towards the royal palace. It took nearly an hour to reach the section of outer wall where Saul had told her to meet earlier that day. Where the city and palace walls intersected, Lyr took a nearly hidden staircase that led underneath the cobbled street. She jumped back upon seeing a palace guard standing beside the wide entrance to the city sewers. The guard said nothing, only nodded towards the entrance, and moved aside. Lyr was aware that the Free Kings had partially infiltrated the palace guard, but she did not feel like abandoning caution just yet. She lowered her head and marched into the gaping mouth of the palace drains.

The drains were a complex infrastructure of sewer tunnels that twisted beneath the palace like buried city streets. Some were wide enough for two horse-drawn carriages to ride abreast, while others were too small for a grown adult to even crawl through. Lyr recalled a story she had heard once about the tunnels being haunted by the ghosts of the men Queen Odessa the Cruel had slaughtered during her bloody reign two hundred years ago.

Lyr ignored the stench that assaulted her. The sound of rushing water was constant. The sewers fed their waste into the Cleo River just outside the city walls. An orange glow up ahead revealed the silhouettes of three people standing near a staircase. Lyr slowed her step as she neared them.

"Ah, Lyr! Thank the gods!" Saul's voice called out softly. The torch in his hand glowed warmly.

Lyr hastened her step and joined the small group. "Is this everyone?" she asked.

Saul sighed. "Four of us should be enough." Lyr grimaced. Though he was trying to project confidence, Saul's nervousness was evident. Saul continued, "We are waiting for our man on the inside to let us in. You have all spent the last few days learning your roles. Now, it's time to become them. Go ahead and introduce yourselves."

The short and stout man at Saul's right smiled unsurely. Lyr recognized the evicted baker from her first Free Kings meeting. "I am Geren. I am a baker. I bake bread. And sweets." With that, he nodded, apparently pleased with his curt introduction, and took a step back.

"I'm Alizia," the young woman next to Geren said flatly.

"No, no, no," Saul said with a hint of panic. "From here on we only use our palace names. I'm Rynard, the butler. And you are—"

"Zinia. The maid." The woman was tall and starkly muscular, beautiful but for the scar that ran down to her chin. Why was someone with such a bold appearance chosen to play a maid? Lyr wasn't sure that Alizia could remain inconspicuous on such a mission, and her poor acting skills were of no further comfort. The woman was solid but nervous. Saul placed a comforting hand on her shoulder. A strange pang of jealousy invaded Lyr. Did Saul also see how beautiful the woman was? How could Lyr's short stature and plain frame compete?

Is this really the time or place to think about that? Lyr chastised herself.

"My name is Yulma, and I will be assisting in the kitchens." The name felt clunky leaving Lyr's mouth. She would have to work on that.

They all remained silent, the rushing of water around them the only sound. Lyr realized that she had grown accustomed to the offal stink of decay and excrement. Somehow, she found resolve in that. Perhaps, in the same way, the city had grown used to the smell of subjugation.

The scrape of an iron door sounded above them, echoing throughout the sewers. The sound of boots descended a staircase.

"AWK!" a voice spat. "It always smells worse than shit down here!"

"Boggar?" Saul called out.

"Yes, yes, it's me." A short man of about forty crept into view, holding a hand in front of his nose. A trimmed salt and pepper beard dusted Boggar's jaw, while no hair to speak of grew underneath his nose or on his head. His eyes were two sunken bruises, and his teeth were yellow and crooked.

"You best put that out," Boggar said, pointing at the torch in Saul's hand.

"Are you certain?" Saul asked. "It gets quite dark further in."

"I know the way." Without another word, Boggar headed further into the dank cavern. Saul dropped the torch to the ground and stomped out the flame. He then joined Boggar, as the rest reluctantly followed.

The tunnel grew darker and narrower, which forced the group to pivot sideways in a single file to squeeze through. The smell of excreta and decay was overwhelming now that her sense of vision was compromised. Lyr began breathing with her mouth, but that only caused her to taste the smell. A large, hairy creature brushed between her legs, then another, and another. *A cat*, she lied to herself, until a slithering tail touched her, making it impossible to ignore that they were wading through a sea of rats.

Eventually, they entered a larger hall. Light filtered in from the grates above. Rainwater cascaded down into the river of filth below them. These grates that lined the streets of Vizen's richer neighborhoods alleviated flooding during the rainy season, while the poorer parts of the city were left to fend for themselves. They caught their breath for a moment on the stone walkway beside the river of shit. The dark water flowed downstream carrying highborn filth into the innocent Cleo.

Out of sight and out of mind.

At the end of the walkway, they reached a three-way fork. Boggar led them down the left and widest path. At the end of that pathway, they reached a narrow staircase. Boggar stopped abruptly. "Up there is the yard. It should be empty at this hour, but just in case I have my man keeping watch. Once we're out, you will make your way to the servant's quarters where you're to be washed and dressed. Leave your clothes on the floor. I'll see to it that they're burned."

He turned to Geren, the baker, and Lyr. "You two will be working in the kitchens. I trust you've already learned where they are." To Alizia and Saul, he said, "You two will be tending to the western wing. I'm afraid you won't be near any royals except during feasts or banquets, but that's the best I could do."

Saul nodded.

Boggar's expression soured. "See to it that you're not discovered. And if you are, ensure that my name remains off your lips. Now, stay put while I ensure all is clear up there." Boggar vanished up the staircase, as the group buzzed with silent anticipation.

Lyr's heart beat nervously and so loudly that she was afraid the others might hear it. The prospect of Saul and Alizia serving in the same wing of the palace filled her yet again with inexplicable jealousy. They were all about to embark on a dangerous mission, so why was this, of all things, what she was thinking about?

A few moments later, Boggar returned and led them upstairs. As promised, the large square courtyard was completely deserted. There was a blacksmith's shack in one corner, as well as a training yard complete with several wooden weapon racks under a wide canopy.

Someone held out a hand to help Lyr up the steps. She looked up to see a tall and handsome young man a few years her senior, with dark focused eyes and hair the color of a copper piece. His black, flowing clothes could not conceal his warrior's build. He smiled at her gently and held her hand as softly as if she were highborn, somehow ignoring the fact that she smelled like proper shit. She couldn't help but blush.

"You all made it," the young man whispered.

"Aye," Boggar gruffed. "Thanks for keeping watch, Dregor."

"My pleasure," the young man replied. "You two," Dregor pointed at Saul and Geren. "With me." He paced away towards the palace, leaving Saul and Geren to scramble after him. Lyr stared at them in a panic. Why were they being separated?

"This way," Boggar said to Lyr and Alizia, leading them through a separate entrance into the palace. Alizia's stiff gait seemed to mirror Lyr's alarm, though they both calmed down once they realized they were being led to the female servants' quarters. Two old women approached them, and Boggar left Lyr and Alizia in their care. They were soon undressed and scrubbed clean. Once they were rid of the stench of the drains, they were given simple brown tunics to wear. Their old clothes were taken away to be disposed of. Moments later, one of the old women led the two of them into the servant common hall, where they were briefly reunited with Saul, Geren, and Boggar.

Cleaning up had taken the better part of an hour, and the early morning sky was beginning to lighten. Their stout guide handed each of them a rolled-up wool blanket and a change of clothes. "You will now be shown your rooms," he said. Lowering his voice further, he added, "Inside the blanket, you will find a small vial containing a clear, odorless, liquid. Keep this on your person at all times. If you're ever found out, or even fear you might be found out, don't hesitate to use it upon yourselves. The result will be painless."

"Sounds like you're describing poison," Geren said, his eyes wide in horror.

"That's because I am," Boggar replied, annoyed.

Before any of them could add another word, they were separated once more and led to their quarters. To Lyr's relief, she and Alizia were quartered together in a room with three other servants. Though Lyr didn't know Alizia beyond the fact that she was a fellow Free King, she welcomed any familiarity in this new environment.

The quarters were small, with unpolished stone walls, a low ceiling, and a single window covered by a wool curtain that blacked out any light. The floor was lined with five cots, three of which were occupied by their sleeping quartermates. Alizia kneeled on an empty cot and unrolled the wool blanket she was given. Lyr followed her lead. As she unrolled it, something small and solid landed on her cot. She picked up the object and examined it: just as Boggar had described, the small vial, about the size of her pinky finger, was filled with clear liquid. As she swirled the vial around, she was struck by how easy it would be to mistake a poison like this for water.

Alizia grabbed her hand and lowered it, shaking her head. She took the vial from Lyr, lifted Lyr's cot, and hid the vial underneath. Alizia then lay on her cot and pulled the covers to her chin. Lyr decided to do the same.

She had only closed her eyes for a couple of hours before waking. Alizia's cot was already empty. The only person still in the small room was a girl a couple of years younger than Lyr. Her skin was milky white, and her hair was red. She was busy tying a thin braided rope around her waist to secure her tunic. The girl turned and looked over at Lyr, who was rubbing the sleep out of her eyes.

"Oh, hello new girl," she said. "What's your name?"

"I'm— Yulma," Lyr replied, clearing the cobwebs out of her throat with a cough. She had nearly blurted out her real name. Suddenly Lyr felt terribly unprepared to face her first day.

"My name is Dora. I heard you arrive early this morning, but I was too sleepy to greet you. How do you find yourself at the palace?"

Thankfully Lyr's past two days of studying paid off and she found herself casually responding, "Though a friend of the family."

"Same with me," Dora replied. "My mother's sister used to serve as the queen's chambermaid before she fell ill and died. The queen loved her so much that she made her daughter, my cousin Bernarda, one of Princess Arisa's handmaids. Bernarda is so lucky. I'm stuck serving in the western wing, so I don't ever see any of the royal family. Where are you serving?"

This one talks a lot. It was best if Lyr kept the information she shared to a minimum. "I'm in the kitchens."

"I hear Flavien is a real pain! He's the head cook. I heard he once beat a servant boy bloody for dropping a teacake from a tray. Gave the poor boy a limp. No one wants a cripple at court, so they threw him out onto the streets. They say he's a beggar in the Pleasants now. How dreadful." Dora looked around the room as if she was about to share a secret. She moved close to Lyr and sat beside her. "Did you see her?" she whispered, her green eyes widening.

"See who?" Lyr asked.

"That other woman they have quartering with us. Had I seen that scar of hers before falling asleep I would have had such nightmares! Who wants such a disgusting creature around? And to think that I'm to serve in the west wing with it! First that scarred child, and now this."

"What scarred child?" Lyr was struggling to keep pace with this conversation.

Dora placed her arm around Lyr's shoulder. "You're a pretty thing, aren't you? Yulma, was it? Don't worry, Yulma. I'll keep an eye on you and make sure no one does you any harm."

Lyr could do nothing but force a smile, hoping her other quartermates were not as pestering. She had a chance to meet them later that day. One was an olive-skinned woman named Leandra whom Lyr would be working with in the kitchens, while the other had to be the 'scarred child' Dora was referring to, although Lyr had observed no scars. She was a quiet little thing who kept to herself. It seemed only Dora would be a concern.

Lyr spent her first day shadowing Leandra, learning what it meant to be a kitchen girl. The job was simple, albeit contradictory: "Always be present, but also stay out of the way. And make sure to do everything Flavien says." Thankfully, Lyr only caught glimpses of the head cook that first day. He was too busy overseeing preparations for the next evening's funeral feast to notice the new girl.

Leandra let Lyr into the kitchen pantry and allowed her a brief moment to observe the space. The small room was a wonder, brimming with fresh produce, dried meats and smelly cheeses hanging from the rafters, barrels of beer, and sacks of grain, beans, tea, and flour. It was more food than Lyr had ever seen in one place, even surpassing the market at the height of the summer harvest.

"If you're lucky," Leandra said, "you will spend more time in here than out there. The sooner you start familiarizing yourself with these shelves and stores, the better." Leandra walked to the back side of the pantry and pulled on a lever in the wall. After a loud click, a large section of the floorboards lowered into the floor. "Down there is the cellar. It's where we store feast day wine casks selected by Flavien."

"That's quite steep," Lyr said, observing the ramp.

"That's why I'm showing it to you now," Leandra agreed. "At some point, you'll have to push a cask up the ramp. It's better if you're mentally prepared for that. Oh, and if the barrel starts rolling back on you, you have two options. You can let the barrel crush you or step out of the way and deal with Flavien. Between you and me, I'd take the barrel."

After the brief pantry tour, Leandra led Lyr back into the kitchen and gave her a long list of chores. Lyr swept the floors, wiped up food scraps, washed dishes, stayed out of Flavien's way, and all too quickly, the day turned to night.

"Good job today," Leandra complimented, walking Lyr back to their quarters to change into a fresh tunic before dinner. "Keep that up and you won't have any problems." In the room, however, they were greeted with an ongoing confrontation. Alizia held Dora against the wall. Dora's feeble struggles against the much larger woman were almost comical. "Leave me alone you dirty Pleasants scum!" Dora sobbed.

"What's going on here?" Leandra demanded.

"She assaulted me without reason," Dora choked.

Leandra stepped between the two and grabbed Alizia's arm. "What happened? Why are you attacking her?"

Alizia eyed the other woman apprehensively, then nodded towards her cot. "See for yourself."

Lyr neared the cot and immediately her nostrils flared as the smell of manure hit them. She plugged her nose and lifted the blanket revealing a brown lump.

"Dora!" Leandra admonished.

"It's just goat dung—and she has no proof I did that," Dora immediately amended. "Besides, I hear that folk from the Pleasants like to roll around in filth." At that, Alizia shoved Dora against the wall harder.

Lyr walked up to Alizia and patted her on the back gently. "Come on. I'll help you clean it up." Alizia eyed Lyr. Her aggression seeped away as if she suddenly remembered their reason for being there. She stabbed Dora with a last deadly look that made even Lyr shudder, before letting go of the crying girl. Along with Lyr, she scooped the manure off the wool blanket. "Thanks," Alizia said.

"I can help you wash your cot and blanket," Lyr offered.

Leandra sighed. "I'll take you both to the wash. You might as well learn where it is. You can grab a fresh blanket there. And you, Dora, I will let Steward Ibessa know about this. I won't tolerate this sort of behavior."

Dora eyed Alizia with bloody contempt.

Perhaps this one will be more trouble than I had first assumed, Lyr thought.

XII.

Petar the Just

The sickly stench of incense permeated the great central hall of the House of the Gods. Its smoke stung Searin's eyes. She wiped a tear from her cheek with the back of her sleeve. Helva, the usually jovial woman who had been Searin's wetnurse, noticed the motion and leaned over to give her a consolatory hug. No doubt she thought the tear was from mourning the king— Searin didn't have the heart to tell the woman that she had no tears to shed for her father. They never had a close relationship. King Petar's heart hadn't held love for his children since his firstborn, who shared his father's namesake, had died at the age of six. A chill had crept into the poor child's chest, turning his every breath into a slow agony.

"Little Petar showed so much promise," the king had once reminisced while drunk. *"You should have seen how he swung his practice sword in the yard. A true warrior-king in the making!"*

Though Searin only possessed a faint memory of her older brother, the ghost of him had cast a deep and dark shadow over her entire existence. Her own talents with a sword served to her father only as a reminder of the potential Petar could have had. She would never live up to Petar the Second—the king that should have been—so she had stopped trying.

When Searin renounced the crown, she had seen relief in her father's eyes. Though he criticized Arisa for being more studious than adventurous, the late king had seen promise in his youngest daughter. No, Searin would not shed a single tear for a man who had only ever viewed her existence as superfluous.

Searin stood with the rest of her family in the middle of the great hall of the House of the Gods. Hovard, her little brother, was positioned next to their mother. The boy's face was pallid and his eyes distant. He had been uncharacteristically silent ever since finding their father's body.

Queen Altima's face, on the other hand, did not betray even the most fleeting ripple of emotion. Whether it was a display of strength before the gathered nobility, or because she had no emotions to conjure, Searin was not certain.

Out of all of them, Arisa wore her emotions most plainly. Tears streamed down her cheeks, her eyes wide and distraught. The realization that the anointment was at hand was clearly weighing on her. Their uncle Clavio placed a hand on Arisa's shoulder and whispered something into her ear. Arisa wiped her cheeks with her sleeve and collected herself with a few slow breaths. Searin couldn't help the prickle of jealousy that wove through her. Not that she particularly cared, but no one besides the old wetnurse had paid her any mind all day.

The Altar of Grace stood at the center of the hall, a large rectangular marble slab snaked with golden vines. Her father lay atop it: King Petar Talessi the First, known to the people of the kingdom as Petar the Just—or at least that was the moniker he had chosen for himself. Searin could think of a few more apt names—Petar the Insufferable, Petar the Neglectful, Petar the Invisible Father... She could not recall a single 'just' thing the man had ever done. Not for his family or for Hovardom.

From impoverishing the kingdom with his inept handling of the war on the Red Coast to closing the Vizenian city gates on all folk seeking healing and shelter after the Tragedy of Albadone, to then forbidding anyone from ever speaking of the Tragedy altogether, King Petar had not been a just ruler. He was a temperamental and fearful man, busier reacting to news than thinking ahead. She wouldn't be surprised if every home in the kingdom was filled with toasts and cheers at the news of his death.

And what of the foreign realms? A strained relation with Toropan to the north, and Boglynd and Earwynne to the south. Their own city-states of Perimat and Sol Forne had been marred by rebellion. *A legacy left in shambles for your children to fix*, Searin thought bitterly.

She glanced over at her sister—Arisa had regained some color to her mournful face. Searin turned ahead to look at her father. His face was more relaxed in death than she had seen it in life.

Arisa will make a greater ruler than you ever were.

The old, drooling High Priest mumbled a prayer, which was rendered incomprehensible by the echoing vastness of the hall, and concluded the eulogy. He then invited the noble guests to approach the altar and to look upon the king's face one last time. As was tradition, each guest placed a smooth river stone atop the king's body as a token of gratitude and honor—a tradition retained by them from the old world.

Searin spied many somber faces among the crowd of nobles approaching the altar that were obviously feigning or, at best, exaggerating their sadness. Bale o'Auldvalley, Amster Sharenton, and Hilda o'Laung were at the front of the line. By king's order, all three of them had lost substantial portions of their lands twenty years prior so that the flow of the Cleo River could be diverted towards the city walls to create a moat. All three sported their most mournful faces as they deposited smooth river stones on top of the king's chest. Behind those teary eyes, Searin knew they couldn't be more elated. Their scribes and lawyers were no doubt drafting a plea to the soon-to-be-anointed Queen Arisa to right the twenty-year-old slight at that very moment.

When Arisa dies, no one will have to pretend to mourn her. Searin often fantasized about her place at her sister's side. As high captain of the King's Guard, she would participate in every closed-door meeting. She would have the queen's ear, and her council would be heeded. She would help her sister shape a better kingdom from the fragments of this current one.

The pile of river stones eventually became so immense that it toppled over and crashed loudly across the floor. The deafening sound made an old noblewoman faint back into the arms of her entourage of servants, who then carried her out of the hall by her arms and legs. Once the last stone had been offered, the procession of nobles paid its respects to the royal family. One by one, hundreds of miserable highborn men, women, and children bowed their heads before Searin. Some whispered prayers and best wishes, while others offered trite words of condolence. Just like the painful ringing of the funerary bells that had blared throughout the city, Searin couldn't wait for this farce to be over.

As the young Thane Ad'ere—a lanky teen who had obviously used the pretense of the king's death as an excuse to visit the capital and who was doing a poor job of pretending to be sad at all—bowed and said a few words, Searin noticed her uncle laying a stone of his own on top of the pile. Clavio then made his way towards them and bowed at a right angle. When he straightened, he kissed the queen on the cheek.

"My deepest condolences to you, my dear, beautiful, Sister-queen," Clavio said in his flowery voice. "May my brother join the Nameless in their eternal Great Hall."

Queen Altima nodded solemnly.

"I am glad I could be in Vizen for this," Clavio added. "I wouldn't have been able to forgive myself if I had missed it." Clavio turned to face Arisa. "Might my niece grace me with a meeting after the ceremony?"

"Of course, Uncle," Arisa agreed flatly. "You may meet me in my chambers later this afternoon."

The queen narrowed her eyes. "My husband hasn't been dead even a week, and you have already begun your machinations. Shame on you."

Clavio looked pained. "My queen, it is a necessity. Tradition dictates that Princess Arisa is to be anointed within the fortnight. Now, more than ever, Arisa needs the counsel of someone who cares for her and for the kingdom."

"And you are such a person?" Queen Altima asked.

"Other nobles and ministers will want nothing more than to fill their pockets with wealth. I am family. I have nothing to gain here other than my family's well-being," Clavio retorted.

The queen stepped forward, defiantly. "Oh, please! And your claim to the throne, as the king's brother, has nothing to do with this?"

Searin had never seen her uncle so taken aback. The flash of affront on his face morphed into hurt.

"Mother," Arisa interjected. "You forget we aren't in our chambers right now."

The queen nodded dismissively. Clearly, the topic would be revisited once they had more privacy.

Clavio bowed again and moved along.

The parade of nobles seemed to never end. Hovard sniffled and was suddenly overtaken by sobs. At Queen Altima's direction, the wetnurse took the boy by the hand and escorted him out of the hall.

"You should come too," Arisa whispered. Searin had not immediately realized she was being spoken to. "When Uncle Clavio meets me in my chambers, you should be there."

"Why?" Searin asked dumbly.

Arisa faced her sister with a confused expression. "Are you not the high captain of my King's Guard?"

"Not yet."

"But soon."

Searin straightened her back. "Of course, my princess."

When the line of nobles finally subsided, the high priest recited the Prayer of Solace, a young boy then sang a long dreary hymn, and by the time it was all over, the sun had already begun its descent. The crowd was at last dismissed and the Great Hall emptied quickly leaving only the royal family and their guards behind.

High Captain Knott approached the queen and fell to one knee before her. "If it pleases my queen, I shall stand vigil in the Great Hall until the morrow, when his grace is to be buried."

The queen nodded and gently touched the captain's head. "I think it is appropriate, Ser Knott. Stand, and may the Nameless bless you."

"And you as well, my queen." The man stood and bowed his head at Arisa and Searin, greeting them with, "My princesses." Before walking towards the altar, he shot Searin a strange look. Searin had perceived some tension between the two of them since the plan for Arisa to name her high captain had been made public last year. When it was time for Arisa to appoint Searin as the high captain of the King's Guard, Captain Knott would be forced to retire from the post. It was not something the man seemed to be looking forward to.

Knott's father had been Minister of Warcraft during her grandmother's—Queen Lorna the Elderqueen's—rule, so he and her father had grown up as close friends. They had sparred, hunted, hawked, and drank together every day as young men. When Queen Lorna died, and Petar was anointed as her successor, his first order had been to appoint Knott as his high captain.

Searin had never cared much for the man. He always seemed to think he knew better than everyone else, especially regarding battle strategy. Just because his father had been Minister of Warcraft—a terrible one, at that, Searin recalled—didn't mean Knott's opinions on the subject were at all valuable. In fact, her father's withdrawal from the war had been necessitated in large part by the losses they'd suffered at the Red Coast as a direct result of relying on Knott's 'tactical brilliance.' Besides that, the things she had heard the high captain say when he was sure he was only in the company of his men, especially the crude japes about the female servants, made her dislike the man even more. Once she became high captain, Searin would put a stop to the culture of mockery and disrespect the man had instilled into the King's Guard.

High Captain Knott walked up to the head of the altar and unsheathed the beautiful ceremonial Greatsword of Ivaran, which had been passed to him by the previous high captain on the day of his appointment. He lowered the tip of the sword onto the floor and began his vigil.

Arisa placed her arm around Searin's and led her out of the House of the Gods. Two carriages were parked outside awaiting them. Hovard's sobs came from the one on the right—let their mother take that one. Searin could not endure any more sadness today. Arisa seemed to agree with her since she led Searin into the left carriage. "To the palace," she called out. The coachman flicked the reins, and the carriage was on its way.

"Thank the gods the bells aren't ringing anymore," Arisa said, breaking the somber silence between them. "I don't think I could take much more of that."

"Will you miss him?" Searin asked, not quite certain why. Perhaps, she simply needed assurance that her sister's feelings were similarly complicated.

Arisa glanced out of the window, at the other carriages leaving the funeral. "Will I miss him?" she asked herself. "I don't know. You?"

Searin hid her disappointment at the question being thrown back at her. Even so, she did not have to think about her answer. "How can I miss what was never there?"

"Oh, he was there, alright," Arisa countered. "Ever since you passed the crown onto me, he was always there, ready to point out everything I did he perceived as a shortcoming. How I preferred reading to swinging a sword; how I preferred the company of servants and guards to that of the nobility; how I did this instead of that. Father was always there. Will I miss the constant reminder that I could never be good enough for him? I don't know."

Searin felt foolish for only then realizing how different her and her sister's relationships with their father had been. She would never exactly understand what the man had put Arisa through, but she shared the hurt. She grabbed her sister's hand. "You'll make a great queen," she said.

Arisa met her eyes—they were glossy with unshed tears—and smiled. "I'd settle for being better than he was."

※ ※ ※ ※

When they reached the palace, they headed immediately to the eastern wing where the royal chambers were situated. Many decades ago, the royals had occupied the top circle of the Royal Tower. Searin could not imagine climbing all of those stairs simply to reach her room. The farthest she had gone on her own was the seventeenth ring, and that was only once as a dare. That ring was said to be haunted by the ghost of a knight who had jumped out of the window after being cuckolded by his lover. It turned out, there was nothing there beyond the unoccupied guest quarters of some eastern thane.

"Where are you headed?" Searin and Arisa turned in unison to see their little brother at the base of the staircase. Hovard was no longer weeping, but his eyes and cheeks were still red and swollen.

"Up to my chambers," Arisa answered.

"Will you be joining the vigil?" There was a pleading tone to the boy's question.

Searin would have preferred to avoid the tradition of sitting silently in the royal chapel with her family and fasting until sunrise, but she felt suddenly guilty for leaving the poor boy to weep on his own. They had never been particularly close, but he was still just a child—and family.

"We're holding a meeting, but we'll join you there very soon," Searin said.

"Are you going to be the queen now?" Hovard asked Arisa.

"Yes," Arisa answered. "But first I must be wed, then I will be anointed."

Hovard burst into a sudden bout of choked sobs. Arisa walked down the stairs and held the boy's face tenderly. "Why are you crying? You should be happy. I like to think I'll make a good ruler."

"I don't want you to be the queen if you're going to become like Father," he cried. Arisa glanced towards Searin, worry creasing her brow.

It appeared Hovard, too, had had a strained relationship with the former king. Searin wondered what that relationship had been like. She had often dismissed her younger brother as petulant and childish. Now she wondered if she had only been perpetuating their father's neglect.

Arisa smiled and wiped Hovard's tears away. "Don't worry. I am never going to become like him. When I am queen you'll never have a reason to cry. Now, let me see a smile." Arisa smiled wide, which Hovard attempted to mimic. "You call that a smile? Let me see those teeth!" Arisa teased as she smiled grotesquely. Hovard giggled despite his tears. "That's better! Now, go on. Don't make Mother wait for you. We'll be there shortly." Arisa kissed the boy's head and resumed her climb up the stairs.

Searin watched as Hovard sauntered away, regretful that she hadn't paid closer attention to her brother's pain until now. She would have to remedy that somehow.

Reiner stood guard in front of the door to Arisa's quarters. He was a pleasant man with a good, honest face. "My princess," Reiner greeted with an unsure tone, "Thane Clavio is inside. I told him to wait out here, but he laughed at me and let himself in. I..."

"It's quite alright, Reiner," Arisa reassured him. "Thank you for informing me." The guard held the door open for them, and greeted Searin with, "My princess," as if noticing her for the first time. Clavio stood in front of Arisa's vast library, scanning the spines of the books with an inquisitive finger.

"I hope you didn't wait too long, Uncle," Arisa apologized. "The funeral seemed to last forever. I feel as if I have been subjected to the weeps of half the kingdom's nobility."

Clavio greeted them with a curt bow and a ready smile. "I've attended more funeral ceremonies than I wish to remember, and by the end, I've always hoped I was the one lying dead on the altar. At least then I wouldn't have to suffer through the droning of the priests and the performative moaning of the mourners."

"May I interest you in some sweet red?" Arisa offered. "Sol Fornian, of course."

"We're supposed to be fasting," Clavio replied.

Arisa rolled her eyes and handed him a filled cup.

Clavio accepted it. "But I've never been known to turn down a good wine. Though Sol Forne and I are not on the best of terms as of late."

"That surprises me," Arisa replied. "I assumed having a rebellion in common would have brought Perimat and Sol Forne closer."

"Unfortunately for us all, that has not been the case. But that's a story for another time." Clavio turned his attention to Searin. "I'm glad you joined us, dear niece. As your sister's soon-to-be-appointed high captain, you best get used to being close at hand," Clavio said, swirling the wine in his glass before taking a sip. "Your father, gods rest his soul, was a bit too free with handing out important positions to rich, inexperienced, nobles. Keeping things in the family, especially while the kingdom is facing several crises, is a wise choice."

Unlike their father, Clavio had always been gentler and more refined. He loved to read and to play the wood harp and had an exceedingly lovely voice that made court ladies swoon, as well as some lords. Searin had always assumed their father was jealous of his younger brother—jealous of his talent, of his beautiful golden curls and dreamy ocean eyes, and of how easily friendliness and charm came to him. Searin had always enjoyed their uncle's company and easy manner, often wishing their father could be more like him. She looked down at the cup of wine Arisa set before her. Though she did not seek to break tradition, a few sips seemed deserved.

"So, to what do I owe the pleasure of this meeting?" Arisa asked.

Clavio took a hearty pull from his wine. "There is a matter of great importance on my mind, if I may, my princess."

"Enough with the formalities, Uncle," Arisa said, not unkindly. "Please speak freely here. We're family, after all."

Clavio smiled and nodded. "The matter is obviously in regard to your approaching anointment."

"I have some idea where this is headed." Arisa sat on a bench lined with a plump purple embroidered velvet pillow. Clavio settled into a chair across from her. Searin remained standing, uncomfortable in the gown her mother had forced her to wear for the funeral.

"As you well know," Clavio began, "tradition dictates that you may not be anointed queen unless you have a husband to name king consort. Until that day, your mother will continue to reign in your stead as queen regent."

Arisa smiled. "Surely you didn't ask to meet so you could explain the ins and outs of royal succession?"

"I have a proposition for you, my dear niece." Clavio paused. When Arisa didn't answer he took it as permission to carry on. "In the days to come, you are going to be approached by every noble, far and wide, proposing to join their house to ours. Your mother has a shortlist of suitors ready for this exact moment. I would like to suggest a match that I'm sure hasn't occurred to her. A great match, if I may say."

Arisa sighed. "Suggest away."

"Reilyn Azurat, son of Thane Ronnan Azurat of Pallew. The man is about your age, and pleasant to look upon, if my emissaries are to be believed."

Searin was taken aback by their uncle's forwardness. By the way she finished her glass of wine in one swallow, even Arisa seemed perturbed. Immediately her eyes scanned the room for the bottle. Searin walked over to them and switched her mostly full glass for Arisa's empty one. Her sister smiled in gratitude.

"I wager you're not suggesting this match based solely on this man's supposed good looks," Searin interjected.

"Of course not, my princess," Clavio said with a grin. "Are you perchance familiar with House Azurat?"

As Arisa took a sip of wine, Searin struggled to recall her knowledge of the several highborn families ministering across the lands and city-states of Hovardom. It had never been her strongest suit.

"Thane Azurat is a very wealthy man," Arisa answered.

"A man your father has greatly wronged, if you'll excuse my bluntness," Clavio added. "Before my brother's reign, the Azurats ministered over a stretch of the Yellow Road from just north of Vizen to Perimat. When your father was anointed, however, he gave me thaneship over that region and sent the Azurats to minister over Pallew to the far east."

Searin thought that sounded exactly like the sort of short-sighted thing her father would have done. "Let me guess," she said, "they gladly accepted and kissed my father's feet in gratitude."

Clavio laughed darkly. "You must take your sense of humor from your mother."

Searin frowned.

Clavio finished his wine. Searin grabbed the bottle and refilled his cup. "Thank you, dear," Clavio said. "Though I was grateful for the appointment, the Azurats did not take the relocation well, even going as far as refusing to move. In response, your father deployed six thousand armed men to Perimat. '*I don't care if they are alive or dead, just move them,*' were his exact words. My brother was quite the impulsive man and didn't think through the consequences of his actions. I offered to accept thaneship anywhere else, but he would not hear it. I think he did it more to rid himself of the Azurats than to favor me.

"As you know, Pallew sits at the south of the Red Coast, and the Azurats have graciously provided the bulk of the force your father has sent to fight back the Sazisani there. However, a man of means such as Thane Ronnan never does anything for free. He has been keeping count of your father's expenditures. And now that your father has foolishly called back the troops, leaving Pallew to defend itself, alone, Thane Ronnan has every intention to charge the crown for fighting the war these past twenty years—with interest. This war has been anything but cheap. The Sazisani are fearsome warriors and adept strategists. They take no prisoners, and subject entire villages to manners of cruelty best not spoken of on such a solemn day. Hopefully, you have the foresight your father lacked and can see what must be done."

Arisa stood and paced about the room, deep in thought. Searin did not envy the mess the late king had left for her sister to resolve. "So. If I understand correctly," Arisa began, "what you're suggesting is that I marry this Azurat fellow, make him my king consort, aid Thane Ronnan in his fight against the Sazisani, then use any territorial gains to cover the value of the outstanding debt."

"You're as sharp as you ever were, my princess," Clavio replied, delighted. "Conveniently for you, the young man is already in Vizen. He arrived at court yesterday to meet with the king. He was there today at your father's funeral."

"How convenient," Searin snarked.

Clavio nodded. "The young man was most excited to see the royal court. The poor boy practically grew up in the shadow of war."

Arisa walked to the far end of the room, facing a large tapestry map of the kingdom. Her hand touched Pallew, the fortified city on the far eastern coast of the kingdom. Searin couldn't help but suspect the display was for her benefit. "Dear Uncle," she said, turning to face them with a warm smile. "Thank you for bringing this to my attention. I shall think it over, and you shall have my answer in the morrow. Now, please, I would like to be left alone before attending my father's funeral vigil."

"As my princess desires." Clavio stood and bowed before heading for the door. Searin followed him, until her sister called out, "Searin, please stay for a moment."

Clavio shot her a grin. "Heed your future queen, and counsel her well," he said before leaving. Outside the door, Clavio clapped Reiner on the shoulder and exclaimed, "Good man!"

Searin closed the door and returned to the center of the chambers. Arisa paced in front of her vast book collection. She scanned the spines until she reached a particular book, which she removed from the shelf and opened on a desk. She turned the pages, lifting small puffs of dust into the air.

"Am I supposed to stand here while you read?" Searin asked, annoyed.

"What do you think of Uncle's offer?" Arisa asked, leafing through the pages of the old book.

"I think it's a bit hasty, but it does have merit," Searin said, moving closer to the table. "Father has left you with a beggared kingdom, and many debts to settle if we want to repair the waning loyalty of the nobles. Acquiring more territory seems like the best way out of our financial troubles, and the only way to give what we've already spent at the Coast any meaning. Meanwhile, the only thing keeping the nobility and peasants from killing each other in the city-states are the Blue Scarabs, a militia large enough to threaten us if it wished. They claim to serve the kingdom, but we do not have any meaningful control over them."

"Anything else?" Arisa asked jokingly.

"Not off the top of my head," Searin deadpanned. "Uncle Clavio's offer is a good one. Marrying you off to one of our biggest debt holders and most vitally located allies can only strengthen us. What are you looking for in there?" When Arisa's nose was stuck in one of her tomes, speaking to her was as effective as wishing into a well.

"Soon after you renounced the crown, Father began to pay closer attention to how I spent my time. Even back then, I loved to read. One day, Father was drunk and in a dark mood. He swiped a book from my hand and split it in half with his sword. He told me that to be a ruler meant to be the strongest in the room. When I told him that he was wrong, he laughed and challenged me to find him a book that could cut as deeply as a blade."

Arisa flipped the pages until she reached a chapter entitled *The Conquest of Amacore*. "Aha!" Arisa exclaimed, pointing at the chapter heading.

"What is this?" Searin asked.

"This is a book of strategy compiled by our great-great-grandfather's Minister of Warcraft during his reign," Arisa explained. "It details the kingdom's northern expanse, and how our forebear forged an alliance with Toropan, one of our greatest historical enemies. Uncle Clavio's proposal is a good one, but I think we have more to gain here than a simple covering of our debts."

"What are you intending to do?" Searin asked, intrigued.

"I don't intend to resume the war, as Uncle Clavio wishes. I wish to end the conflict, once and for all with resolve, diplomacy, and alliance," Arisa said. "I intend to prove Father wrong and show that the knowledge contained in a book can cut deeper than any blade."

A swelling of pride and trust arose within Searin. Her sister was already proving to be the wise ruler Searin had expected—wiser than she would have been. "Anything you need, I am at your service," Searin swore with a bow.

"Why do you think he did it?"

The question shocked Searin. She wiped the red flash of her father's blood from her eyes with the back of her hand. "I don't know," she whispered. "He was a miserable man."

Arisa raised her eyes from the tome and met hers. For a moment, it seemed as if she intended to cry. But that moment passed as soon as it came. "Yes," she said. "He was." Arisa's attention returned to the book in front of her, Searin entirely forgotten.

XIII.

A Jar of Dirt and Maggots

The prickling fumes of the onions she chopped assaulted Lyr's eyes. She tried to wipe the sting away with the back of her hand, but that somehow made it worse. She hurried towards a washbasin and rinsed her face, but only because Flavien, the head cook, wasn't around to see her escape her station. That morning, for the crime of tasting a nibble of hard cheese, the stout cook had walloped her behind with the large wooden spoon he kept tied around his neck. The spoon had left an angry bruise on her buttock about the size of an apple and made it painful to sit—though, with all the work there was, Lyr had no time for rest anyway.

She finished cutting the onions and moved on to chopping carrots, a few fragrant leeks, and finally long sticks of celery. It seemed as if tonight's meal would include some kind of stew. Flavien, who was usually ever-present, had left along with Geren, her infiltration companion, and the stronger kitchen servants. It had just been her, Leandra, and two older kitchen servants there since the late morning, keeping the place tidy, prepping the vegetables, and simmering stock over the fire.

"You're going to have to be quicker than that," Leandra scolded. Though coming from her, it didn't sound malicious. The woman pointed at the pile of vegetables in front of Lyr. "You mangled the poor things. Hasn't anyone ever taught you to chop?"

"Not really," Lyr replied. "I'm better at sweeping or washing things."

Leandra's eyebrows were always raised as if she was perpetually worried. But now, she managed to raise them further than Lyr thought possible. "How is it you landed a spot in the kitchens then?"

Lyr's eyes wandered from the woman to the pile of roughly diced carrots, onion, and celery in front of her. In the letter she had been made to study for this mission, they had written the name of the person in charge of staffing for use in such an occasion—Myrna? Or was it Bryma? Lyr could feel the sweat rising to the surface of her palms.

"I— I asked Myrna for a maid position, but I guess she has a cruel sense of humor." Lyr waited for Leandra's reaction.

Leandra frowned and shook her head. "She really does, that one. Probably hoping you get flogged, the wretched crone! Maybe give those another pass," she counseled, nodding towards the vegetables. "Flavien likes them nice and thin."

The relief Lyr felt was indescribable. It took till the afternoon, but she finally finished chopping everything that needed chopping and placed all the vegetable pieces into a large wooden bowl. She turned to Leandra and asked, "Is there anything else that needs to be done?"

"If you haven't cleaned up your station yet, you best do that," the young woman answered. "But until Flavien returns, there's not much more that needs doing. Whatever you choose to occupy yourself with, be sure to stay out of sight."

"The nobles don't much care to see lowborn girls running around the palace," one of the two other women interjected.

Out of sight and out of mind. Just like the waste flowing from the palace drains.

Lyr decided to return to the servant quarters. She could use a nap since the little sleep she had gotten that night had been plagued by anxious thoughts—nightmares of her mother refusing food and wasting away as she blamed Lyr for abandoning her. Lyr feared the state she would find the woman in upon her return.

If I return, that is.

The dark hallways that snaked into the servants' quarters were sparsely occupied. The other servants were hard at work preparing for that evening's funeral feast. Lyr wondered how Saul was faring. Why couldn't she be with him instead of Alizia? What did Alizia possess that she didn't? A tall, strong, physique, for one. Skin the color of varnished wood, like that of southerners, unlike Lyr's commonplace provincial hue. At least Lyr's face wasn't scarred like hers.

Lyr shook her head as if to shake out those thoughts. Alizia had done nothing to her. She was a Free King, just like Lyr was now, and they shared the same mission. If Lyr didn't allow herself to trust Alizia, that could become a problem.

The door to their quarters was open, a shadow moving within. Lyr slowed and approached the room cautiously. Inside was Dora, hovering over Alizia's cot with a jar in hand. The jar appeared to be full of dirt dotted with white moving shapes Lyr couldn't quite make out from the doorway. "What are you doing?" Lyr asked.

"Nothing you should concern yourself with," Dora said venomously, a devious smile on her face. As she turned her back, Lyr caught sight of a few red welts disappearing into the back of the girl's tunic. Whatever beating she had received in punishment for her antics the previous day seemed only to have vindicated her hatred. The girl opened the jar and poured its contents under Alizia's pillow. Seeing them land on the bed, Lyr recognized the wriggling shapes to be, to her horror, dozens of maggots. "I can't wait to see her face when she lays down in her little cot and feels these squirming crawlers all over her."

I have to do something. Lyr stood there watching the girl enact her devious plan. Dora must have noticed Lyr's discomfort because she turned towards her and smiled. "You're not going to tell on me, are you?"

Lyr sighed deeply. *When Alizia finds out, she's going to beat you to a pulp.* She shook her head.

"Good," Dora said. "I've had all I can take of snitches."

Once the jar was one-third of the way emptied, Dora lifted Alizia's cot to pour some more there. The girl stopped and set the jar aside. Lyr felt like throwing up at the realization of what had happened. Dora reached under Alizia's cot and pulled out the small vial of clear poison. Alizia must have forgotten to take it with her when she dressed that morning.

"What do we have here?" the girl asked playfully, uncorking the vial and sniffing its contents. "Doesn't smell like anything. Probably liquor." Lyr was shocked at just how naive this girl was about the world. "The lowborn do love to get drunk, I hear. Wait until Steward Ibessa finds out. She'll be stripped naked and flogged far worse than I was. If we're lucky, they'll do it in the courtyard. And we'll get to watch."

Dora replaced the cork and sauntered to the door. Lyr blocked her path.

"What are you doing? Move!" Dora commanded. Lyr stood her ground. Dora narrowed her eyes. "Move or I'll tell them this is yours."

"You can't," Lyr begged, pathetically.

"And why not?" Dora asked, crossing her arms.

Because anyone else will be able to tell immediately that it's not liquor. Because I have its sister vial tucked at my chest as we speak and I don't want to be forced to take it because of you. Forced to take it...

Lyr felt her stomach twist into knots as bile crept upwards and she burped up the rasher of bacon and black bread she had for breakfast. Lyr had agreed to join this plan with an awareness of what the risks would be. She was prepared to take her own life for the cause but being discovered with poison could mean death for all four of them. It was an outcome she could have accepted in other circumstances but not for this spiteful girl. Not for Dora. Lyr closed the door behind her.

"What are you doing?" Dora asked playfully, still of the mind that this was all some sort of game. Dora shoved her way towards the door, but Lyr pushed her onto the cot behind her. Fury darkened Dora's eyes. "You bitch! How dare you? I'm going to have you tarred and flayed as well!"

Lyr launched herself onto the servant girl and held her down. It was easy, much easier than she expected. Dora was soft and weak, having only lived the sheltered life of a royal servant. Lyr was a survivor of the Pleasants. She was quick and scrappy, and Dora was neither. The girl just lay there under Lyr's weight, barely putting up a fight. Lyr felt dreadful.

"Get off of me!" Dora yelled.

"You mustn't tell," Lyr insisted.

"I will tell whomever I please," the girl rebutted, shaking angrily. Her face reddened from the struggle.

It was at that moment that Lyr realized that reasoning with Dora was not possible. Lyr looked into the girl's eyes and knew how simple it would be to make this all go away—make it as if they had never been caught. She knew she could do it. And it scared her.

Lyr snatched the small vial from the girl's hand, quickly uncorked it with her teeth, and spilled a few drops of its translucent contents over Dora's face. The glassy droplets fell right into the girl's gnashing mouth. Dora screamed once the poison hit her tongue. Lyr wasn't concerned by the noise—there was no one in the hallways that would intervene.

Almost immediately, Dora's mouth began to fill with foam. Her eyes turned red, and her skin grew taught as gray veins webbed across it. Lyr jumped back to her feet, watching as Dora coughed, choked, and spasmed. The girl's eyes rolled to the back of her head, making them appear entirely red and bloodshot. Dora's death was quick but painful—so much for Boggar's assurance. As soon as it was over, Lyr tucked the small vial beside her own at her breast and fled the room in a hurry.

She would need to return to the kitchens soon to not raise any questions from the others, but before that, she needed to find Alizia and share what had happened. By some tremendous mercy of fate, Lyr didn't have to venture far through the corridors to find her.

Alizia was walking towards her in the servant hall that led into the western wing of the palace. She had likely just realized she had left her vial behind. Lyr wasn't sure how she must have looked but it was enough to stop Alizia in her tracks, concern instantly lining her face.

"Dora found it," Lyr whispered. Alizia's eyes went wide, her hand clutching for a sword that didn't exist except in muscle memory.

"So that's it, then," Alizia replied, sounding strangely resigned to her fate.

"No, I... I handled it." Lyr's hands were shaking.

"What do you mean?"

"I... She's dead," was all the explanation Lyr could summon.

"And the corpse?" Lyr felt the heat from Alizia's body filling the few inches between them. "How did you get rid of it?"

"I didn't."

Alizia's eyes snapped up to meet her own and, for a second, Lyr thought the woman might slap her.

"You just left a dead body lying about the palace for anyone to find?"

Lyr forced herself to not lower her gaze. "That wasn't my first thought." She reached into her tunic, producing the small vial and burying it into Alizia's hand.

Alizia breathed out loudly. "Where is she?"

"In the quarters. I did—"

"You did what needed to be done. I will take care of the rest."

With those words, Alizia placed the vial in her pocket and paced down the hall, towards their quarters.

Lyr returned to the kitchens right as Geren and Flavien were walking in carrying a large hog. Leandra helped them set the heavy sow onto the table.

"What a beautiful animal!" one of the old kitchen servants exclaimed.

"Isn't she?" Flavien smiled. "Geren, help me gut it. Tonight, we're serving roast!"

XIV.

BUNCH OF SCOUNDRELS

Rovan awakened. The steady purple and blue light of the *dreadhall* lanterns made it hard to tell it was before dawn. He stood and glanced over at his sleeping companions—he would allow them some more time to rest. He donned his boots and exited the small shack. The cave village was still slumbering, though a man in his middle years was tending to some morning chores. The man greeted Rovan with a nod and a taught smile.

Rovan walked to the mouth of the cave and peered out. To his surprise, it had stopped raining, though the sky was still tented by dark and angry piles of storm clouds that promised more to come. Rovan stepped out into the brisk morning air and bathed in its diffused blue light. A few droplets of rain grazed him.

He faced the upward path to the left of the cave and decided to follow it. The black earth was still slick, but it wasn't as treacherous as it had been the previous day. After a few paces, the path turned inwards, then opened into a wide canyon riddled with honeycomb-like caves, not dissimilar from a large empty lotus pod. The rain had filled where the canyon sloped downwards, creating a sort of pool in the middle, where an elevated stone path had been built leading to a cave at the far end of the canyon—a cave that had a wooden wall and door built at its entrance.

The enchantress, Mother Adriel, was kneeling on the floor near the entrance to her home when Rovan almost stumbled into her. The breeze swayed the shimmering feathers in the woman's hair. Rovan turned to leave, not wanting to disturb her.

"You know it's rude to intrude upon others' business," the woman said.

"I didn't mean to interrupt," Rovan replied. "I was just curious to see where the path headed."

"Come here," the woman commanded. Rovan took a few tentative steps towards the enchantress. He had not been able to take stock of her looks the previous day in the dimness of the cave. She was younger than she had seemed the previous evening—only a few years older than him, in fact. Attractive in a wild and dangerous way, though the severe lines of her face did not quite become her. They seemed to belong to someone else, as if they were borrowed. The only thing that betrayed the woman's true age were her hands, which, though they were calloused and caked with old clay, dirt, and dyes, were undeniably youthful.

What really gave the enchantress an ancient and forbidding air was what she wore. Her clothes were old and dingy, much more suited for a matron than a woman in her mid-twenties. The feathers in her nest of hair could not be called adornment—a happy accident at best. Around her neck was a necklace that looked more like a collar, accented by a single glowing yellow runestone. Within it, Rovan recognized the etching of *Binding*.

The enchantress indicated a pile of spherical stones placed in a spiral shape on the ground. "What is that?" Rovan asked.

"How does it make you feel?"

Rovan started at the enchantress' question. He felt uneasy, but in truth that had more to do with the woman than the pile of stones. "Pay close attention," she said. "Clear your mind and listen."

Rovan stared at the strange, entrancing, spiral. What was the enchantress getting at? "I don't understand."

The enchantress sighed. "Have you ever seen a male enchanter?"

Rovan shook his head. The words 'male enchanter' sounded strange, like a fiction. It was something he had never wondered about, especially being from Sol Forne where enchantresses were altogether uncommon. Why were all enchantresses women?

"It is a long-held tradition that an enchantress shall bestow her teachings upon an apprentice of a very young age," the woman explained. "In Albadone, when a new enchantress takes over for the old, the woodsfolk gather their children aged seven and below and present them to the new enchantress. She then tests each child and finds the one with the most promise—with the strongest connection to the Cycle of Nature. That's how an enchantress selects her apprentice. Now, tell me, Rovan, how many parents do you think include their sons in this offering?"

"I don't know," Rovan replied, unsure.

The enchantress smiled toothily. "Not many, if any at all. We enchantresses choose girls to be our apprentices, not because boys lack a connection to the Cycle, but only because folk seem to regard girls as more disposable. The common folk need enchantresses. We keep the Cycle of Nature from degrading by balancing enchantments with their costs and by guarding the Cycle from those who would do it harm. Though people may not always see our works, most are at least aware of their importance. Yet, they still keep their boys away from learning our ways. I wonder what they fear."

"Why are you telling me this?"

"As I've said before, I sense a strong connection to the Cycle within you. Perhaps, in another lifetime, you would have been a fine enchanter, first of your kind."

The thought disturbed Rovan deeply. But not as deeply as the look the enchantress was giving him. It was predatory—the eyes of a wolf. He changed the subject. "So, this girl, Sesha, is your apprentice?"

"Apprentice, yes. And daughter, truly. It was a blessing that her birth mother would surrender her to me at such a time of need—for the forest, the Cycle, and myself. I had recently lost my teacher and required an apprentice of my own. Raising the babe from such a young age, I was able to instill within her ancient knowledge that few other living enchantresses have been able to master. The girl is quite powerful, more so than I am even. I'm worried what will happen if the abilities she possesses were to fall into the wrong hands."

Rovan's back stiffened, recalling all too well the damage a rogue enchantress could inflict. "We will find her," Rovan promised.

"Then what?" the woman confronted him. "You'll take her away to be with a woman the girl has never really known?"

"I—" Rovan could not meet the woman's fiery eyes. He looked down at the spiral of stones, suddenly feeling a strange pang of anxiety wash over him like a buzz. He balled his clammy fists and took several steps away from the spiral and enchantress.

Adriel's face brightened. "You do feel something, don't you?"

"Maybe. I don't know." Rovan turned around, feeling the tension dissipate from him. "I don't know," he repeated, this time referring to the enchantress' first question. "When we find the girl, we shall see what she wants to do."

"With your connection to the Cycle, I trust that you will do the right thing," Adriel said. "It will be unavoidable."

"Do you have any idea of where to start our search once we're in the city?" Rovan asked.

"I'm able to track her generally through our mutual connection to the Cycle," the woman answered curtly.

Rovan remembered how Ashe had tracked the child using the now spent runestone of *Guidance* and found himself retrieving it from his hood.

"What do you have there?" Adriel asked.

"It's nothing," Rovan said, quickly repocketing the runestone.

"I've been around long enough to recognize a spent runestone, boy," Adriel snarked.

Rovan sighed. "It's a runestone of *Guidance*. The girl's mother gave it to me. She used it to find the girl."

The enchantress stared at Rovan with greedy eyes. "Give it to me," she ordered.

Rovan was taken aback by the woman's sudden firmness. "I'd rather hold onto it if it's all the same."

"It's useless to you. Give it to me."

"I understand, but I'd still prefer to keep it." Something about the way the woman demanded the runestone made Rovan suspect it held some value. At the very least, he would not allow the woman to boss him around a second time.

The enchantress scanned Rovan as if he was diseased. She begrudged him a smile, then turned to face her home. "Of course, of course. Hold on to it, and don't lose it."

Rovan was still uncertain how much trust to place in the woman. The inhabitants of the cave seemed to hold her in high regard, but why did Rovan get such a sense of dark foreboding from being near her?

The sunlight had begun to crest over the canyon, filling it with light. Specks of rain danced like dust in the breeze. "I think it's time to go," Rovan said.

"I will gather my things," the enchantress agreed.

※ ※ ※ ※

The cave village had sprung to life while Rovan was gone. The tables beneath the tents were now filled with families breaking their fast on boiled eggs and porridge. This time, when offered a plate, Rovan could not refuse. The egg was welcome, but the porridge was a bit too bland for his taste, although graciously free of lizard. He muscled it down—no sense in traveling hungry. Due to the enchantress' limp, and having to avoid the Red Road, the trip to Vizen would take at least two days.

Scintilla and Tieg were dining among the folk. There was a cordial stillness between them. It wasn't coldness, Rovan was pleased to see, but it wasn't quite friendly. Rovan patted them both on the back, and the three exchanged their good mornings. "The enchantress is finishing her preparations," Rovan said. "We should leave after she joins us."

"I've never been to a place as big as Vizen," Scintilla admitted.

"Me neither," Tieg added.

The two eyed Rovan as if expecting something from him. Reassurance, perhaps? Out of their group, he was the only one who had been brought up in a large city. The rest were from smaller towns and anonymous villages. "I've never been to Vizen, either," Rovan said. "But if it's anything like Sol Forne, then we just need to keep focused on our task and remain together. We'll be alright."

Tieg seemed to gather some comfort from those words, but Scintilla still looked distant and distracted. "What's wrong?" Rovan asked her.

"It's nothing," she mumbled. Rovan accepted the non-answer. No reason to press her for what she wouldn't willingly divulge.

Mother Adriel soon reached the cave. A woman offered her a bowl of porridge, which the enchantress waved away curtly. Her brow was a flat, severe line. "Time to go," Rovan said, heading for their replenished supplies. He selected his rucksack, then approached the mouth of the cave. "Thank you for your hospitality," he greeted Tonja, who stood beside the enchantress. The older woman smiled politely and bowed her head. Tieg and Scintilla joined them and, without further fanfare, the four headed out of the cave and down the mountain path.

Though the rain was not as incessant as it had been the previous two days, it was not altogether gone. Rovan was thankful that the sun could, at least, cut occasionally through the thick dark clouds drifting above. It wasn't a warm light, but it gave the day a more inviting air. From the side of the mountain, however, a downpour was visible to the northwest, right where they were headed.

"You know where to go?" Mother Adriel asked.

"We'll take the woodland path north then intersect with the Red Road about a mile south of the city," Rovan explained.

"Why don't we take the Red Road now?" the enchantress asked.

"It's those damned Blue Scarabs," Tieg cursed.

"We're not on friendly terms with them," Scintilla added.

"Why are you concerned about some bugs?" Mother Adriel asked.

The three friends glanced at each other in bewilderment. "You don't know about the Blue Scarabs?" Tieg asked.

The enchantress looked irritated by the question. Rovan spoke before the woman could pelt Tieg with whatever she was about to say. "They're a militia group that now controls the entirety of the Red Road and has a presence in most cities and towns along it."

"A militia that big? I'll bet the royals are shitting themselves trying to figure out how to handle them."

"Well, they're loyal to the king," Rovan explained.

"BAH! I'm sure both the royals and these beetles would want it to look that way."

Rovan was taken aback—Mother Adriel had a surprisingly insightful mind when it came to politics for someone who lived in such isolation from surrounding events.

"The long route will work just fine," the enchantress said, placing herself at the head of the party. Since she was the slowest, she would set the pace. Tieg and Scintilla walked side by side behind her. From his spot at the back of the group, Rovan noticed the two exchange a telling grimace. They would be lucky to reach Vizen by tomorrow afternoon at this rate.

The spotty showers of that morning solidified back into the downpour they were accustomed to. While the three friends raised their hoods in response, the enchantress seemed altogether unbothered by the elements—in fact, to Rovan, she seemed to relish being in them. "You like the rain?" Rovan found himself half-asking.

The pleasantness in the woman's face was instantly replaced by a neutral expression—perhaps she did not wish for her enjoyment to be perceived by others. "Rain is the True One's blessing," she said, and left it at that.

A shift in the air forced Rovan's eyes closed. When he opened them, his vision was blurred and unsteady. Rovan wiped his eyes with a balled fist. Mother Adriel turned to face him and placed a stabilizing hand on his shoulder. "You felt that too, didn't you?" she asked.

"Felt what?" Scintilla asked.

"I don't know," Rovan answered.

"You did," the enchantress insisted, removing her hand. "There's something emanating a strong *life energy* nearby. Something dark."

"What does that mean?" Tieg asked.

"I don't know," Rovan repeated. The wave of darkness that overtook him moments before was suddenly gone. It had felt like panic blanketing him. Only, more concentrated—as if someone had distilled the essence of fear into a single moment.

"We should move on," he pushed.

"That would be wise," Mother Adriel agreed, returning to the head of the group and picking up her limping pace.

Tieg and Scintilla flanked Rovan as they walked. Both wore worry plainly on their faces. "Are you all right?" Tieg asked quietly, trying to exclude the enchantress.

"I think so," Rovan answered.

"What was that?" Tieg asked. "I can't be the only one to think that was strange."

"What did you feel?" Scintilla asked.

Rovan sipped in air, wondering how to explain such a strange sensation. "I felt... an anxiety so strong it blurred my vision... It was probably nothing," he added when his friends appeared dismayed.

"You don't think what you felt was..." Tieg said, leaving the thought unfinished. His glance towards Scintilla made his meaning obvious.

"No," Rovan offered, regretting the lie immediately. "Maybe," he amended. Now that Tieg had voiced his concern, it was clear to Rovan that what he had just felt was similar to the dread he had sensed before their previous close call with the *reaverlord*.

"Maybe what?" Scintilla asked in alarm.

"Sin, I need you to be ready for the worst," Rovan cautioned, touching her arm. "Can you do that?"

"I'm not sure."

Rovan could feel her arm shaking. He lowered his touch and took her cold hand in his. "If we hear a *reaverlord* again, I need to know that you'll stay with us," he said. Scintilla nodded unsure, her grip tightening around his hand.

"A *reaverlord*?" Mother Adriel asked. How much of their quiet conversation had the woman overheard?

"When we headed this way from Pevine, we heard one screaming in the distance," Tieg explained.

"Ah," the enchantress replied flatly. "That explains the darkness in the air. We must tread very carefully around such wretched beasts."

"Have you ever encountered one?" Tieg asked.

"Only once before," she answered. "A long, long time ago." Once again, Rovan was caught by the incongruity between the way the woman spoke and her obvious youth.

"What makes them so evil?" Scintilla asked.

Mother Adriel glanced back at her, then returned her sight to the wooded path ahead. "What does evil mean to you?" she asked.

"A *reaverlord* destroyed the orphanage I was raised in. Killed nearly everyone—even the children."

"An evil deed. I'm sorry." To Rovan's surprise, the enchantress' apology sounded genuine. "But you see," the enchantress continued, "if we were to ask a *reaverlord*, they might share quite a few stories of evil deeds done to them by humanfolk."

"Do you mean to say *reaverlords* can be spoken with?" Rovan asked.

"Not in their current form, no," Mother Adriel said. "Are you familiar with the Ancient Guardians?"

Scintilla shook her head. Tieg and Rovan nodded. "They used to tell stories of the four Ancient Guardians in my village," Tieg explained. "*Melk, dragons, griffons,* and... What was that last one?"

"The *mer*," Rovan answered. Though he had never seen the thing fully, Rovan had gotten far too close to a *mer* during the attack at the port of Sol Forne and had witnessed the destruction the sea monster was capable of. He knew, better than his friends, that there was truth to be found in the old legends.

"Yes, the *mer!*" Tieg agreed. "They're all just myths, though."

"Not just myths," Mother Adriel corrected. "A history. One that has returned to fulfill its duty to the Cycle. The Ancient Guardians were created by the True One to protect this world. The humanfolk, however, had a poor time sharing space and drove the Guardians from their lands as they spread. But the Guardian's duty to protect is still their driving force. Just before the fires in Albadone, the *melk*—the Guardians of the Forest—returned to set things right and protect the land from those set on exploiting and destroying it. But they failed, and the Cycle of Nature paid for that failure."

Tieg seemed confused by Mother Adriel's words. "And what do the *reaverlords* have to do with the Guardians?"

"When the humanfolk began driving the Guardians away by force, each of the Guardians chose a place to escape to. The *griffons* flew to the distant lands in the north. The *melk* retreated to their native forest of Albadone. The *mer* hid in the dark depths of the sea. And the *dragons* burrowed within the Womb of the World."

Rovan thought back on the canyon where the enchantress was living and the many unnatural circular caves that lined it. Could those really have been... *dragon* burrows?

"The *dragons*, however, did not burrow to hide away. They hatched a plan, and changed themselves into a form that would help them destroy what they saw as the biggest threat to the Cycle of Nature."

"The *reaverlords* are... *dragons*?" Tieg asked, astonished.

"*Were dragons*," Adriel corrected. "*Dragons* had wings that could fly, and claws that could dig into the earth. They had the power to cause storms and shape mountains. But they gave all that up, to roam the earth on two feet in the image of their enemy."

"But why?" Scintilla asked breathily.

"Maybe they thought that by assuming an approximation of the human form, they could blend in with the rest of you and pick you off more easily. Maybe it's a type of madness they are suffering from." The enchantress stopped and turned to face Scintilla darkly. "Can I ask what you would do to the *reaverlords* if you could?"

"Kill them all," Scintilla answered without pause.

"Hmm..." was all the response Mother Adriel offered, seeming content to have proven to herself whatever point she had hoped.

Scintilla's restless eyes scanned the woman's face. "Those children—my friends—were of no threat to the *dragons* or the Cycle. They were just children!"

"Yes," Adriel agreed solemnly. "But they could have grown up to become threats. The *dragons... Reaverlords* would rather destroy that possibility than wait and find out they were right once it's too late."

Rovan had the overwhelming urge to step between them and diffuse the tension, though he remained still, allowing the enchantress' words to wash over him. It wasn't exactly what she had said but how she had said it. There was an ageless and detached note to those words as if discussing the wiping out of all humans involved her as little as the migration of birds. The way the enchantress spoke reminded him of Vaelin, the djinn he had accompanied in Sol Forne—the djinn he had betrayed. He cringed at the memory.

"Look!" Tieg said, pointing into the woods.

The enchantress turned abruptly, the worry apparent on her face. Scintilla's glare lingered on the woman a few moments longer before turning to face where Tieg had pointed.

"There, on the ground," Tieg insisted. When no one in the group appeared to see what he was indicating, Tieg huffed and walked towards a nearby thicket. Rovan followed and then stopped short.

A person lay on the ground, their face pressed into the dirt. They wore a motley of armor pieces from several different sets, though their boots were missing. Their right hand still gripped a large sword, while their left was... gone—severed. "Gods," Rovan cursed softly.

"Did a *reaverlord* do this?" Tieg asked.

"No," Adriel answered. "This is too clean. A *reaverlord* would have scattered him about."

"Oh!" Scintilla gasped. She was looking at something else entirely. Rovan moved to her side and immediately stepped back when he saw a second body slumped against a tree, its throat slit. The rain had washed the blood away, pooling it into the mud surrounding the corpse. "What happened here?" Scintilla wondered.

Through the trees, Rovan could see a few more mounds that were almost certainly other victims of whatever had transpired here. Several were punctured by arrows. Arrows that had missed their marks were sunken into nearby trees. "A battle," Rovan said. "It must have happened yesterday while we were on the Womb."

Adriel shook her head in distaste. "Folk killing folk. How predictable." She said it as if she were a parent disappointed in her children rather than a young woman witnessing so much carnage. "We better move," she said, turning and trudging into the woods, leaning heavily on her staff.

Scintilla shot Rovan an admonishing glance as if the enchantress being there was his fault somehow. Even Tieg's shrug seemed to agree with her.

They carried on quietly and steadily through the woods with a newfound wariness of their surroundings. They saw only one more body—a man who had been skewered to a pulp by an unreasonable amount of arrows. Beyond that, the woods were as eerily silent as their group. Soon, however, sounds began to trickle to them—chatter and laughter. The smell of a cookfire caused Rovan to salivate. It was well into the early evening, and they had not eaten except for some bread and cheese that afternoon.

"Should we go around whoever that is?" Tieg asked.

"A good proposal," Adriel said.

Rovan agreed, though unfortunately, their options were limited. "Shall we try the Red Road? That'll only take us a couple of miles off course," he asked the group.

"And risk being turned away at a Blue Scarab outpost again?" Tieg asked. "What if we went north? Isn't Vizen that way anyway?"

"The terrain north from here is intersected by the Cleo," Adriel said. "The rains are sure to have swelled the crossing. Unless you'd like to swim in treacherous waters, I'd avoid that way."

"And who might you lot be?" a voice demanded.

The group turned to face a group of soldiers with their swords drawn. They all wore shiny pristine armor, a large cross engraved at the front of each breastplate. *Great,* Rovan grimaced. *Errant–fucking–knights.*

Before Rovan could supply an answer, the enchantress took charge of the situation. "I am Mother Adriel, enchantress of Albadone," she said. "And you?"

"Enchantress of Albadone?" one of the knights—weaselly man—repeated. A shit-eating grin widened upon his face. "I've heard of you!" He turned to his companions and said, "She's the one Yugo's always going on about."

Rovan shuddered at the sound of the errant knight's name. He had met Yugo years ago, in Sol Forne. Rovan had been impressed by the man at first but had quickly grown disturbed by the knight's methods.

A sturdy woman to the man's right laughed like a chair being dragged over wooden floorboards. "I can't believe the odds!"

The enchantress' face soured. "We'll be off," she announced.

"Better if you stay near us," the errant knight cautioned. "A *reaverlord's* been spotted in the area."

"We are aware," Adriel deadpanned. "Now, leave us be."

"At least dine with us!" a third knight offered. He was shorter than the others and not at all what Rovan would have thought of as the type to be an errant knight. "It would be an honor to have *the* Mother Adriel grace our cookfire." The other knights snickered.

"We are overdue a rest," Tieg suggested.

Rovan wanted nothing more than to leave these errant knights behind, but he would not make that call on his own. He faced Scintilla to gather her input. "I wouldn't mind," she admitted. "Being near these knights might keep us safer while we rest."

"Very well," Rovan sighed.

"I don't think so," Adriel countered. "We're not stopping with these brutes."

"That's not how our group does things," Rovan said. "We decide together."

"I am not part of your group," the enchantress retorted.

"Well, we're the only escorts you've got."

The enchantress narrowed her eyes but not in a way that could be described as a frown. Before she could reply, Rovan turned to the errant knights and lied, "We would be honored to join you."

※ ※ ※ ※

A plump goat crackled above the smoldering cookfire, infusing its savory aroma across the air. A canopy had been erected over the blaze to protect it from the rain, while the knights sat carelessly on the muddy ground around it. Tieg had laid a blanket across the soggy earth for the four of them to sit on. Mother Adriel, however, had decided to stand apart from them, instead sullenly leaning on her staff and brooding.

Though Rovan enjoyed the warmth and the prospect of eating a hot meal, the company of the errant knights made him uneasy. Yugo, the only errant knight he had spent any time with, had turned out to be a madman with almost no limits to what he would do to achieve his ends, including assaulting a defenseless noblewoman. He wanted to believe that other errant knights were different from Yugo, though, observing those around him now, they all seemed to be stamped from the same mold.

"So, you're the enchantress Yugo told us so much about," a rugged, bearded man grinned. "A bit dingy, but I get the appeal."

Mother Adriel frowned deeply. "I would watch your tongue if you intend to keep it."

The man only smiled wider, and mocked, "'Twas only a joke, milady." He removed a large knife from his belt and began to carve the meat, placing the slices into a wooden bowl. "I am Pilons, the leader of this band of errant knights."

"I am Rovan, this is—"

"Rovan?" another errant knight repeated. "From that little group of kids running around the countryside?"

Rovan grimaced. "Sounds like you've heard of us."

"I'll say! I hear you do errant knight work for free."

"Well, I wouldn't say—"

"Stealing work from us, are you?" Pilons asked, arching an eyebrow.

Rovan shifted nervously.

The man barked a horrible laugh. "Look at him! We've scared the poor pup." The man handed Rovan the bowl filled with steaming slices of glistening goat meat. "I don't mind the competition. In fact, I welcome it! It's a shame about those fingers of yours. If you were a decent swordsman, I'd have to press you to join the Guild."

Rovan smiled politely but his grip on the bowl tightened. He hated reminders of the missing digits on his right hand, even when they weren't dripping in condescension. He passed the bowl to Scintilla. She and Tieg picked at the meat voraciously. "Is Yugo here?" Rovan asked, in part, to change the subject, and in part to save himself any unpleasant surprises.

"No, he's not here," Pilons replied. "The life of an errant knight is over for that one."

"No one wants to hire a wobbler," another knight laughed.

Pilons thrust an admonishing glance at the man, who immediately lowered his head. "Yugo was injured in combat a few years back. Lost his leg up to the knee. He was a boastful arse, but he was a good knight." Several of the errant knights nodded in solemn agreement.

"I'm sorry to hear that," Rovan said, and, surprisingly, found that he meant it.

"Sounds like you know the man," Pilons said.

"I met him a long time ago, in Sol Forne."

Pilons nodded to himself. "Make yourselves at home in my camp. Though, we will be moving along in the morning."

"Where are you headed?" Scintilla asked.

"We've been chasing a *reaverlord* since Rondhill. The monster has caused a lot of destruction in a village near the city. It headed towards the Womb, then switched course and made north towards Vizen. We're hoping to catch it before it reaches the city."

"Catch it? Don't you mean *kill* it?" Scintilla confronted.

"Usually, that's the case. But this time, someone's paying us a lot of coin to capture it."

"Is it even possible to capture a monster like that?" Scintilla asked.

Pilons grinned wickedly. "I guess we'll find out."

"And all those dead men back there in the woods?" Tieg asked.

"You saw that, eh? The *reaverlord's* band. They put up a decent fight! We caught them and killed most of them, then dispersed the rest. Mostly brigands out of Rondhill hoping to pick up some loot wherever the *reaverlord* destroyed."

"Bunch of scoundrels," a nearby knight declared.

"Yeah," Scintilla agreed softly.

Pilons cut himself a hunk of meat and slurped it down in one swallow. "Our scouts have it that the *reaverlord* is only a few miles east of here."

"Towards the Red Road?" Rovan asked.

"Aye," Pilons replied. "It's not ideal, not with those fucking Blue Scarabs about. We'd hate for them to take our credit. Please excuse me, now. I have pressing matters to attend to." With a curt bow, Pilons walked away towards a small cluster of knights at the far end of the camp.

Rovan reached into the bowl of meat and selected one of the few remaining slices—Tieg and Scintilla had already picked out the choice cuts. The tender and flavorful meat coated his mouth with savory fat. The other knights began to slice the meat for themselves. Someone came by and offered them ale from an overfilled skin. Scintilla and Tieg declined, but Rovan could not—having been raised in Sol Forne, it never quite felt right to eat a meal without pairing it with a strong drink. From his rucksack, Tieg produced four bread rolls. He set two of them on a plate near the fire, offering them as a sort of payment for the knights' hospitality. It didn't take long for them to vanish.

The enchantress, however, remained standing, pensively staring into the woods to the north. Rovan ripped a piece of bread and used it to pick up a small bit of meat. He stood and walked towards Adriel. "Aren't you hungry?" he asked.

"We need to go. And soon," she replied.

"We will go. As soon as we're done eating and resting."

The enchantress faced him, and suddenly he noticed something in her eyes he had not seen there before: worry. "This might be just another job for you all, but, for me, this is life and death. My child is in a city, all alone. She has never been anywhere larger than the cave village at the Womb. I don't know what I'll do if..." She shook her head as if to dispel her fears.

"I'm sorry," Rovan found himself saying. "I should have been more understanding of your urgency. But it serves no one if we travel all night in this rain, hungry and tired." He handed the bread and meat to Adriel. She glanced at the food then tentatively accepted it and bit into it hungrily.

"We will be on our way at first light," Rovan reassured.

XV.

The Funeral Feast

The funeral feast was somehow even less bearable than the funeral ceremony the previous day—at least the funeral had been quiet. The assembly hall teemed with nobility of the highest order, the collective stench of their flowery perfumes coalescing into something viler than any body odor she had ever smelled. Searin surveyed them from the royal table, which was raised on a stage at the back of the hall.

Her mother, as stately as ever, was seated in the center. The empty chair to the queen's left would have, at any other feast, been occupied by the king. The chair beside it was for Arisa, though she was busy drunkenly flirting with Ser Dregor across the hall. Searin shook her head at the embarrassing sight. For someone so well-read, her sister could be so flippant in regard to formality.

As the eldest, Searin should have sat next to her mother but had instead decided to cede that spot to her little brother. Their mother had not protested—what was one more custom for Searin to surrender?

Hovard was both startled by the celebratory noise of the assembly and exhausted by the late hour. Searin sympathized with the boy—she too had begun to feel the weight of tiredness slouch her shoulders and droop her eyes. The barrage of toasts hadn't helped. It seemed as if every minute another noble would stand and raise a glass to the late king. Searin could only take so much wine. For the last few toasts, she had only pressed her lips against the cup and pretended to sip. She heard this was supposed to be some esteemed vintage made from grapes grown during the fifth summer of her father's reign, though, to her, all wine tasted the same.

She caught herself nodding off and quickly straightened her back. Though she hated every moment of this feast, she knew she must endure and put on a good show. Unlike her sister, she would at least feign properness. She decided to focus her attention on Arisa to stifle the boredom. Her sister was brushing her long black hair with her hand while snickering at the handsome young knight's words. To his credit, Dregor remained impassive and stoic, though a quick smile briefly cracked the facade. Searin rolled her eyes. *Let the man do his job, Arisa!*

Their uncle intruded upon the two and dismissed Dregor, who casually marched to the other side of the hall. Arisa did not seem amused—in fact, she seemed rather annoyed at their uncle for spoiling her fun. Clavio gestured with his hand towards a nearby table, where a young man stood and bashfully made his way towards the two, accompanied by what Searin guessed was a handservant. The young man was a pretty little thing, sheepish in all but his attire, which was flamboyant in the Eastern style, with their colorful embroidered cloaks and golden chains. His face was delicate and his lips dark, like plumbs—Arisa seemed to approve.

So that must be the Azurat heir, Searin thought. *Reilyn, was it? Poor guy.* No one could have missed Arisa's careless flirting. What must he have thought of that?

"So that's your uncle's little pawn," the queen said. The woman's stern eyes were locked on Clavio. Searin thought it best to not say a word. She could sense a darkening storm in her mother's mood.

Reilyn and his servant both bowed deeply. Clavio said a few words and Arisa suddenly seemed to don a mask of soberness. She curtsied slightly and smiled at the young man.

Someone walked in front of Searin, blocking her view of the scene. A servant woman retrieved the empty bowls and plates from their table and placed them onto a silver tray. Searin tried to glance around the tall woman, but then quickly gave up once she realized how conspicuous of an action that was.

"Apologies, my princess," the servant said in a deep, mellow, voice. She quickly moved aside and walked to the other end of the table, clearing Searin's line of sight.

"It's alright," Searin began to say, but the servant was already too far to hear the words. The servant woman was taller than most, Searin observed. Her shiny dark hair was pulled neatly into a bun. Even though she wore plain servants' garbs—not drab or ugly but meant to ensure that the servants did not stand out—there was a powerful elegance about her that took Searin aback. The woman's face was long and defined, though a scar ran across her cheek down to her chin. Searin recognized the cut immediately—it wasn't the result of a childhood accident or a servants' mishap, but a sword's slash.

She followed the woman with her gaze, her sister and uncle entirely forgotten. The servant balanced several bowls and plates on her silver tray—her arms bulged beneath her sleeves as its weight increased with each dirty dish. Sure, servants required some degree of strength, especially those whose occupation was carrying things, but something about the way this woman held herself—head high and back straight—combined with that strangely defined musculature, and the sword scar across her face, resulted in something that felt very out of place for a servant.

Searin stood with every intention of finding out who this woman was. Then the hall spun around her, and she caught herself on the back of her chair. Her mother shot her a cold stare. "From your sister, this sort of public drunkenness is expected," the queen said. "But from you..."

She had to concede the woman her point. Searin had not realized just how drunk she had become. Those stupid toasts... The cacophony within the hall felt sweltering and overwhelming. Searin looked at her mother. The queen's eyes morphed from coldness to pity—a very subtle difference, but one that Searin was not too intoxicated to notice. "Go," the queen said. "Take your brother to his chambers, then retire."

It was the greatest kindness her mother had shown her in years. Searin reached her hand out towards Hovard. The boy took it tentatively. Together, they walked towards the back door that led towards the royal sleeping quarters. Before exiting, Searin stole another glance at the servant woman. *Perhaps the wine is making me see things,* Searin thought. Either way, she resolved to take a sober look at the woman the following day.

The quiet that greeted them in the empty halls once the door had shut behind them was a stark contrast to the jovial noise they left behind. Searin and Hovard remained silent as if reverently basking in the stillness, which was only interrupted by the soft padding of Hovard's ever-bare feet. Up the stairs, Searin made a right turn, headed for Hovard's chambers. The boy stopped unexpectedly, and Searin found herself tugging on his arm.

"What is it?" Searin asked.

Hovard's head remained low. Quietly, he muttered, "I don't want to be alone."

Searin looked around as if anyone would be there to attend to the boy's request. But it was just the two of them, and her brother's plea now fell squarely on her shoulders. She fought down the spiky irritation that pricked at her. Unlike her brother, Searin wanted nothing more than to be left alone. Yet, she found herself unable to refuse his request. She would compromise and remain with Hovard until he fell asleep.

"Fine," Searin surrendered. The look Hovard gave her warmed her heart, and in an instant, the distance between them did not feel so unfathomable. Searin was at once reminded that they both shared the burden of what their father had done to himself—and to their family. Perhaps not quite the same burden, but a burden, nonetheless.

Peshyr stood next to Hovard's chamber doors. The guard was broad and severe—unfriendly and untalkative towards all, though a decent guard. Hovard smiled and waved his hand emphatically at the man.

"My prince, my princess," the guard greeted with a curt bow, then opened the doors for them. "Would you like me to call up a servant?" Peshyr asked with a faint smile. Searin was somewhat shocked by the fondness she saw on the guard's face.

"No, thank you, Peshie," Hovard replied.

"My pleasure," the guard said. As soon as they were inside the room, Peshyr closed them in.

Searin realized at that moment that she had never been inside Hovard's chambers. The aroma of sweet cinnamon and tree-nut-scented candles gave the room an inviting air. The hearth was already blazing an inviting fire. The decor was homey, the bed, desk, and every chair begging to be used. The walls were covered in tapestry representations of some of the most well-known fables in Hovardom. Searin recognized one as having once hung in her own room before she had decided to adopt a more austere aesthetic.

"Mother was going to throw that one out," Hovard said, noticing Searin studying her old tapestry. "But Father refused."

"Anything to start a strife with Mother," Searin soured.

"He said he had it made for someone special, and he didn't want such a priceless thing destroyed. So, it ended up with me."

A foreign emotion crept through Searin. Was it shame? She turned away from the tapestry, no longer able to bear its sight.

Hovard removed his belt, then unbuttoned his shirt and allowed it to fall to the floor. He grabbed a neatly folded night shift from his dresser. As he slid his head into the silky garb, he became stuck, unable to pull the garment down. Searin watched her brother struggle for some time, noticing that Hovard had forgotten to unfasten the buttons at the shift's collar.

"Some help would be appreciated," Hovard grunted.

Searin stifled a laugh and moved to help Hovard, unfastening the buttons at the collar and guiding the shift down over his head. The boy scowled at her behind his now-messy locks. "Not sure what's so funny."

"Sorry, I..." Searin scratched her neck. "I'm not very good at this sisterly stuff."

"I'll say," Hovard teased. The boy pulled back the thick blankets and hopped into bed. He left the blankets open and stared at Searin. "Are you just going to stand there?" he asked.

Searin rolled her eyes and approached the bed. Hovard pointed at Searin's boots. "You're not coming in here with those." Searin removed her boots with a huff, dropping them onto the carpeted floor. "And your day clothes too," Hovard added. "Mother says it's not good to sully a bed with what you've worn all day."

Searin furrowed her brow. "I only have my small clothes beneath this."

"So?" Hovard rebuffed.

She could leave and go to her own chambers, Searin thought. This sort of thing was beneath her. She didn't have time to waste on a child's whims—especially not when that child was Hovard. She glanced about the room with resentment. In all that surrounded her, Hovard embodied everything a prince should be. They were so unlike each other that, if Searin hadn't known any better, she would never have imagined them to be related.

Searin felt she had no choice but to comply. She unbuttoned the horrid funeral gown her mother had made her wear two days in a row, and let it slip onto the floor. Searin felt relief wash over her, as if by slipping the dress off she had also removed the baggage of the day from her shoulders. Hovard nodded towards the empty side of the bed, and Searin slid in and pulled the covers over herself.

"Gods!" Searin exclaimed, jumping up. "Your feet are frigid!"

"Then warm them up," Hovard taunted, prodding Searin with those icicles.

"Stop that!" Searin cried out, squirming to avoid her brother's freezing touch. "Stop, or I will leave!"

"Leave? That's what you two always do." Hovard's voice was soft. "All you do is train, and all Arisa does is read. Mother is the only one that ever talks to me. Even Father doesn't... didn't..." Hovard choked out a quickly stifled sob.

"What could we even do together?" Searin asked, and it felt like a cruel question to pose.

"Train."

"Train?" Searin repeated, baffled.

"I don't know," Hovard huffed. "You're the best in the yard. That's what everyone says. What if I could also be good at swinging a sword? I won't know unless I try. I could learn from the best. You."

Searin stared at the back of Hovard's head, as the boy's shoulders rose and fell with each breath. Suddenly, Searin had a great urge to move closer to her brother, to hold him and tell him everything would be all right. She regretted not sharing the warmth of her body. It wasn't something she could offer now—that would sting her pride too much. Such a silly thing to worry about, pride.

"I wanted to show him Uncle Clavio's gift," Hovard whimpered.

A knot formed in Searin's throat from the abrupt statement. The poor child. Hovard was just like his room: clean, polished, comfortable, and soft. Searin could not imagine what seeing their father in such a way had done to him. Would Hovard ever be able to forget that sight? Would she?

XVI.

THE DOOR

The smell of roasting pig would have made anyone else salivate, but it was having the opposite effect on Lyr. The day passed her by, and suddenly evening had come. She was seated in the servants' common hall, a bowl of cold stew and bread set in front of her. Nothing that had happened between her killing Dora and now had been retained by her mind.

I killed someone. It was true but the thought did not feel real. *I killed Dora.* It wasn't something she had planned to do. It was just something she had done—something she had been forced to do. Had she not, Dora would have brought that vial to someone in charge, and Lyr and the other Free Kings would be lying in a cell right now. Or a grave. Lyr could easily imagine how little sympathy Dora would have had for any of them had their circumstances been reversed. No, Lyr had done what needed to be done. Simple as that.

She picked up the spoon, realizing then that her hand was shaking. She wished Saul was here. At least then she would be able to share her guilt with someone who could understand. Even Alizia would be a welcome presence, though she and Saul were in the western wing this evening serving at the king's funeral feast.

Lyr sighed and pierced the spoon through the orange film that had formed across the surface of the stew. She resolved to consider what had happened with Dora as self-defense. It was a grim thought. She needed to eat, to keep up her strength, and to hold out until their mission was complete. Lyr desperately hoped that would be sooner rather than later.

"Did you hear?"

Lyr started, then chastised herself for doing so. The servant child that quartered with her sat across the table, staring at her with wide eyes. She was a scrawny little thing. The webbing of light burn scars climbing her neck and arms hadn't been visible to Lyr until she was sitting this close to her. "Hear what?" Lyr asked.

"Dora got beaten yesterday as punishment and today she left her post and never returned," the girl said in a hushed tone. "People are saying she ran away."

Lyr let go of her spoon, sending it clinking loudly against the bowl. "Sorry," she said, nervously scratching her forehead.

"Don't worry," the girl continued, "We won't get blamed for her leaving. Nobody around here really liked her much." The child took a sip of her stew. "Too bad for her family though. I heard from Enye—one of the chambermaids, have you met her?—that they punish your whole family if you run away like that."

Lyr contemplated the stew, wondering if she had it in her to take a bite after all. She looked up and realized the child was staring at her. "I really hope she doesn't come back," the child said. "She was a bully and a tattler. I like you better."

Lyr feigned a smile at the compliment, then stood. "I think I'm going to go to sleep. I've had a long day."

The girl nodded. "The kitchens sound tough. I'm glad they have me cleaning the chambers instead. Though I guess my style of cleaning isn't up to 'the royal standard' according to Steward Ibessa." The girl rolled her eyes, "You'd think these people had never seen mud on the floor before."

Lyr picked up her bowl and began to walk away, but the child stood as well and followed. "I'm Falma," she said.

Lyr nodded. "I'm Yulma."

"I know."

A conversation with a child was more than Lyr had stamina for at this time. She smiled pitifully and increased her speed. She poured her untouched bowl back into the cauldron hanging over the large hearth and turned back to face the hall. Several servants had begun to clear it, preparing to return to their chambers. Falma had returned to the table and was now seated by herself, splashing her spoon in her bowl of stew. Something dawned on Lyr—what was a child doing here all alone? She must have some connections to land a job in the palace at such a young age. Based on what Lyr had learned from the other servants, Falma had most likely been delivered here by her family. Being a palace servant was a much better option than living in the Pleasants or most other districts, especially for a little girl. But at least Lyr had friends in the Pleasants. Falma seemed all alone.

Lyr left the hall and made for the sleeping quarters. She did not have the mental fortitude for it today—especially after all that had happened—but she made a promise to herself that she would try to be more pleasant towards Falma.

Perhaps faking a disposition would also help her distract herself from thoughts of what she had done.

The door to the quarters was closed. Lyr pushed it open cautiously and entered. She feared finding Dora's body still there, gray and decaying. But Alizia had done her job well and there was no body nor any trace of one having been there. Lyr removed her day clothes and replaced them with her night shift. She climbed into her cot and pulled the covers tight. Instinctively, she reached into her small clothes for the vial, fearing it had somehow vanished. She felt its glass shape between her fingers, to her relief and horror. She would be carrying it on her even while she slept from now on.

Dark visions of Dora's pallid death throes stalked Lyr's sleep. She resigned herself to staring up at the stone ceiling. Falma soon entered the room and assumed her cot. The child removed only her shoes and did not change into her night shift, Lyr noted. Leandra did not return to the room that evening, nor did Alizia. Lyr knew it was ridiculous, but her sleepless mind wandered to thoughts of Saul and that woman. Perhaps that was why Alizia hadn't returned—she and Saul were holed up somewhere, kissing and touching one another. Lyr imagined how broad and strong their children would grow to be.

The unwelcome thoughts irritated her, but they were better than the alternative—better than dwelling on the girl she had murdered.

Hours passed in this self-inflicted torture, until something shifted in the room. Lyr remained still as Falma furtively stood from her cot and headed for the door. Her bare feet made no sound against the stone floor. The girl vanished into the dimness beyond the room and softly closed the door behind her.

Curiosity overtook Lyr, supplanting her guilt and jealousy. She jumped from her cot and opened the door just a crack to peek outside, catching the back of Falma as she tiptoed around a corner. Where was the girl headed at this hour of the night? Should Lyr follow? What excuse would she conjure if she was caught?

Lyr padded her way out of the room and down the hall Falma had just crossed. Lyr looked around the corner in time to see the child turn into another hallway. It was a stupid thought, but if Falma could remain undetected, so could she. Lyr followed, then peeked around the corner to ensure no one was there. The hallway before her extended into a deep darkness, but even then she could make out a door closing a few paces away. She glanced back to check for followers, then, once she was certain no one was there, Lyr headed for the door. Lyr remembered this hall from the map of the palace she had studied. There wasn't supposed to be a door here. Lyr reached for the handle and pushed— it was locked. Perhaps that was for the best.

Nearing footsteps reverberated through the hall. Lyr had no intention of being caught here, especially not in her night clothes. She retraced her steps back to her room and opened the door. A tall, dark figure stood before her. Lyr jumped back and yelped.

"What are you doing?" the figure whispered. It was Alizia.

Lyr sighed in relief. "I'm sorry, I— You startled me."

Alizia untied the belt around her waist and unfastened the buttons at the front of her shift. "I just got back from the funeral feast. They had so many guests that they called all servants of the western wing to attend."

Lyr sat on her cot. "How was it?"

"It was... loud. I got a good look at the royal family. I even managed to attend to their table at one point."

Lyr nodded, though she wasn't sure Alizia could see her in the darkness. Lyr raised her blankets and returned to their warmth.

"They're saying she ran away," Alizia said suddenly, breaking the dark silence. "That Dora girl."

Lyr's throat tightened. "Yes," was all she could muster, though she wasn't sure why she said it.

"We're lucky for that. We're lucky you were so quick to react. We do what we must to protect our comrades. And what we must do is not always easy," Alizia seemed to sense how conflicted Lyr felt. "You did the right thing, Yulma."

The door to the room opened, and Lyr thanked the True One for the interruption. Leandra plodded into the room. The faint torchlight from the hallway painted her features with startlement. "What are you two still doing up?" the woman asked.

"I only just returned from the funeral feast," Alizia replied.

Leandra closed the door and quickly hurried into bed, fully dressed. "You two better get some sleep soon. These next few days will be some of the busiest you'll ever work here."

"Where's the girl?" Lyr asked.

"Dora?" Leandra asked, before quickly adding, "If she's smart, she's begging Steward Ibessa for forgiveness after disappearing on such an important day."

"No, Falma," Lyr corrected.

"That girl has her own tasks that occupy her. Worry not and get some sleep."

Lyr settled in the darkness, attempting to do just that. Just as sleep was within grasp, she felt something tickling her. She reached beneath her blanket and pulled a speck from her forearm. A ghost-white maggot wriggled between her fingers.

XVII.

THE RED ROAD

They did not linger long at the errant knight encampment once day broke. After breaking their fast on bread rolls, Rovan instructed Tieg and Scintilla to pack their things and prepare themselves for the rest of the journey. "Have we decided which direction we're headed in?" Scintilla inquired.

"A large river crossing to the north, or the Red Road to the east crawling with Blue Scarabs and very likely a *reaverlord*. A bad hand," Tieg observed.

Rovan passed a roll to the enchantress, who had finally awakened and had taken a seat on a nearby stump. "What do you think?" he asked her.

"Now you value my input?" Adriel snarked.

Rovan frowned. "Never mind, then."

"Take the Road," the enchantress advised. "If we meet the *reaverlord*, I will know how to deal with it."

"And what about the Scarabs?" Tieg asked.

The enchantress snorted. "Sometimes it's best to trust the flow of the Cycle."

Rovan was not particularly fond of surrendering plans to fate, though he had to admit sitting around was only good for wasting time. "The Red Road it is," he announced. "If the weather holds, we should reach it in a couple hours."

The campsite was now teeming with activity as the knights began to pack. Though they were errant knights—each working for themselves—they were surprisingly efficient at clearing the camp as a team. Pilons was an adept captain. Rovan wondered if the man had any past military experience.

"We should move unless we want to spend our time journeying alongside errant knights," Adriel urged.

"Oh, they're not so bad," Tieg said.

"They can be. Best to not overstay our welcome," Rovan said. The group collected and proceeded through the woods, leaving the buzzing camp behind. Their hope for clear weather was immediately quelled, as the rain resumed its constant companionship—the fifth member of their party. Not only did it render the hike unstable, but it also made conversing difficult. It was hard to hear what anyone said through the constant downpour, which is why it took Rovan a few moments to hear that Scintilla was calling out to him.

"What?" Rovan asked.

"Look," she said, pointing to the ground with a shaky hand.

Embedded within the mud were what appeared to be the footprints of a large man. Though Rovan had never seen a man with claws that long.

"A greatwolf?" Scintilla asked, retrieving the bow holster from her back in preparation.

"I don't know," Rovan lied. The enchantress shot him a severe look. "Let's keep moving," he said.

Time did not seem to matter in the hazy grayness of the forest. Two hours had passed, Rovan was certain, and they should have reached the Red Road by now. Yet they were still surrounded by trees and more trees. And rain. For a moment, Rovan wondered if they had taken a wrong turn somewhere. The dark gray sky above concealed the sun, making it challenging to orient himself. Yet, though she limped and leaned heavily on her staff, there was a certainness to the enchantress' step that made Rovan trust that they were headed the right way. Could there be anyone more familiar with these woods than an enchantress of Albadone?

The scream that pierced the air sapped the strength from Rovan's limbs. He buckled under the weight of his bundle. Tieg reached out and steadied him. Rovan grunted, "Thank you," then faced Scintilla to gauge her reaction to the sound. Her face had drained of all blood, melting into a gray pallor. "Scintilla..." Rovan called out gently.

The young woman swallowed, then faced him with a strained expression. "I'm all right," she assured.

Rovan nodded, then turned to the enchantress. "Did you feel that?" he asked.

"The *reaverlord* is nearby," Adriel said. "We must tread carefully."

"And you are sure you know how to handle it?" Scintilla asked.

"As sure as I'm alive."

Rovan caught his bearings, positioned himself in front of the group, and carried onwards. The feeling of exhaustion didn't leave—it was a lingering presence within his body, like the symptom of an illness after the fever has broken. Rovan glanced about the forest, ensuring that the *reaverlord* was nowhere in sight. "How much farther to the Road?" he asked the enchantress, abandoning all pretense that he had any idea of where they were headed.

"An hour," Adriel said.

"Let's pick up the pace," Rovan pressed, sensing a dark presence looming close—just behind his shoulder.

Scintilla yelped, then immediately covered her mouth. Tieg hovered over her protectively. The four stopped and looked out into the forest. A figure stood several paces away, its back rising and falling with heavy breaths. It looked like an animal doing its best impression of a human. Though it stood on two legs, it seemed as if it was not meant to. Its breathing was more like heaving, and its fingers twitched constantly, scratching the air in front of it. Bulky armor covered its entire body, including its head.

The simple sight of the *reaverlord* was enough to fill Rovan with the greatest dread he had ever experienced.

"Stand back," Adriel commanded, moving ahead of the group and towards the beast.

Rovan grabbed her arm. "What are you doing?" he whispered.

"I'm making myself known to it. Better to deal with it now that it's calm than later after it has whipped itself into a frenzy."

Rovan reluctantly let go of the woman, hoping to all higher powers—named and unnamed—that she actually knew what she was doing.

"We need to run," Scintilla whispered.

"And leave her alone?" Tieg asked.

"She's giving herself up as bait, is she not?"

"What? Don't be stupid!"

"Quiet!" Rovan shushed. "And stay back, in case anything happens." Scintilla and Tieg turned to hide behind the nearest tree. Rovan remained standing in place, prepared to either defend the enchantress or run—he had not decided which.

The enchantress reached the *reaverlord*. The creature spun, revealing that what had appeared to Rovan as a helmet was its face. In fact, on a lingering look, Rovan realized that the creature was not wearing armor at all. Its entire body was covered by hard, hulking scales that shimmered silver and emerald in the light.

The *reaverlord* grunted, then belched a horrible scream. What Rovan had confused for the helmet's slit opened to reveal two sets of razor-sharp teeth. The enchantress did not budge an inch beneath the intimidating roar. The creature raised an arm as if to attack, but before it could swing, the woman began chanting in a strange, foreign tongue. Slowly, the *reaverlord* lowered its arm, and tilted its head from side to side, as if understanding the woman's words.

Rovan could feel the easing of the tension in the air as if it was something palpable—solid. The relief came to him instantly and he was finally able to catch his breath. Strain dissipated from the *reaverlord's* posture, and it suddenly did not look as dangerous as it had a moment earlier. From its horrific mouth, the *reaverlord* emitted several guttural sounds that seemed to mimic those of the enchantress. Rovan could not avert his gaze. The two conversed for some time until Adriel bowed her head and turned back towards the group. On her face was a placid look, as if the matter of the *reaverlord* had been resolved.

"That's that," the woman announced.

"So, it seems," Rovan agreed in astonishment.

A whizzing sound zipped through the forest, growing nearer and nearer until it reached where the *reaverlord* stood. An arrow bounced off its carapaced head and landed, broken, into the muddy earth. The *reaverlord* screamed—this time, Adriel fell to the ground from the startlement. A tidal wave of anger and confusion washed over Rovan, threatening to drown him. He collapsed to the ground under its weight. Tieg and Scintilla reached them both and raised them to their feet.

"Don't let it get away!" someone yelled from the nearby brush. The battalion of errant knights entered the thicket and began encircling the *reaverlord,* Pilons at their head. Their drawn swords and bows were pointed forward. The creature did not allow itself to be surrounded—it sprung toward the nearest knight with near-imperceptible speed. With a swipe of its hand, it sliced the man's sword in half, then grabbed his head and pulled it upwards until it came free. The *reaverlord* dropped the man's dangling body to the ground, then moved on to its next victim.

Disorder quickly arose within the battlement. Pilons stood aside, barking commands, expecting the knights to resume their places, but no one heeded his call. For all their orderliness at the campsite that morning, they now appeared like children wildly swinging toy swords, hoping to nick the frenzied *reaverlord.* But none of their attacks seemed to make a single dent in its hard scales. Arrows flew every which way, hitting the creature as often as they did trees and even fellow knights. All the while, the monster continued making quick work of knight after knight, severing limbs with tooth and claw as easily as one might snap a twig.

A slap in the face returned Rovan to his body. He had not realized that he had become a captive audience to the slaughter while his friends stood near, awaiting his word. Some leader he was. The slap had come from the enchantress. "We have to go," she said frantically. "It will kill us if we don't."

Rovan nodded, doing his best to regain his composure. The enchantress jogged in front and, yet again, Rovan was happy to have someone else lead. The four of them ran eastward through the woods, quickly leaving the sound of battle behind. Even in her injured state, the enchantress managed a swift and steady pace. The trees tunneled around him, and Rovan was sure that, had he led the group, he would have gotten them lost. Some time later, the enchantress finally stopped and leaned against a tree to catch her breath. Rovan noticed her clutching a purple runestone to her leg.

Tieg's face was red and blotchy, his eyes anxiously scanning the tree line. Scintilla, however, looked as if she was about to sick up. Rovan felt guilt and embarrassment for the way he had frozen earlier.

"All good?" he asked no one in particular.

"Oh, yeah," Tieg said between winded breaths. "Very, very good."

"We almost died," Scintilla murmured. She suddenly broke into the most morbid laugh Rovan had ever heard. It broke his heart.

Tieg placed his hand on her tense arm and Scintilla crumbled in his grip. Though they were of equal height, she suddenly seemed smaller and more fragile to Rovan. She placed her head on Tieg's shoulder and took in several strained breaths.

"We're safe now," Tieg said.

"No," the enchantress disagreed. She rolled her shoulders and continued onwards through the forest. "Those damn fools. What were they thinking?—attacking that creature! They will all meet a tragic end."

Tieg rubbed Scintilla's shoulder. "Can you make it, Sin?"

Scintilla raised her head and nodded. She looked tired—haggard. She followed the enchantress forward as if by rote. Tieg followed but, before he could join the two women, Rovan halted him with a gentle hand on his chest. "I'm sorry," Rovan said.

"What for?" Tieg asked, an unfamiliar tremor in his voice.

"For all of this. If it wasn't for this job, you would be halfway to your family's home by now."

Tieg frowned. "You think I'm doing this because of you? I said I would do it, so I am. I may be stupid, but I don't back away from my word."

"You're not stupid," Rovan countered.

"I know what you all really think of me."

Rovan narrowed his eyes. "What are you talking about?"

"Let's just go, before we lose them." Tieg shrugged away from Rovan and joined the two women ahead.

Rovan was left dumbfounded by his friend's words. Had something happened that Rovan was not aware of? Had there been infighting in their group, or had someone made Tieg feel unwelcome? Was this why he had decided to leave? Rovan was once again disappointed in himself for not realizing any of this before it was too late. Tieg didn't want to state it outright, but Rovan knew the truth—this was his fault. All of it. His focus on saving Pevine had made him ignore his friends' needs. He had done the opposite of what Terreck had asked of him by using no discernment at all in continuing this journey. He had endangered those he cared for.

Just for a moment, he had thought that maybe people had been following him for a reason—that maybe he was actually cut out to be a leader. All that had been a delusion.

Half an hour passed before the soil beneath their feet gave way to the red sediment that delineated the Red Road. None of them were in a mood to celebrate, but rather quietly joined the beaten dirt road and followed it north, towards Vizen. As predicted, they spotted a Blue Scarab outpost just ahead.

"These must be the bug boys you mentioned," Adriel wondered aloud.

"If we're lucky they'll let us through without asking for our documents," Tieg said.

"What sort of documents?" the enchantress scoffed.

"Travel permits," Rovan replied. "The Blue Scarabs check them at outposts along the Red Road. Everyone must carry them when going from city to city."

"And you have such permits?"

The three friends glanced at each other uneasily. "We do not."

The enchantress narrowed her eyes. "And how did you intend on entering Vizen without them?"

"We always find a way," Scintilla said.

"True One blind me," Adriel cursed.

It didn't take long for the Blue Scarabs at the encampment to take notice of them. They were instructed to stand aside and wait since the soldiers were busy with someone else. A mule cart was parked to the side of the road, the mule chewing lazily on some wet liontails. The cart's driver argued animatedly with one of the Scarab soldiers. The argument seemed to have something to do with the cart's lack of cargo. "It's suspicious, s'all I'm saying," the bald soldier explained.

"I'm tired of repeating myself. The mule and the cart *are* the cargo!" the driver shouted. "I purchased them in Rondhill and I'm taking them home to Urstway."

"And you have no papers to prove this transaction?"

"Papers!?" the man fumed. "I wasn't stopped at any of the other ten patrols! Why am I being treated so terribly now?"

Rovan closed his eyes as a sudden wariness overcame him. He addressed his companions. "Let's just go around them." But, before they could attempt this evasion, another Scarab approached them and said, "You'll have your turn," perhaps sensing their intent.

"Are you certain?" Tieg asked the soldier. "Seems to me like you've decided to keep this man here forever."

"That's what I'm saying!" the driver agreed.

"Wait your turn," the Scarab repeated, then retreated under the canopy of the outpost. The driver and soldier resumed their argument—it sounded muffled and distant to Rovan's ears. He was so tired. So, terribly, tired.

"Are you all right, Rovan?" Scintilla asked, touching his arm.

The enchantress perked up as if hearing something in the distance. "Oh, for fuck's sake!" she grunted.

A scream brought all arguments to a halt. Birds left their comfortable perches atop the nearby trees and fled into the gray sky. "What was that?" the driver asked. The swollen moment of silence that followed his question was chilling.

The *reaverlord* emerged from the tree line, sprinting towards them. Dark blood oozed from gashes covering its body. Several of its shimmering scales had been hacked to shreds by what Rovan guessed were enchanted swords.

"What in the Nameless—" The Scarab could not finish his curse before the *reaverlord* plowed directly into him, its razor-sharp claws obliterating his armor instantly. The man landed on the ground, blood pouring from his mouth and pooling all around him. The *reaverlord* stood over its kill and growled, pleased with its work.

The mule started and galloped up the road as fast as it was able, dragging the empty cart behind it. The driver averted his astonishment away from the *reaverlord* and dashed, chasing his runaway cargo. The other Scarab unsheathed his sword, which glowed red with the heat of a very powerful enchantment of *Power*. "Try that with me, shadowbeast," he challenged. The *reaverlord* appeared eager to test the man. The creature lunged and slashed at the Scarab. To his credit, the man parried the slashes well, then backed away to compose an attack.

"Let's go!" Tieg exclaimed, taking both Rovan and Scintilla by the hand. Once again, the *reaverlord* had captivated Rovan's attention entirely. He was not sure why, but he was unable to divert his gaze without aid.

"Where is the enchantress?" Rovan asked as he was being dragged away from the scene by Tieg.

"Who cares?" Tieg replied.

I do, Rovan told himself. He let go of Tieg's hand and looked at Scintilla. Her eyes were wide and distant. "Go north up the Road. Don't stop until you reach Vizen. We will regroup at the city gates."

"What are you thinking?" Scintilla asked.

"I'll be fine." Rovan stared into his friends' worried eyes, silently communicating the urgency of his request. Scintilla looked like she wanted to protest, but Tieg dragged her away.

At the outpost, the Scarab soldier continued to adeptly parry the beast's attacks. Sweat beaded the man's shaved head from the effort. This was nothing like fighting another soldier—the *reaverlord* was faster than any human, animal, or djinn, Rovan had ever seen. For each blow the soldier fended off, there were three more awaiting him.

With great strain, Rovan forced himself to look away from the fight, seeking the enchantress. The woman wobbled atop a stool that she had removed from under the outpost canopy. She raised her arms, attempting to make herself seem as large as possible. For a moment, it distracted the *reaverlord*. The Scarab took that as a chance to hack at the beast, slicing through its shoulder blade. The *reaverlord* screamed and lunged at the soldier, who barely managed to avoid the onslaught.

"Stop fighting it!" Adriel shouted.

The Scarab did not pay her any mind, as he remained locked in mad combat. It could not last long. It was evident that the man was growing tired and sluggish. Rovan had to do something to distract the beast. But what?

"Take it alive!" a man's voice shouted. Pilons ran out of the tree line followed by two of his errant knight companions. All three were covered in blood—it was hard to discern if it belonged to them, to the beast, or to their fallen companions. Pilons's face was drenched in red pouring out of a gash at his hairline. He shouted and, along with his companions, joined the assault.

The, now four, combatants attacked the *reaverlord,* alternating swings and parries with no rhyme or reason. There was no precision or strategy, just red-hot fury. The *reaverlord* killed one of the two knights by grabbing their head and smashing it heavily against the ground. Rovan turned away from the gory display to face the enchantress. Adriel still stood atop the stool, swinging her arms wildly and yelling, "Stop!" It was no use—the knights were intent on taking the *reaverlord* down.

Rovan reached the enchantress. "They won't stop," he said. "Come down and run."

"*Reaverlords—dragons—*are the Guardian of the Mountains," the enchantress explained. "All it wants to do is to protect its home."

"Yes, but it's also killing every human it can find," he countered.

"If you can get them to stop fighting, I can—"

A gurgling sound like water boiling came from the *reaverlord*. Rovan turned in time to watch the creature hunch over and spit out its foul blood. Only Pilons and his fellow knight remained standing—the Scarab lay crumpled over, cradling his severed arm in an embrace. Pilons's eyes were barely visible behind a mask of blood. A frightening grin widened the other knight's face. "All yours," the man said, respectfully stepping aside to allow Pilons the killing blow.

"Please, stop!" Rovan called out.

Pilons and the knight turned to face him. It was as if they had just realized he and the enchantress were there. "Have you come to watch me slay the beast, little pup?" Pilons asked. The man's voice was loud and frantic.

"Don't kill it!" Rovan begged. He wasn't sure why, but he felt a tremendous surge of foreboding.

Pilons's face soured grimly. He turned to face the creature and thrust his sword through its neck. "NO!" Adriel screamed.

Blood sprayed from the creature's mouth. In blind dying fury, it lunged ahead, collapsing atop Pilons. The man heaved a cry, which the *reaverlord* silenced by sinking its teeth into his skull. Both stilled. Rovan instantly felt the grip of the *reaverlord's* essence release him as a sigh escaped his lungs. Mother Adriel seemed affronted by his apparent relief. "A tragedy," she murmured.

The remaining errant knight laughed and cheered, as if every other one of his companions had not just been killed. The life of an errant knight was a solitary one, Rovan had to remind himself. That lot were fast friends and even faster rivals when it came down to being paid. This man had apparently forgotten their role was to capture the beast alive. The knight sat heavily in the red mud and stared at the bodies of Pilons and the beast, locked in eternal combat. His smile faded briefly, though his laughter remained.

"Poor fool," Adriel said. "Deep down, within the *life energy* that flows through his body, he is aware of the great evil that was committed here." The enchantress reached a hand out towards Rovan, who helped her step off the stool. Adriel knelt before the felled beast. The errant knight stopped his laughter and observed the woman with taught nervousness as if she somehow could steal his kill. Adriel placed her hand on the *reaverlord's* head and closed her eyes. She chanted quietly for some time before finally standing up.

"Let's go," she said, before proceeding north, up the Red Road.

XVIII.

A Change in the Winds

Leandra's warning that the day after the funeral feast would be busier than the feast itself had not been an exaggeration. Yesterday, Lyr had been tasked with the chopping of vegetables, sweeping of floors, and stirring of pots, but today she was confronted with the remnants of the feast. Hundreds of dirty plates, bowls, pots and pans, and an army of cutlery were carelessly scattered about the kitchen. Leandra sighed at the sight. "Let's get to it before Flavien arrives and starts stirring mud into our morning tea," the woman grumbled.

Lyr soaked the grimy pots and pans in scalding water, then scrubbed them with salt. The food was caked onto the inner sides of the cookware, and much effort was required to scrub through it. The entire morning was spent like this: soaking, scrubbing, soaking, scrubbing. At first, Lyr had been wary of skipping breakfast that morning, but now she was glad she had, as the smell and soft feel of wet foodstuff was making her nauseous.

Eventually, Flavien entered the kitchen, like a dark midday storm. He scolded Leandra for not having finished the dishes already. The woman apologized, though Lyr was not sure how much more the two of them could have done. The other servants in the kitchen had been occupied with prepping food for yet another feast that was to be held later that day. Lyr asked if it was customary to have a feast the day after a funeral feast, to which Leandra replied, "Nobles just like to feast."

There was such a coming and going in the kitchen that Leandra directed Lyr to transport all remaining dirty dishes in crates to an unused ballroom. They then brought in a copper tub and filled it with scalding water so they could resume their cleaning undisturbed and without being in the way. Lyr preferred this to circumventing frantic cooks, servants, and Flavien's hungover ire.

The two of them sat on the floor next to the tub as they worked. Besides the occasional comment on the ineffectiveness of Lyr's scrubbing technique, Leandra was not a very talkative companion that day.

"How did you end up at the palace?" Lyr's voice reverberated deeply through the empty ballroom.

Leandra kept her eyes on a particularly stubborn crust on the pot she was scrubbing. Lyr half-expected the woman to remain silent, but, to her surprise, a reply finally came. "I've been here longer than you've been alive. My mother was a chambermaid to Lady Forrester, who was one of the queen's best friends in childhood. When I was younger, I was groomed to be a chambermaid to a future princess. Lady Forrester, however, fell out of favor with the queen after some incident. My mother was demoted to a kitchen hand, and that's where she spent the rest of her life. So, here I am too."

Lyr was astonished by how much that simple question had managed to get out of Leandra. More astonishing was the level of passiveness in the woman's tone. This was a life Leandra was resigned to, but not one that she felt any passion for. Lyr wondered how many other servants felt similarly stuck. "Why was your mother demoted when it was Lady Forrester who fell out of favor?"

Leandra stopped scrubbing the pot and met Lyr's eyes. "Does it matter? Do you think the royals care about what happens to servants?"

"Surely they put some thought into their actions," Lyr replied.

Leandra smiled sourly. "Yulma, we are but boats in their mercurial wind. You either learn to stay afloat and navigate it the hard way, or you drift away and sink. It may not seem fair, but what are our lives without the wind?" Leandra lowered her eyes back to the pot and gave it an animated scrub as if to add finality to her statement. The woman was no longer in a mood to speak, Lyr understood.

In the world the Free Kings envisioned, without nobility or royalty, what role would someone like Leandra take on? For that matter, how would the rest of the servants fare? They were little more than livestock to the royals, with none of the skills needed to survive the streets of Vizen. Would they see the Free Kings as liberators or as usurpers driving them into the wilderness? One servant had already died at her hand for this cause. How many more would have to pay for a choice she was making for them?

It was well into the afternoon by the time the last of the pots had been cleaned. Leandra left the ballroom as Lyr wrung gray water out of the towels. The woman soon returned with a pair of steaming meat pastries. The smell made Lyr feel faint—she had not realized how ravenous she had become. She thanked Leandra and took a nibble of the pastry, doing her best not to swallow the whole thing in one bite.

"That new baker is quite adept," Leandra complimented, after taking a neat bite of her pastry. "Let's return to the kitchen and see what needs to be done there. If we find we are not needed, I suggest you wash up and make yourself scarce."

The kitchens were operating efficiently when they arrived. Leandra gave Lyr a knowing nod, so Lyr decided to take the opportunity to remove herself from the post. On her way out, Geren, the baker, bumped into her, dropping a tray of pastries onto the ground. "Oh, apologies Yulma," he said, bending to pick up the tray. Only one of the pastries had not survived the impact, rolling off the tray and onto the floor. Lyr kneeled to pick it up, and Geren, the fellow infiltrator, took the opportunity to bend closer to her and whisper, "We're meeting in the south hall storage room during the feast. Be there."

Lyr nodded, though her eyes had broadened like a startled cat's. Geren stood with the tray and hurried to place the steaming treats to cool on a wire rack. Lyr hurried out of the kitchen, still holding the warm pastry she had picked up. She took a distracted bite from it, having forgotten that it had fallen onto the dirty kitchen floor. The inside was a warm custard, rich and creamy—it was perhaps the best thing she had ever tasted.

The life of a palace servant was not at all what Lyr had expected it to be. Sure, there was work to be done, much of it tedious and draining. But there was just as much leisure. There was not nearly enough work to occupy every palace servant at the same time. Moreso, Lyr noticed that all some servants did was walk around the palace, tidying up the halls by dusting and straightening portraits. These servants stood out because they were dressed in colorful robes, adornments in their hair, and confidence in their strides. When thinking of servants, Lyr had always thought of meek and badgered people. This was not at all what she had envisioned. Having now lived both the life of a peasant and that of a palace servant, Lyr struggled to make the two worlds meet.

One thing about the life of a servant that Lyr could not quite adapt to was the infrequent boredom. It wasn't too dissimilar from the boredom she had felt in the Pleasants when there was no work to be had in the market, but at least there she could go on a walk through her neighborhood or visit a tavern and listen to some songs or a story. Here, there were no such activities. The servants' common hall was quiet and austere. Servants who were not busy at work sat alone at the various tables doing absolutely nothing, none of them allowed to leave the palace.

So, Lyr waited for the day to pass, and eventually, the hall grew abuzz. This was the time of day the servants lived for—the evening meal where they could meet and share gossip about the lives of those above their station. Like the previous night, the hall was only partially populated. Many servants were working at that evening's feast. Alizia made her way towards the table carrying two plates of sausage and pungent boiled cabbage. She set one of the plates in front of Lyr and took the seat across from her.

"Did you hear about the meeting?" Alizia whispered. She poked the sausage with her fork and bit into it—its juices ran down her chin.

Lyr nodded. She stared at the plate before her. Though she had already eaten, she was still hungry. With the fork, she cut off an end from the sausage and took a bite—warm, savory, pleasantly spiced.

"Saul says there's an update to the plan." Alizia chewed with her mouth open. Lyr found that strangely charming.

"Do you know what it is?" Lyr asked.

"Perhaps they figured out where the documents we're looking for are stored. I don't know about you, but I am becoming wary of this place. The work is demeaning, and I'm glad to have gotten the night off. How is it in the kitchens?"

"Not so bad," Lyr replied. It occurred to her that she could ask Alizia the question that had been pressing on her mind all day. "What do you think will happen to them when we..." Lyr glanced about, though no one was paying the two of them any mind. "When the royals are gone, what will happen to the servants?"

Alizia arched an eyebrow as if baffled by the question. "I don't see how that matters," she replied after brief consideration.

"What do you mean?" Lyr pressed.

"We know what must be done for the good of all. That's all there is to it."

"I know, it's just..."

Alizia set her half-eaten sausage back on the plate and reached for Lyr's hand. The tenderness of the gesture startled Lyr. The woman's hands were rough and calloused—the hands of a fighter. "Many servants share our vision for the future, even though they may not yet realize it. Others will curse our names or even try to stop us. Nothing scares the complacent more than change. All that matters is that we remain strong in our will and conviction. We will succeed and save them from their lives of servitude, whether they like it or not."

Lyr wasn't sure that she liked that answer, but she couldn't bring herself to say anything in reply. She picked at the cabbage—it was too sour for her taste—and ate half the sausage before the time came to meet with the rest of the group in the storage room. Saul stood near the room's door, ensuring that no one would follow them inside. This precaution was mostly unnecessary as the storage room was located in the least trafficked hall of the palace. Lyr doubted even long-term servants were aware its door could even be opened. Surely, she would have been unable to locate it herself had it not been specifically marked on the map the Free Kings had given her to study prior to the mission.

Alizia and Lyr entered, then Saul. Geren was already inside, as was Dregor, the handsome man who had escorted them in when they had first arrived. The young man was concealed in an oversized dark cloak. Lyr wondered who he was and what role he had in the remainder of their task. The room was much smaller than Lyr imagined it would be, with a maze of angular veiled furniture cast-offs looming ghostly in the torchlight around them.

"Can we get this moving along?" Geren asked while wringing his hands. "I have very little time before Flavien will come looking for me. I've inadvertently made myself essential to the kitchen. Unlike others here." He glared at Lyr when he said it.

Lyr only shrugged in reply.

"We will make this brief, then. Dregor," Saul prompted.

The handsome man perked up and brandished a smile. "Ah, yes. I believe it's time I come clean to you all." Dregor unfastened his cloak and swung it open, revealing the splendid set of golden armor beneath. Geren and Lyr gasped in unison. Alizia tensed. "I am Ser Dregor, knight of the King's Guard."

"Oh, gods! You've gotten us all killed!" Geren exclaimed accusingly at Saul.

"Relax!" Saul said placatingly. "Ser Dregor is one of us. It's only through him that we've been able to come so far." Saul looked at each one of them, his eyes landing on the unmoving Alizia. "You can all trust him," he promised.

Alizia sipped in a breath and nodded, though Lyr could see tension remained in her arms and chest. Geren took a step back, wringing his hands, while Lyr stared at the knight's armor in bewilderment.

Saul resumed his pitch, "We've come to learn through Ser Dregor that Princess Arisa is to be wed within the week. Four days, if our information is right. The Free Kings have been informed, and they've already started to enact their part of the plan."

"Which is?" Geren interjected.

Saul shrugged off his obvious irritation at being interrupted. Lyr noticed that Saul was tired. His red eyes floated into purple, sunken pools. Was he getting enough sleep? Or any at all? Saul's back tensed with the weight of the entire mission. "The Free Kings are arming themselves for insurrection. They will await our portion of the plan to be enacted before they rush in and secure the palace."

"They intend to attack?" Alizia blurted out, her calm facade wavering.

"Not an all-out attack," Saul corrected.

Dregor raised a hand and added, "Many Free Kings have already infiltrated the palace guard over the course of the past year. More than you imagine. Once your task is successful, the palace will be thrust into utter chaos. It will be left up to the guard to restore order."

"And, of course, the guards know about us and will keep us safe," Saul assured.

"Safe?" Geren exploded. "You're talking about insurrection! We came here to find documents!"

"Documents..." Alizia grumbled. "This doesn't sound like an update to the plan. This sounds like an entirely different one."

"The documents, while important, were never going to shift the tide of power in this country on their own. But now we have a real opportunity with this wedding to do something more," Saul explained.

"So, what is it? Out with it!" Alizia prompted.

"Our new mission is to assassinate the royals."

The already claustrophobic storage closet shrunk down to the size of a mousehole. Lyr tried to catch her breath but there was no air to be had. She must have heard wrong. Assassinate? The royal family? Lyr looked over at Geren. The man was as white as the sheets covering the furniture behind him.

"And how exactly are we supposed to do that?" Alizia asked in frustration. "Take those tiny vials of poison you gave us and hand them to the queen to drink?"

Saul looked utterly embarrassed.

"You fuckers..." Geren cursed.

"There's a reason you two are in the kitchens," Saul said to Geren and Lyr. "A special cask of vintage will be selected and stored in the kitchen cellar for the feast. You two will poison that wine cask before it is taken to the grand hall. The poison acts very quickly." Saul glanced at Lyr with a grave expression. Had he heard about how Lyr had killed

Dora? Lyr looked away from him, focusing instead on some small cobwebs near her feet.

"Why don't we poison the food directly?" Lyr asked.

"Poison what? The meat? The sides? The sauces?" Dregor countered. "It needs to be something everyone will consume at the same time. The wedding toast is our moment."

"Poisoning a cask seems fairly simple, but how do we ensure that the poison isn't detected before it's given out at the feast?" Alizia asked. "Surely there is some sort of security when it comes to food and drink intended for the royals."

"The King's Guard is responsible for testing food and drink for poisons or rogue enchantments," Dregor explained. "I will ensure that our tests find the wine to be safe for the royal family's lips."

Alizia seemed satisfied with that answer—or, at least, as satisfied as she could be.

"I don't like any of this!" Geren huffed.

Saul touched the man's shoulder. "We're all in this together, Geren. We will succeed. You must believe in our mission."

"We've been sent here to die! Oh, gods, we're going to be caught and executed." The man had begun to shake, his pale cheeks bobbing up and down with the movement. It would have been comical if he wasn't also exposing Lyr's deepest fears.

Dregor moved Saul aside and grabbed Geren by the front of his shirt. "Listen to me clearly, *baker*. If you don't steel yourself, your companions will be the ones to suffer for it. Understood?"

Though Dregor had not raised his voice, the intensity behind his words made Geren freeze. "You have me and the Free Kings on your side," Dregor continued, releasing Geren's shirt.

Geren blinked rapidly as if to allow Dregor's words to sink in. "I must— I must go now," he said. "I must return to the kitchen."

"Stay strong Geren," Saul encouraged. "We have each other's backs."

Geren quickly fled the storage room.

"I don't trust that one," Dregor confided. "Men like him could be our downfall."

"Don't be so dramatic," Saul said. "Geren is a good man. He will not fail us."

"I sure hope you're right. Saul. Ladies." Dregor bowed deeply at each of them, refastened his cloak, and then left the room.

"We should all disperse as well before people start to wonder what four servants and a knight were doing in an unused hall," Alizia said.

"Of course," Saul agreed. "I just hope..." Lyr wasn't sure what he meant to say before he cut himself short and left the room. Moments later, she and Alizia left the musty space, returning to the servants' commons. They resumed their seats across from one another and sat in anxious silence.

"Do you trust Saul?" Lyr asked. The question seemed to startle Alizia out of a daze.

The woman furrowed her brow. "He trusts me. That is enough," she replied. "It's been a long time since someone has told me they need me."

A memory assaulted Lyr. "*I need you.*" Those words had seemed so personal when they first reached her ear. Had Saul said that same thing to Alizia? Had he accompanied her home as well, holding her hand in the dark? "*I need you.*" The words had made Lyr feel special. Now, they made her feel like nothing but a tool—something that is needed, then discarded after use.

But was that not exactly what she had turned herself into?

Lyr had felt so much pity for Leandra when she had described herself as nothing but a boat carried by the will of the royals. And now Lyr recognized that she was also being steered by winds outside of her control.

She made herself look into Alizia's dark eyes and ask, "Do you trust me?"

Alizia's expression changed to a more determined one. "I do," she said without hesitation. "You proved to be worthy of trust when you took care of that girl. I know you have what it takes to do what needs to be done."

Lyr swallowed the lump in her throat. She wasn't sure that she did now that she understood the full breadth of what they were tasked to do, but the woman's confidence alleviated her fear, replacing it with a kinship she had never felt before. "I trust you too," Lyr said, and Alizia cracked a warm smile.

XIX.

Passed the City Gates

Exhaustion from the chaos of that morning had overtaken their bodies. Though they had wished to reach Vizen by early afternoon, both Rovan and Adriel knew they needed to stop for a brief rest. From his sack, Rovan produced a journeycake. The cloth it was wrapped in was entirely rain-soaked, and even the cake itself was soggy. Nevertheless, he split it in half to share with the enchantress. She nodded gratefully and took a bite.

They continued for another hour before the city walls came into view. They were taller than those of Sol Forne, though not much wider, encircling their section of the western coast in a stark stone embrace. A final Blue Scarab outpost interrupted the Road before them, and Rovan found himself annoyed by the prospect of having to speak with their ilk again. To his relief, the Scarabs were waving folk through one by one without question. But, when their time came, a Scarab halted them.

"Where are you coming from?" she asked.

Rovan glanced at the enchantress, hoping she would provide him with some insight on how to answer the question. Should they say they were coming from Pevine or the Womb?

"Albadone," the enchantress answered.

The Scarab raised a non-existent eyebrow. "Did you see anything suspicious at the previous outpost?"

"Suspicious?" Rovan echoed.

"Lots of blood. Everyone was dead," the enchantress answered.

Rovan felt his blood cool. Now they would surely be questioned further. And so close to the city...

"That's what we've heard," the soldier nodded. "Did you see what might have caused it?"

"Luckily, we did not," Adriel lied.

"All right, go on ahead."

"No papers?" the enchantress asked. Rovan squeezed his eyes shut at the woman's stupidity. It was like being caught committing a crime, then asking for punishment after being let go.

"No papers needed today," the soldier said. "All are welcome into Vizen on the week of King Petar's death and the anointment of the new Queen. Move along."

"The king is dead?" Adriel inquired.

Rovan couldn't care less about whether the king lived or not and did not have to be told twice to proceed. He placed a hand on the enchantress' back and pushed her along past the outpost. The woman did not look too pleased, but Rovan did not care. His directive was to find Tieg and Scintilla as soon as possible. Though the city loomed before them, there were a couple of miles between this outpost and the city gates. His friends could be anywhere along that stretch of road. And the closer they got to the imposing walls of Vizen, the more the task of finding a child within them seemed insurmountable.

They walked in heavy, uncomfortable, silence, but Rovan didn't have it in him to make conversation. His entire body ached from the strain of running through the woods that morning. The small rest they had taken had not been enough. He sorely missed the drafty little room he had occupied in Pevine and even his lumpy floor cot. He wondered how long it would be before he returned.

"How do you feel?" Adriel asked.

"I could use a lie-down," Rovan admitted. "Why do you ask?"

"Am I not allowed to check on the wellbeing of my travel companion?" she snarked. "But I am more specifically asking about earlier. You appeared to go faint each time we neared the *reaverlord*. Its *life energy* really affected you."

"Is that what that was?" Rovan asked.

"I wasn't exaggerating when I said I sense a great connection to the Cycle within you. The closer you are in your life to birth and death, the stronger you feel *life energy's* song. That's why the younger a child is, the better they can be taught to hone their enchanting skills. Are you sure you never felt that sort of feeling before, when you were a boy?"

"I am certain."

"And you do not look close to death. So how is this possible?"

Rovan glanced at the enchantress, gauging how much he should share of his past. He decided some honesty on this subject couldn't hurt. "Several years ago, I made a blood pact with a being of pure *life energy*. She said it was a *Sealing* enchantment. If I had to guess, I'd say that's what caused this... connection."

Adriel stared at Rovan inquisitively. "A blood pact, you say? This being of pure *life energy* wouldn't happen to have been a djinn?"

Rovan nodded. "You know Vaelin?" he asked, somehow both surprised and strangely not.

The enchantress chuckled, "If you've been *Sealed* to that one, it would certainly explain your sensitivity towards *life energy*."

"But I'm no longer *Sealed* to her," Rovan clarified. He instinctively rubbed his palm.

"That doesn't matter. Even if the *Sealing* is gone, your connection to the Cycle has been permanently amplified. It's something you'll have to contend with for the rest of your life. Or you can learn to ignore it if you are so inclined."

The idea of this connection felt invasive to Rovan—just another thing to add to his ever-increasing pile of troubles. His hand hovered over the pocket that contained the spent runestone of *Guidance* Ashe had given him. Was it entirely in his head, or could he feel it pulling him towards the city? He moved the hand away as soon as he realized Adriel was staring at the spot. As much out of wariness as out of tiredness, Rovan resolved to remain silent until they reached the city gates.

They passed the flooded muddy remains of previously tilled fields. Whatever had grown there was long gone. Even so, dozens of all ages trudged knee-deep into the muck, their backs hunched and forearms sunken into the wet earth.

"What do you think they're doing?" Rovan asked.

As if in answer, a young girl raised a large brown clod into the air, and excitedly exclaimed, "I found another one!" A woman joined the child and wiped the dirty lump with a rag, revealing the small potato within. The pitiful thing joined others in a burlap sack at the woman's back.

The woman touched the girl's face affectionately, leaving a streak of mud behind.

"You're free to join us in the field, but you'll have to put whatever you find in the pile, and we're splitting them evenly in the end. No pocketing," a woman said. Her work clothes were caked with mud up to the elbows and knees.

"Has it been a bad harvest?" Rovan asked, wondering if Vizen had fared as poorly as Pevine.

"It's been decent, though the Royals have picked us clean for all their feasting. King's dead, and all that."

"Are there any inns before the city gates?" Rovan figured that would be a good place to start their search for his friends.

"A couple. Nothing as nice as in Vizen. Hey! Drop that!" The woman marched towards a pair of boys who were making off with a burlap sack.

The sparse outcropping of homes thickened into a dense town the closer they drew to the Vizenian walls. They followed the road all the way to a sort of town square. Several taller brick buildings stood in a semicircle—an inn, a bank, and a carriage and goods transportation service. Though the space was small, it was strangely uncrowded.

He entered the inn and headed straight for the bar, behind which lounged a middle-aged woman. She eyed Rovan and Adriel with bored disinterest. "Good day," Rovan greeted. "We're looking for our two companions. A young woman and man about my age. Perhaps they stopped here for lodging. She has dark—"

"No need to describe them," the innkeeper interrupted. "I know who you're looking for. Very few guests stop here as of late."

"That's great!" Rovan said. "Where can I find them?"

"How should I know?" the woman shrugged.

"You said you knew where they were," Rovan rebutted.

"No. I said I knew who you were talking about. Your friends had no pieces on them. My inn might be empty, but I still need to make a living."

Rovan frowned. "Do you know where they ended up?"

"Again, how should I know? I didn't follow them."

Rovan felt a flush of anger, amplified by his tiredness, color his ears. "If you don't need a room or drink, you better scram," the innkeeper threatened. Rovan gladly obliged.

"There he is!" Rovan heard Scintilla call after him as soon as he stepped out of the inn. The young woman reached him and hugged him tightly.

"We knew you'd be looking for us at an inn, so we stayed in the area to wait," Tieg explained.

"Smart," Rovan commended his friends. "How are you?" he asked.

"Tired," Scintilla complained.

"Have you eaten?"

"Yes, though our provisions are almost depleted," Tieg replied.

"We will replenish them once we're in the city," Adriel said. "Let's not waste any more time." The group agreed and made for the city gates.

The rain had mostly cleared, though gray clouds still curdled overhead. The Vizenian gates opened across a wide drawbridge that encroached over the Cleo River, which encircled the city like a moat. Beneath the bridge, the waters widened and raged onwards, spilling west into the Emerial Sea. The gates themselves were the tallest structures Rovan had ever seen, taller than anything within his native Sol Forne, even the Academy. Rovan had heard that the Royal

Tower at the center of the circular city reached even further into the sky. Had the circumstances of his visit been different, he would have loved to see it.

A crowd formed at the mouth of the city, though it was nowhere near as dense as what Rovan had expected. It didn't take long to get through and into Vizen proper. What greeted them within was a collection of tall, yet thin, stone habitations lining the street. The road split into three paths, each leading deeper into the city. Tieg and Scintilla seemed immediately overwhelmed. Even Adriel looked put off by the place. Rovan decided it was time to take charge of the group once again.

"We need to find an inn," Rovan announced.

"What for?" Adriel asked.

"Because we're all exhausted, for one. This search could take some time. We need a place where we can rendezvous as needed."

The enchantress reluctantly agreed to Rovan's reasoning. Was she expecting this to be an easy task? Even with her help, finding the child would be as simple as finding a drop of rain in the ocean.

"Excuse me," Rovan approached a passerby—a tall, clean-shaven man with a gaunt face. The man kept his eyes on the road ahead, not dignifying Rovan with even a cursory glance.

"Rude fuck," Scintilla grunted.

"Hello!" Rovan greeted another passerby—a plump woman carrying a baby in a basket. She glanced at Rovan, though her face seemed strained by worry. "We're looking for an inn," Rovan began, with as much of a friendly tone as he could muster.

"Preferably somewhere affordable," Tieg added.

"Could you point us in the right direction?" Rovan asked.

The woman's apprehension eased somewhat. Her baby began to fuss, so she quieted it by rocking the basket. "Affordable," the woman repeated. "You mean cheap, by the looks of you. Head that way, to the Pleasants, and look for *Chanter's Cove*. The woman that runs it takes in anyone these days." After pointing at the easternmost path, the woman hurried off the opposite way.

"The Pleasants. Doesn't sound too bad," Scintilla mused.

The path led them further into the belly of Vizen. The capital of Hovardom was not a colorful city, like those in the southern reaches of the kingdom. The unadorned buildings were made of gray stone, just like those of the outer town. There was also a general sense of ancient disrepair—the homes looked slanted and weathered, and the deep cracks in the cobblestone street were filled with rainwater and mud. A morose gray, like the sky above, seemed to be Vizen's only color. And the cityfolk's disposition matched that of their surroundings. Perhaps this was due to the recent death of the king, or maybe this was just the way these people were.

Rovan kept a watchful eye on the businesses that lined the street—here a cobbler, a smith, or a drygoods man. The following stretch of road was entirely devoid of such business, instead being composed of the shabbiest habitations Rovan had ever seen. Even the poorest districts of Sol Forne had a sort of charm to them. But the horribly misnamed Pleasants turned out to be nothing short of a shantytown.

"Are we sure we're in the right place?" Scintilla asked, her eyes darting from a tent home to a hastily assembled wood hut.

"I believe we are," Adriel replied, pointing with her staff to where the street opened up into what appeared to be a plaza. The circular space was occupied by a few empty wooden stalls. A pair of ragged beggars seemed to have made one of them their temporary dwelling. Was the rain the cause of such desolation, or was something else going on here?

Across the empty market plaza stood a three-story building. The chipping painted sign above the door announced it to be *Chanter's Cove*. Rovan pulled the rickety door and held it open for his companions to walk inside. The heat of the fireplace within was a balm on his wet body.

"I just cleaned the floor, and look at this! You're tracking mud inside!" A woman approached them gripping a broom as one might a spear. They all took an instinctive step back. The woman shook her head. "How can I help you?"

"We're seeking a room," Rovan explained.

"Only one?" the woman asked, eyeing Adriel and Scintilla.

"Two, if we can afford it," Rovan replied.

The woman sighed. "What can you afford?"

Rovan reached into his hood and retrieved a small coin purse. He opened it and, for a moment, stared at its contents in alarm—eight coppers and two silvers. That would cover them only for one night, two at best. What would they do for food in the meanwhile?

"We have this," Rovan admitted. He handed the woman the coin purse. She weighed it on her palm warily. "We can work the kitchen for food—"

"Don't be a bull's bullock," the enchantress interrupted. "Give the boy his coin pouch. Here." Adriel handed the woman two gold pieces. Everyone's eyes widened at the unexpected wealth.

"Two rooms it is," the innkeeper said. "Give me a moment to set them up. In the meantime, please make yourselves comfortable by the fire. I'll have some food and drink sent out for you in a moment. My name is Amya. Do not hesitate to ask for anything. I only have one request: please take those sodden things off your feet before you ruin my floor."

They all gratefully obliged, setting their muddy boots against the wall near the entrance. Tieg removed his hood and set it on the floor in front of the fireplace. Rovan and Scintilla did the same. The three friends collapsed into chairs across from the fire and allowed its hot kiss to thaw their souls. Adriel, however, remained standing, impatiently pacing the hall.

"Thank you," Rovan told the enchantress.

"What for?" the woman asked.

"For covering the costs of the rooms."

"Oh, that? I have more if we need it."

"Why don't you sit down?" Tieg asked the woman. "It's nice and warm here."

Adriel grunted. "Must I remind you all that we're here on a temporary basis? We are only in this cursed city to find my child, not to indulge in the comforts of a drab inn."

"Suit yourself," Scintilla scoffed.

"In fact," the enchantress continued, "we should be out there, not here wasting precious time."

Scintilla frowned and faced the woman. "We just barely escaped with our lives from a rampaging *reaverlord*. I think we have earned ourselves a bit of respite, don't you think?"

"Earned?" Adriel spat. "I pay for your lodging, and you want to talk about what you've earned?"

Rovan stood and said firmly, "If you're going to hold that over our heads, I will request that the innkeeper return the gold pieces to you, and we'll make do with what we have."

A cold anger lit up Adriel's eyes, but it vanished as quickly as it was conjured. "No," she spoke. "Have your rest."

Rovan nodded and resumed his seat. The innkeeper soon returned to the hall carrying two keys. She handed one to Adriel ("For the ladies") and the other to Tieg ("and this one is for the sirs"). Afterward, the woman walked behind the bar and filled four goblets with spiced wine and handed one to each of them. It was instantly clear to Rovan that the spices had been added not for flavor but to cover the souring age of the wine. Tieg and Scintilla didn't seem to mind—sometimes Rovan wished he had not lived so long in the kingdom's cultural capital of wine. Adriel swirled her goblet, then set it on the bar untouched. She exuded the same anxious air as a caged cat.

Amya picked their hoods from the floor. "These will get singed so close to the flame! I'll set these in the ladies' room by the window. There's a nice breeze in there."

After the wine came the meal: a bowl of sour turnip soup with chopped bits of fatty meat thrown in. It was warm and delectable and instantly raised the groups' spirits. Scintilla and Tieg bickered amicably over the best way to cook turnips. Even the innkeeper and the only other tavern patron joined their friendly debate. Rovan watched them all with a quiet tranquility. Though he did not join their discussion, there was a peace that came with watching his friends return to their normal selves after their rough journey.

Rovan glanced back to the bar, but Adriel was no longer there. In fact, it seemed she had left the hall entirely. He stood and placed his empty bowl on the bar, then headed down the hallway that led to the bedrooms. "She's not there," a feeble voice said.

Rovan turned to see a gaunt, wiry, woman standing at the edge of one of the bedrooms. As soon as Rovan looked at her, the woman glanced away and said, "She made a terrible racket next door. I peeked out of my window and saw her jump into the alley."

"Thank you," Rovan said, and the woman retreated into her room. Rovan placed his hand on the door of the next room and pushed lightly. The door swung open revealing the empty chamber within. From the rafters hung their three dripping cloaks. The window faced into an alleyway that tunneled the wind, causing a strong cool breeze to circulate the room. Rovan shivered as he watched the hoods sway to and fro.

He looked out into the empty alleyway outside. Why had the enchantress left through the window? None of them would have protested her leaving through the front door of the inn. Something had happened here. Rovan groaned at the realization.

He reached inside the inner chest pocket of his hood—it was empty. Adriel had taken the runestone of *Guidance* Ashe had given him. Did she intend to search for the child on her own? He cursed himself for carelessly revealing the item to the woman and returned to the main hall of the inn. He would allow his companions a few more moments of merriment before informing them of the enchantress' departure.

XX.

A Sparring Partner

Searin categorically refused to attend another damned feast. There were so many other things that still needed to be done—so many preparations. Arisa had only informally met with the young man Clavio wished for her to marry. The queen had labeled Reilyn a "pawn" and there was some truth to that. It was expected for royals to marry their offspring off in exchange for wealth and status. This marriage would make good on debts their father had accrued towards the Azurats. Though it felt unfair for her sister to have to take on the burden of their father's broken promises, Searin knew that was the weight of the crown.

How many more of their father's mistakes would there be to amend? Searin would be there to lessen her sister's burden.

Soon, after Arisa's anointment, Searin would become high captain of the King's Guard, and would then be able to handpick her team of eleven trustworthy knights. She would keep the team mostly as it was—they were a collection of valiant and capable men and women. The only knight of the eleven that she foresaw posing problems was Dregor. It could risk a scandal if Arisa married the Azurat boy while carrying on her less-than-covert relationship with the knight. Arisa had assured Searin that it was only a temporary fling, but that was difficult to believe after how flippantly she had acted at the feast the previous night.

Oh, right. The feast. Searin scowled. All the hungover guests of the previous night were invited once more to get drunk and toast her father's memory. Searin could not think of a worse way to spend the day. Her mother had insisted on having things her way the previous days, so tonight Searin resolved to be comfortable by dressing simply in pants and a linen tunic.

The feast was already underway by the time she entered the hall. Her mother posed at the high table like a statue watching the world pass by. The queen glanced at Searin. Her nostrils flaring was the only sign of her anger—the pants and tunic were having their intended effect. Hovard was seated next to the queen, sipping on a steaming cup of tea. The boy's eyes bounced off of Searin indifferently. How she wished the previous night could have gone better between them, but there was no sense in lingering on that regret. Searin sat next to her brother and bid him, "Good day," which garnered only a grunt in response.

Of Arisa, there was no sign. It shouldn't have surprised Searin as much as it did. "Where's Arisa?" she asked. Neither her mother nor her brother replied, which irritated her greatly.

A servant poured her a cup of tea. Searin nodded in thanks and took a sip of the fragrant and spiced beverage. Scanning the room, she saw many of the same faces as the previous night, albeit more haggard and hungover in the mid-morning light. Sunken bloodshot eyes, bountiful grimaces, and sour red faces made this yet another sordid affair. Perhaps, this was what her father would have wanted: a hall full of his most hated acquaintances united in hungover misery.

Though the feast would last until dusk, Searin had no intention of seeing it through. If even her sister could not dignify it by being on time, why should she be made to stay longer than necessary? And where was her sister exactly? Another person missing from the feast was Dregor. Searin briefly wondered if the two could be fooling around until she realized that Uncle Clavio appeared to be missing as well. Something else was afoot. She stood from the table, intent on finding out what.

"And where are you going?" the queen probed.

"To find our queen-to-be," Searin replied.

"She's not even anointed and she's already proving to be just like her rotten father."

Searin did not dignify the remark with a response. She descended to the level of the other tables and crossed the hall. At each table she passed, the seated nobles raised their cups and slurred some cheers in her name. *What a farce,* she thought. A minor lord dropped his cup, sending purple wine splashing across the stone floor, and suddenly she was transported back to her father's chambers—his red blood streaking down the side of the tub and onto the floor.

"Are you all right, my princess?" a woman asked.

Searin blinked the image away, realizing she had wandered into one of the hallways used by the servants to remain out of the nobles' way. Her head spun dizzyingly. The woman in front of her touched her shoulder. Searin shrugged out of her grasp, yelling, "Don't touch me!"

The woman quickly backed away and bowed in apology. It was then that Searin took a real look at the servant that stood before her. Her plain tunic could not hide her broad shoulders and strong musculature. When the woman lifted her angular and scarred face, her eyes met Searin's—something a servant should never do.

"Who are you?" Searin demanded.

The woman averted her gaze as if suddenly remembering her station. "I am Zinia, your servant, if it pleases my princess."

The rote way the words were spoken was common among the servants, but Searin was not convinced. "You're not familiar to me. How long have you served at court?"

"It hasn't been long, my princess."

"How long?" Searin insisted.

The woman swallowed nervously. "Three days, my princess."

"Three days, and you're already serving at royal feasts?"

"I'm quite good at it, my princess."

"Give me your hand," Searin commanded.

"What?" Zinia asked, stepping back.

Searin frowned and grabbed the servant's wrist. "Any other servant would have obeyed their princess without protest." She flipped Zinia's hand upwards and traced her index finger across the woman's palm, feeling her thick calluses. "What did you do before joining the court servants?"

"I was a blacksmith, my princess," Zinia replied. Her tone had greatly meekened.

Searin scowled at the woman. "You don't get callouses like these swinging hammers. Do not lie to me again unless you want to be punished for it."

"I— My princess..." The servant struggled to formulate a defense for some time. Beneath her tightening grip on the Zinia's wrist, Searin could feel her taught forearms, and the quick beating of her heart.

An idea incepted itself in Searin's mind. It was an absurd thought, but one that intrigued Searin far more than the vapid festivities in the other room—more even than searching for her sister. "Come with me," she commanded, dragging the woman further down the hall.

Each servant they passed bowed and stepped aside. Many eyed Zinia with reproach, as if interacting with the royals had earned their disapproval. Even an act as simple as asking a distraught princess if she was all right could be punishable by, at best, a night in a cell or, at worst, a beating. This woman was no servant, and Searin was going to expose her the only way she knew how.

After taking a right bend, Searin opened the door that led out into the practice courtyard and shoved Zinia outside. The rain was a faint drizzle, thank the gods. The yard was empty besides the few guards standing alert on the parapets. Most other guards were within the palace, monitoring the feast, or patrolling the palace gates. Searin reached the canopied weapons rack, Zinia reluctantly followed behind. Searin plucked a blunted practice sword from the rack and tossed it at the servant. Zinia caught it and flourished it dexterously, before immediately halting as if she had been discovered doing something she wasn't supposed to.

"As I suspected," Searin said, grabbing a practice sword for herself. "You're no blacksmith. You have a callus between your index and thumb that you would have only gotten from wielding a sword. And besides, blacksmiths tend to have more musculature on their swinging arms than on their off arm. You, on the other hand, are quite evenly built." Searin raised her sword, then lunged into a rapid attack.

Zinia parried the attack and jumped back as gracefully as if she was half her size.

Searin smiled, exhilarated. "You're a swordswoman!"

The woman did not try to deny it, as she deftly parried Searin's oncoming assault. It was intoxicating to finally fight someone as capable as herself, though Zinia never seemed to go on the offensive. "Attack me!" Searin commanded, swinging her sword at Zinia's hip.

Zinia spun, avoiding the blow, then quickly entered a defensive stance.

"I said," Searin charged, "attack me!"

Zinia parried the attack aimed at her chest, then counterattacked with astonishing power. Searin swiped her sword upwards, deflecting Zinia's blade, which was aimed directly at her head. Searin felt giddy with delight, but the laughter quickly died in her throat—any other swordswoman would have allowed that move to open their front to a counter, but Zinia did not appear to be an ordinary swordswoman. Using the momentum of Searin's parry, Zinia spun into another attack, forcing Searin into the defensive.

The barrage of swings continued until Searin was forced to pull away. There was nothing more dishonorable than disengaging from a duel, but Searin saw no other option unless she tried something drastic. Just when Zinia's confidence in her swings was at its peak, Searin planted her feet and used her next parry to guide Zinia's sword towards her left. The maneuver resulted in a shallow grazing of her shoulder but succeeded in unbalancing the servant.

Stabilizing herself, Searin swung at the woman's neck. Somehow, Zinia's weapon was already there. The two blunted blades rang dully against one another. The shock of impact vibrated up Searin's arm, taking her by surprise for only an instant.

An instant too long.

Zinia switched her sword to her off hand and struck down at Searin's arm. The blow made her drop her sword, which clanked loudly upon the stone. Searin glanced around the yard. One of the men guarding the parapet turned to face away, pretending as if he hadn't just witnessed her loss. She turned back to face Zinia, who held her sword pointed at Searin as if daring her to make another move. Remembering her place, Zinia lowered the weapon and fell to her knees.

"I am so sorry, my princess," the woman begged, fear quivering in her voice.

Searin stood frozen before the woman while rubbing her stinging arm. Her pride was in shambles. She had been bested—something that had not happened in years, either because no one could or because those with the ability feared offending their princess. But now, looking at the woman who had just defeated her, Searin felt a burgeoning excitement rising taller than her hurt pride.

"Stand," Searin commanded, and the woman obeyed. Zinia had the downtrodden look of someone aware of Searin's position of power. "I'm going to ask you again and, this time, you're not going to lie to me. Who are you?"

"My name is Zinia," the woman stated in a firm voice. "I am a swordswoman."

"Why are you here?" Searin asked.

"Because I am a servant."

"I told you not to lie," Searin snapped.

"I am not lying, my princess. I am a servant at the palace. But I was a mercenary, once—in another life."

Searin could hear the plain truth in the woman's words, but what should she do with it? Who had allowed a former mercenary to serve in the palace? The part of Searin that was prepared to bear the responsibility of captaining the King's Guard knew what precautions should be taken: Zinia needed to be questioned to ensure she posed no threat and then cast out of the palace—or out of the city, even.

But was there a need to rush that? Couldn't she spend a few days observing the woman and benefitting from her sparring skills? The woman might turn out to be no threat at all. Could Searin really fault or punish this woman for who she used to be? She hadn't done anything wrong besides interacting with a princess.

Searin had never had true companions or friends. Her family did not understand her. The knights were too weak or refused to spar with her altogether, and the court softies avoided her at any cost, preferring the company of her mother, brother, and sister. Searin examined the woman—her long, angular face, the scar that defined her jaw, the dark hair that was somehow still collected in a bun as if the woman had not strained one bit—and she saw something there she had never seen in anyone else before.

"What are your duties?" Searin asked.

"So far I've served at two feasts and kept the western wing tidy," the woman answered.

"I want you here, after dark, each evening," Searin said.

"My princess?"

"I need a partner—a sparring partner that is as good as, or better, than myself. Someone that will pose a challenge."

"Is that appropriate, my princess?" Zinia asked.

No, it was not, Searin knew. "Worry yourself with obeying. Understood?"

The woman bowed meekly. "Tonight, then?"

"Tonight," Searin confirmed. And, as simply as that, she had her own secret, just like her sister Arisa. "Now, return to the hall before the other servants begin to wonder where you've gone."

"Will you also return to the hall?" the woman asked. "My princess," she added abruptly.

"I don't know. I cannot bear another feast," Searin admitted.

Zinia smiled. "At least you have the privilege of being able to avoid it." It was as if she was testing the boundaries of their newly formed bond. Searin flashed a smile, then reached her hand out for Zinia to return the sword. The woman approached her and set the hilt of the blunt weapon in Searin's hand. Their fingers brushed for an instant. Searin had held the woman's hand, felt her sword calluses, but this quick and furtive touch felt alarmingly intimate. Searin looked up, meeting the taller woman's eyes, and suddenly she wasn't sure she possessed the strength to keep her gaze still.

"Until later, my princess," the woman said, then marched to the door they had first emerged from.

Searin found herself in the courtyard, alone. She suddenly had the strange urge to return to the feast, to allow her time and thoughts to be filled, even by something as mindless as drunk nobles' bawdy japes. Or, perhaps, to have the chance to be in the same place as Zinia—to study the woman. Searin gripped the hilt of the practice sword—her hand where Zinia's was moments before—and swung it. The familiar act gave her a sudden sense of clarity. She was not as foolish as her sister, to flagrantly flaunt her secrets for all to see. And besides, her secret was nothing like Arisa's.

She was not having any sort of inappropriate relationship with the servant—it was simply training.

The relationship was already inappropriate by virtue of it being between a royal and a servant. But why should that stop her? She had never done anything wrong in her life and always sought to obey and do right. Was that why this left her feeling so conflicted? Was this really just about training?

Of course, it was! Searin shoved the practice swords into their holder and stormed off just as the rain was beginning again. She entered the palace and quickly made for her room, avoiding all interactions with the drunk nobles that littered the halls.

As always, her chamber was unguarded, though Stervo stood at the end of the hall watching its entrance. She had demanded that the hall be free of guards as she could not sleep knowing one of them stood outside her door at night. Her parents had reluctantly agreed, though they still kept a guard at a distance at all times just in case.

Her room felt stripped and cold after being in Hovard's the prior night. The wall where her old tapestry had once hung looked startlingly bare. She lay back on her hard bed and closed her eyes. The image of blood oozing out of a slit wrist reappeared and Searin felt panic overtaking her. She focused on the only other thing she could think of to vanquish the horrible vision: fighting Zinia. The woman was so fast and precise. All Searin wished to do at that moment was to spar with her again. Evening could not come soon enough.

※ ※ ※ ※

Searin awakened roughly in her bed. Her head pounded behind her eyes. Whatever that unexpected nap was, it could not have been called restful. She sat up and rubbed her forehead with the ball of her wrist. There was always some peppermint kept in the kitchens for this exact reason—she would either brew it as a tea or chew on some leaves to alleviate her pain.

She stood, walked to her shuttered window, and opened it to let in the rain-chilled air. Her eyes widened in startlement as she realized that she had slept through the entire afternoon. The sun was already deeply setting behind the palace walls, tinting the sky crimson and deep blue.

Her day clothes were quickly removed, folded, and placed on the bed. Searin opened her wardrobe and removed her new armor, applying each individual piece, and fastening them to herself with the assistance of Stervo, who still loitered outside her room. At least he was good for something. She left the helmet in the wardrobe—it was more decorative than practical. And there was no need to mess up her hair any further.

The drunk nobles from earlier in the day now slept along the floors of the palace hallways. The ones who were still awake played chase and pinched each other's bottoms while giggling gleefully. It was a wretched display. A red-faced man halted his drunken run in front of her and stared in derision, then quickly bolted away upon realizing who she was. Searin shook her head and headed for the kitchen.

Several servants were still there cleaning pots and pans while sneaking the occasional bite of leftovers. They bowed deeply when she entered.

"How may I assist you, my princess?" Leandra, the kitchen mistress, asked.

Searin explained her predicament, and the woman quickly produced a bundle of herbs from a small wooden chest and handed Searin a few strands of peppermint and feverfew. The princess thanked the woman and headed out of the kitchen, chewing on the leaves, their floral and minty herbal flavors flaring her nostrils.

She resolved to finally find her sister, though that task was long overdue by this point. She peeked within the great hall, only to find it filled with only a few talkative nobles and many others who slept in their seats or on the floor. Her mother and brother no longer occupied the high table. She decided to head upstairs, to Arisa's room. There was still time before nightfall when she had told Zinia she would meet her in the yard—the thought provoked a foreign mix of embarrassment and excitement in her.

Arisa's solar was guarded by three knights of the King's Guard, which could only mean she was inside. Searin reached the door and nodded at the knights, but they did not move aside. "I'm here to see my sister," Searin said.

"The princess is busy conferring within, my princess," Sabbant said in his usual, overly formal, way.

Searin narrowed her eyes. "I'm aware that she is. Now, move aside."

"I'm afraid we cannot do that, my princess."

"What did you say?" Searin's headache only fueled her indignation.

"My princess," Telmo, another one of the knights, interjected. "We're under strict orders by Princess Arisa and Thane Clavio to not allow anyone within."

"My uncle is inside?"

"I've said too much, my princess," Telmo chastised himself.

The knights were only doing as they had been instructed, which would, on any other day, please Searin greatly. But the thought of Arisa secretly conferring with their uncle, without her, filled Searin with an immense jealousy she was not ready to contend with. She stood rigidly across from the knights. "I will wait here if it's all the same with you."

"Of course, my princess," the three knights said in unison while bowing. Searin noted the stress on their faces and postures at having to deny their princess access to the room. It was common knowledge within the ranks of guards, soldiers, and knights, that Searin would be elevated to high captain of the King's Guard someday soon. That would give her jurisdiction over all of their functions, and she was certain that some of them had recently started to go above and beyond to please her in fear of potential retaliation or replacement.

Had they instead got to know her more, they would have known that Searin did not possess a vindictive bone in her body. In truth, Searin was often hurt by the lengths the guards and knights went to avoid her—no different than the nobility. Would she ever find a place where she could neatly fit in?

The armor began to feel cumbersome on her. Her old set felt lighter. Standing still in this hallway for an hour was not a good way to get accustomed to its weight. While the pain in her head was mostly alleviated by the herbs, her joints had now begun to ache dully. The knights in front of her remained alert and still. Perhaps this was a good opportunity to allow them to get to know her. But what did she know about them?

Ser Telmo was a veteran of the First Red Coast Expansion. He was a valiant soldier turned guard captain, and then ultimately raised to knight. He was even-tempered and strong with a sword and spear. Ser Sabbant was the son of a noble who was savvy enough to have been a scholar but had instead chosen the life of a knight. The third was Lady Glaston whom Searin knew the least about. Searin resolved to start with her.

Before she could utter a word, Clavio emerged from Arisa's solar. "Searin, my dear," he said jovially. She could tell that his mood had been somewhat aided by wine. "Where were you? We looked everywhere!"

"Not everywhere, it seems. I was in my room," she deadpanned.

"I knocked, but no one answered."

Searin cringed. How could she have allowed herself to sleep through the day like that? It was inexcusable. "What's she doing?" she asked.

"Your sister? Turning in for the night, I believe. She has a very important meeting in the morning that she cannot miss. I was going to tell you all about it," he added, sensing her unease. "You could have let her in," he scolded the knights.

"No, no," Searin said. "You told them not to allow anyone inside, and they did just that."

"I will phrase my orders more carefully next time," Clavio said, eyeing the knights with a contempt that didn't suit him at all. *Definitely drunk,* Searin realized.

"So, what is this meeting tomorrow about?" Searin asked.

"Come, come, away from these ears," Clavio said, pushing Searin down the hall with his hand on her back. Once they were several paces closer to the stairs that led down to the halls below, Clavio whispered, "Your sister is to be introduced to her potential consort."

"You mean, in a formal setting?" Searin asked.

"Yes, we must do this right—in accordance with tradition—if we are to please the Azurats and secure the kingdom's future. Though, if I'm honest, not much of this is very traditional. Reilyn's parents are not here and your mother refuses to attend, so your sister needs you there."

"Why won't Mother be there?" Searin asked. The queen was known to have her moods, but to not attend the future queen and a potential consort's formal introduction could be seen as negligence.

"Your mother doesn't see eye to eye with me on many things, including this," Clavio said. He seemed hurt by this knowledge. "She believes she has better potential suitors for your sister. I do not doubt she could make a good match, but she somehow got it in her head that I am trying to control Arisa in some way that I do not understand. I am aware that she just lost her husband and king—may my brother's soul find rest—but the kingdom can't mourn forever. Things must move along. And change."

"I will be there," Searin resolved.

"Thank you, dear. We will meet in the small council hall in the second ring. Oh, and expect a surprise announcement."

Searin's heart soared into her throat. Could this mean that Arisa had decided to make her appointment as high captain public? "What sort of surprise announcement?" she asked.

"Actually, I shouldn't have said anything," Clavio caught himself. "Just forget I've mentioned it."

"Very well. Now, if you'll excuse me, Uncle, I have something to attend to," Searin said, heading for the stairs. It was dark outside and time that she met Zinia in the courtyard for their scheduled spar.

"One last thing," Clavio said. Searin faced her uncle, the smile on his face assuming a strangely cold cast. "I've heard a little rumor. One that involves you fighting in the practice yard with a servant earlier today."

Searin felt her blood run cold.

"Don't worry! It's nothing serious." Clavio laughed abruptly, in a clumsy attempt at levity. "But it is something I must inquire about before it spreads any further. So, care to put my fears at ease?"

"It's as you said, Uncle: nothing to worry about," she replied.

"I sure hope not, because if people see you swordfighting with a servant, they may get strange ideas about you. Do you understand?"

"I'm not sure I do," Searin admitted.

Clavio stepped towards her, and it took all of Searin's resilience to not step back. "Your sister playing with a knight, who possesses noble blood, is one matter. Arisa will soon be queen, and all her wrongs can be erased. But a princess associating with a servant cannot be so easily forgiven. Don't forget what blood runs in our veins. Be worthy of it."

Searin forced herself to meet her uncle's severe eyes and nod. Clavio smiled and padded her shoulder, then disappeared within the inky darkness of the hallways. Searin walked in a daze downstairs and headed for the door that led out to the practice yard. She had never held secrets before, and maybe it was for good reason since this one had been uncovered so quickly. Her uncle was right—it was wrong for royals and servants to interact in such a way. But then why did she want nothing more than to duel with this woman?

Searin glanced outside one of the windows facing the yard. Zinia's dark silhouette stood beneath the canopied weapons rack. The longing that filled Searin was unbearable, but she forced herself to look away and walk in the opposite direction.

XXI.

ON THE HOUSE

Tieg and Scintilla had not taken the news of the enchantress' disappearance well—at least that was one thing they could agree on. Without her help, they were back to their original plan: scour Vizen for any trace of the child. It was a terrible plan. There was no sense rushing such a hopeless task. The inn was a comfortable place to rest, and the events of that morning still dogged them, especially Scintilla. There was an edge to her voice, even in friendly conversation, as if any levity was put on for their benefit.

They would take the rest of today to rest their bodies and minds, then spend tomorrow worrying about finding the girl. Vizen was an enormous city and, even worse, they had no concrete proof that the girl was here beyond what the enchantress had told them. She could be anywhere. That was, if she was still alive—though Rovan preferred not to dwell on that possibility for now.

"If one was to look for a missing person, where would they begin?" Rovan asked the innkeeper at the bar.

"Depends on the person," Amya replied.

"What about a child?"

The innkeeper raised a suspicious eyebrow. "Is that what brings you to Vizen?"

Rovan nodded. "A friend's daughter has gone missing. We know she's in Vizen, but we're not from here and don't know where to even start."

"I'm sorry to hear that," Amya said, although her tone was guarded. "There are some orphanages that might have picked her up, though I wouldn't bet on it."

"Why do you say that?"

"The lost often get eaten by this city, never to be seen again." There was a startling soberness enveloping those words. "A lost child is just as likely to be picked up by an orphanage as they are by any other disgusting vulture. It can be a cruel place, this home of ours." Amya eyed him levelly as if to say that was all the help she would provide. Rovan understood her position well. For all she knew, he was one of the disgusting vultures hunting down a child who had rightfully escaped some type of abuse.

Rovan thanked the woman, then returned to the sitting area near the fireplace. Having finished their meal and spiced wine, Scintilla and Tieg sat with their feet up, holding warm mugs of herbal tea. A sleepy air had descended upon them. Tieg's eyes were lightly lidded while Scintilla held onto wakefulness for dear life.

"So, what's the plan, Ro?" Scintilla asked. Tieg did not stir.

Rovan smiled at the scene. "Don't worry yourself over it just now," he said. "Just relax and recuperate your strength and spirit. We have a lot of work ahead of us."

Scintilla frowned. "You're just as exhausted as we are. Allow us to share the burden."

Rovan reached for the tilting mug of tea in Tieg's lap and rescued his friend from a wet and steaming crotch. The tea was still warm, so he took a sip—it was thinly flavored but soothing, nonetheless. "We'll try some orphanages to see if the child is there. Unfortunately, we can't use the enchantress' connection to Sesha to guide us, so we're on our own."

"Why do you think she went off like that? And what was the point of stealing a useless runestone from you?" Scintilla asked.

Rovan sipped the tea. It was a question he had been pondering since he had discovered the theft. "Approaching the city gates, I felt... *something* from the runestone. It almost felt like I was near the *reaverlord*, but different. It's hard to put into words."

"But the runestone was spent. You couldn't have felt anything from it."

"When I was fifteen, I was involved in a *Sealing* enchantment that seems to have done something to me. Or at least that's what Mother Adriel thinks. I guess I can feel some things others can't. Maybe she thought I could use the runestone in some way. And she didn't want me to."

"What if she took it to prevent us from finding the girl first?" Sesha suggested.

That hadn't occurred to Rovan, but it seemed likely.

Scintilla turned to face the flames. The inn glowed orange. "I don't need any sort of special senses to know that enchantress is trouble. I don't like her."

"Neither do I," Rovan agreed. "We don't have enchantresses where I'm from, and the entire practice is a bit strange to me."

Tieg shifted in his seat. "We had an enchantress in my village," he said sleepily. His eyes were still closed, but he seemed to be awake. "She was old and weird. She was also a diviner—could see the future in chicken shit and fish eyes."

Scintilla and Rovan chuckled. "She told me my future, once. Said that if I ever left my home, I would never return."

Scintilla eyed her friend apprehensively. "Is that why you're going back? To prove some crazy old enchantress wrong?"

Tieg frowned. "Maybe? I don't know. It's just something I need to do."

"No. It's something you're choosing to do," Scintilla corrected.

Tieg straightened in his seat, now fully awake. "Yes, I am. Rovan always talks about the power of choice. This is something I am choosing to do. No one is making me do this, and no one can make me change my mind."

"No one is asking that of you," Rovan said. "We're just... a bit confused, is all."

"Yeah," Scintilla agreed. "Confused about why you would leave us for them."

Tieg stood. "I'm going to the room. I could use a bed."

"Tieg," Rovan said, standing as well. "We should talk about this."

"There's nothing to talk about," Tieg snapped.

"We're just trying to help," Scintilla offered.

"Has it ever occurred to you that I don't need anyone's help? I can't change what my family did to me, but I am choosing to confront it. And yet, you all think I'm so stupid to put myself in that position. But you know what? I am much stronger than you all give me credit for. And I don't need any of you to talk down to me!"

Tieg stomped away and disappeared into the darker hallway. Rovan returned to his seat, feeling deflated. "Aren't you going to say something?" Scintilla asked. There was a dark cast to her eyes, as if she wasn't sure whether to be angry or sad.

"Didn't you hear him?" Rovan replied. "I think it's best if we give him some space."

"I can't believe that's what he thinks of us," she huffed.

Rovan sipped the remaining tea—its already bland flavor had entirely vanished along with its warmth. "I'd rather not discuss this when Tieg is not around. I think we should rest. We have a long day ahead of us tomorrow."

The late afternoon dipped slowly into evening. Scintilla remained seated by the fire next to him, though she did not speak much. Rovan wished he knew which words to say to appease her, but nothing he came up with seemed like enough. Once it became dark outside, she retired to her room. He would attempt a new start in the morning with both her and Tieg.

Rovan was surprised by how few patrons populated the tavern. He had expected it to grow crowded as the evening progressed—men and women grabbing a bite to eat and a drink after their day's work—but no such crowd ever materialized beyond three thirsty locals. Rovan sat at the bar and Amya's husband, Filli, who had taken over her shift once it became dark, immediately served him a glass of mead. Rovan thanked the man, though he had no taste for the stuff—just the smell of it reminded him of the headache that followed the last time he had tried something similar.

"I expected Vizen to be a bustling center of commerce, but the city seems to be slumbering," Rovan said to the innkeeper. "Can't possibly be the weather."

"You're joking?" Filli chuckled. "Haven't you heard the king died?"

"I have, but I didn't realize that would send the entire city to a standstill."

"It isn't by choice." The broad-shouldered man poured himself some mead, then raised his cup. Rovan had no choice but to share a drink with the man. It burned as it went down, but it was a lot smoother than Rovan had anticipated. "You like it?" Filli asked with a smile.

"I must confess, I'm not much of a mead drinker, but this makes the shit I've had in the past taste like... well, shit."

Filli laughed loudly. "This is my own batch. My father taught me how to brew it the old way—the right way! It makes all the difference." Filli poured them two more cups. Rovan did not have it in him to refuse, though he already felt the heat of the previous drink seeping through his body.

"So, the king died, and now the city is forced to shut down?" Rovan reprised.

"'Forced mourning' is what they call it," Filli replied. "All markets are closed, so no one can buy or sell goods. Which means no one has pieces to spare at this tavern, hence the lack of clientele. It's all hogwash if you ask me. Why should I be forced to mourn someone who has never done me no good? You're not a royal footstool are you?"

"No, no," Rovan answered. The sharpness of the question gave him pause, but the drink in his belly lent him the confidence to admit, "I have no love for the nobility myself. A bunch of stuck-up wastes of space."

"To their downfall," Filli said, raising his glass. Rovan smirked and followed suit, downing a second shot of mead. "Where do you and yours hail from?"

"Pevine," Rovan answered.

Filli's eyes broadened. "You don't say? You're not from there, though, are you?"

"No. We only moved there a few months ago. It's still in disarray after the fires and the riots years ago. We're helping rebuild the place—fixing up houses, roofs, that sort of thing. It's hard work, but if the town can return to being a home its inhabitants can be proud of, it will all have been worth it."

Filli studied Rovan attentively. "That's mighty noble of you. Not the sort of noble that sits on golden chairs in golden rooms. But proper noble. Heroic."

Long ago, those exact words were everything Rovan had ever wanted to hear. He had hungered to become a better version of what a noble was supposed to be. Though that dream had been abandoned, he couldn't help the swelling of pride that the words stirred within him. "And you're from Vizen?" Rovan asked.

Filli grinned. "Pevine, actually. Isn't that something?"

"A fine coincidence," Rovan agreed with a smile. "And what brought you to Vizen?"

"My wife and I left our home due to the fires, five years ago."

"Seven," Rovan corrected.

"My, has it really been that long?" Filli shook his head, grimacing. "We moved to Vizen only days before the royals shut the gates, thank the gods! I had a great uncle here in Vizen. He set us up nicely working at his inn, which we then inherited after his passing a couple of years later. All things considered, we've been blessed. Not many others in Pevine can say the same." Filli glanced towards the hallway opposite the bar.

"We witness it every day," Rovan said. "The way the people of Pevine have been abandoned by their kingdom. They live so close to Vizen yet have received no aid in all these years. Not even the Blue Scarabs want anything to do with that place."

"That's by design," Filli said, downing the rest of his mead. He then reached for the bottle and poured himself another glass. He made to pour some more for Rovan, but Rovan placed a hand over the glass to stop the man. "Had enough?" the bartender asked.

Rovan smiled. "Unfortunately, I am not great at holding my liquor. I do better with wine."

"I'd pour you a glass of that, but all we have on hand tastes of piss."

Rovan laughed. "What did you mean when you said the royals ignoring Pevine was by design?"

Filli inhaled deeply and frowned. "Ask anyone in the city about the fires, and most won't know what you're talking about."

"But everyone knows about the Tragedy of Albadone, even as far south as Sol Forne."

The bearded man frowned. "Not here. At first, I thought it was because people simply didn't care—too absorbed in their city lives to give a shit. But then, I found out the truth. Whatever caused the fires, all that digging in the woods, somehow the royals are connected to it. They buried any discussion of the fires so they could hide their involvement. But trust me, whatever happened in Albadone all those years ago leads straight to the top of the Royal Tower, if you catch my meaning."

Filli scrutinized Rovan thoughtfully for a pregnant minute, before asking, "Have you ever heard of the Free Kings of Hovardom?"

"I can't say that I have," Rovan admitted.

Filli smiled. "Good. They like to keep it that way." Filli lowered his voice. "The Free Kings are a group who seek a world beyond the shackles of bloodlines and nobility—a world where every man's labor is his own. A world where riches no longer mean gold and silver, but a helpful community and a life with dignity. Doesn't that sound like a world you'd like to live in?"

"I suppose it does," Rovan admitted.

The barkeep cleared his throat, adopting a more serious tone. "But it'd be best not to mention the name 'Free Kings' outside this inn. Most people consider them a myth, but others prefer the term 'enemies of the crown.'"

Rovan nodded. "Understood." This Filli man was clearly a fan of this group, although from how he spoke of them, Rovan couldn't help being reminded of his first encounters with the Blue Scarabs. They had described themselves similarly—as part of a greater cause to help the regular people of Hovardom. He had seen where that road had led the Blue Scarabs. Now, they saw themselves as the sole keepers of law and order in the land, ahead even of royal soldiers and knights. Rovan wondered if these Free Kings were any different.

It had gotten late, and they would need to wake up early tomorrow. Rovan placed a copper piece on the bar, but Filli waved it away. "For a new friend, who longs for the same world as I do, these drinks are on the house."

XXII.

The Hearth Beneath the Palace

The day vanished before her. Time in this place drained away as if it was nothing but waste. Lyr trudged back to her quarters and crawled into her cot. The only other person in the room was Falma, the child's small shape rising and falling with each breath beneath her covers.

Exhaustion fell weightily over Lyr, reminding her that she had barely gotten any sleep the previous night. But though her body craved rest, her mind seemed intent on scrutinizing every single conversation and interaction she had ever had with Saul. Were any of his words genuine? No matter how many times Lyr told herself that she had joined the Free Kings out of her own search for justice, she could not help but wonder how much Saul had influenced her decision. A lot, she had to admit.

Thoughts of her mother and father inundated her, causing Lyr immense heartache. How her mother had kept the truth of her father's death from everyone, including her own daughter, must have strangled the woman from the inside out. The weight of such a lie would have crushed Lyr too. She wanted to cry from the guilt of having seen her mother as merely a burden.

Faint candlelight touched Lyr's eyelids. She hadn't even heard Falma get out of bed. The child crept from the room and quietly shut the door. Perhaps it was sleeplessness that found Lyr quickly standing and following the child like she had the other night. Lyr needed something to occupy herself with—anything to stop dwelling on her parents and Saul. The hallway was ice to her naked feet, but she padded onwards, following the path she knew the girl would take.

No candles illuminated the dim hallway Falma led her into, but Lyr could see movement just ahead. Falma entered the door that should not have been there. Lyr pressed her hand against the wall to help guide her through the darkness. She quickly reached the door the child had entered and slid her foot in to stop it from closing.

Lyr took a step beyond the door and nearly tumbled down a set of stairs—in the darkness, it was impossible to see how far down it extended. She briefly considered if following the child any further would be wise. What would Saul say to her, she wondered? That thought alone made her take the first step down the stairs. She knew Saul wouldn't approve of this, so she was doing it. This act of defiance could be what she needed to set her mind right. Or perhaps, she was simply being a curious fool. Regret encroached as swiftly as the darkness.

The stairs continued downward for some time. Beyond the door Lyr had entered, there didn't seem to be any other point of access to this staircase. Lyr's only guide was the soft sound of Falma's bare feet on cold stone and the sound of her nose sniffling every once in a while. Lyr kept her distance, remaining as quiet as she was able. An orange glow illuminated a space below—waves of heat from within, as well as a crackling sound, revealed its source to be a hearth. What was a hearth doing down here?

Falma entered the lit chamber, hastening her step. Lyr remained back, peeking inside from the edge of the entryway. Several steel doors lined the long hallway-like room. If it hadn't been for the hearth that roared at the far edge of the hall, Lyr would have assumed this to be some sort of dungeon.

The child paced quickly toward a door, caressing it as if it were an old friend. Lyr realized then that the girl's sniffles were not to stifle a cold; she was crying. "It's alright. It's going to be alright," the girl sobbed lightly. Suddenly, a man materialized in the room. Lyr almost jumped back at the sight. How had he entered?

Falma did not have to look at the man to know he was there. "She's sad," the girl said. "You can't keep her in there forever."

"I don't plan to. You know this very well." His voice was as warm and dangerous as the heat from the hearth.

"When will you free her?" Falma asked.

"I can't say for certain. Soon, I hope. But that all hinges upon many factors."

Whatever was within the cell growled—if that's what the sound could be called. It was more like the rasping of a rake against a sheet of steel. "Tell it to settle down," the man commanded.

Falma faced the man and stomped towards him. "She will die, you know? She needs *life energy* to survive."

"Why do you think I allow you in here?" the man countered.

"She needs more than you're giving her. A lot more." The girl's tone sounded resigned, spent.

"Listen to the girl," a feeble voice creaked. Lyr couldn't quite tell where it had come from.

The man shook his head, ignoring the voice entirely. "This arrangement will have to do until the time comes. Then, it can have all the *life energy* it could ever want. Now, it's time for the feeding."

A pair of armored figures entered the room carrying a large crate. Based on where they appeared, Lyr realized there was another entrance into this secret room. Backlit by the hearth, she couldn't make out many details about them. But by the shine of their heads in the firelight, she could tell that the two were bald and that they weren't wearing normal guard armor. They seemed more like soldiers. They placed the crate in front of the door, then one of them produced a set of keys. After unlocking the door, they cautiously opened it.

A low hum, like that of an earthquake, vibrated through Lyr. An angry, sorrowful, bitter feeling overtook her, and she found her knees threatening to give out. Falma quickly ran inside the cell and, just as it had appeared, the strange feeling vanished, along with the hum. The two soldiers picked up the crate and set it in the cell. A bleating sound like that of a goat or lamb came from within, followed immediately by a strange noise—like a strained growl. The two soldiers exited in alarm. The growl subsided. It sounded to Lyr as if Falma was sweetly shushing someone or something within the cell.

The bleating grew louder and more desperate. The bald soldiers flinched and instinctively took a step back at the sound of a loud wet crunch. The man, however, stared impassively into the cell. Though Lyr could not see his expression, she could somehow tell he was bemused. Goose flesh pimpled her skin as the horrible sounds continued. Once they stopped, the man spoke, "Alright, Falma. That's enough."

The girl exited the cell with her head low. Her arms dripped with a dark liquid—it almost looked like blood. *True One! That is blood.* Lyr covered her mouth.

The man placed his hand on Falma's head. "Thank you, Falma. This service you have rendered for us will not go unrewarded."

"I don't care about any rewards. I just want you to free her." The girl's voice did not carry any strength or resolve. It was as if something had sapped all the strength she had held moments ago.

The man addressed the soldiers. "Get her cleaned, then take her to her quarters."

"Yes, Master," the two soldiers replied, placing a fist to their hearts. The man walked to the other side of the room and vanished through whatever hidden door was there. One of the two soldiers picked Falma up as easily as if she were a sleeping baby, while the other closed and locked the cell door.

A flash of alarm suddenly made Lyr stand upright. *They're taking Falma back to her quarters. Our quarters!* She stood and quickly padded up the dark stairs. In her hurry, she tripped over a step and crashed loudly onto the floor. Her knee exploded with pain, but she bit back her yelp and sat quietly on the cold step, listening for any sign that she had been heard. When nothing came but the muffled sound of the hearth below, she stood and carried on upwards.

She finally reached the top of the staircase after what felt like an interminable climb. The ache in her knee was sharp—she had most likely scuffed it; she prayed there was no bleeding. The door that led back to the hallway stood before her. Lyr reached for the handle and pushed. It didn't budge.

No. NO! Panic made her hands shake uncontrollably. She pushed and pushed, but the door would not move. How was this possible? She ran her hands across its length, looking for a latch, a lock, a switch, anything! *You're a fool! Worse than a fool, even: an idiot.* Her blind search led her hands to the top rail of the door. There was something there, cold and metal—some sort of latch. From her tiptoes, Lyr could barely lift it. When she eventually did, the door swung outward, and she tumbled gracelessly into the hallway.

"What's this?" a man shouted from around a corner. A guard came into view, the lantern in his hand giving the lines of his face a skull-like gauntness. "You can't be in there!"

"I know," Lyr said, lowering her head. "I walked in and got stuck—" She couldn't even begin her lie before the guard pulled her by the hair and dragged her to the floor of the hallway. Lyr yelped from the pain at her scalp.

"That door should remain locked. No one is allowed in there!"

Lyr reached for her head. In the darkness, she could not see the blood, but she could feel its sticky wetness on her fingers. "I was just saying, I... I..." Lyr's voice quivered in fear. Whatever excuse she was about to come up with had vanished.

"You're spending the night in the pen," the guard said, gripping her arm tightly and standing her up. "Someone in charge will figure out how to deal with you. If I have a chance to recommend it, you'll be flogged!" The man paced through the hall, forcefully dragging Lyr by the scruff of her neck. How stupid she had been. She had doomed herself, but she refused to doom her fellow Free Kings. She would rather take the poison and end it all than allow herself to give them up when she would be inevitably questioned.

The guard opened an iron door and walked Lyr through the guards' quarters. The stone walls were exposed here. The place had an older air, as if it had not been updated or repaired throughout the years as the rest of the palace had been. Not many guards were awake at this time of night. The few that were shot Lyr disinterested, sleepy, glances. Beyond another heavy door was a larger room lined with cells. They were mostly unoccupied except for the last one which held two young women.

The guard pulled a ring of keys from the wall and unlocked one of the cells. He shoved Lyr inside. She landed against the hard stone floor on her already-hurt knee. If it wasn't before, it was definitely bleeding now.

"How much longer are you going to keep us in here?" one of the prisoners asked.

"Shut up," the guard shouted. Then, to Lyr, he said, "You'll need all the rest you can get for what's to come." He then closed the cell door, leaving the room and taking the light with him. Lyr was plunged into darkness once more. And, just like before on her cot, she found the same ghosts waiting for her in the inky black, preventing any rest.

It must have been early in the morning when the jail door opened, allowing in a sliver of blue light from the windows lining the outer hallway. It was impossible for Lyr to be sure how long she had been there—the span of time between now and when she had been locked up was a sleepless blur of dread and boredom. She raised her head and focused on the three people that stood outside the cell. One of them was the guard that had apprehended her, thumbing through a ring of keys, saying, "She's awake," in a disappointed tone of voice—perhaps he had wished to shake her awake himself.

There was another guard, a woman with a hard Vizenian jawline, and the last of the three was none other than Ser Dregor, the knight and fellow Free King. Lyr fought to keep relief from appearing on her face.

"Are you sure you want to sully your time with such a wretch?" the guard asked.

"She was found trespassing in an area reserved for royal affairs," Dregor said. "This is the King's Guards' jurisdiction."

"As you wish, Ser," the man said, sliding the key through the hole and opening the cell. "Up with you," he barked as he kicked her foot.

Lyr stood, sharp pain in her knee flaring. Dregor grabbed her wrist and walked her out of the room. His grip was firm but not aggressive. "You're in a world of trouble," Dregor said calmly.

Lyr could do nothing but nod. "What will become of me?"

Dregor sighed heavily—the only indication that he was in any way concerned by her predicament. "Don't speak until we're alone."

The guards' bunker was now quite full of armored women and men, as well as others in simple day clothes not dissimilar from those worn by the servants. Lyr was afraid that their eyes would skewer her with hateful glances, but she was surprised to see that most averted their gazes entirely. They were avoiding Dregor, she realized. Was this done out of fear or reverence? She was not sure.

Instead of walking her through the main halls of the palace, Dregor took an inconspicuous route through the windowless dark halls of the guards' bunker. He opened a door and led her outside, into a wide courtyard where several guards and a pair of knights were sparring. At the far end of the yard, Dregor led her through another door and into an area of the palace that was entirely deserted. "What is this place?" Lyr asked.

"A place you will hopefully never find yourself in again."

Down another windowless hall, and through a steel door, Dregor let go of Lyr's arm and had her sit down on a stool. The walls of the cramped room were bare stone. Against the far wall was a table covered in all sorts of tools—hammers, wires, rods, knives... A chill crept down Lyr's back upon realizing what sort of grim place she had entered. As soon as the door was closed behind them, the facade of steel resolve melted from Dregor's face. There was another stool in the room, but Dregor did not take it—it must not have been very comfortable to sit down wearing all that armor.

"When did you decide to betray the Free Kings?" Dregor asked.

"I didn't betray the Free Kings!" Lyr exclaimed, perhaps a bit too harshly.

"Then why would you do such a stupid thing as to threaten the entire mission?" Though his voice remained flat, there was an imposing quality to his tone.

"It's simply as you say. I did something stupid."

"Why?"

"Because... I don't know why." Lyr lowered her head in embarrassment.

"Let's start from the beginning," Dregor said, leaning against the wall. "What were you doing in there?"

"I was following that child, Falma, who quarters with me. I know it was stupid of me. I was told she had her own tasks to attend to, but I just couldn't leave it at that, knowing a young girl was being called away every night." Lyr held her head in her hands—she knew how pitiful she sounded.

"So, you followed her down?" Dregor asked.

Lyr looked up at him. Something about his expression told Lyr that her fate was directly tied to what she had witnessed in the hall below. Dregor was a Free King posing as a knight. She could trust him, right? How much did she truly know about the man?

"No," Lyr lied. Somehow she found her resolve strengthened by the lie. "The door closed behind me. I immediately tried to push it open, but it had locked me in. I didn't know doors could do that."

Though he stood still, something in Dregor's posture visibly relaxed. "Then what?" he prodded.

"Then I found some kind of latch that opened the door. But a guard heard me and dragged me to that cell."

"Very well." Dregor crossed his arms and approached her. "You're lucky I was the first one to hear about this. Any other knight would have had you whipped and expelled for life. Or worse. The royals are very protective of their secrets."

Lyr swallowed the lump of fear in her throat. "Thank you, Ser," she said.

Dregor turned towards the table and ran his fingers across the collection of tools scattered about. "Unfortunately, I cannot let you return to your post unscathed."

"What do you mean?" Lyr felt dizzy with alarm.

"It wouldn't look right if you went completely unpunished. What you did was very, very stupid. Highly improper. Do you understand?"

Lyr fought the tears of fear that formed at her eyes and nodded as bravely and proudly as she was able.

"It can never happen again," Dregor reiterated. "It *must* not happen again. You will remain focused on your mission."

"Yes, Ser," Lyr choked.

"I'm happy to hear it." Dregor picked up a rod from the table and whacked it loudly across his palm. Lyr jumped. "Now, please lift your shift and let us get this over with."

XXIII.

The Appointment

The Royal Tower was one of the oldest structures in the entire city—a remnant of the long-gone age before the First Folk colonized the continent. It was a commonly held belief among the peasantry—and some of the lower nobility—that the royal family still resided at the top of the tower. In truth, Searin had only ever been to the very top ring once before when she was a baby. As was tradition with every royal heir, her father had carried her up there to receive the blessing of the Nameless so that her future reign would prosper.

Thankfully, there weren't many floors to climb to reach the small council hall, which was situated in the second ring of the tower. Arisa sat on her father's throne atop a raised platform. It was an uncomfortable old wooden thing that creaked under Arisa's constant shifting. It brought Searin a sort of pleasure seeing her sister squirm about—a small, secret, revenge for having been denied entry to her sister's chambers the previous evening. But this would not do. As the soon-to-be queen, Arisa had to show some modicum of stoicism in front of the council.

Searin approached the throne and leaned into her sister's ear. "Sit still," she whispered. "And where is Mother? Shouldn't that be her seat?"

"Mother is actually the subject of our first piece of discussion. I don't understand how Father sat on this blasted thing," Arisa complained.

"Either sit still or stand," Searin reprimanded, then returned to her chair at Arisa's right. Arisa shot her a viperous glance before begrudgingly settling into the uncomfortable seat.

Behind the throne stood High Captain Knott in his oiled golden plating and red cape. Searin sized up the old man, coveting his armor, ceremonial sword, and station with a burning impatience. Behind the high captain stood four of the eleven knights of the King's Guard—the rest were posted at each corner of the hall, and outside the doors. To Arisa's left sat Uncle Clavio, his face freshly shaved and his blonde curls collected into his customary tail. Searin noted that Clavio wore his ceremonial dress—a blue velvet cassock that lent his slender build wider shoulders and the illusion of extra height.

Everyone was wearing their best attire despite the queen's absence. Had the queen been present, Searin would have received ample side-eye from her for having donned her armor and decorative helmet, its red plume raised in salute, rather than another horrid gown. Her sword, Vow, sat familiarly at her hip. It felt good to be seen this way by the men and women who sat before her—this is who she was and who she would be to them going forward.

"Shall we begin, my princess?" Clavio asked.

Arisa nodded. "You have by now all observed that the queen regent will not be joining us today." The lack of surprise on the faces of the surrounding ministers spoke volumes. "The loss of my father has sat heavy on her heart to the point of compromising her health. In her wisdom and consideration for the kingdom, she has temporarily vested her authority in me until my anointment renders the transfer permanent. As proof of this exchange, I present her seal and signature upon this official scroll." Arisa waved over an attendant from the back wall who carried with him a plush velvet box. The man opened the lid and unfurled the scroll within before holding it up and turning slowly to afford each seated person a good view of the queen's yellow primrose seal.

Searin's eyes widened. What had Arisa said to their mother to convince her to sign such a document? Whatever it had been, the relief on the faces of the ministers, especially Lord Trett, at not having to field any further unreasonableness from the queen was apparent.

Arisa continued, "With that announced, we may begin in earnest by welcoming our guest."

They didn't have to wait long before a short, handsome page walked in and announced the arrival of Lord Reilyn Azurat trailed dutifully by his escort of hand servants and bodyguards. The small group walked into the hall and bowed politely in front of the dais.

"Please stand," Arisa commanded, and the group obeyed.

Searin's eyes were immediately drawn to Lord Reilyn. In the firelight of the feast two days prior, he had seemed young and meek, but there was a confidence in his eyes that Searin had not noticed before. The young man was about Arisa's age, with smooth raven hair that fell effortlessly about his shoulders, and large gray eyes like pools of liquid cinder. He wore a blue stole that shimmered with his every movement and brought out dark blue highlights in his pitch-black hair.

Arisa smiled sweetly, which disarmed the young man's collectedness.

"My princess," Clavio began, "it is my utmost pleasure to introduce you to our guest and good friend of the crown, Lord Reilyn Azurat, eldest son of Thanes Ronnan and Priscenda Azurat of Pallew." The young man stepped ahead of his escort and bowed.

"My lord, while these circumstances are tragic, I am gracious that they have allowed us the opportunity to meet. I hear this is your first time at court," Arisa greeted.

"It is, my princess," Lord Reilyn replied in a melodious voice, his Eastern accent effortlessly gliding over each word. "Though my mother and father have been at court many times in the past. My mother was a good friend to Thane Clavio Talessi's wife, Thane Oma, back when she was Lady Oma o'Kendry."

Searin's eyes bounced between the young man and her uncle. The connections between him and these Azurats ran much deeper than Searin had realized.

Clavio nodded at the man, a reminiscing smile lightening his features. "My lady wife remembers your mother fondly."

"And my mother often recounts glad memories of her time at court. She hopes to visit you and your wife in Perimat someday soon," Reilyn replied. He returned his attention to Arisa. "The Azurats would like to offer the royal family our deepest condolences over the passing of his grace, King Petar. He was a good man and did a lot of good for the kingdom. His absence leaves an unmendable hole in each of our lives."

Everyone in the hall mumbled in agreement. It was all Searin could do to not roll her eyes. *It's likely this man's father is celebrating the king's death at this very moment,* she mused.

"You are most kind, my lord," Arisa acknowledged. "I'm saddened that your father and mother could not attend the funeral."

"I hope my presence was enough to satisfy my princess."

Arisa's eyes sparkled. "Indeed, it was."

Clavio cleared his throat. "While Princess Arisa is honored to host you at court, I must confess this summons concerns a much more pressing and urgent matter."

Reilyn's demeanor changed, worry blooming on his face. "What sort of matter?" he asked, his voice betraying concern, and perhaps a tinge of fear.

Clavio seemed to sense the man's worry and applied his most disarmingly cordial smile. "While it is important, it's not a grim matter. Unless my lord fears matrimony."

The color drained from Reilyn's face. "Matrimony?" he echoed. The lord's servants glanced at one another knowingly. Murmurs droned throughout the hall.

"Allow me to explain," Clavio continued, raising a hand to placate the audience. "I know it's quite unorthodox to speak of these matters without the presence of your parents or the queen regent, but," Clavio reached into his smock and pulled out a small scroll bearing the seal of House Azurat—two hands cupping a coin. "I have here a written testament of their consent to this union. As you know, Princess Arisa is next in line for the throne. However, custom dictates she may not be anointed queen until she has a consort at her side to share in the anointment."

Arisa stood from her uncomfortable seat, candidly rubbing her backside. "As children of noble blood, we grow up with the understanding that we are often the last to be consulted on the matter of our own marriage partner. That said, I hope you will indulge me in the rather performative act of me asking for your hand as my King Consort." She allowed the young man a moment to process her words. "So, what is your answer?" For the longest time, no one spoke a single word. The only sounds in the hall were the shuffling of seats and furtive whispers.

Clavio coughed, breaking the silence. "I don't mean to offend my lord, but I believe your princess has asked you a question. What will your answer be?"

"My princess," Lord Reilyn began, in a slow and calculated manner. "It would be the honor of my life to join our houses." He bowed deeply.

"How wonderful," Clavio answered, the director of a play going exactly as scripted. "And congratulations to you both on your engagement."

Arisa stepped off the dais and approached the man. Standing in front of him, she extended her hand. After a brief hesitation, Reilyn took it in his own and lowered his head to plant a soft kiss upon it. Arisa curtsied low in response, a sign of deference no one else could have been granted. Reilyn blushed a deep crimson.

Clavio interrupted the tender moment, "This letter also contains the sincerest regrets of Thanes Azurat for having to forego the events of today. They wish to host the wedding at their castle in Pallew and have offered to cover all preparations and expenses to this end."

"Your family's generosity honors me," Arisa said to Reylin.

"I hope my princess will find my home a deserving venue for this joyous occasion," the befuddled lord supplied.

The hall was immediately alight with conversations that no longer aspired to subtly.

Arisa smiled. "Then it is decided. We shall all travel together to Pallew and carry out the wedding ceremony there."

"Princess Arisa," High Captain Knott's booming voice brought all other conversations to a halt. "Do you think it is wise to leave Vizen so suddenly in the wake of the king's passing? Will your mother resume charge in your absence?"

"You are right, High Captain, that someone must be appointed to serve while I'm away," Arisa said. "That brings us to our next point of order. I am appointing my uncle, Thane Clavio, as prime regent of the city."

Searin was truly shocked by this. There hadn't been a prime regent in Hovardom for generations. She faced her uncle—the man smiled and nodded in acceptance of this new role. The council seemed greatly pleased by this, reacting with robust applause.

"It is a great honor to serve Vizen and the kingdom," Clavio said when the clapping died down.

"If I may share another concern, my princess," Knott resumed. "To reach Pallew, a caravan must travel the Red Road. There have been troubling sightings of *reaverlords* as of late."

"It's very kind of you to show concern, High Captain," Arisa replied. "I will require most of the King's Guard as escorts." She faced Reilyn. "I assume you were escorted by an armed retinue when you first made for Vizen?"

"I was, my princess," the lord replied.

"Then we shall combine our forces and travel together. I'm certain we will be more than safe. And it will give us both a better opportunity to grow acquainted."

Reilyn smiled broadly and bowed.

Clavio stepped beside Arisa. "I will see that horses and carriages are readied and that provisions are stocked for the lengthy trip."

"Thank you, Uncle," Arisa said. "I know this is a lot to place upon you all at once, Lord Reilyn. But I hope you are pleased by this turn of events."

"More than pleased, my princess," Lord Reilyn replied, "Honored, even."

"That is most pleasant to hear," Arisa smiled. "We shall leave within a couple of days."

"That's too soon!" the lord exclaimed, before quickly regaining his composure. "That's so soon."

"I fear the kingdom cannot wait. Now, if you'll excuse us, we have much more to discuss."

Reilyn bowed at the dismissal, as did his servants. They all then turned to leave, though Reilyn smiled back at the princess before disappearing behind the heavily carved doors of the hall. Once they were gone, Arisa took a deep breath.

"I think that went splendidly! What do you all say?" Clavio asked the hall. In response, the council nodded and mumbled their assent. Clavio turned to Arisa, "We will have a messenger sent ahead to Pallew to confirm your upcoming visit. I'm sure the Azurats will be most pleased." Clavio pointed at Isander, one of the most attentive of the King's Guards. Isander nodded then headed out of the room in haste to send out the message.

"I must say, my princess, I am quite surprised by all of these sudden developments," Captain Knott said.

"And that brings us to our next piece of business," Arisa smiled.

"My princess," a wispy voice called out. Lord Kell Trett, the Minister of Coin, stood. "The wedding feast is still under preparation. May we call it off in a timely fashion to save on the expenditure?"

"That's a good point," Arisa agreed.

Lord Trett seemed pleased by Arisa's consideration, but Clavio quickly interjected. "I recommend that we move forward with the feast."

Lord Trett scowled. "And why is that?"

Clavio turned to Arisa. "Many have traveled in haste to Vizen, not only to pay their respects to your father but also to witness your anointment. They may feel cheated when they hear that you have decided to head to Pallew instead."

"My princess, I have not brought the urgency or extent of this problem to your attention out of respect for your grief, but it would be irresponsible of me to not warn you that this additional feast would greatly strain the royal coffers and food stores. I sincerely hope you will reconsider," Lord Trett pleaded.

"My lord, surely we can spare enough to placate the travel-weary nobility," Clavio insisted.

For all its strangeness, Arisa seemed to be pondering Clavio's suggestion. "Lord Trett raises a valid concern. While my father was known as Petar the Just, I do not wish to begin my reign as Arisa the Miser. See about cutting back on cakes or performances."

"I'll see what can be done, my princess." Lord Trett retreated back into his seat.

Arisa returned her attention to the audience. "There is one last thing to tend to before we adjourn. An appointment I'd like to make."

The hairs on Searin's neck raised at her sister's words. Could this be the moment she had been waiting for? High captains of the King's Guard were traditionally appointed after the anointment ceremony, but there was precedent for such unorthodox timing. She glanced at her sister for some sign, but Arisa continued to face the crowd.

Arisa turned to Knott, who also seemed to suspect where this was going. "High Captain, you have served my father well for many years, not only by leading the King's Guard but also by being a true friend to him. You've more than earned a rest."

"My princess?" the high captain said in poorly concealed resignation.

"Your time as high captain of the King's Guard has come to an end. We will ensure that you are adequately rewarded for your years of service and will provide your family with a new home within the palace, or wherever you wish it to be if you have the desire to relocate."

Knott's face fell. Searin couldn't feel too bad for the man—she was about to assume his station. Arisa cleared her throat. It was time. Searin steadied herself and prepared to accept her destiny.

Arisa continued, "I hereby entrust the position of high captain of the King's Guard to Ser Dregor Lonseley, who has valiantly proved himself to be worthy of the honor."

A rote round of applause broke out, but Searin could not hear it. Dregor's name rang in her mind like a dissonant bell. Dregor approached Arisa and kneeled before her. Air was not reaching Searin's lungs.

"Ser Knott, please hand over the ceremonial Greatsword of Ivaran to High Captain Dregor," Arisa said.

Knott appeared unaware he had been issued a command. "The sword, Knott," Clavio repeated. Knott unfastened his belt and held the sheathed ceremonial greatsword in his hands. He handed the sword over to Dregor with a deep and proper bow. As soon as Dregor took the sword from him, Knott faced the crowd and then stormed out of the hall.

Searin wished she had the resolve to do the same. Her sister had betrayed her. She had handed Arisa the right of rule in exchange for leadership of the King's Guard, and in turn, she would be left with neither. She fought to keep her face still and her jaw unclenched as she watched Dregor recite the Seven Rites while kneeling before Arisa.

This was a nightmare—it had to be.

At some point, the recitation must have ended because Dregor stood and faced the hall. "I am honored to follow the legacy of the faithful high captains of the King's Guard that came before me," he said. "I vow that, with this new title, I shall protect our ruler and our kingdom with my life." The hall answered his words with applause but also confused murmuring. Searin, too, applauded halfheartedly, her eyes fixed upon her smiling traitor of a sister. She could feel the gazes of others fixed upon her, gauging her reaction.

The council was soon dismissed, and the hall was quickly vacated. Dregor, Clavio, and Arisa remained in their seats, talking amongst themselves. Searin watched the three with a bloodlust she had never felt before. She wanted to take her sister by the throat and throw her from her uncomfortable gilded throne onto her bony gilded ass. Her face must have betrayed her thoughts because Clavio stood and approached with his hands held up in an irritatingly placating manner.

"I can see that you are angry, my dear," Clavio said. "Perhaps it is best if you go cool off somewhere. Maybe take a bath."

"I don't want a fucking bath," Searin said through gritted teeth. Her voice echoed petulantly through the empty hall. Arisa and Dregor turned to face her. "I want what was promised to me."

"Searin," Clavio sighed. "I'm sorry this is how you had to find out about our plans. Had you been at our meeting yesterday, this would not have caught you so off guard. We all have roles we must play in what's to come." Clavio placed a cool hand on her cheek, making her realize just how hot with anger her face had become. "Your role, unfortunately, does not involve you becoming high captain of the King's Guard."

She faced her sister who, to her credit, seemed sickened by what had just happened. "I'm sorry," Arisa said. "It wasn't an easy—" Searin stood and stomped out of the hall. Another word and she would have clawed Arisa's eyes out. Searin knew better than to act in this fractious manner, but she could not stop herself. Every aspect of her life had been precisely plotted to lead up to her appointment as high captain. Now that her future had been stripped from her, she would act however she felt—and she felt feral.

The nobles and lordlings she passed in the halls parted before her as if avoiding a stampeding beast. They sickened her. She caught a glimpse of a knight and immediately turned away. Searin didn't remember taking any stairs or opening any doors, yet she found herself suddenly in the western wing of the palace. The servants there were still tidying up after the previous day's feast. Among them, she caught sight of Zinia.

The woman was dusting a tall shelf, unreachable by most of the other servants. Searin grabbed the woman by her arm. "Hey!" Zinia exclaimed, before realizing who was dragging her out of the hall and through the servants' quarters. "My princess, what is—"

"Quiet!" Searin interrupted. They reached the door leading into the practice yard and Zinia stopped, planting her feet on the floor.

"You said you'd meet me last night, but you never showed," Zinia said.

Searin scowled at the woman, then exited into the courtyard. The servant followed reluctantly. Guards were sparring beneath a light mist of rain. Searin approached them and yelled, "Clear the yard!" The men and women bowed and returned their practice weapons to the canopied rack before retreating.

"My princess, what is the meaning of this?" called Henter, the old palace guard captain.

"Clear the yard!" Searin yelled in the man's face.

Henter scowled darkly, then joined his guards in funneling out of the yard. That would come back to haunt Searin, but she was beyond caring. She removed her helmet and tossed it aside with a clank. Its once proud feather melted pathetically into a puddle. Beneath the canopy, she scanned the rack for a practice sword. None of them seemed suitable to embody the rage and betrayal she felt. She reached for her side and unsheathed her sword, Vow.

"A beautiful weapon," Zinia complimented. Searin turned to face the woman, who stood a few paces away.

"Pick a sword," Searin barked. Zinia approached the rack, but Searin halted her by raising her hand. "No. From there." She pointed at another rack across the yard.

"Those are real swords," Zinia said flatly.

Searin nodded.

The servant hesitated only for a moment before heading for the weapon's rack and selecting a sword. She sliced the air tentatively before returning to the center of the yard. "So, you want to draw blood?" the woman asked.

"We'll see what happens," Searin answered, approaching Zinia.

"You know what will happen if I hurt you. Why are you putting me in this position?"

"Shut up, and fight!"

Searin lunged towards Zinia and swung Vow as if intending to cut the woman's arm off—perhaps she was. Something told her it wouldn't be so simple to maim the woman. Zinia backed away from the swing, allowing Searin an opportunity to strike again. Zinia parried, then disengaged.

"Are you trying to kill me?" Zinia asked. "It will only take a few parries for that sword of yours to obliterate mine."

Searin knew this to be true, but she didn't care. She needed to feel her blade hitting another. She swung again, and this time Zinia parried, her sword reeling from the impact like a sheet of hot steel hit by a smith's hammer. To Searin's surprise, Zinia switched to a quick counterattack. Searin raised her sword to parry, but Zinia had other plans. The woman crouched and kicked Searin's legs, sending her falling to the ground. Zinia then stood and stomped on Searin's wrist, forcing her to drop Vow to the ground.

"That was dirty!" Searin complained.

"You left me no choice," Zinia replied coolly. "If this is your idea of a duel, then why not ask for my neck and be done with it?"

Searin looked away from Zinia's towering gaze in shame. Anger was no justification to stack the deck against her opponent. "Release me," she said calmly, and the woman obeyed, removing her foot from Searin's wrist. Zinia held out a hand and Searin took it, allowing the woman to help her stand.

"There's a fury in you that was not there in our last spar," Zinia said. "Is everything all right, my princess?"

"Nothing to concern a servant," Searin spat.

"Very well," Zinia said. "But I would appreciate a warning next time, so I know what I'm in for."

"Next time," Searin chuckled. She looked at the woman and realized that her words had been serious. Zinia truly expected these duels to carry on, even after Searin had almost killed her. There was something in the woman's expression—a quiet expectation—that disarmed Searin and made her want to open up. Zinia would never understand what Searin was going through, but it might feel good to say her piece to someone who had no stake in the royal game.

"I was promised something by my sister, and instead she gave it to someone else without so much as a warning," Searin said. "I abdicated my station as next in line to the throne for it. I don't understand how she could betray me like this."

"Next in line?" Zinia echoed. "You are the eldest daughter?"

"How could you possibly not know?" Searin was dumbfounded.

The woman shrugged. "I don't tend to pay much attention to what goes on around me beyond the scope of my tasks. As a mercenary, I fought for a living. As a servant," she chuckled, looking at the sword in her hand, "it seems not much has changed."

Searin found herself smiling. "Fighting for a living. Sometimes it feels like the opposite is true for me. I live to fight."

Zinia placed her hand on Searin's shoulder, something that in any other circumstance would have been highly inappropriate. But the woman's touch grounded her. "I'm sorry," the woman said, and that was all Searin needed to hear.

Searin touched the woman's hand, its roughness now strangely familiar to her. Searin backed away, suddenly remembering the insurmountable distance between their stations. "It wouldn't sting as badly if I was at least invited to travel to the wedding."

"Travel?" Zinia asked.

"My sister has decided to go to Pallew in a couple of days." Searin shook her head. "The whole affair is very rushed."

"And what about the feast?"

Searin shrugged, though she sensed a note of worry in the woman's tone. "The nobles will have their feast, but there will no longer be a wedding here in Vizen." Zinia's forehead creased. "What's wrong?" Searin asked.

"Oh, it's nothing, my princess," Zinia said. "I just have some servant friends who will be quite disappointed that their hard work will be for yet another feast, and not a wedding."

"A disappointment shared by many, it seems. Shall we spar?"

Zinia nodded. "I would love to. But this time, can we return to the practice swords? I'd rather keep my head."

XXIV.

No Children Here

Rovan opened his eyes and glanced at the empty right side of the bed—Tieg had already gotten up. The rain had reduced to a gentle pitter-pattering against the window sill. That would make their search for the girl somewhat more bearable. His stomach groaned, having soured from the sweet liquor he had imbibed the previous night. No hangover, though—another thing to be grateful for.

He stood from the bed, dressed quickly in his annoyingly still-damp clothes, and went to find his friends. A small cluster of people huddled around the fireplace, warming themselves and breaking their fast on bread, hard cheese, and ale. Scintilla sat at the bar eating a steaming bowl of soup. Though it was the same sour turnip soup they had enjoyed the previous evening, its smell today almost made Rovan retch.

"Good morning," Rovan greeted her.

"Morning," she returned flatly.

"Where's Tieg?"

"Bathing in the back room," she replied. "I already had my turn. You should have a go too, before the water turns cold."

Rovan could only imagine how road-ripened he must smell. "That sounds like a good plan. How are you?"

Scintilla scooped the soup with her spoon and let it fall back into the bowl. "You should be asking Tieg that question."

"I will."

Scintilla let go of the spoon and turned to face him. "I'm all right, all things considered. I could be much worse. We escaped a *reaverlord* for gods' sakes." She shook her head. "I'm disappointed in myself. The way I froze... It's embarrassing."

"It's only natural for you to react that way in the face of such a beast. There's no need to feel embarrassed. We all froze—well, except Mother Adriel."

Scintilla smiled. "It's a nice sentiment, but I would've felt better if I'd at least loosed an arrow into one of its disgusting eyes."

"Where's the bathroom?" he asked, changing the subject.

"At the end of the hall." Scintilla pointed towards the rooms.

Rovan thanked her. The hallway that led to their rooms bent right, revealing a door at the far end. Rovan opened it. "Occupied!" Tieg exclaimed in a panic. The top of his head emerged from a copper tub filled with sudsy water.

"It's just me," Rovan laughed.

Tieg lifted his head and relaxed against the tub. Foamy suds clung to his chest. "You could have announced yourself before barging in."

"I'm sorry," Rovan said, stifling his laughter with a grin. "How's the water?" he asked.

"Still warm, but not for much longer," Tieg replied.

"Then finish up so I don't have to freeze."

Tieg frowned and picked up a wooden bowl that sat next to the tub. He scooped the bath water and rinsed himself of the suds. "I'm done anyways." Tieg stood and stepped out of the tub, splashing water across the wooden floor.

Rovan quickly turned to the door, feeling his face heat up. His friends were more comfortable with nudity than he was. It had to do with where he'd been raised, he realized. In big cities like Sol Forne, nakedness was seen as improper, whereas in smaller towns and rural villages, it was just part of everyday life. Rovan could not bring himself to be naked around anyone, nor was he comfortable around anyone who was naked—even his friends.

"All yours," Tieg declared. Rovan allowed a few moments to pass before turning around. Tieg had not bothered to dry himself before donning his trousers. He picked his shirt from a chair and pulled it over his head. "So. Orphanages?"

"It's all we have to go by, unfortunately," Rovan said.

"Very well." Tieg moved for the door.

"Tieg," Rovan called out, stopping his friend. "I..." The words struggled to form, "I... want to say—"

"It's nothing." Tieg cut him off, leaving Rovan to puzzle out what he had been trying to say on his own.

※ ※ ※ ※

A warm breakfast and a few unclear directions later, the three friends found themselves roaming the uneven and, in many places, flooded streets of Vizen. The citizens of Vizen were a rude lot, bumping into them in ways that seemed at times intentional, or clutching their bags and pockets distrustfully as they walked by. The light gray sky above was merciful today, but they had seen it turn dark without warning before. Their hope to remain dry was a restrained one.

They almost missed the first orphanage due to how well it blended in with the surrounding buildings. Three stories tall and slightly crooked, its windows were either shuttered or entirely too dark to see within. Planting pots lined the entrance and the window sills of the first floor like a graveyard of dead plants. But it wasn't the disrepair or drabness of the building that gave Rovan pause. It was the silence within. The only thing marking it as an orphanage was the mostly faded signage above the door.

"I don't like this place," Scintilla said.

"Neither do I," Rovan agreed. He reached for the door and swung the knocker, sending three firm knocks reverberating through the building's interior. Moments later, a young woman opened the door just a crack and peeked at them from within. Her face was deathly pale, her round eyes floating in the dark pools surrounding them. "Yes?" she asked sleepily.

"Hello madame," Rovan greeted with a nod. "My companions and I are searching for a child that has gone missing. A little girl named Sesha. Are you by any chance housing a child by that name here?"

"Children?" The woman said it as if she had never spoken the word in her life. "No children here."

"What do you mean?" Rovan asked.

"This is an orphanage, yes?" Tieg pressed.

The woman eyed them suspiciously, then repeated, "No children here," before shutting them out.

Rovan turned to face his friends. "That was strange."

"Very," Scintilla agreed. "I say we break in and see for ourselves."

"I don't think we should cause that sort of commotion," Tieg countered.

"How else are we supposed to know if the child is in there?" she pressed.

"We need to be certain," Rovan agreed. "But we can't do it by breaking down the door and storming in. Let's circle around and see if there's a window we can get a better view from, or a back door."

Having agreed to this plan, the three proceeded down the line of identically drab buildings until they reached a turning point. The road arched left then sunk downwards into a cramped and foreboding back street. A pair was huddled in the cramped path having an animated conversation. When they saw the three of them approaching, their eyes turned suspicious, and the volume of their words lowered to a whisper.

"I don't think we should be here," Tieg said under his breath.

They passed the two men in uncomfortable silence, heading for the back side of the orphanage. Here, the building was covered in dark, fuzzy, mold that veined its way through the stonework. A single window was next to the rickety back door, nailed wooden planks concealing the view within.

"What do we do now?" Rovan wondered aloud.

Scintilla reached for the handle of the back door and turned it. "Would you look at that!" she marveled as she pushed the door open. She faced Rovan and Tieg with a grin. "No need to break in at all."

Rovan sighed. "Let's be quiet and careful."

They proceeded into the dark building cautiously, leaving the door open a crack to permit them a quick escape, if needed. They found themselves in a kitchen, though no fire was lit beneath the grimy cauldron. A smoky haze filled the air, filling Rovan's nostrils with a pungent aroma. It wasn't a smell he was familiar with, and it instantly made his head feel as light as a cloud.

They crept into the larger room across the kitchen, then stopped when they noticed three figures clustered on the floor, surrounding a bowl. One of the three—the woman that had greeted them at the door—blew across the lip of the bowl, reddening the coals that sat within. More smoke lifted into the air.

"We should get out of here," Tieg whispered.

The thumping of footsteps upstairs made the ceiling creak. Scintilla headed for the stairs. It was a terrible idea, Rovan knew, but he quietly followed her up. Tieg grabbed his sleeve and pulled him back. "Rovan, we have to go."

"We need to be sure," Rovan replied. As he padded upstairs, his eyes began to water, and the room swirled around him as if he was standing in a boat. He passed room after room in what felt like an infinite hallway. Within the rooms, more people were gathered around smoking bowls, their skeletal bodies splayed across the floor like lizards in the sun.

Scintilla ducked into a room ahead. She was saying something, but Rovan could not hear. He followed and tried to call out to her, but the words felt stuck in his head, just behind his mouth. He knew he should react strongly to the room full of children that he found himself in, but the most he could manage was to remain standing.

"Have you seen a girl?" Scintilla asked them. "Sesha?"

There were a dozen children, ages ranging from four to twelve, Rovan estimated. Their sunken eyes glided over him, not really seeing him. "Sesha? Are you here?" Scintilla called out before bursting into a coughing fit.

"Whassat??" someone in the other room slurred.

Rovan felt a tug on his arm. Tieg was behind them, dragging both to the door while yelling, "We have to go!" Rovan found that he could not move. His legs felt heavy and rooted to the floor, while his head wished to float upwards until it reached the ceiling. Tieg continued to pull until finally, Rovan's legs responded. The people in the other rooms yelled and cursed, but no one followed them downstairs or out the back door.

"I feel sick," Scintilla said between coughs. "What was that stuff?"

"That was poppium," Tieg answered. "Are you all right, Rovan?"

Rovan had his hand flat against the outer walls of the old orphanage. The mold felt slick and delightful beneath his touch. "I... don't know," Rovan said.

"Should we head back to the inn?" Tieg asked.

"No, no," Rovan mumbled. "I think I'll be fine in a few moments. I just need to walk it off." Scintilla leaned forward and dry heaved. She spat on the ground and rubbed her eyes. "Sin?" Rovan called—he couldn't muster much else.

Scintilla filled her lungs and breathed out slowly. She nodded. "I'll be all right."

Rovan felt a sort of pit forming in his stomach, as if he too would sick up. Out of the three of them, only Tieg seemed to be unaffected, though not entirely since his eyes looked red and glossed over.

"I hate to say this, but we'll have to go back in there to be certain Sesha isn't inside. But I don't know how we'll manage with all that blasted smoke," Rovan lamented.

"She's not in there," Tieg stated.

"How can you be certain of that?" Rovan asked.

"Poppium messes with life energy. The enchantress in my village told me that. An apprentice enchantress would never stay in such a place."

"Let's move to the next orphanage, then," Rovan said.

"Rovan, but those kids," Scintilla began.

"I know. But what are we supposed to do? Let them out onto the street?"

It was not what Scintilla had wanted to hear from him, but from her resigned expression, she seemed to know he was right. *At least they have shelter*, Rovan told himself, as if that helped.

Amya, the innkeeper, had told them there was another orphanage northwest of there. The road ahead swam as if Rovan was drunk. The buildings around him were breathing. He focused his attention on his feet, afraid of taking a misstep and falling into a puddle. Next to him, he could hear Scintilla's heaving breath, as if she could not hold enough air. He glanced up at her for just a moment and noticed her hands opening and closing frantically. His own hands felt clammy.

They had only been in contact with the poppium for a short time and yet were already deeply affected. How could people choose to subject themselves to such a thing? And those poor children, who did not even have a choice... Rovan found himself thankful for the rain, which had begun to pick up. Its wet coolness felt soothing to his feverish head.

The other orphanage was in a much nicer neighborhood. The buildings here were cleaner and the streets that cut between them were wider and in good condition. But, as was often the case, this nicer neighborhood was inhabited by a more dismissive breed of folk. The glances their group drew from the people on the street could not have been called friendly. Perhaps it was due to their travel-worn clothing, or, more likely, the inhalation of the poppium had lent them a strange cast. Rovan knew that neither he nor Scintilla would get anywhere with these people, so he asked Tieg to solicit directions from the passersby. Even Tieg, in his surprising lucidity, struggled with this task. Most people simply ignored him or turned away.

After many failures, Tieg eventually managed to learn from an old woman that the orphanage was just around the next bend. As Rovan followed, the poppium mist that had hovered over his head began to lift. Finally, he was feeling like himself, though a slight haze lingered. Scintilla's gait had also resumed its usual confidence. "Better?" he asked her. She nodded and replied, "Better."

The two-story, sandstone orphanage was immediately apparent. This time, light shone from within each window—a sign of the life and activity that should fill an orphanage. Rovan knocked on the door and moved back. When the door opened, a child stood behind it. Her dark stringy hair was cut short around the ear. Dark circles surrounded her eyes, but she otherwise looked well-fed and cared for. She looked up at Rovan without saying so much as a word. "Hello," Rovan greeted. "Is there a grown-up in there?" The child stared dumbly into Rovan's eyes.

Scintilla approached the door and kneeled to the child's eye level. "Do you know a girl named Sesha?" she asked.

"Portia! What did I tell you about opening the door?" a woman's voice called out from within the building. The child quickly retreated down the hall leaving the door wide open in her wake. Scintilla stood as a robust woman reached them and bowed in greeting, her mousy hair pulled up in a disheveled bun. "Apologies, how may I—" At the sight of them, her expression changed from demure to fearful. "What do you want?" she asked, moving the door closed ever so slightly.

"My name is Rovan, and these are my friends, Scintilla and Tieg," Rovan introduced. "We have been hired by a woman to search for her missing daughter. The child is around seven, and her name is Sesha."

The woman shook her head. "There's no one by that name here."

"She could have gone by a different name," Scintilla said. "Do you have a ledger that we may look at?"

"What for?" the woman asked.

"We have a general idea of when she went missing. A list of dates could help us figure out if she's been picked up."

"Picked up?" The woman sounded affronted. "Do you think I prowl the streets looking for children to snatch up? That is not how orphanages work."

"How does it work, then?" Tieg asked, crossing his arms.

"Parents leave their children here when they can't care for them. Or I take in children who come here or are brought by the city guard. But I don't go seeking 'em out. Do you have any idea how many needy children there are? The place is already overflowing as it is…"

"We didn't mean to insinuate anything," Rovan cautioned.

"It's all right," the woman sighed. "I've heard it all before: baby-snatcher, baby-eater, witch... I don't have time to care."

"So, has a girl of around seven come here on her own in the last few months?" Scintilla asked.

The woman frowned, but it seemed to be because she was attempting to recall something. "In truth, yes. There were two such girls. But neither was called... What was it?"

"Sesha," Rovan said.

"No Seshas here."

Tieg took a step forward. "Are these girls still here? Could we ask them questions?"

"I'm afraid I've run out of time to spare, and I must run back inside and care for the children. It's just me running this place, you know?"

"By yourself?" Rovan asked, shocked.

"So long, then," the woman said. But before she could close the door, Rovan called out, "Wait!"

The woman opened the door and narrowed her eyes. "What is it now?"

Rovan sighed, knowing well what must be done. He reached into his hood and produced their coin purse. He handed the purse to the woman, who took it reluctantly. "It's not much, but it's all we have. Could we come in and speak to the children?"

The woman eyed Rovan apprehensively but eventually opened the door fully and allowed them inside. The interior could not be called tidy, but it was at least clean and serviceable as a living space. The stone walls were covered in children's charcoal sketches of large dogs and cats fighting crudely rendered stick people, among other fantastical scenes. The sounds of children playing could be heard emanating from every which way. It was, by all appearances, a happy place. As they followed the woman through the rooms, and up a creaky set of stairs, each child they encountered either froze or fled.

"They don't like strangers," the woman explained.

"Have you been doing this for a long time?" Rovan asked.

"All my life," the woman said. "I was abandoned here as a child, and now I run the place. It might not seem like the most glamorous life, but someone needs to take care of these children."

The woman led them into a room crammed with dozens of beds. A few children were playing within. "Issica, please come here," the woman said. A child with a dark complexion and unkempt black locks faced them. "These people want to speak with you."

"Hello Issica," Rovan said, kneeling in front of the child. "My name is Rovan. I'm looking for a girl. Maybe you know her? Her name is Sesha."

Issica lowered her head, her body tense and nervous. "Are you all right?" Tieg asked.

The child turned to her caretaker. "Don't let them take me! Please!"

Rovan stood and faced the woman. "What does she mean by that?"

The woman's face paled, her eyes darting around the room. "Well, it's just— It's nothing you should concern yourself with."

"Don't worry, we're not going to take you anywhere," Tieg reassured Issica.

"You said there were two children that came around the same time," Scintilla said, moving closer to the woman. "Was the second child taken?"

The woman lowered her gaze. "I... Well, I couldn't..."

"They took Falma!" the child shouted.

"Who took her?" Rovan asked the caretaker.

The woman sighed in resignation. "It was Blue Scarabs. They paid."

"Paid?" Scintilla repeated, startled. "You sell children?"

"No!" the woman blurted out. "I do no such thing. This was the only time. You must understand, that the only support we get comes from the House of the Gods, and it's barely a pittance. No one helps! Just me! The Blue Scarabs could have taken the girl by force, and I couldn't have stopped them. But instead, they offered me gold to take her. They said they'd look after her," she added the last as a means to paint herself in a better light.

Rovan looked away from the woman, not able to bear the guilt that contorted her face. What would he have done in her place?

"Where did they take her?" Scintilla asked in a hard voice.

"I don't know," the woman answered.

"Nor do you seem to care," Rovan muttered under his breath. "There's no telling if this Falma is even who we're looking for. Are there any other orphanages in Vizen we could visit?"

"There is another one just outside the city," the caretaker answered. "The only other one is abandoned."

"Not so abandoned," Scintilla grunted. The woman nodded, obviously aware of the state of the other orphanage.

"Was Falma your friend?" Tieg asked Issica. The child nodded sadly. "Is there anything you can tell us about her? Do you know where she came from, or who her mother was?" Issica shook her head. "We want to make sure she's not in any trouble. Anything you remember could help us find her."

Issica raised her eyes. "She always got sad at night."

"Why was that?" Tieg asked.

"She said it was too quiet in the city. Where she was from, she could always hear the trees singing to her."

XXV.

A Chant of Life

She was pathetically thankful for having been forced to spend the day in the cell since there were only two captive pairs of eyes to witness her crying. When Lyr was finally released to the servants' quarters that evening, she hobbled through the halls, her backside on fire. Even now, tears came to her unbidden from the slightest movement, but she was no longer choking on sobs at least. The pain was only part of it. The utter humiliation of having been caught was the rest.

Her stomach grumbled, but Lyr did not have it in her to seek the kitchens or the servants' hall for a meal. All she wanted was the comfort of her small cot and a few hours of uninterrupted rest away from prying eyes. Dark shadows sliced through the hall floors. Even with her head held low, Lyr could sense the judgment of the passing servants.

She entered her room and sighed, relieved that it was empty. Leandra was most likely still in the kitchens, while Falma and Alizia were likely tidying elsewhere. As she removed her shift over her head, the fabric rasped against her bottom sending fresh stinging jolts up her body. She did not dare wear her bedtime shift—she opened the blanket and entered the bed naked. She lay on her stomach and allowed the coolness of the room to soothe her bare bottom.

Another cry was pried from deep within her. The humiliation she felt extended its reach back home. If she had been caught by anyone other than Dregor, she would have been tortured and interrogated. Her mother could have been implicated. And killed. How could she have been so stupid?

Lyr wasn't sure exactly how long she had been crying and wallowing in self-pity before the door of the room creaked open. "Yulma. Yulma." Alizia whispered in a panicked voice, quickly confirming the room was empty besides the two of them and closing the door firmly behind her. "The anointment has been delayed!" Lyr wiped her face and sniffled deeply but made no move to turn to face the woman. "What's wrong?" Alizia asked.

"It's nothing," Lyr whimpered.

"If it's your monthly, I know Leandra has some rags you can use, and some herbs for the pain," Alizia said.

"What are you talking about?" Lyr grunted as she lifted her head off the pillow and turned to face the woman. On the floor, between the cot and Alizia, was Lyr's shift, dark blood staining its back. Had she been bleeding all the way here? Lyr lowered her face into her pillow and sighed hotly.

"Are you injured?" Alizia asked.

"I did something very stupid," Lyr let out. Alizia stood silently, awaiting Lyr's next words. "I..." Lyr trailed off, biting back more tears of shame. "I got caught in a part of the palace I wasn't supposed to be in. I was punished."

"You..." Alizia whispered. The woman leaned in closer to Lyr. "You didn't say anything, did you?"

"No. I was caught by that knight, Dregor. I still had to be punished by him to not raise suspicion."

"Stupid, stupid girl," Alizia seethed.

"I know! I'm stupid!" Lyr choked. "You don't have to remind me." In truth, part of her wished to be reminded, wished that Alizia would brandish Lyr's failure as a rod of discipline and beat her further with it. Instead, the woman sighed, seemingly in relief. "Unfortunately, that's the least of our problems right now."

"What do you mean?" Lyr asked.

"There is not going to be an anointment ceremony here at the palace. Not for a while at least."

The news was so startling that Lyr momentarily ignored her pain to roll over onto her side. "And what about the wedding?" she asked.

"It will be held in Pallew," Alizia answered.

"Where is that?"

"It's a city to the far east of the kingdom. Princess Arisa has decided to hold the ceremony there instead of here for some reason. It's a last-minute change of schedule, or so it seems."

"What are we going to do? Does Saul know?" Lyr's mind was split between her pain and the panic caused by this news. She suddenly longed to return to her mother and live out the rest of her life as a subjugated peasant.

"I made Saul aware," Alizia replied. "We will all meet tomorrow in the storage room at sunset, like last time. Instead of the ceremony, they will be throwing yet another feast for the nobility the day after next. We can use the commotion of that occasion to slip out of the palace and regroup. We will know more tomorrow."

Slip out of the palace—the words bore into her mind. She actually could return to her life and leave this all behind. But then what would all this pain have been for? She was sharply aware of the fact that she had killed a girl on the very cot she now occupied. Dora's gray-veined face stared accusingly from behind Lyr's closed eyes. Would Lyr be able to contend with what she had done if it was all for nothing?

The door to the room opened and Leandra walked in. Alizia immediately began removing her shift, as if that's what she had been doing all along. "You are well ripe!" Leandra exclaimed, wrinkling her nose.

"Lots of running around today," Alizia replied with a feigned chuckle.

Leandra raised her shift over her head and folded it neatly over her cot. "The nobility will be very active tomorrow. You best wash up."

"Of course," Alizia replied. "Wouldn't want them to smell a real person."

For all her straight-faced propriety, Leandra laughed. "Wouldn't that be something! And you," she said, facing Lyr's back. "I've brought you something for the pain. We will get you properly bandaged in the morning." Lyr didn't have to see the woman's face to sense her concern. Of course, Leandra had already heard about Lyr's punishment. A small bundle of fragrant herbs was deposited onto the bed next to Lyr's head. Leandra remained quiet for a few moments, perhaps expecting Lyr to reply. Eventually, the woman huffed and donned her nightgown.

Alizia shot Lyr a knowing glance as she climbed into her cot. Lyr nodded and then closed her eyes. A long, sleepless night followed. Barbs of pain bit into her backside, sending flashes of white heat traveling up her shoulders and down her legs. She cried silently before finally succumbing to exhaustion. When she finally opened her eyes, Leandra stood over her, gently patting her forehead. The woman's cool hand was a balm on Lyr's feverish skin.

"Let's get you cleaned up for the day," Leandra said quietly.

Lyr attempted to stand, but the pain had settled within her body like a boulder in a river. Leandra reached for Lyr's arm and helped her to her feet. Someone grabbed her other arm to lend her some stability. At first, Lyr assumed it to be Alizia, but then she realized the hands were much smaller. Falma's concern would have touched Lyr deeply had her pain allowed it. The woman and the child helped Lyr redress in her soiled shift—"We'll bring you a new one for after you've bathed," Leandra reassured. Next, Lyr was led to a nearby chamber, where a large tub filled with steaming water sat ready for her. A medicinal, vegetal, smell infused the air. The servants normally washed themselves in a basement bathhouse fed by frigid river water. Leandra had gone out of her way to procure this tub and hot water for Lyr.

"I don't know if I can," Lyr choked. The heat of the steam reminded her of the hot pain she still felt.

"It will burn, but it will be good for you," Leandra said. "The water is infused with marigold."

Lyr allowed herself to be undressed and lowered into the tub. The heat of the water felt like fire on her tender flesh, but it didn't take long for the infusion to soothe her.

"I must go to the kitchens," Leandra said. "Falma will watch over you and help you wash, won't you?" The child nodded emphatically. "There's a towel and clean clothes on the stand over there. When you're done, come find me. You'll have to work today, but I'll make sure you aren't doing anything too taxing. I trust this won't happen again."

Lyr lowered her gaze and nodded in reply. Leandra left the chamber and shut the door behind her. Lyr wasn't sure why, but she had expected more anger or reproach from

Leandra. Instead, she had received care and understanding. Leandra's promptness in pulling together this setup made Lyr wonder just how many times servants were beaten for misbehaving or simply for any reason at all.

Falma reached within the clothes that had been laid out for Lyr and retrieved a bundle, then approached the tub. She placed small objects into the water one by one: a strand of dark hair, a gold ring, and a wriggling spider.

"What are you doing?" Lyr asked, moving back from the drowning spider.

Falma placed her hands on the tub and chanted in a foreign language for some time. The strange monotone was entrancing, causing Lyr to forget about her pain and her worries. She suddenly felt lighter, as if her body was floating inches above the water. Only when the chanting stopped, sometime later, was Lyr's focus returned to the then and now. "What was that?" Lyr asked.

"A Chant of *Life*," Falma replied. "Your back should feel much better."

It wasn't just that the chanting had distracted Lyr from the pain—it had removed it entirely. "How? Without a runestone?" It had been years since Lyr had seen a purple runestone of *Life,* but she had hazy childhood recollections of her parents using them to soothe their patients' discomfort during healing treatments.

"You don't need the runestones if you know the required enchanting ingredients," Falma recited, matter-of-factly. "The hair was mine. The ring and the spider were simple to find in a palace. The water was already in the tub, so that was easy. All I had to do was to release their energies, and the rest was the Cycle."

"You stole that ring?" Lyr asked in a panic, but she shook her head and dropped the subject when Falma only blinked at her in response. "How do you know these things?" Lyr probed.

Falma shrugged. "My mother taught them to me."

"Your mother?" Lyr swallowed. "Falma... Is your mother an enchantress?"

"What were you doing downstairs?" Falma asked suddenly.

Lyr recoiled from the question with a yelped, "What?"

"I wasn't sure at first, but I'm sure of it now. I sensed you down there. Why did you follow me?"

Lyr had been asking herself that question for the greater part of a day and a half. "I don't know," she said dumbly. "I thought you might be in trouble. I wanted to see where you went at night. I was curious. I was... stupid."

"Mother told me it's important to be curious," Falma said. "It's the only path that leads to discovery. But it's also important to not be an idiot."

"That is a skill I seem to lack."

"You still have time to learn it," Falma said.

"What were you doing down there? I saw... I don't know what I saw. Those men. And all that blood..."

Falma shook her head. "We shouldn't talk about that. I don't want to get you in trouble again."

The two remained silent for the remainder of Lyr's bath. Lyr had to be careful when cleaning her wounds—the soothing from the enchantment of *Life* had removed much of their sensitivity and, if she wasn't mindful, she could accidentally reopen them. Once she was done washing, she stood out of the tub and wrapped herself in the soft towel Falma handed to her. Once she was dry, Falma treated her backside with a poultice then bandaged it. She then dressed Lyr in the new shift Leandra had left her. It wasn't as soft as the towel, but at least it was clean.

"I'm off to the kitchens, then," Lyr said.

"Be careful," the girl replied, leaving the chamber and wandering off somewhere before Lyr could thank her.

※ ※ ※ ※

There was a frantic air about the kitchen when Lyr arrived. Flavien was barking complaints at no one in particular—something to do with the lack of "proper onions." Lyr was suddenly uncertain she could last the entire day. As if summoned by her wariness, Leandra appeared at Lyr's side and hurried her into the pantry. Many of the items were in disarray, scattered about the floor, or piled incomprehensibly atop the shelves.

"Has he been in a mood all day?" Lyr asked.

"When is he not in a mood?" Leandra huffed. "Your bottom has already seen its fair share of beatings, so stay out of reach from his wooden spoon. Cooks and kitchen servants will be coming in and out—"

On cue, an old kitchen servant stormed through the door, prodded at his back by Flavien's shouts. He frantically selected a bag of flour and dragged it out of the pantry, leaving a trail of white on the floor.

"Like I was saying," Leandra continued. "Servants will be in and out of the pantry all day to make messes they won't have time to clean." She indicated the streak of flour.

"Understood," Lyr said, anticipating her role there.

"Good. And don't get into any more trouble." Leandra teasingly smacked Lyr's shoulder, then left her alone in the pantry.

The monotony of the work was a balm, at least until the pain in her back began returning in bursts. Focusing on organizing sacks and boxes, sweeping the floor, and rearranging shelves distracted Lyr from her self-pity and the anxiety of the upcoming meeting with her co-conspirators. What would they think of her when they learned how she had nearly fumbled the mission and risked all of their lives? And would Dregor be there? The dread of seeing him again made her clench muscles that immediately screamed in protest.

A distracted servant knocked over a jar of brine, sending it smashing onto the floor. The man shot Lyr an alarmed look, as if the accident had been her fault, then left the pantry in a hurry, carrying out bundles of rosemary. Lyr sighed and kneeled to sweep the shattered jar into a dustpan. Her backside pulsed with hot pain causing her eyes to water.

A few more hours went by before Leandra returned to check on her. The woman handed her a hunk of day-old bread. She sliced a wedge from a wheel of hard cheese with her kitchen knife and handed it to Lyr. "Flavien is still going at it," the woman said. "First it was the onions, now the sauce is too thin. I envy you here, all alone, in peace and quiet." Leandra lingered a moment longer to ensure that Lyr had a few bites of the bread and cheese, then returned to the kitchen once she was satisfied with the amount Lyr had consumed.

Every now and again, Lyr peeked her head out of the pantry into the kitchen—not to watch the rush of activity, but to get a glimpse of the sunlight that entered through the narrow windows. When the light of the sun had deepened enough to lend the kitchen a golden hue, Lyr decided it was time to head to the eastern hall.

It was surprisingly easy to sneak out of the kitchen in the confusion that was transpiring there. Leandra was the only one to notice Lyr, but the woman's glance only breezed by her since she was so busy tending to the cookpots. Flavien's face was red and sweaty, the veins at his temple and neck at a full boil. "What do you mean, you need a moment?" the cook screamed.

"My hands are cramping!" Geren complained, wiping his flour-dusted hands on his apron.

"Out of my sight!" Flavien barked. "I have no need for time-wasters."

Geren scowled, his thick arms tensing. Flavien puffed his chest as if sensing the baker's desire for a fight. Geren turned to the door and left, eyeing Lyr with anger as he did so. Lyr glanced back to see Flavien's relish at the baker's retreat. The cook abruptly clapped his hands as he turned towards another baker. "Move it!" he bellowed.

It took Lyr some effort to catch up with Geren, who was stomping down the hall and cursing under his breath. "If not this mission, then that cook will be the death of me!" Geren fumed.

"He's insufferable," Lyr agreed.

"I do not understand how a man who doesn't know the difference between a tart and a pie has any say in a royal kitchen!"

Lyr allowed her companion to air out his frustrations all the way to the inconspicuous storage room.

"There you are!"

A mixture of longing and shame overtook Lyr upon seeing Saul. He looked even more gaunt and haggard than she had seen him last. He had likely not slept a lick any of the previous nights. From the worry that painted his face, he had heard about Lyr's punishment. But there was something else in his demeanor—panic that had never been there before—that told Lyr that her mistake was the least of their concerns.

Saul touched Lyr's shoulder, then paced to the other side of the cramped space as if he could not stand still. Alizia stood in the corner with her thick arms crossed—a picture of brooding calm that contrasted deeply with Saul. At the other side of the room stood Dregor in a fancy gold-plated suit of armor and red cape. Humiliation inked Lyr's vision. Dregor smiled at her knowingly. Suddenly Lyr could sense an aura of danger about him.

"There's been a sudden change of plans," Saul began without preamble. Lyr tore her eyes away from Dregor and forced her attention back onto Saul. "The wedding will no longer happen here at the palace."

"What!?" Geren exclaimed. "Then why in the Nameless' skulls are we cooking up all that food?" The question seemed to have more to do with Geren's frustrations towards Flavien than with the mission.

"There's still going to be a feast tomorrow, just not for the wedding," Saul said.

"So, what's next for us?" Alizia asked.

"We managed to get a message to the Free Kings, thanks to Dregor. Our plan stays the same. The Queen Regent and Princess Searin will be at the feast, as will many other nobles. As for Princess Arisa and Prince Hovard, they will be in a carriage on the way to Pallew tomorrow, along with the princess' betrothed."

"I have been tasked with escorting them, as I have been named high captain of the King's Guard," Dregor announced. Lyr shivered at the man's calm voice. "It won't be a large convoy, and many of those guarding it are Free Kings infiltrators. We will eliminate the princess and prince, while you deal with the rest of the royal family."

"So, are we still poisoning the wine?" Geren huffed.

Saul nodded. "The queen and princess will lead a toast after which every noble in the hall will take a drink. Our Free Kings comrades will already be on-site to secure the palace after the poison takes effect."

"How will they get in?" Alizia asked.

"It's all taken care of," Dregor dismissed.

"What happens after that? We stay put in the kitchens?" Geren asked.

The question had the effect of accenting Saul's wariness. For a moment, he seemed to have no answer—as if he had not spared a single thought to that part of the plan. It was Dregor who eventually spoke: "Yes. Stay put. Act as if nothing is amiss, and all will go smoothly. If you see guards wearing these around their arm," Dregor held out a white handkerchief, "they are one of us. They have been instructed to look for you escort you out of the palace."

That seemed to placate Geren, though Lyr wasn't so convinced. If anything went wrong with the poisoning of the casks—say, if anyone stole a sip from their cup before the toast—the kitchen servants would be the prime suspects in the matter. Lyr wished to voice her concerns, but the unease she had felt before stilled her tongue. Though the knight had only been covering for her when he beat her, Lyr couldn't justify the strange glee she had sensed in him as he had carried out her punishment.

Soon, the meeting came to an end, and it was time for her and Geren to slip back into the kitchen. Before she could leave, Saul took her aside and looked at her, pained. "I'm sorry," Lyr heard herself say.

"We're so close," Saul said. "Please don't make me regret bringing you here."

A sudden anger rose within her at the words—she had not asked to be mixed up in this business. For as much as she agreed with the Free King's agenda, for as much as she even understood the Free King's agenda, this mission now felt as if it was something that had been inflicted upon her by Saul. It was a danger that she was placed into, not something she had sought out. She found no answer to give to her old friend, so she simply nodded and looked away.

Once the exchange was done, he left her and returned to whatever duties he had to tend to. Lyr couldn't bear being in this place any longer.

A strong hand touched her shoulder. "It will all work out," Alizia said, and, at that moment, Lyr believed her.

XXVI.

Cloth, Dishes, Cutlery...

Rovan realized he should have been feeling hunger pangs, but his stomach still felt closed and unsettled from the poppium. Scintilla was similarly disinterested in food, but they all agreed to return to the inn for a meal and to formulate a plan.

Could this child, Falma, be the one they were searching for? Rovan thought it very likely. But if that was the case, why had the Blue Scarabs taken her?

"So, do we break into the Blue Scarab base?" Scintilla asked. The steaming potato and leek soup in front of her remained largely untouched, as did Rovan's.

"Breaking in is your solution to everything. We could simply knock on the door and ask," Tieg suggested between mouthfuls of broth.

"Ask what?" Scintilla snorted. "*May we have that child that you purchased from the orphanage?*"

Tieg grunted. "And breaking into a base crawling with soldiers is much smarter? How do we know the girl is even there? And how do we know that it's the right girl?"

Rovan spooned the soup into his mouth and tried to muscle it down. "I've been held in a Blue Scarab lodge before. My sister and... a friend managed to gain entry and smuggle me out. But that took a lot of luck that we cannot possibly rely on at this moment."

"We could post ourselves outside the Blue Scarab lodge in shifts and watch until we see a way inside," Tieg suggested.

"But that could take days. Weeks, even!" Scintilla complained.

"It could," Rovan sighed. This task was beginning to resemble the great mountain where their search had begun: large and looming, yet so far from their grasp.

The door to the inn shot open and Adriel stumbled in, her unhooded hair sopping wet from the evening rain. She allowed the door to slam behind her and frantically approached them. Her staff rang loudly against the floorboards along the way. "I know where she is," the enchantress blurted out.

Rovan frowned. "How very nice of you to return after stealing from us."

"This?" Adriel placed the runestone of *Guidance* on the table in front of Rovan. "You can have it back."

"Returning it is not the point. It's that you felt the need to steal it and leave without consulting any of us."

Adriel's face assumed a severe cast. "You all needed rest. I needed to find my daughter." She eyed Scintilla and Tieg dismissively. "May we take this somewhere more private?" Adriel asked.

Rovan narrowed his eyes. "We're all in this together."

Adriel did not like that answer one bit, her face turning frigid. She removed her soaked hood, then took a seat at the table, across from Rovan. The woman remained silent as if awaiting permission to speak—or, rather, as if taunting one of them to break the silence first.

"Do you really expect us to believe you stole the runestone because you care so much about our rest?" Scintilla dared.

Adriel met her gaze but said nothing.

"Let's not kid ourselves," Scintilla continued. "You got what you needed from us and left. You stole that runestone to find the girl on your own. Now you're back because you need us again. Do I have that right?"

A grin tugged at Adriel's lips. "Smart mouth on you," the enchantress said. "Our temporary alliance is a means to an end for both of us. But now that I know where my child is, I can finally take a moment to breathe." Adriel sighed and relaxed her composure. Rovan realized just how tense the woman had been up until that very moment.

"We know where she is too, despite your efforts," Tieg bluffed.

Adriel arched an eyebrow. "Then we shall all head to the royal palace in the morning."

"What do you mean, the palace?" Scintilla asked.

"Seems I was right to underestimate you," Adriel smirked.

"We heard at an orphanage of a child named Falma," Rovan explained, irritated by the enchantress's mockery. "This Falma spoke of singing trees to one of the children there. That sounds a lot like something an apprentice enchantress would describe. The Blue Scarabs paid the headmistress of the orphanage to take the girl with them. We assumed she was being held at their lodge."

"Falma?" Adriel straightened her head and smiled.

"You know that name?" Tieg asked.

"It's the name of Sesha's favorite character from a bedtime story I used to tell her." Her eyes shone with fond reminiscence.

"The Blue Scarabs took her to the palace, then," Scintilla prompted.

"Sounds like it," Rovan agreed. "But what could they want with an apprentice enchantress? And a child, at that?"

Adriel's expression hardened. "Be ready to leave at dawn."

"Ready to leave? What are you talking about?" Scintilla asked, in astonishment,

"We are going to the palace to get my girl," Adriel continued as if it was the most obvious thing.

"But how exactly do you plan on getting in?" Rovan asked.

Adriel stood, placing the bulk of her weight on her staff. "I leave that up to you. Didn't you say you always find a way?" The woman smirked, then headed for the bedroom she was to share with Scintilla.

"That woman is not all there. Will we ever get a straight answer from her?" Scintilla complained.

"Don't count on it," Rovan agreed.

"I'd rather sleep out here than share a room with her."

"So how exactly are we getting into the palace?" Tieg sighed.

Rovan stood. "A very good question I just do not have the willpower to grapple with at the moment."

"The poppium messed you both up," Tieg smirked.

"It's more remarkable that it affected you so little," Scintilla teased.

"Seems I'm just better at handling that sort of thing than either of you."

Rovan bid the two goodnight. He approached the bar and asked for another glass of the barkeep's special mead, which flattered the man into a quite generous pour.

Amya, the innkeeper, took a seat at the bar next to Rovan. "I see Filli's peddling his mead again."

"By request this time," Rovan said, taking a sip.

"Don't start that!" Amya chastised playfully. "Now he'll try to push a glass on every new guest." After a short spurt of laughter, Amya leaned her head in towards Rovan and whispered, "I heard that you need a way into the royal palace."

Rovan met the woman's dark eyes in surprise. "How did you—"

"Next time your companion with the staff suggests moving your conversation to greater privacy, I'd consider it," the woman replied with a coy smile. Rovan felt immensely foolish. "We could help you enter the palace if you're willing to do us a small favor."

"What's the favor?" Rovan asked, intrigued but wary. If Amya's request was as legitimate as she was making it out to be, she shouldn't feel the need to whisper it.

"We have two wagons of supplies that need to be transported into the palace. The guards are already aware of their arrival and will allow them in without issue, as long as they are shown the order papers. One of our drivers pulled out of the job this morning, so we urgently need one more. The wagon needs to be driven inside and parked in the courtyard. No need to unload the cargo. Quite simple, don't you think?"

"So, if I leave the wagon in the courtyard, how am I supposed to get out?"

"You asked for a way in."

"What's the cargo?" Rovan asked reluctantly.

"Feast supplies," Filli whispered. Rovan immediately understood why he let his wife do the covert talking, as the man's whispered voice still boomed and carried across the hall.

"There's to be a feast at the palace in two days," Amya resumed. "We have been hired to provide surplus supplies for the occasion."

"That's great and all," Rovan said. "But you haven't truly answered my question. What sort of supplies?" Terreck's words resonated in his mind—it was time for Rovan to show some discernment.

"Cloth, dishware, cutlery..." Amya answered flatly.

Rovan nodded. Something did not add up. "Two days, you say?"

"Our goods must be delivered tomorrow night," Amya confirmed. "It's a guaranteed way into the palace for you, and a way to complete a job for us. I can tell you now, you won't be able to walk through the front gate otherwise. On a typical day, it would be a miracle to gain entry. But during a feast? Forget it! Help us with this simple task, and you're in."

There was truth in the woman's words. If Sesha was in the palace, she likely needed their help. Time was not on their side. Terreck's words hounded him yet again, like an echo of reason. He had promised to walk away if things became too dangerous. The previous evening, Filli had explained to Rovan that there was a group in the city working to oppose the will of the royals. And now, there was a request to transport supplies into the palace for a feast. Rovan wasn't sure if it was discernment or just awareness of his own penchant for bad luck that told him the two things were connected.

And yet, along with Terreck's voice, he was reminded of Ashe and Alanda's plea. "*Ashe felt now was the right time. That the girl needed her, somehow,*" Alanda had said. If the child had been taken by Blue Scarabs and was being held at the Palace, the woman was right to fear for the girl's wellbeing. He'd seen the ways the Scarabs used enchantresses as mere tools. *Discernment my ass*, he thought to himself. Once again, Rovan found that his mind was made. But if he was going to take this risk, the least he could do was not inflict it upon Tieg and Scintilla. He would have to find a way to exclude them without alarming them.

"Very well," Rovan said. "But please allow me to speak to my companions before committing to this."

Filli smiled and filled his and Rovan's cup with more mead. Rovan sipped the sweet drink and found himself hounded by an incredible tiredness. He bid the couple farewell, then stood and headed for his room.

Within, Rovan found two mounds beneath the covers—Tieg and Scintilla slept soundly, holding one another in a tight embrace. Heat rose in Rovan's face as he quietly closed the door. He felt embarrassed at having caught his friends in such an intimate moment, but under that was another more subtle feeling—a hollowness. He'd felt it before whenever Tieg brought up leaving, or when he pictured the future, a future in which his friends all found places to belong and he continued to wander, alone.

He knew he should be relieved seeing them self-reliant, but it also made him feel superfluous, spare. He told himself all the time how much they needed him, but it was more accurate to say that he needed to feel necessary to them.

They would be angry once they realized he was gone, but they had each other for that.

He rapped lightly on the door to the enchantress' bedroom. The woman cracked it open, a dark suspicion barely concealed by her disheveled locks. "What?" she asked.

"We need to speak," Rovan said.

※ ※ ※ ※

At some point in the night, the fire in the hearth had burned out, and the cold had wasted no time in claiming the space. Someone—one of the two innkeepers most likely—had placed a thick wool blanket over Rovan, to which he was greatly thankful. The chair by the hearth was not the most comfortable place to sleep. But since Tieg and Scintilla were sharing a room, Rovan's other option was to quarter with Mother Adriel, which he flatly refused.

The sounds of a poorly hushed argument had awakened him. At the bar, Filli, Amya, and another man in a soaked cloak bickered quietly. Rovan didn't catch much until Filli spoke in his rumbling baritone. "We will have to make do."

Rovan stood from the chair, a sharp ache traveling across his back all the way to his neck. He vowed to sleep on the floor next time. "This him?" the newcomer asked, finger jabbed at Rovan.

Amya and Filli nodded. The man approached Rovan and stood inches from him, glaring furiously. His angular face was almost as red as his hair, his green eyes as sharp as a blade of grass. "Can I help you?" Rovan asked when the man remained still and staring.

"I don't trust you," the man accused. "I don't know you."

"I don't know you either," Rovan countered. "Am I supposed to?"

The man ignored the question. "How am I supposed to trust you if I don't know you?"

Rovan shifted his eyes towards the bar—Amya seemed embarrassed by the man. "Rob, this is Rovan," she attempted.

"Rovan," Rob grunted. "Stupid name."

Rovan found himself chuckling at that, though it seemed Rob had not intended it as a joke. "So, Rob, I take it you're the other wagon driver," Rovan assumed.

"The name is Robbin, and I don't trust you."

"So you've already said." Rovan grimaced and headed for the bar.

"You can trust Rovan," Filli interjected. "He seems like a very decent sort of... driver."

If they were trying to fool him in some way, Rovan wished they could be less obvious about it. "Must I remind you that this is a favor I have been asked to do?"

"He's right, Rob," Amya said. "We need a third driver. We don't have time to find anyone else."

"Atrew and Isaan are not going to like this," Rob said.

Rovan tapped his fingers on the bar—it was time to ask the question that had been plaguing him since the previous night. "I'm involving myself in Free Kings' business with this, aren't I?"

"Quiet!" Rob shushed. "Don't speak that name aloud, you imbecile."

Rovan ignored the man's protest, turning his question to the two innkeepers. "Cloth, dishware, and cutlery, right?" he challenged. The two seemed uncomfortable by his unspoken accusation. Rovan decided to speak plainly. "What are you really asking me to transport? Weapons? Rebels?"

"Does it matter?" Amya asked. "I thought all you required was a way into the palace. We're not asking you why you need to go in, are we?"

"Yes, but I'd rather know if I am transporting honey or bees into this ursa's den."

Amya sighed and lowered her voice to a whisper. "The reason we have no one else we can trust with this job is because everyone we can trust will already be hiding within those wagons."

"Amya, shut up!" Rob said, pounding his fist onto the bar.

"Do not speak to my wife in that tone, boy," Filli gruffed.

"He needs to know if he's to agree to this. Besides, come tomorrow the entire city will know the Free Kings exist," Amya said.

"Bees, then," Rovan mused. "What are you planning?"

"That is for us to know." Amya reached into her skirt pocket and pulled out a few white strips of cloth. "No harm will befall you or your companions as long as you're wearing these, be assured of that. The palace guard is on our side."

Rovan did not like any of this. It was starting to sound like this group was attempting some sort of coup. An ursa's den? This was more like walking directly into a hangman's noose. So much for his promise to Terreck. But the child, Sesha, was in more danger than he had originally thought. Beyond his reservations, he found himself accepting the offered cloths. "Very well, I will do it. But on one condition."

"What is it?" Filli asked.

"Do not speak a word of this to my friends. I will tell them about this when the time is right."

"Done." Filli uncorked a bottle of his mead and poured three glasses.

"Now hold on a moment!" Rob intoned. "I haven't agreed to anything just yet."

"Drink, you fool!" Filli slammed a glass of mead before each of them, excluding Amya, who appeared to have a great dislike of her husband's homemade liquor.

Rob frowned and narrowed his eyes as he sipped. "Midnight. Be ready." Rovan nodded but did not take a sip—it was too early for him to start drinking.

Rovan had the bad habit of committing thoughtlessly to tasks that he saw as heroic, and his friends had a bad habit of following his lead. This task would be the dumbest and most dangerous he had ever agreed to. And, because of that, he would not put his friends at risk. He would do this alone.

XXVII.

Ser Knott

Servants spilled into the breakfast room in the early morning blue, setting bowls of fruit and cream, plates of fragrant pastries, and a steaming tea kettle onto the table. An old woman drew the curtains, then yelped in startlement at the sight of Searin, who sat across from the unlit fireplace.

"Apologies, my princess," the woman bowed. "I did not see you there."

Searin dismissed the woman with an absentminded nod. She was usually the first to be seated at the breakfast table, but she had never arrived this early before. Thoughts of her sister's betrayal had impeded her from any sleep that night. In the quiet hours of early morning, Searin had made her way down to the breakfast room and sat in the darkness.

She glanced over at the chair she had occupied the day of her father's death and mourned the future that had so thoroughly shattered before her eyes.

As the servants continued setting the table, Searin stood and walked towards the incomplete painting of her brother Hovard. The impression of the boy was much more jovial than Hovard had been as of late. The painter had done a good job—a few embellishments in Hovard's cape and the details of the background were all that remained to finish.

Searin had also posed for her share of portraits when she was Hovard's age. At the time, everyone had assumed she would grow to inherit the throne, so every little change in her physiognomy was meticulously documented by paintings and sketches. All of that changed when she had abdicated to Arisa. Searin didn't care much for portraits, though she had always imagined her next one to depict her in the splendid armor of a high captain.

"He did a good job, didn't he?" Searin turned to find the voice belonged to her sister. Arisa's hair was shiny and freshly braided. Instead of her normal day tunic, she had opted for a fetching yellow gown. Arisa was never on time for breakfast, often still in bed until late into the morning. Searin wondered what had spurred this sudden punctuality and neatness.

Arisa poured some fruit wine from a carafe into a chalice and sipped it. She reacted to Searin's astonishment with an annoying smirk. "I know, I know. Arriving at breakfast so early is a rarity for me. But since I am to leave tomorrow, I wanted some time to speak privately with you about what happened yesterday."

Searin frowned. A myriad of degrading insults formed on her tongue like spears, but she could not find the strength to launch a single one. "Why, Arisa?" was all she managed after several attempts.

Arisa sighed. "I know you have no patience for politics, but you have to understand—"

Searin stomped towards her sister and thrust her index finger into her collarbone. "You made a promise to me, you bitch! I gave the kingdom to you! All you had to do was keep your word."

"Don't be so full of shit, Searin! You gave up the throne for yourself, not for me." Arisa's sudden anger morphed into regret. "I'm sorry, but there's more going on than you can see."

"Then help me see it!"

Arisa stepped away. She sipped on her wine, thoughtfully. "There is some information I have been made aware of that has forced me to change our plans."

This was not what Searin had expected to hear. She collected her outrage, or at least did her best to leash it. "What sort of information?"

"I can't tell you more than that for now. You're going to have to trust me."

Anger returned to Searin like a destructive wave. "I *was* trusting you, and look what it has yielded me. You're not queen yet, and your guard is nowhere in sight. Perhaps I should take back my birthright."

"Spare me the threats, Searin!" Arisa said sternly. "You may want me dead right now but we both know you have no desire for a fiancé. I have a very important place for you in my kingdom. But it won't be as high captain of the King's Guard. Not just yet."

"What will I be then?" Searin fumed. "The spinster princess everyone is too embarrassed to acknowledge?"

"You're not listening to me!" Arisa shouted, slamming her cup onto the table. Fruit wine splashed about, dotting the tablecloth in speckles of purple. "You're the only person I can trust to care for Vizen while I am gone."

"What?" The question came out as a gasp.

"When I travel to Pallew tomorrow morning, I will need my King's Guard to accompany me, including my newly appointed high captain. I'll be leaving the remaining palace guards and knights in your command. Uncle Clavio's job as Prime Regent is to legislate and enact judgment," Arisa explained, as if Searin was unaware of this. "He and the queen must be protected. Think of it like a trial run for the job of high captain. Do this well and no one will question that you earned your appointment when I return."

"So, you still intend to..."

"Make you my high captain? Yes. Just not when I must split my defenses and not when I have the eyes of Pallew to consider. Dregor was a boring choice for high captain, but I need their attention to be solely on me for this trip. I hope you'll pardon my ego," Arisa explained, smiling.

Arisa was right, Searin had never been one for politics. But she had to admit her sister's reasoning was fair. She knew her abdication had been shocking to the kingdom and that her appointment to high captain would cause a similar stir. Perhaps it was too much to add to an already rushed and unexpected anointment. If Searin was to be a good high captain, having the patience for this kind of strategy was necessary. Arisa had blamed her ego mostly for Searin's benefit. There was nothing about this move that wasn't shrewd and pragmatic, but Arisa was still giving her sister room to be angry at her for it. Searin's rage ebbed and allowed room for a feeling of pride towards the future queen.

Searin bowed her head. "The terms are acceptable."

Relief dawned on Arisa's face. "I am glad to hear you say that. I hated the thought of leaving on a sour note. The paperwork for your appointment as interim commander of the palace guard has already been signed by Uncle Clavio. All that is left is for Mother to sign and seal it. It... It hasn't been easy to talk to her lately."

"I know she does not approve of you and Reilyn's match," Searin offered.

"That's only half of it. She worries that I have chosen too quickly and that Uncle Clavio has influenced my decision."

"Well, hasn't he?" Searin asked.

Arisa smiled. "In a way, yes. But I'm also very capable of making my own choices. I've studied my histories, so I know this is the best path forward if we are to win the war on the Red Coast once and for all."

"Win the war?" Searin furrowed her brow. "Didn't you say you wished to use diplomacy to end the war?"

Queen Altima and Hovard entered the room, and it seemed as if the light of the rising sun had suddenly dimmed a touch. Their mother had worn a perennial scowl since the funeral feast, one that poor Hovard had started to mirror. "Good morning, Mother, Hovard," Arisa greeted with a bow.

Hovard took his usual seat, displaying none of his customary cheer and eagerness. Searin's chest hurt at seeing her little brother like this. Leaving the city was perhaps the best thing for him. New scenery could work well to distract him. Searin wondered how their uncle had convinced the queen to allow her son to accompany Arisa to Pallew.

Their mother approached the painting and tilted her head in judgment. "At least he fixed the forehead."

Arisa looked at Searin, then nodded towards their mother. Searin approached the queen and cleared her voice. "Mother, there is a document that is in need of signing."

The queen's eyes remained fixed on the painting. "I'll have the painter finish it, even though, by the time you're back in Vizen, you will most likely need a new one. Don't you think, dear?"

"Yes, Mother," Hovard replied, distantly.

"Mother," Searin called out. Queen Altima turned to face her daughter as if she had heard her for the first time. "About the document?" Searin insisted.

The queen headed for her seat at the breakfast table. "Your uncle had that thing delivered to my chambers this morning. I've barely had enough time to read it."

Arisa took her father's seat at the head of the table. "The document appoints Searin as temporary commander of the palace guard."

"The last thing you asked me to sign stripped me of any relevance," the queen said. "I'm not sure why I'm needed at all, seeing as your uncle is the prime regent now."

"It's a formality," Arisa explained.

The queen smiled bitterly. "A formality," she repeated. "I thought we had done away with formalities when you decided to abandon the palace."

Arisa rolled her eyes. "Must we do this again? I am not abandoning anything. I am solidifying an alliance that is critical for the wellbeing of this kingdom."

"For the continuation of a foolish war, is more like it..."

The argument that ensued was a blur to Searin's senses. Her eyes landed on her brother. Hovard sat quietly, glancing at the empty plate in front of him. Searin found herself unable to bear the pitiful sight. She walked out of the breakfast room and headed for the practice yard—Hovard's sad eyes followed her out.

Only a few guards were sparring in the yard at this early hour. Some servants swept the stone floor of the space with wide-brushed brooms, lifting rolling clouds of dust into the air. High Captain Knott stood beneath a canopy—well, not high captain any longer—hitting a dangling practice dummy with a sword. His swings had a martial precision that came from a lifetime of rigorous training. The man had always been among the most feared in the yard, especially in his youth. She had seen him spar with others and had always been curious about what it would be like to go hand-to-hand with the man.

"Would you prefer a livelier sparring partner?" Searin offered.

Knott lowered the sword and turned to face her. The man's face was hard, each scar and wrinkle carving out the story of his years of service to the throne. He nodded and made room for Searin to select a weapon from the rack. The wooden swords were arranged from the lightest at the top to the heaviest at the bottom. Searin grabbed her usual one—three notches down from the top—noting that Knott had taken the heaviest sword at the bottom.

Searin warmed up her arm and wrist by slicing the sword across the air. "It's been a while since I've seen you in the yard, High Ca—uh, Ser Knott."

Knott smiled, though his eyes remained hard and focused. "It's going to take a while to get used to not having that title. How are you faring?"

"What do you mean?" Searin asked.

"The knights of the King's Guard were very aware that you were to be appointed as high captain. That was the plan, wasn't it? We were all shocked when your sister named Ser Dregor instead of you." Knott shook his head. "Perhaps your sister has a certain preference for how he wields his blade."

Searin frowned. "You best watch your words. Years of being high captain seems to have made you too candid with how you speak of my sister."

"No offense was intended," Knott bowed.

"High Captain Dregor and most of the King's Guard will accompany Arisa to Pallew for the wedding, while I will be appointed commander of the knights and guards who remain behind. I'll be named high captain upon my sister's return."

Searin could not tell if Knott wore a smile or a scowl. "Congratulations are in order, then," the man said. "But if you'll permit me to continue speaking candidly... Your sister may think she has a handle on things, but this whole business reeks of Clavio."

"I always thought you were fond of my uncle," Searin said.

Knott smiled and lunged at her, his huge practice sword leading him like the tip of an arrow.

Searin dodged, then immediately sprung into a counterattack. Knott lifted his sword, his arm bulging under its weight, and parried the counter as if his sword weighed no more than hers. The man's strength had always been remarkable, even now in his middle years.

"You should be wary of your uncle's insatiable lust for power," Knott said, striking once again.

Searin parried the massive blade, its weight pushing her back. She planted her feet and held strong. "Don't most nobles share similar ambitions?" she asked.

"Not like him." Knott slammed Searin back, then swung his sword once again. The tip of Knott's sword brushed against Searin's waist as she sidestepped a moment too late. The hit unbalanced her, causing her to fall back. Knott pointed the tip of his sword towards Searin's throat, but she quickly rolled away and jolted to her feet.

The man continued, "Why do you think he sought the Thaneship of Perimat to begin with? Why do you think he allies himself with the Blue Scarabs, whom your father detested?"

Searin caught her breath. "What do you mean he sought the Thaneship?"

"No, not sought—he *begged* your father for Perimat. And now, I hear your uncle has convinced your sister to continue fighting against the Sazisani, which is..." Knott shook his head. "It's an impossible war to win. The land is treacherous and the Sazisani know it too well. And if that wasn't enough, those savages possess a powerful dark magic we do not understand. But your uncle sees glory where only a meat grinder exists."

Searin resumed a fighting stance, which Knott reciprocated. They stood unmoving as if daring one another to pounce first. Searin decided to break the tension with a rapid barrage of attacks. Knott blocked each one, then quickly countered. They exchanged hit after hit until, finally, Searin noticed a slight, near-imperceptible, opening right after one of Knott's swings. She took it and found herself standing behind Knott, her sword tip pointed at the nape of his neck.

"Very good, my princess," he surrendered. "You've improved much since the last time I saw you spar."

Searin lowered her weapon and did her best not to show how much that compliment meant to her. "Thank you, ser," was all she said. Knott approached the weapon's rack and returned the practice sword to its proper place. "What will you do, now that you are no longer high captain?" she asked.

Knott wiped the sweat from his brow with a distant look. "In truth, I don't know. I've been doing this for most of my life. Perhaps I'll return to my estate down south near Rondhill. Haven't seen my wife in a few years. But what then?" Knott rolled his shoulders and stretched his arms. "Who can say what the days to come will bring? But we must remain vigilant. Challenging times are coming for us all."

The man bowed his head. "Until next time, my princess. Or, I should say, Commander Searin," Knott said, then left the yard.

The fight had energized Searin, but being called "Commander" invigorated her. She headed for the wooden dummy and began practicing her forms. Knott's words of warning echoed through her skull. Ever since her recent conversation with Uncle Clavio, something had shifted in her perception of the man. He had always been very invested in the lives of his nieces and nephew, but his recent involvement in Arisa's rule was concerningly overbearing.

Clavio was well-liked at court, so no one saw any issue with it, but the fact that the man had appeared, after so much time, the same day the king had died was not lost on Searin. It was obvious that the king had inflicted those injuries upon himself. Suspecting her uncle of any foul play felt distasteful. Perhaps Clavio's recent push for power could be reduced to simple opportunism. Really, all of Knott's concerns could be boiled down to that—Clavio's thaneship, his alliance with the Blue Scarabs, his new role as Prime Regent, and now the push for war.

Then why did Searin feel like there was more to all of this—more to her uncle's motives? And why had Clavio lied about being thrust into the Thaneship of Perimat, when Knott claimed he had demanded it?

Swinging a sword always brought Searin soberness and clarity. It would be best to voice these concerns directly with her uncle, instead of wasting time on speculation. Surely, Clavio would never intentionally exclude Searin, the future high captain, from understanding his plans. Working beside him as commander of the palace guard would give them ample time to discuss such things. Searin smiled. Just that morning she had felt so unmoored, rudderless. Now, she found her future still intact, still before her, and, at last, closer than ever before.

XXVIII.

A Rescue in Vizen

It took nearly two hours for them to reach the palace walls. The surrounding squat buildings were in a more decent state than those of the Pleasants, though Rovan was surprised at how subtle the delineation between the poorer city districts and the nicer ones was. Nearly everything in Vizen was built from the same weathered gray stone and seemed in some state of disrepair. The outer palace walls were not on par with even the most pedestrian of Sol Fornian structures as far as beauty was concerned. "*The bigger the city, the greater its problems,*" was a saying he had heard from an Albadonian woodsfolk. Vizen's problems were especially hard to overlook.

The city guard was on high alert that day—clusters of them were gathered around the palace gates. Or, maybe, this was just the palace's normal level of security. Rovan grimaced, thinking about the job he had agreed to do for the Free Kings. If Filli and Amya had been honest about the guards' involvement, there was a chance it could work. But if they had lied, he was a dead man.

Besides the city guard, Rovan had noticed a strangely high number of Blue Scarabs patrolling the neighboring streets. Not quite patrolling as much as strolling. Almost exclusively in pairs, the blue-armored soldiers casually bantered amongst themselves. There was a palpable animosity between the Scarabs and the city guard. Each time one of the pairs of Scarabs ventured too close to the palace walls, the clusters of guards grew tighter and tenser, which the Scarabs seemed to find hilarious.

"How are we supposed to get in?" Scintilla wondered.

"The Cleo is just on the other side of the wall," Tieg began.

"Are you suggesting we swim?" Scintilla asked.

"No. We could take a boat," Tieg countered.

"Ah! So, they won't let people walk in, but sailing in is just fine," Scintilla laughed.

"Well, we can't very well climb *that*," Tieg said, pointing at the walls. "And with the palace being so thickly guarded, I'm all out of ideas."

Rovan sighed and shook his head.

"Are you all right, Rovan?" Tieg asked. "You don't seem like yourself."

"It's nothing," he said. It didn't feel good to lie to his friends. He had suggested they reach the palace wall to see if they could spot a way in, but this was simply a time-wasting diversion. A plan was already in motion for him and the enchantress to infiltrate the palace without Tieg or Scintilla. He was protecting his friends, Rovan convinced himself. They had already survived a *reaverlord* attack and traveled miles of countryside. Things could have gone worse than they had, so Rovan would not take any chances with their safety now.

Tieg and Scintilla shared a concerned look. "About last night," Scintilla began.

"Over here, I think I see something," Rovan exclaimed, pointing at the far edge of the wall, then pacing in that direction. He did not turn to see if the others were following him. What was he doing? He was acting like a panicked child. He was making the right choice for their own good, so why did it also feel like he was betraying them?

"Where are you going?" Scintilla asked, irritated.

Rovan realized he had trudged further than where he had pointed. He stopped, then faced his friends. He expected them to be annoyed, but all he saw on their faces was concern—and that was somehow much worse. He sipped in a few breaths, and said, "I'm sorry."

"What for?" Tieg asked.

He glanced from Tieg to Scintilla, wondering how much to divulge about what he had agreed to do. If the Free Kings were truly attempting a full-scale infiltration of the palace, keeping the information he shared with his friends to the bare minimum was a good idea. "I think it would be best if you both were on your way out of the city and to Tieg's home," he said.

The two stared at him for a long while before anyone spoke. Though both wore confusion, Scintilla's was stained by anger. "What are you talking about?" she asked.

"We always finish what we start. Together," Tieg said.

"Yes, but..." Rovan floundered, unsure of what to say. "I've... We've reached a wall—literally and figuratively. There's no way inside the palace. Not a safe one, at least. I think it's time we walk away before this gets any more dangerous."

Tieg frowned in disappointment. Scintilla scowled. "You're keeping something from us," she accused.

"No," Rovan refuted dumbly. "I just—"

"You are, aren't you?" Tieg asked, taking a step closer to Rovan and inspecting his face, as if he could plainly see the lie.

"All I'm saying is—"

"What is it you're not telling us?"

"Enough!" Rovan exclaimed. Scintilla and Tieg stepped back, recoiling from his outburst. Several guards directed their inquisitive eyes towards them. Rovan shook his head, feeling the heat rise in his face. "You're right. I am keeping something from you, but for good reason. I just need you both to let me do this on my own."

"What did the enchantress say to you?" Scintilla's eyes narrowed.

"The enchantress?"

"Where is she anyways?" Tieg wondered.

"No, no," Rovan waved his hand for emphasis. "This has nothing to do with her. This is all me. And I need you out of this. Please."

Scintilla approached Rovan and, for a moment, he thought she meant to strike him. Instead, she glowered at him, then turned and walked away. Tieg struggled with which expression to wear, settling on something between neutral and a grimace.

"Tieg, you have to understand," Rovan said. "I would tell you what's going on if I could."

"No, I understand," Tieg said, raising his hands in a placating manner. "We're just your burden to protect."

"Tieg, no." Rovan stepped towards his friend, reaching out a supplicant hand.

Tieg backed away, then turned and joined Scintilla. "Don't worry, we'll stop slowing you down now."

Tieg and Scintilla took the path back to the inn, and Rovan decided it was best to give them some space. He chose a different street, a wide one with an inviting air. He got the impression that, on a normal day, the sides of the street would have been lined with merchants and peddlers. He wasn't sure if no one was there due to the rain or if it was still part of the forced mourning for the late king. Besides the occasional city guard or Blue Scarab, the people he did see mingled in small groups and spoke in hushed tones. An old woman glared at him as he walked by. Rovan recognized this creeping feeling of foreboding from his youth in Sol Forne. The citizens sensed something was coming.

Rovan took an alleyway that would lead him towards the inn. Though the rain was more of a mist today, he felt irritatingly damp. The inn's hearth called out to him.

This alleyway was not as cramped as some of the surrounding ones, but it was rather dark, even in the middle of the day. He kept his head high, chest wide, and eyes focused—he did not want to seem like easy prey for pickpockets or other ruffians. The alleyway took a sharp turn left, sending him off-course from the inn. Rovan chastised himself—he should have just taken the route he knew. No one else seemed to be in this area, which couldn't be a good sign.

After an abrupt right turn at the end of the path, Rovan found himself in a small square courtyard encircled by tall, shabby abodes. An old well squatted in the center of the yard, and at the far side was what looked like a small shrine. Rovan approached the shrine—it was built from sanded light wood. Unlit candles consumed to varying heights covered it, as well as small bowls filled with various objects—sewing needles, spent runestones, buttons, locks of hair...

"Please don't touch it," someone pleaded.

Rovan turned with a start to face a person covered in a dark hood from head to toe. A hump on their back forced their head low, making it impossible to see their face.

"What is it?" he asked, indicating the shrine.

"That's all we have left from those we lost," the person implored.

Rovan examined the shrine with new eyes. The wood he now recognized as being from the same pale trees as those that surrounded Pevine. "You're woodsfolk," Rovan said, turning to face the person.

The person's head perked up just enough for Rovan to be able to see the bottom of their face. "I am," they confirmed.

"I've met several woodsfolk," Rovan said. "You're good people. Very neighborly."

"That we are."

"What is a woodsfolk doing in Vizen?" Rovan asked.

The person's head lowered once more. "After the fires, soldiers came to my home in the woods and ordered me to pack my belongings."

"You were a healer."

"Aye," the person continued. "We were rounded up and relocated here by force. They told us it was to ensure our safety, and that we would eventually be able to return to our homes. It's been seven years since. And here we are..."

"Why don't you leave? Albadone isn't too far. Just a two-day journey."

"We would if we could," the person said, raising their arm and rolling up the sleeve of their robe. Upon their right wrist was a brand that read 'NP'. "It means 'No Passage'. We healers are prisoners of this city, never allowed to return to our homes, nor to make a living doing our craft or any other labor. The people of this city call us the Marked and treat us as pariahs."

"But why would they do this?" Rovan asked. "It doesn't make any sense."

The person shook their head. "We've been wondering that ourselves for many years now. Long enough to stop asking. Most people in this city aren't aware that the fires ever even occurred."

"That's..." Words escaped Rovan. His thoughts were suddenly consumed by plans to free these marked healers and lead them out of the city. Must he always make everything about being a hero? "I'm sorry," was all he could say.

The person faced the shrine. "It's all right. If no one else will, at least we remember."

❦ ❦ ❦ ❦

After returning to the inn, Rovan approached the closed bedroom door. Within, he could hear Tieg and Scintilla's animated conversation. Rovan could guess what it was about. His fist hovered near the wood of the door, but he lacked the courage to knock. He instead retreated to a seat at the bar.

Moments later, Tieg and Scintilla left the inn without saying so much as a word to him. Besides their hoods, Rovan noted they had not taken their belongings. They did not intend to leave Vizen just yet.

Unlike the previous days, the inn was popular today. Several patrons surrounded him at the bar, while a pair of old women perched near the fire. Filli stood behind the counter, dispensing drinks and conversing amicably, while Amya was mostly confined to the kitchen, a savory scent emanating from the door there each time it was opened. The minute, skeletal, woman who had warned Rovan of Mother Adriel's escape through the window was out as well, sweeping the floor of the main hall. Rovan had not realized that she was also employed there.

He paused, narrowing his eyes. There, on the woman's right wrist, was a startlingly white scar of the letters "NP." This woman belonged to the same group as the cloaked person he'd encountered coming back from the palace wall—the pariahs known as the Marked. By allowing her presence here, Amya and Filli were likely doing something any other inn owners would think too risky. Rovan couldn't help admiring them for it.

Filli set a glass of mead in front of him. Rovan shook his head. "I'm all right."

"You ready?" Filli asked.

Rovan looked down at the glass and wondered if he truly was. He picked it up and made himself sip the heat within. "I will have to be," he answered.

After he finished his glass, Filli set another one on the bar. Rovan waved it away. First cup for courage, second cup for the reprise—a common bard's saying. When Amya set the plate of roasted hare and mustard greens in front of him, Rovan accepted it graciously, though he could not bring himself to eat any of it. He was nervous. He was sad. He was too many things all at once, and he wished only to find this child and be done with this cursed task entirely.

A tap came on his shoulder. Rovan opened his eyes and turned around. Had he fallen asleep? The tavern was now mostly empty, the hearth staining the place in a honey-orange glow. Amya stood behind him. "What is it?" he asked.

"It's time."

Rovan nodded, stood from the bar, and headed for the hallway. He stopped in front of the room Mother Adriel occupied and then glanced at the door beside it. Maybe he should knock on that door and apologize to his friends, beg for their forgiveness. Say he was a fool to make them feel like he didn't trust them. The crack below the door showed that there was no light within the room. The two were either asleep or gone.

Had he slept through their departure? Had they left without saying goodbye? He couldn't blame them if they had. As always, he was the only one there was to blame.

He rapped on the first door. Mother Adriel walked out and headed into the hall without a word. "Rob is waiting outside," Amya said. "May the gods watch over you."

Outside, they were immediately accosted by Rob. The man's scowl seemed to be a fixture of his prune-like face. "Took you long enough," he complained.

"No reason to prolong the wait any further," Mother Adriel said.

"Who is this?" Rob asked, stepping close to the enchantress.

"If you don't step back, I will bite your nose off, boy," the woman threatened. By her tone, Rovan knew she meant it.

Rob took a step back. "I only agreed to you," he said, pointing at Rovan.

"Things have changed," Rovan explained. "It's both of us or neither."

Every muscle in Rob's face seemed to tense at the same time. The man turned and stomped away, well aware that he could not afford to lose a driver now. It took a moment for Rovan to realize that Rob had intended them to follow. They headed a few blocks south on the adjacent street. Mother Adriel managed to keep her pace equal to Rovan's, though leaning on her staff seemed to cause her more strain than usual. Rob took a right, leading them into an enclosed courtyard where three mule-drawn covered wagons were parked.

"Thought you said it was only one," a woman asked. Rovan did not see her right away in the near-pitch blackness of the yard. The floating red embers of a pipe revealed her round face to him.

"I misspoke," Rob grunted as he climbed atop one of the wagons. "Can we get moving?"

The woman slapped the side of one of the wagons. "This one is yours," she said to them. "Know how to drive?"

"Yes," Rovan replied. In truth, he had only ever driven one carriage before a few years back, and that had been drawn by horses, not mules. There was no sense in telling the truth now. And besides, how different could this be?

"Good," Adriel said. "Because I don't know shit about these animals." The driver actually chuckled at that.

"Let him do the driving, then," the woman replied. "Follow me and you'll be all right." The woman then climbed atop her wagon and gripped the reins.

Rovan climbed into the driver's seat of the wagon he was charged with, then held out his hand for Adriel. The enchantress glanced at it as if he had offered her a rotten fish. After setting her jaw, the enchantress took Rovan's hand

and allowed him to hoist her up. Rovan settled next to the woman and picked up the reins.

Ahead of them, Rob flicked his reins while making a clicking sound with his mouth, and his wagon was on the move. The other driver did the same, her wagon following Rob's closely behind. Rovan imitated them. At first, his two mules only budged a few feet before coming to a halt. After a second go at it, this time with a sharper flick, the mules fell into a steady walk and soon joined in pace with the other two wagons.

Puddles splashed beneath the wagon wheels, reminding Rovan to be thankful that the rain had stopped, at least for the night. Dark clouds hid the stars and the moon, making the midnight hour feel much more vacant and ominous than it usually did. The distant rumbling of thunder cautioned that a storm could surprise them at any time. The slow pace of the wagons emphasized the weight of their load. Rovan pictured armored rebels prepared to take over the palace, then quickly decided to think of anything else.

"Will we sense where she is within the palace?" Rovan asked Adriel. His voice sounded too loud at this strange hour.

The enchantress nodded solemnly. "I have no doubt. We will follow Sesha's essence wherever she may be and retrieve her."

Rovan was not too sure that it would be that easy. They were infiltrating the royal palace after all. Getting in was already a challenge—one that they had been able to circumvent only by a stroke of luck. But getting back out of there, especially with a child who, as far as they knew, was being held captive, could prove even harder. Rovan didn't like relying on luck—it was a fickle thing that took more often than it gave. He much preferred relying on his friends.

Rovan wondered if he'd done the right thing by excluding Scintilla and Tieg from this mission. Sure, he had told himself it was to keep them safe, but after seeing how much it had hurt them, it now felt like the height of selfishness and condescension. They'd be safe, all right. They'd be safe, and they'd hate him, and they'd probably never speak to him again if by some miracle he walked away from all of this alive.

The palace gate soon came into view, tall and imposing. Instead of heading straight for it through the main street, Rob's wagon took a turn into a cramped side alley. The buildings at the wagon's flanks were so close that Rovan feared the wagon would become stuck. After one more turn, a wide gate came into view. Once they reached it, their convoy halted. Rovan stood and craned his neck to see beyond the two wagons ahead of him.

"What's going on?" Adriel asked.

"A guard just approached Rob," Rovan described. "No, two guards. They're talking. I can't tell what's being said, but it doesn't seem—Oh! One of the guards nodded and now they're both heading back to the gate. I think we are in the clear."

"Blessed be the True One," the enchantress sighed. Rovan was surprised—she had given no indication that she had felt any sort of anxiety until now. The enchantress made it easy to forget that she was human like the rest of them.

The guards opened the gate, and the two wagons ahead slowly proceeded through. Rovan clicked his tongue and flicked the reins, joining them. As he passed, the guards sized him up. Rovan kept his eyes on the road ahead, doing his best not to acknowledge the appraising stares.

Bumpy cobblestones made way for a smoothly paved yard where other carriages and wagons were parked. The leading wagons stopped near a wall on the far side of the yard. Rovan followed their example and halted his wagon next to Rob's.

Rob knocked three times on the back of his wagon, then walked over to do the same to Rovan's. "Looks like we made it," Rovan said.

"Not yet," Rob disagreed. "That was the easy part."

Rovan hopped off the wagon, then offered his hand for Adriel to step down. This time, the enchantress refused it, opting for handing him her staff and lowering herself slowly off the side until her feet touched the ground. She held her hand out and Rovan returned the staff to her. "Do you feel her?" Adriel asked.

"Here? I don't think so," Rovan answered. "Do you?"

The woman nodded. "I feel something else, too. A great amount of *life energy* within the depths of this place. It's so large that I cannot comprehend if Sesha is near it or within it."

Rovan nodded as if he understood what that meant, then turned to the pipe-smoking driver, who had approached him. "Thanks for the help," the woman said. "I think it's best if you make yourself scarce unless you want to get caught up in some nasty shit. Oh, and from now on, you should both be wearing those arm bands that were given to you."

Rovan pulled two strips of cloth from his pocket and handed one to Adriel before securing the other around his arm. The enchantress shook her head and stuffed hers into her satchel.

The curtains of Rob's wagon shifted. A man hopped out, and Rovan felt as if he was going to faint at the sight of Leano, the Blue Scarab lieutenant. He had met the man in Sol Forne when he was fifteen. Leano had been a handsome man back then, but time had not been kind to him. Though he retained much of his proud stature, his face had grown gaunt, and his musculature was leaner than Rovan remembered. A lawn of dark hair had grown unevenly atop his head. He also wore the uniform of a palace guard rather than the ornate armor of a Blue Scarab lieutenant. If there had been any doubt that this man was Leano, the gaping hole where his ear had been was confirmation. The unsightly wound had been a parting gift from Vaelin, Rovan's former djinn companion.

Rovan turned to face Adriel, afraid of being recognized by the man. What was he doing here, among these Free Kings rebels? Were the Blue Scarabs somehow involved in their plan? It didn't make sense, and Rovan wanted nothing to do with any of it.

"It's hot as a hearth on a summer's day in there!" Leano complained.

"Comfort was not our aim," Rob explained.

"Of course not. We made it in—that's all that matters!"

Rovan leaned in close to the enchantress. "We have to go. Now."

Adriel seemed to recognize the flash of panic in Rovan's eyes. She pointed towards an unassuming door. "Let's start there." Rovan did not ask why the woman chose that particular door and immediately walked towards it.

"Hold on a moment," Leano said, blocking their path.

Rovan locked eyes with the man and felt suddenly ill.

Leano smiled at him with no recognition. "I just wanted to personally thank you for volunteering to drive the wagon. Your contribution to the Free Kings' cause will not be forgotten."

How could the man not remember Rovan? Had he changed so much in the past six years? Rovan forced himself to return the smile but could not find any words to say. It was Adriel who replied for him. "We're here to find someone," she said. "Helping you was only cursory. Now, if you will excuse us." Adriel grabbed Rovan's sleeve and tugged on it until his eyes broke from Leano's gaze. Rovan could hear Leano exchanging hushed words with the two drivers but could not make out the specifics. He felt the urgent need to turn back and alert Rob and the pipe-smoking woman that a Blue Scarab was in their midst—and not just any Blue Scarab: a lieutenant!

Adriel opened the door and thrust Rovan inside, closing them into a dark hallway. "You know that man?" she asked him.

"He's a high-ranking Blue Scarab," Rovan replied. "I think these Free Kings are in trouble. Their infiltration may be compromised. The Blue Scarabs are not the type to change their ideology so radically, and especially not that one!"

Adriel held up a hand and shushed him. "Banish those thoughts from your heart and focus. Do you feel her?"

It wasn't an easy feat for Rovan to forget that in the yard, just beyond that door, stood a ghost from his past. He closed his eyes, as if the hallway he was in could get any darker and tried to do as the woman said. Something, like the light touch of a crawling insect, caught him by surprise.

"I think I feel something," he said. "But it's so far. It feels like the palace has a heartbeat."

"Yes," the woman said, placing her arm on his shoulder. "Follow the heartbeat. That's where we must go."

Adriel walked ahead, then turned left at a bend in the hallway, her staff hitting the floor as softly as she was able. They encountered no servants or guards as they progressed, which was quite strange. This was the palace—shouldn't there be guards posted everywhere? The only ones they had seen were those at the gate. Something strange was happening that left Rovan feeling a deep sense of foreboding.

The enchantress' hand shot up, halting Rovan. "Do you sense that too?" she asked. "That deep sadness?"

Rovan shifted his focus away from his thoughts, only then realizing that the anguish he was feeling was not his own. Rather, it was reaching him from somewhere nearby. He walked up to a door and placed his hand against it.

"Yes," the enchantress agreed. "Through there."

"Is that really Sesha? This pull feels very powerful," Rovan said.

"My child is strong."

The door was unfortunately locked. "We'll have to find another way," Rovan said.

"There may not be another way. Step aside."

Rovan moved away from the door and the enchantress handed him her staff. She placed her hands on the metal frame surrounding the door handle and closed her eyes. Under her breath, Rovan could hear her uttering a chant. A ghostly red glow began to emanate from her gloves. At first, Rovan wasn't sure if he was simply imagining it. But as the red glow grew brighter, it was obvious the woman was tapping into the essence of *Power* imbued within her gloves.

The door smoked and sizzled beneath her touch until she pried it open.

Adriel fell forward. Rovan caught her and returned her staff. The door frame where the woman had touched was charred and warped from the heat. "You've done that before?" Rovan asked.

"Never," Adriel smirked. "But figuring out unconventional uses for enchantments is the most fun part of my line of work."

Rovan followed the woman inside, pulling the door closed in hopes no one would come this way. It was pitch black inside. Rovan could hear the clicking of Adriel's staff as it probed ahead. "Watch out, there are stairs," she warned.

There was a strangeness to walking down spiraling stairs in the dark that Rovan could not quite describe. A strangeness amplified by the ever-growing sense of anguish and loneliness that was overtaking him. They must have descended three or four floors, though Rovan could not be certain. There didn't seem to be any end in sight until he started to feel warmth caress his face. A faint orange light began to give shape to the stairs. Finally, they reached the bottom floor, which led into a sort of cellar illuminated by a large roaring hearth.

Rovan and Adriel entered the vacant cellar, only then noticing the cell doors that lined the right wall. "True One!" Adriel exclaimed, tentatively nearing one. Rovan could feel despair radiating from within its iron depths. He moved closer to the door, and something inside growled in response.

"Don't get too close, unless you wish to have your arm ripped off," Adriel warned.

"What is that?" he asked. A large shape distinguished itself from the darkness within. Rovan could tell it was big and covered in feathers.

"I don't understand who could do such a thing." Adriel's voice was confused and sorrowful. "This is a *melk*, an Ancient Guardian of Albadone."

Rovan's eyes widened in surprise as he took an instinctive step back.

"We can tell you who did it," a voice said from the other cell.

Rovan and Adriel shared a startled glance, then walked to the opening of the neighboring cage. A person was inside, sitting on the stone floor. Though they too were obscured by darkness, Rovan could see they were dressed in rags. "Who are you?" Adriel asked.

The figure stretched its bony arms. "We are... We are... We *are*."

Adriel wrinkled her mouth in something resembling pity, or disgust. "Don't trust this one," she said. "Its *life energy* is... wrong."

"Have you seen a child here?" Rovan asked, returning to the task at hand. "A little girl around seven years old?"

"We don't see many down here, but yes, a little girl. She comes here often," the prisoner said. Their voice was dry and thin, as if they hadn't had a sip to drink in some time.

"You have seen her?" Adiel said, her interest in the prisoner rekindling.

"Almost every night, the child descends and feeds the *melk*. Never feeds us, though."

"Where is she?" Adriel asked.

"We have to wait for the Master to feed us. But we're always so hungry."

"Where is she?" Adriel repeated, impatience rising in her voice.

The prisoner stared at them through the iron slats, then slowly stood, their frame looking skeletal in the darkness. "We remember you," they said, pointing a bony finger at Rovan. "Before two became one, a part of us met you. It was not so long ago."

Rovan drew closer to the cell door and looked in, but he could not make out the person's face, nor did he recognize their voice. "You must have me mistaken for someone else," Rovan said. "How did you find yourself here?"

"No, no mistake. After two became one, we tried to forge our own path, but then the Scarabs took us. They poked and prodded, sliced, and bled us dry, to figure out what we were and how to best use us. A part of us was a tool once, eager to be used. But not anymore."

"This is useless!" Adriel exclaimed. "Tell us about the girl."

"Easy!" Rovan admonished. As strange as this prisoner was, there was no point in antagonizing them. Adriel's eyes shot daggers at Rovan. He had obviously struck a nerve, but he was beyond caring about the woman's feelings.

Rovan faced the cells and continued his questioning. "These Scarabs, they bring the girl down here?"

"She meets them here," the prisoner answered. "They bring the food for the *melk*, but they fear it and will not come near. The child does not fear the *melk* for she is touched by the True One. Sometimes the Master is here, too. But he never looks like what we remember."

"The Master? Master Eggar?" Rovan asked. He had met the Blue Scarab leader in Sol Forne but had heard that he had been killed when a crazed *mer* destroyed the city's port.

"Yes, and no," the prisoner answered. "He wears many faces. If you saw him today, you would not recognize him from when you met him at the banquet."

Rovan's eyes widened in surprise. "How do you know that?"

"Is this line of questioning necessary?" Adriel scoffed.

"This one is very annoying," the prisoner said. "If you wish to meet the girl, she will descend soon to feed the *melk*. She does so almost every night. But the Scarabs will be here too. You must hide or you will be caught."

Rovan took in the sparse space—beyond the large hearth there was not much else. "If only we could kill that fire, then we could hide in the hearth," Rovan suggested.

"Not a bad idea," Adriel agreed. She reached into her hood and produced a smooth gray stone. Though it looked like it was almost spent, it had the faint shimmer of an active runestone. Adriel tossed it into the fire and chanted a few words in an ancient tongue. The fire glowed green, its light becoming blinding for a moment. Rovan shielded his eyes with his arm until he realized they had been plunged into darkness.

"What was that?" Rovan asked.

The prisoner clapped their hands. "*Transference*! Brilliant!"

"I always keep a runestone of *Transference* on hand," Adriel said. "When attuned, its essence can greatly aid an enchantress' work. But when released, the essence of *Transference* can reduce energies to their base components and scatter them."

Rovan could not deny he was impressed. He stepped into the hearth and was shocked to find it cold to the touch as if the fire had been out for hours. "This will do. At least, until someone decides to light it once more."

"The hearth is always lit. They will be suspicious of it, but we won't say a word," the prisoner assured.

Adriel walked into the hearth and leaned onto her staff. She placed the still-glowing runestone of *Transference* into her bag, returning them to absolute darkness. Rovan focused on the sounds that surrounded him: on the rumbling breathing of the *melk*, and Adriel's similarly ragged breath. It had been obvious to him for a while that the enchantress was straining herself at the edge of her strength. How much longer could the woman hold out? Hopefully until they had freed Sesha and escaped.

Rovan observed the nothingness before him and waited.

※ ※ ※ ※

"What happened to the fire?" a child's voice trickled through the hall.

Rovan opened his eyes. It was hard to tell he had even closed them in the pitch blackness of the strange dungeon. The imprisoned beast let out a deep chirp and the girl nodded as if understanding.

"Who knows why the Master does what he does," the other prisoner said, as if answering something the beast had asked.

"Hush, you!" the child scolded. "I don't wish to speak to you."

"Oh, why not?" the prisoner taunted. "What did we ever do to little Falma?"

"I'm not *allowed* to speak to you," the girl amended. "If the Master finds out—"

A loud click made Rovan's back straighten. After a sound of stones rubbing against each other, a man entered the room through a passage in the wall revealed by a sliver of light. The man faced the hearth and crossed his arms. "Someone was supposed to tend that," he said. The man then approached the child. "It seems there won't be a feeding today."

"But she's hungry!" Sesha argued.

"We're hungry too," the prisoner chimed in, but they were ignored entirely.

"She will be fed soon, don't you worry," the man assuaged. "I need you to stay here until I return."

"Why?" Sesha asked.

"There are things happening in the palace that I do not want you to be involved in. You will be safe here. I will have someone rekindle the hearth fire and bring you some bedding. Is there anything else you require to be comfortable? It might be some time before you will be able to return to your quarters."

The girl huffed. "No."

"Very well," the man said. The man retreated into the passage but left it open to allow some light into the dungeon.

"What am I supposed to do, stuck in here?" Sesha complained.

The *melk* growled in sympathy—Rovan was beginning to recognize its intonations as if they were human speech. He shifted and a half-consumed log tumbled out of the hearth.

The child gasped. "Who's there?"

A million ways to introduce himself spun through Rovan's foggy mind, but it was Adriel who broke the silence. "My child," the woman said, stepping into the shaft of light spilling from the open doorway. "My baby. My Sesha."

Sesha's eyes grew wide in what Rovan could only describe as horror. "No. True One, no!"

"I've come for you, my child," Adriel continued, the fondness in her voice morphing into something Rovan could not quite place.

"Stay away," the girl cried out, rushing towards the *melk*'s cell. The beast stood, filling the entire cramped space. Its feathers bristled like thousands of daggers.

"We must go now before they return. I'll take you home." The nearer the woman got, the further Sesha backed into the cell. The *melk* growled, filling Rovan with savage anger. Why was the girl cowering from her mother? This wasn't right.

"Back away, Adriel!" Rovan called out, stepping out of his hiding place. He was aware that his emotions were being amplified by the *melk's* distress. The enchantress' focus remained on the girl, but Sesha's eyes widened in startlement at the sight of him. "Who are you?" she asked.

"My name is Rovan. I've been hired by your birth mother to find you."

"My... birth mother?" Sesha asked, her eyes darting between him and the enchantress.

"Her name is Ashe," Rovan said. "She's in a town called Pevine waiting for you."

The child seemed unsure of what to make of Rovan's words. "Why are you with her?" she asked, nodding towards Adriel.

"She said she would help me find you," Rovan explained. "Why do you fear her?"

Adriel turned to face him—even though her expression was shrouded in darkness, Rovan could feel the seething anger in it. "Our secrets are our own, Sesha," the woman seethed. "Do not tell this man anything."

"She kills people," Sesha said firmly. "And she tried to kill me."

"Sesha, quiet!" Adriel rushed the girl. The *melk* reached an enormous paw through the cell bars, wrapping the child protectively in its claws. Sesha's eyes were set in determination, taunting the enchantress to see what would happen if she attempted to touch her. Adriel halted and backed away.

"Why did she try to kill you?" Rovan asked the girl, still facing Adriel.

Sesha lowered the collar of her shirt. It was hard to tell in the dim light, but Rovan could see a red scar on the side of the child's neck. "I came home one day. Mother asked me to taste something at her desk. While I had my back turned, she put a knife at my neck. But I was faster than her. I ran and ran until I arrived here."

Rovan remained silent to allow Adriel to defend herself. But the woman held her tongue. Rovan took a quiet step towards the woman just in case she planned to do anything sudden and asked, "Why would you do that?" He didn't doubt the child's words—in his mind, the enchantress seemed entirely capable of such a thing.

"You wouldn't understand," Adriel said, shaking her head.

"Try me."

"This is bigger than you, or Sesha, or myself. You cannot imagine the destruction I am trying to spare you from."

Continuing this line of questioning would not do. Rovan turned to the child, noting the fear in her wide eyes. He regretted leaving his friends behind—Tieg would be offering the child comforting words, while Scintilla would know exactly how to confront the enchantress. Telling them to leave had been a mistake.

"Sesha," he said as gently as he was able. "I can take you out of the palace. Come to Pevine with me. Meet your birth mother—or don't! But I can take you somewhere safe."

"I'm not going anywhere with *her*," Sesha said, pointing at Adriel. "Besides, I can't leave her behind." This time, '*her*' was referring to the *melk*.

"Someone's coming," the prisoner crowed.

Footsteps sounded through the open passage. Rovan grabbed Adriel's arm and dragged her to the far wall near the hearth, away from the light's reach. The wall was pushed open by an armored man carrying a large cloth sack. "Was told to bring these to you," the man said, placing the bundle on the floor. "Pillow, and a few blankets. I've got firewood in the other room. Gonna get the hearth started. It's right chilly in here!"

"Thanks," Sesha said, tentatively.

Rovan could feel the tension in Adriel's posture. Was the woman preparing to do something?

The armored man returned through the secret passage. Adriel shoved Rovan with more strength than he'd realized she possessed, and he went crashing onto the floor. The fall sucked the air out of his lungs. In the darkness of the room, Adriel's gloved hand glowed red.

"What was that?" The armored man walked through the door carrying a log. Adriel dropped her staff and hobbled towards him. The man released the log in confusion and reached for his sword. "Who the—?"

A blinding red light flashed as Adriel's fist collided with the man's chest. The man dropped to the floor a few paces away, grunting and panting as though he could not catch his breath. Adriel grabbed the man's sword and hoisted it, pointing its tip at Rovan. "Take her," she commanded.

"What?" he asked, shaking his head.

Adriel limped towards Rovan and pointed the sword inches from his face. "Stand up and take her. We're getting out of this palace and this cursed city." Each word was strained by her phlegmy and ragged breathing.

Rovan stood slowly, his palms raised. "Adriel, you don't have to resort to this."

"If you can't do this one thing, then I have no use for you." Adriel raised the sword as if to strike.

A metal *click* sounded behind them, followed by the creaking of an iron door. "Hey!" Sesha called out. The deafening screech-like roar that followed did not seem to affect the child. Adriel turned to face the girl, allowing Rovan time to retreat into the other corner of the hall. In Sesha's hands was a jangling ring of keys, which she must have taken from the unconscious guard. Behind the child stood the now freed *melk*, its black eyes fixed on the enchantress.

"I want you to leave me alone," Sesha commanded.

"My child, please..." Adriel whimpered. "You know as well as I that I cannot do that. You're my everything. I need you."

Sesha took a step forward, as did the beast. "Why did you try to kill me?"

Adriel mouthed something tentatively. She glanced at Rovan as if he would offer aid. Or, rather, it seemed like she did not wish to say what she was being compelled to in his presence.

"Mother, speak!" Sesha commanded, the *melk* accenting her words with a deep screech.

The sword clamored to the stone floor as Adriel leaned against the wall for support. "My child, I am dying. I may seem young, but... But this body is withering away from the inside."

"What are you saying?" Sesha asked, her voice lowering to a trickle.

"I've been alive for many, many, centuries, my child. I have survived using the bodies of my apprentices. But each time I perform the ritual of *Transference*—each time I take possession of one of them—my connection to the Cycle grows weaker. And so do I. One can only stay alive for so long before the Cycle catches up to them."

Though he did not quite understand what he was hearing, Rovan could sense the astonishment in Sesha's heavy breathing. He glanced at the sword on the floor near the enchantress, then at the still-open secret passage, weighing his options carefully.

"So, you were going to kill me to take over my body?" Sesha asked.

Adriel nodded. "I am dying, and you are already so powerfully connected to the Cycle of Nature at such a young age. I need your body to stay alive, and to carry out my mission."

"And what mission is that?"

Adriel's voice grew solemn. "There are those in this world that wish to use *life energy* for their own selfish, and destructive, gain. If I don't keep myself alive those who threaten the Cycle will go unchecked. That cannot be allowed. Your life, like those of all my apprentices past, is a necessary sacrifice."

The prisoner spoke. "You are a Remnant: one of those left behind by the elvenfolk who sacrificed their lives in the Great Return. You are the one who broke the Oath. Calthesya: the First Enchantress!"

Adriel faced the prisoner with shock. "How do you know that name?"

"A part of us has been alive for many, many, centuries too."

Adriel studied the dark figure for a moment, before returning her attention to Sesha. "Child, come with me."

The girl balled her fists and stood her ground. "I would rather stay locked in here forever than go anywhere with you."

"Sesha, obey your Mother!" Adriel approached the child, but the *melk* jumped between them, its snarl like the grinding of steel on stone. To her credit, the enchantress did not buckle at the beast's threat. The woman raised a gloved fist and punched the *melk*. When the red flash cleared from Rovan's vision, he saw the *melk* collapse in a daze against the cell doors.

"No!" Sesha screamed.

Adriel struck the girl with her ungloved hand. Sesha fell unconscious to the floor. The enchantress buckled over, panting. "Take her," she said between breaths. It took a moment for Rovan to realize she was talking to him. "Take her!" the woman repeated.

"Are you really going to kill her?" Rovan asked.

"Stupid boy," Adriel spat. "Do as I say!"

Rovan eyed the sword lying on the floor. He lunged towards it and raised it in front of him. His grip was not as tight as it needed to be due to his missing fingers, and he had never been an adept swordsman. But the enchantress did not know that. He pointed the blade at the woman, hoping to seem more confident with it than he felt. "No," he said. "I am going to take the girl, but you are staying right here."

Adriel laughed venomously. "If you take my child from me, I will hunt you down until my last breath. Until I run out of bodies to possess. I will find you, and I will kill you."

Rovan approached the unconscious child, careful to keep the sword between him and the enchantress. He kneeled and scooped up the girl, carefully draping her light body over his shoulder. "Stay here," he commanded.

Adriel smiled and reached her gloved hand out towards the sword and squeezed the blade. The metal sizzled and smoked beneath her grip until it was nothing but a thin lump. Rovan dropped the useless weapon and backed away, towards the secret entrance. "You have underestimated me for the last time, Rovan. Either do as I say or die!"

Suddenly, the enchantress was pulled into the darkness. Adriel's scream was cut short, and all that was left was the *melk*'s violent screech as it wetly tore into the woman's flesh with its beak and claws.

Rovan carried Sesha through the secret passage, quickly sealing the door behind them. The *melk* roared and scratched the wall from the other side which seemed to wake Sesha, who squirmed in his arms. "Let me go!" she yelled. Rovan set her on the floor, and the girl immediately ran towards the wall. "We can't leave her here," she begged. "She's all I have left." The girl was suddenly overtaken by sobs.

"I'm sorry about your mother," Rovan said.

"She was going to kill me." Sesha looked offended by his apology.

"Yes," Rovan replied stupidly. He found himself wishing once again that Scintilla and Tieg could be there.

"We need to free her," the girl insisted. "She will die if she stays down here."

"She... You mean the *melk*?" Rovan asked.

"I was brought here to care for her. We are bonded, like sisters. I don't know how it happened, but it's like we share the same mind. She can't survive away from the forest for much longer. She needs to return to her home. To Albadone."

It seemed Rovan did not have to convince the child to follow him to Pevine, if only for the benefit of the *melk*. But did he trust Sesha's connection to the creature enough to be sure it wouldn't attack him, or anyone else? And, besides, how would they get something so huge out of the palace unseen? Time was running thin. "Do you think you can keep it—*her*, calm?"

Sesha wiped her tears on her sleeve. "Yes," she promised firmly.

It would have to do. Rovan felt around the wall for some sort of latch that would open the secret door. "What are you doing?" Sesha asked.

One of the bricks felt hollow to the touch. He pushed his weight into it, and the secret door *clicked* open a crack. "That!" he exclaimed.

Sesha pushed her weight into the wall, but it barely budged. Rovan helped her, and together they managed to open it. Sesha immediately dashed towards the *melk* and hugged it like an old friend. Though it was dark inside, Rovan placed himself in front of where he knew the enchantress' ruined body lay—it was best if the child did not see. Even so, the smell of blood and death was quite stark.

The *melk* growled at Rovan. "No, no," Sesha said, gently. "He's a friend. Please, do not hurt him. Stay calm. We will get you out of here soon."

A chill ran down Rovan's spine.

"What about us?" the prisoner asked.

Sesha glanced at the cell, then walked over to where she had dropped the ring of keys. Rovan pivoted with her movement, remaining between the girl and Adriel's body the entire time. Sesha walked up to the cell and handed the prisoner the keys.

"We will remember this," the prisoner said warmly.

The sound of a door creaking open made Rovan's blood run cold. Someone had opened the door upstairs that led into the dungeon and was now descending the stairs. Rovan whispered a curse, then faced the others. "Someone is coming," he alerted them. He glanced over at the secret passage, the stone door not opened wide enough for the *melk* to fit through. "Be quiet and lay flat against the wall. It's dark enough that they shouldn't see us."

"Get in there," Sesha told the *melk*, referring to the hearth. The beast entered the cramped space, filling it entirely. Rovan rushed towards the downed guard, grabbed his legs, and dragged him across the hall towards the far wall. The guard was much heavier than he looked, but eventually, Rovan managed to get him into the darkest corner of the dungeon.

Their eyes had grown used to the darkness, so it was difficult to estimate how visible they would be. Rovan hoped that it was dark enough to conceal them all, at least until whoever was descending had gone.

"Keep moving!" a man's distant voice ordered.

XXIX.

INFILTRATORS

Servants chopped vegetables while others carved thick slabs of meat from a large ham. A pair of older women stirred two enormous bubbling cauldrons. Flavien drifted through the chaos, observing and taking occasional spoonfuls of whatever was being prepared. He offered reprimands more liberally than praises. When the head cook approached to try one of the steaming tea cakes Geren had just removed from the oven, the baker swatted at Flavien's hand.

"They need to rest," Geren reproached.

Flavien grabbed one anyway, then immediately dropped it to the floor when it burned his hand. The cook leered at Geren as if the heat of the cake had been some sort of retaliation rather than an expected outcome. Geren puffed his chest out, taunting Flavien to say a word. The cook instead stalked away, rubbing his burned hand.

Lyr raced to sweep the fallen tea cake into a dustpan then moved to the other side of the kitchen where one of the other servants had piled the leaf-like skins of several dozen onions onto the floor. Cleaning an active kitchen involved a lot more movement than the previous day spent tending to the pantry, but Lyr was content with the work if it meant not being bossed around by Flavien. Her backside still stung as if scorched. Shivers of pain clawed up and down her legs at each movement no matter how subtle—although, none of her movements could afford the luxury of subtlety today anyway.

Perhaps later, Falma could perform another soothing chant of *Life* for Lyr. The thought shriveled immediately. That would not be possible. There would be no 'later' for her here. Today was the day their mission would be enacted. If they succeeded, this would be the last time Lyr would ever set foot in the palace kitchens. All she and Geren had to do was poison the celebratory wine cask Flavien had painstakingly selected and set aside for this event in the cellar. Then their part would be complete. The small vial of poison was nestled in her pocket, heavier than anything she had ever carried before.

The news that there would not be a wedding feast had only recently reached the kitchens, but Flavien had decided to treat the preparations for this evening's feast as if they would still occur. Even so, it was obvious by his excessive brusqueness that he was greatly irritated by having the ceremony demoted to just another feast.

"Head!" Leandra called out. Lyr ducked as a tray of roasted carrots zipped over her. Leandra placed the tray onto the table where other servants were dressing porcelain plates with a slathering of deep crimson sauce, then wiped the sweat from her forehead with her sleeve.

"How are you faring?" Leandra asked Lyr.

"Better than you are, it seems," Lyr answered.

"How about we switch?"

Lyr smiled. "Not on my life."

Leandra playfully swatted Lyr's shoulder then reentered the surrounding frenzy, snapping back into the fray like a soldier running into battle. A hand gripped Lyr's arm and dragged her aside. For a moment, Lyr was sure it was Flavien. It was finally her turn to receive his ire. Instead, she found Geren dragging her into the pantry.

"What is it?" Lyr asked, pulling her arm back from the baker's forceful grip.

"My pastries are resting. I don't know if we'll get a better chance than right now."

Bile bubbled in Lyr's stomach. She wished she had not eaten anything that morning. Geren returned the instinctual nod she gave him—each a mirror of the other's horror. "How should we proceed?" Lyr whispered.

"I'll keep watch while you're down there," Geren suggested.

"I don't know if I can climb down. My back is still very sore. Maybe it's best if you go down there."

Beads of sweat freckled Geren's blotchy face. "No," he whimpered. "I cannot. Please, I cannot do it. Standing watch, I can do. But going down there. I can't... I can't do that." Geren reached a shaky hand into the pocket of his apron and produced his vial of poison. He grabbed Lyr's wrist and forced the vial in her hand. "You must. Please, you must!"

"Fine!" Lyr snapped. The baker's sudden cowardice was unseemly. And worse, it was contagious. Lyr's legs shook as she made her way towards the cellar door at the back of the pantry. She lifted the hatch, revealing the ramp that led into the cavernous space below. She glanced back at Geren, then immediately looked away from the man's horrid pallor. "Keep watch," she said. "Don't let anyone in here."

"Yes, yes," the baker replied, his voice stained by desperate relief.

Lyr descended the ramp and quickly paced across the first row of barrels, towards where she knew the cask had been set. But there was nothing there, just the disturbed silt of where it used to sit. She rushed back to Geren.

"What's wrong?" he asked.

"It's not there," Lyr panted.

"What do you mean?"

"The cask. It's gone. They must have already collected it for the feast."

Geren shut his eyes as if he could not bear the sight of her. "It cannot be. Why so soon?"

"Why, no longer matters," Lyr said. "We need to figure out what to do now."

"What to do?" Geren huffed. "There's nothing to do! We've failed, Lyr. It's over." The baker leaned into the pantry door and made to leave.

Lyr gripped the back of the man's shirt, holding him in place. "We have to warn the others."

"Let go!" Geren said, shoving Lyr back, then returning to the kitchen. Lyr watched the door shut behind the man in disbelief. How easily he had given up, and how she wished it would be so simple for her to do the same. But she had to warn Alizia and Saul, and, perhaps, there would still be a way for their plan to be salvaged.

With her heart beating in her throat, Lyr paced across the kitchen with her head low, avoiding cooks and servants alike. She exited into the bustling halls, where still more servants dusted shelves, swept floors, and set the decor in order. Some eyed her apprehensively. Lyr glanced down, realizing that she still wore her kitchen apron. It was clean, as she had not had to deal with any foodstuffs, but it made her stand out. She quickly unlaced the apron and dropped it covertly behind a large potted fern.

Two doorways and a few right turns later, Lyr found herself in the western wing of the palace. The decor grew denser and more opulent. The somber faces of past and current royalty cast their heavy gazes down on her from ornate filigreed gold and silver frames. Gemstone-studded candle holders glittered atop polished wooden dressers inlaid with gold. Multicolored rugs spanned the length of every hall, while the air was choked with dizzying incense that stung Lyr's eyes. Nobles awaiting the evening feast chit-chatted in small clusters. Chirps of laughter and rowdy bellows filled the wide space. The smells, sights, and sounds were enough to make Lyr nauseated.

As she passed the crowd of nobles to head towards the western wing's servants' halls, Lyr yelped in pain as someone pinched her bottom. She turned to witness the preying grins of a group of noblemen. She did not hear the jeer that caused the group to laugh, but she knew she had been the butt of it. All she could do was smile, lower her head, and continue on her way.

The servants' halls of the western wing were not nearly as chaotic as those bordering the kitchens. Here, so close to the nobility, the servants could not raise their voices, as Flavien often did, without being heard. Though these servants did not have to worry about the fickle whims of the boisterous head cook, their proximity to the nobles and royals made their station no more enviable.

Lyr kept her pace quick without alarming the other servants. Her hastening heart and breath did not at all match her mask of calm. She pushed past the pain in her backside, ignoring it as much as she was able, though she could not help but let out infrequent strained grunts of air through her gritted teeth.

She spotted Saul almost instantly, due to how he towered over the rest of the servants. Along with a dozen others, the young man stood behind a table polishing silver plates, cutlery, and serving ware with a cloth in preparation for the feast. His tired eyes were intent on the task as if it was the only thing that mattered to him. He looked even more haggard than he had the previous day.

As she approached the table, Saul's eyes widened in confusion, though he did not pause his work. Lyr leaned in close to him and whispered, "We have a problem."

Saul cleared his throat but said nothing. He finished polishing a fork, placed it in its proper silver box, and then set the cloth on the table with care. Only then did he encircle the table and join Lyr. "Why are you here?" he asked in a thin, low, voice.

"The cask of vintage was collected earlier than we anticipated," Lyr replied.

"What? Why?"

"I don't know. It's not where it ought to be. They must have transported it to the feast hall early this morning."

Saul cursed under his breath. His eyes scanned the space around Lyr's head as if it might contain the answer to this problem. "We knew something like this could happen. We have other options."

Lyr followed Saul's gaze to the row of silver serving pitchers waiting to be polished. "What do you have in mind?" she asked.

Saul took a silver pitcher from a lineup on the table. He dabbed a cloth onto a small canister of oil then used it to polish the surface, and the inside, of the pitcher. His eyes remained on Lyr's as he repeated the motion. He meant to poison the polishing oil. "I will let Zinia know of our change of plans," he said. "Now, go back to the kitchens. You shouldn't be seen here."

"Good luck," Lyr said, extending her hand to him. He took it, accepting the two vials of poison Lyr passed to him in the process. He'd need them more than she did. Saul returned to his polishing task.

On her way back through the western wing, Lyr avoided the clusters of nobles entirely, keeping her head low and her pace quick. Upon reaching the hall that led to the kitchens, a voice called out, "There she is!" Leandra approached her followed by none other than Boggar, the squat man that had led her and her comrades into the palace through the drains. So, the time had come for Lyr to make her escape.

"Yulma, where did you go?" Leandra wondered.

"I was—" Lyr started before being interrupted by Boggar.

"Never mind that," the man said. "Your presence is required elsewhere."

"She's not in trouble, is she?" Leandra asked, in a pleading way that broke Lyr's heart.

"Not at all," Boggar reassured. "That will be all, Leandra."

Concern did not entirely leave the woman's eyes. Leandra examined Lyr in a way that made it clear the woman knew they would not see each other again. "Be good," Leandra said, then she retreated into the kitchens.

"This way." Boggar led Lyr back the way she came, his pace quick and steady.

"Where's Geren?" Lyr asked.

"We already got the baker out of there. Not very smart of you to wander the palace on a day such as this."

"I had to reach Saul," Lyr explained. "When we went to poison the cask of wine, it was gone."

Boggar halted and shot Lyr a tempestuous look. "What are you talking about? Gone? But who—"

"We don't know. It just wasn't there."

"And Saul knows?" Boggar asked.

"Yes. I told him. He has another plan."

Boggar shut his eyes tightly, then resumed his fast walk. "Well, whatever he's got planned, it better work. Otherwise, we're all as good as dead. In here." Boggar held a door open for Lyr. She entered the dark room apprehensively and could barely make out dozens of people in armor within. They all tensed and reached for their weapons before Boggar said, "It's just me. I got the other one."

"Who are they?" Lyr asked.

"Why, they're your comrades," Boggar explained. "The Free Kings, awaiting orders to storm the festivities and secure the palace."

"Secure the palace..." A question that had been nagging at Lyr for some time reared its head. There was no better time than now to get a definite answer. "When the palace is secured, and our mission is complete, what will happen to all the servants?"

"The servants? Don't bother with them," Boggar said, placing a hand on Lyr's shoulder and leading her across the room to where Geren stood. The baker dry-washed his hands while wearing the most nervous scowl Lyr had ever seen on a person. "What I've learned from my years of being among them is that servants will never understand," Boggar resumed. "The gods made them that way. Loyal to a fault. There is no place for them in the world we are forging."

"No place... What do you mean? What do you intend to do to them?" Lyr begged.

"Who cares!" Geren blurted out. "Can we get out of here now?"

Boggar nodded to a guard, who approached the two. "Cerian will escort you out. Though the mission did not quite go as planned, I thank you both for your participation."

While Geren was simply eager to leave, Lyr felt haunted by Boggar's words. Alizia had previously suggested something similar, but now that their revolution was underway, the reality of the woman's words finally set in. What would happen to Leandra if she did not accept the Free Kings' way? Would she be thrown out to the streets? Exiled? Killed? And what about Falma? She hadn't seen the poor child amongst the servants in the halls, or in the kitchens— Lyr hoped the girl was someplace safe.

The guard led Geren and Lyr through several halls. The frenzy in Lyr's mind impeded her from noticing where they were headed until they reached the door through which Lyr had followed Falma only two days before. "Why are we here?" she asked.

The guard pulled the door open and inspected the melted lump of metal where the door handle should have been in confusion. "In here," he said finally after a moment's consideration.

"We shouldn't go down there," Lyr warned. Why would a Free King posing as a palace guard be escorting them here? Something wasn't right. "Geren stop." Lyr grabbed the baker's arm.

"What are you doing? Let go!" The baker shoved out of her grasp.

"There is a dungeon down there. There's a beast there, too."

"A beast? What are you... And how would you know that anyhow?" the baker asked.

The guard's sword slithered out of its sheath. "In," the man said firmly, pointing into the darkness past the door with the tip of the blade.

Even in the dimness of the hallway, the baker's eggshell pallor was unmistakable. The two lowered their heads and walked through the door. The guard closed it behind them, then said, "Keep moving!" Lyr and Geren proceeded down the dark spiral stairs, feeling the ghostly tip of the guard's sword at their backs. The room below was lit only by a sliver of light entering from where a passage in the wall lay open. The dormant hearth was entirely concealed by the darkness—had Lyr not known it was there, she would have assumed it to be a solid wall. The offal smell of decay assaulted her nose. That had not been there the last time she was here—even the guard seemed surprised and put off by it.

"Go," the guard grunted, pulling the passage door wide open.

They found themselves in a sconce-lit storage room. Stacked firewood and a mess of crates lined the far wall, while a well-stocked weapons rack stood near a cramped doorway. Next to the rack was a chest containing pieces of blue-tinted armor. "Is this the way out?" Geren asked, still hopeful that the guard's brusque manner was some sort of misunderstanding. Lyr knew better than that.

A set of booted footsteps paced into the room from the adjacent hallway. The dim light revealed a woman's shiny bald head, and the polished blue armor she wore. "This is them?" the woman asked.

"Yeah," the guard confirmed, removing his helmet. He, too, was bald. "The doors were already open, both upstairs and the passage. What's that about?"

"Don't know," the woman confessed. "Maybe Captain had them kept open to help us move quickly. Doesn't matter. The others are getting ready. Let's get rid of these two."

"Are you sure you don't want to make a show of it? Set an example?" the guard asked.

"Excuse me! What is this about?" Geren called out, his voice quaking in fear. Lyr wanted to add to the protest, but her throat felt dry and tightly sealed. And it would be of no use anyway.

Their captors ignored Geren's words. "Captain Velden said the show we have planned will be plenty," the soldier replied. "Just get rid of these two."

"Here?" the guard asked.

"We'll send someone to clean up later," the other said coldly. "We have to move."

All the work she had done for the Free Kings had been for nothing. It was obvious now that the group had either been discovered long before her foolish mission had even started, or they had been betrayed. How did the Blue Scarabs fit into all this? The Free Kings had infiltrated the palace guard, but had the Blue Scarabs infiltrated the Free Kings?

None of these questions mattered. They would all go unanswered now that she was going to die.

Lyr spared a thought for her mother—the woman had already lost her will to live after her husband's death. Lyr wondered how she would fare after learning of her daughter's equally miserable demise. She had surrendered the quick relief of poison to help Saul, but thankfully these soldiers did not seem interested in interrogating her. Her mother would be safe—Lyr allowed herself that respite.

The guard's eyes grew cold as he faced them. "For the crime of treason against your kingdom, you are both sentenced to die."

"Please, wait a moment!" Geren begged.

The swing was so fast that Lyr had no time to register it. Blood bloomed around Geren's throat, and his head leaned forward until it smacked wetly against the floor. His body followed an instant later. A confused, choked, sob erupted from Lyr's lips. The guard faced her and lifted his sword. Lyr closed her eyes.

The ensuing wet impact made Lyr instinctively reach for her throat. But she didn't feel pain or blood there. She was very much still intact. She opened her eyes.

An enormous creature, like a silver feathered bear, held what remained of the guard's head in its sharp beak. It flicked its head upwards and the guard's decapitated body fell lifelessly to the floor. The beast crunched on the head as if it were no more than a berry.

"Nameless' breath!" the Blue Scarab woman cursed. She unsheathed her sword, which glowed red in the dim room, and entered a fighting stance. The beast turned its attention towards her and charged. The soldier attempted to slice the beast, but the monster had already trampled her. It took the glowing sword in its beak, drinking its red glow until it was extinguished. Then the monster bit down, shattering the sword.

The beast's night-black eye was suddenly upon Lyr.

"Not her!" a child's voice called out. Falma ran into the room, then shoved her face into the creature's silver feathers.

"Falma?" Lyr called out faintly, in disbelief. "What's going on?"

XXX.

A Toast

Servants fastened luggage straps atop the carriages and festooned their interiors with cushions. A royal caravan of this caliber had not been seen since her great-grandmother's journey to Amacore nearly one hundred years ago. Since then, the royals had never left Vizen. Arisa had always made it clear to Searin that her reign would operate differently than her father's. The girl had not yet been anointed, and she was already keeping true to her word.

Six carriages were neatly lined in the front yard of the palace, the horses at their fronts observed their surroundings with disinterest. On their journey to Pallew, Sers Fervon, Staff, and Berenton would ride in the carriage at the front, while the rest of the knights of the King's Guard flanked the convoy on horseback. High Captain Dregor, however, would be occupying the second carriage with Arisa and Hovard. Lord Raylin and his escort would trail them in the following two, while the carriages at the rear transported servants and cargo.

Near the carriages, Clavio and Dregor were conferring quietly. From Dregor's clenched jaw, it appeared Clavio was giving the young man a lecture. '*Keep my niece and nephew safe!*' was no doubt the meat of it—a reminder that, as high captain of the King's Guard, Dregor did not need.

Searin approached the pair, extinguishing their conversation with her presence. Dregor exchanged his usual low bow for a slight nod—now that he was high captain, his new station allowed him that privilege. Clavio wielded his usual disarming smile. "Hello niece," he greeted. "The rains seem to have given us some reprieve today. A blessing from the Nameless, and a harbinger of a good voyage for your sister and brother."

Searin glanced up at the sky still heavily mottled by thick gray clouds, then nodded. "Is there anything I can do to help out here?"

Clavio and Dregor exchanged a strange glance, and Searin was now certain she had intruded in some private matter. Good. "I think we are all set here," Clavio said. "High Captain?" he added.

Dregor scratched his jaw, his eyes bouncing around the yard. "All is in order."

"Very well," Searin confirmed. She remained quiet for an uncomfortable moment, offering either of the men leeway to speak. When neither accepted, she added, "Well, I will go see if my sister needs anything."

"Of course, my princess," Clavio said with a bow, then quickly turned away from her. Dregor's eyes lingered on her before facing Clavio and resuming their conversation.

Searin did not want to admit to herself just how anxious that interaction had made her. It should be her there instead of Dregor, overseeing the caravan and protecting her family. Arisa's reasoning for choosing Dregor was sound, but Searin's instincts still screamed out that this was what she had trained for—had dreamed of doing for so long. She felt the weight of her sword, Vow, more than ever. For the first time, she wondered why she even carried the thing at all. It had been given to her by her uncle in return for the vow to protect her family, always and forever. But now that they were leaving without her, the metal blade felt awkward and useless at her side. Wasted like so many long afternoons of training.

Searin glanced up at the palace and noticed the shadow of a woman standing at one of the windows. Queen Altima did not approve of Arisa's chosen consort but could not publicly oppose it at this stage either. Instead, she was playing the one card at her disposal to express her displeasure—pretending to be too ill to see the caravan off.

Searin sighed. If she could not be there for her siblings, at least she would be there for her mother. The two of them had never had a great relationship, but perhaps that was something Searin could also treat as a proving ground. Relationships were much like dueling, in a way—or all-out warfare, when it came to her mother.

Lord Reilyn and his servants were clustered around the carriage that was to be their transport. Searin thought it appropriate to wish the young lord a good journey, as they would soon become family. "I wish you could join us, my princess," Reilyn replied to her well wishes, though from his tone, Searin was not convinced. The man seemed baffled by her appearance and relieved when she excused herself.

Arisa and Hovard finally entered the yard, followed by Ser Fervon and Ser Staff, their capes catching marvelously in the morning breeze. Searin approached them and smiled. "Good morning," she greeted.

"I wish we could have one more breakfast together before leaving," Arisa lamented. Were nerves getting the better of her?

Searin nodded in agreement. "Everything is in order, thanks to Uncle Clavio and Ser—uh, Captain Dregor. Seems there's no need for me here."

"I can have you load a trunk or two if you need something to do."

"Tempting," Searin chuckled. "But I suppose I have my work cut out for me now that I'm the interim commander of the palace guard."

"I know I leave the city in good hands," Arisa said. "Just don't work yourself ragged."

Searin kneeled before her brother. "And how about you? Are you excited to be on your way?"

Hovard shrugged, his eyes falling to the ground.

"Tell you what, if you promise to behave and have a good time in Pallew, when you return to Vizen I will teach you how to swing a real sword."

The boy's bright eyes gazed into hers. "Really?"

Searin nodded, then stood. "Really. But you have to promise to at least try and enjoy the trip."

"I promise, I will try." Hovard hugged Searin tightly, before heading to the carriage, eager to get the trip over with and receive his reward.

"I'll miss you." Arisa's eyes shined with tears.

Searin reached out and embraced her. It dawned on Searin that she could not recall the last time she had hugged her sister. Being held in return made her feel safe and relaxed as if she could entrust Arisa with anything—even the entire kingdom.

Arisa smiled as she released Searin. She wiped the tears from her cheeks and headed towards the carriage. Before entering, Arisa glanced up at the palace—at the silhouette of their mother, still staining the window. The shadow vanished out of sight, as did Arisa's smile.

Searin could feel the weight of Clavio's presence behind her as he joined in waving the caravan goodbye. The flags atop the carriages unfurled, revealing the Talessi green sparrow on its field of red. The palace gates opened, and the carriages proceeded out, flanked by the three knights on horseback.

"There they go," Clavio sighed. "May the Nameless guide them." After speaking the prayer, her uncle placed his hand on her shoulder. "I think it's best you speak with your mother. Her behavior as of late has been, frankly, inappropriate. The people need to see their queen."

Searin shrugged out of her uncle's touch. "I don't think you've realized this yet, Uncle, but I am not Arisa."

Clavio wore surprise on his face for just a moment, before replacing it with a warm smile. "Of course not," he said, confused at what she was implying. "I would never dream of making that mistake."

"Then you know that I am not as welcome in my mother's chambers as her other daughter."

"Still more welcomed than myself, I'd imagine," Clavio mused, his smile dropping. "I don't wish to push you to do anything, but the queen's behavior must be addressed."

"You've already handpicked my sister's consort and convinced her to resume a war that my father wished to end. Pushing people to do things seems to come naturally to you." Searin said the words with the bland tone of observation but cringed inwardly at how accusatory they sounded. She turned to excuse herself from this horrible conversation, but Clavio reached out and grabbed her arm.

"Searin, you wound me. I... I don't like hearing that is how you see me or what I'm trying to do for the kingdom. I understand how you feel. You lost your father. I lost my only brother. We've both been suddenly thrust into roles that are not what we expected."

When she relaxed her arm, Clavio released it. "Let's be allies in this—friends, even. You are, after all, the interim commander of the palace guard." Clavio reached into his pocket and pulled out a small box, holding it out for Searin to take. "I wanted to wait until the feast this evening to present this to you."

Searin took the light box and opened it. Inside was a golden pin in the shape of a sparrow. "Uncle..."

"Since there's not going to be a wedding this evening, we must still give the palace nobles something to celebrate. I will make your new station public tonight. Your mother will be expected to have rallied from her illness by then."

Searin closed the box and returned it to Clavio. She couldn't stop a small grin from blossoming on her face. "I will speak with Mother," she committed, then returned to the palace.

An air of disappointment thickened each hall. The nobility had all been formally notified that the anointment ceremony would be delayed until after Princess Arisa's wedding in Pallew. Because of the length of the journey there and back, the nobles would have to return to overseeing their lands and then make a second journey to Vizen in several more weeks. They seemed put out at needing to make two long trips for the price of only one dead king. To add insult to injury, only the queen and Searin remained to see them off. The queen they adored, but Searin? She didn't need to see the way they glanced at her to know just how lacking they found her as a spectacle.

Searin headed up the stairs that led to the window where she had spotted her mother. The woman was not there, of course, but her chambers were nearby.

"Is my mother in?" Searin asked the palace guard who stood outside the queen's chambers.

"Yes, my princess," the graying man replied. "But she does not wish to be disturbed."

This would not do. If she was to be a commander to the palace guard, the time had come to assert herself as such. "Step aside. That is an order from your interim commander."

The guard looked at her askance.

"I am to be named to the post at this evening's feast," she clarified.

The man bowed his head. "My prin— Uh... commander," he corrected, before moving away from the door.

Searin entered her mother's chambers. More a cave than a room, Searin thought. The dark, heavy, curtains restricted the light of day from entering within, while a thick fog of incense clogged the air. "Mother?" Searin called out tentatively. There was no immediate reply, but a dark shape lying on the canopied bed came into focus. "What are you doing?" Searin asked.

"Oh," Queen Altima sighed. "You're still here?" Though her voice came at a trickle, it contained just as much malice as it always did when Searin was its recipient.

Searin stomped to the window and forcefully drew the curtains, letting the day invade the room. The light revealed her mother's pallor and sunken eyes—it looked as if she had not slept since Searin last saw her. Her hair was disheveled, and the only nice thing about her appearance was the stale funerary gown she still wore. *Has she taken the thing off at all?* Searin wondered.

"I will fetch some servants to ready you for tonight's feast," Searin stated.

"Why?" Altima asked.

"Because you are the queen regent, and the palace needs to see you," Searin said.

Altima sat up on her cushions and leered at Searin. "You only want me to be there because of your appointment as temporary commander. You don't care at all about me—none of you do. Otherwise, my children wouldn't have left me."

Searin sighed. "I didn't leave you," she countered. No matter how much she did not see eye to eye with her mother, Searin did not enjoy seeing her reduced to this moping husk.

The anger left Altima's eyes, replaced with the most pitiful look Searin had ever seen. "And what am I supposed to do with only you?"

Anger rose within Searin like a flame. She set her jaw and balled her fists, afraid that she would hit her mother. "You will be at the feast," Searin said flatly. The woman lowered her head back on the bed in resignation, appearing to take Searin's words as the order they were intended to be.

Searin stormed from the room and headed gods-knew-where. She wanted desperately to find Zinia and spar a few rounds, but that would not be appropriate today of all days. After finding some servants and ordering them to bathe and dress the queen, she headed for her room to wash up and polish her armor—she resolved to look her best this evening. This was her time to finally be seen by the court as she saw herself. Princess Searin would no longer be the lame horse of the Talessi family, but its strongest representative at the palace in her sister's absence.

After bathing, she decided to spritz herself with a few puffs from an old bottle of perfume her sister had gifted her years ago. Searin was not typically one for scents, but she had always enjoyed the subtle spiciness of this one. It would be good to have something that reminded her of Arisa today. Everything that came after tonight would be to prove to the court—and her sister—that Searin was cut out to be the permanent high captain of the King's Guard.

She lost herself in the routine of oiling her armor and sword, then polishing them with a clean cloth. The task took the better part of an hour. When she donned the armor and the helmet, and affixed Vow to her hip, she finally felt whole. She gazed at herself through the small, seldom used, looking glass that she kept in a drawer and smiled.

※ ※ ※ ※

Unlike the two previous funeral feasts, this one took place in one of the smaller ballrooms of the western wing. This rendered the event much more intimate, which was not a good thing in the least. There was no platform that elevated the royal table above all others and, therefore, a disturbing lack of separation between them and the annoying nobles. No, this was a mingling sort of event, where Searin would be the center of attention, and it could not be over soon enough.

An elongated table covered in hors d'oeuvres divided the room in half. Servants fixed small plates, setting them at the guest tables scattered about. This more intimate setting seemed to confuse or, in a few cases, irritate the guests. By now, they would have all made their preparations to depart. At least some of them were as eager to get this over with as Searin was.

The worst part of the entire ordeal was how alone Searin felt. Sure, her uncle was there. And so was her mother. But she greatly felt the vacancy left by her sister. She missed little Hovard too and wished nothing more than one more chance to accompany him to his chamber and warm his perennially cold feet.

Searin was seated at Clavio's right hand with the queen at his left. Her mother had arrived late, but at least she had arrived. She was dressed in a clean crimson velvet dress dotted with sparkling stones that did well to distract from her haggard visage. Searin had halfway expected the queen to remain locked in her room in some grand defiant gesture. There was a lot Searin could say about her mother, but the woman ultimately did understand the importance of ceremony.

Among the servants buzzing about the tables, Searin spotted Zinia. She seemed worried, her eyes darting this way and that. The ex-mercenary still had a lot to learn about what it meant to be a servant. A servant did not stand out or show concern—a good servant was as useful and inconspicuous as a chair. But Searin did not fault the woman, nor did she wish her to shed away any part of herself. Zinia's earnestness was what made the woman so exciting to begin with.

Searin imagined herself as the high captain, and Zinia standing beside her. Not as a knight, of course. But with her swordsmanship skills, Searin could easily secure a position for her somewhere—perhaps in the palace guard. A command position. Something respectable. As soon as this ordeal was over, Searin would ask her about it. The giddiness she felt at the prospect was strange yet enticing.

Lady Shenna o'Dower, the Minister of Warcraft, approached their table and bowed. She was a handsome woman, though her look was more starkly neat than luxurious—Searin had always respected that about the woman. "My queen, my princess," she greeted. "May I steal the Prime Regent?"

"Steal away," the queen said, waving the back of her hand. "I have no use for him."

"My sister-queen, I know you don't mean that," Clavio said, playfully. Altima did not dignify him with a response, instead choosing to nibble on a stuffed date. Clavio smiled as he stood, then facing Searin, he said, "You should join us."

The minister shot Clavio an alarmed glance. Searin gathered that she was not welcome into whatever this conversation was about, and resolved, for that reason alone, to make herself part of it.

Searin stood and bowed to the queen before following her uncle towards a circle of people at the other end of the room. Searin turned to catch a glance of her mother—though she was still the queen, the woman had never looked more powerless to her than she did now.

The group they joined consisted of Lord Kell Trett, the Minister of Coin, Lord Koren, the Minister of Information, and a sturdy, hairless, old man Searin had never met before. The two ministers eyed Searin with inappropriate distrust, contrasted starkly by the bald man who smiled at her in a grandfatherly way. "Princess," the two said, bowing their heads. The bald man's eyes widened in surprise, as he joined the others in a bow.

"Ah, Captain!" Clavio greeted the older man. "It's been a long while since I had the pleasure of your presence."

"It's a pleasure for me as well, my Thane. Or, I should say, Prime Regent," the man retorted, jovially.

"I am still getting used to the title myself," Clavio mused. "Allow me to introduce my niece, Princess Searin." Then, turning to Searin, he added, "My princess, this is Captain Velden, of the Order of the Blue Scarab."

Searin briefly stared at the man in astonishment. The late king, her father, would have never allowed a Blue Scarab anywhere within the palace, and now here was one of their leaders at her appointment feast. She was aware Clavio would bring change, as would Arisa, but this was quite strange and very fast. Her father had never trusted the Blue Scarabs, no matter how much they had insisted they wished only to enact his will for the betterment of the kingdom.

"The captain and I have known each other for many years," Clavio continued. "I believe he and the Blue Scarabs will be instrumental in bringing about the end of the war at the Red Coast."

"How so?" Searin asked.

The captain smiled. "My princess, one of the reasons this war has been a challenging one is because Hovardom's soldiers are spread too thin. Able-bodied men and women are stationed here in Vizen, or in other cities such as Sol Forne, guarding palaces or city streets. Meanwhile, the bulk of our army is made up of, at best, what the eastern cities can muster or, at worst, mercenary bands that hold no loyalty to the kingdom."

"So, you're sending the Blue Scarabs to fight?" Searin asked.

"That's part of it," Velden replied.

"We will have time to talk about the war in a more appropriate setting," Clavio interrupted. "Now, what did you call me over to discuss? There are announcements that must be made, and this room seems quite impatient for things to begin."

The ministers glanced at one another as if daring each other to speak. "What is it?" Clavio pried.

"My lord," Koren said. "It has come to our attention that the royal carriage has not yet reached the third outpost."

"What do you mean?" Searin asked.

Koren's lip quivered faintly as if Searin's voice caused him great distress. "Since the Blue Scarabs have outposts along the Red Road, Captain Velden has instructed them to relay back to the palace each time the royal convoy passes one of them."

Velden nodded and folded his arms behind his back. "We received word when they passed the first two outposts, about two hours apart from each other. The third outpost is about an hour further south at their pace. We should have already received communication of their arrival but have yet to hear a word."

"Lodging was set up for them in Rondhill for the night," Lord Trett said. "But, even from the greeting party I placed there two days ago, there is no word."

Panic settled in Searin's stomach like ice. Her uncle's face was so still it seemed carved from stone. "We need to make sure that they're all right," Searin said.

"Dispatch Ser Montrose and a dozen men with our swiftest horses." The words had barely left Clavio's mouth before Lady Shenna paced away to set them to action.

It wasn't enough. Searin wanted to leave this cursed feast and ride a horse down the Red Road herself. She should never have allowed her sister and brother to leave without her. Vow hung heavily at her hip.

As if sensing her anxiety, Clavio placed a firm hand on her shoulder. "The knights of the King's Guard are there to protect them," he said. "I trust that they are safe. Perhaps they have stopped before reaching Rondhill due to inclement weather."

"It is possible," Lord Koren agreed. "The rains have rendered the Red Road unpredictable and unstable."

"We should inform Mother," Searin said.

The ministers nodded halfheartedly, though Clavio did not seem to agree. "Why worry her for no reason? It is best if we maintain the semblance of composure throughout the feast and then deal with this later. The matter might resolve itself by the time the feast is over." Clavio turned away from the group and returned to his seat. Searin followed a few paces behind.

Once he reached the table, Clavio raised his hand. Such a simple subtle gesture, but enough to bring servants and nobles alike to a halt. He stood, signaling that his speech was to begin. A line of servants carrying polished silver pitchers of ceremonial wine flowed from a side door and began circulating the room, pouring into each person's cup.

The room quieted as every eye turned to face Clavio. He smiled—the man always did love an audience. "All of you know Princess Arisa is currently on her way to Pallew, escorted by the King's Guard, and accompanied by young

Prince Hovard. Along with her travels Lord Reilyn Azurat, who Princess Arisa has decided to marry. Their union shall be a grand affair overseen by the Thanes Azurat, who apologize that they could not be here with us today due to illness. Upon the happy couple's return, invitations shall be dispatched notifying you all of the date of the anointment.

"While I know this is not the celebration we all were hoping for, it is not without special occasion that we are gathered here tonight." Clavio placed a hand on Searin's back, pushing her gently ahead of himself. "As Prime Regent of this Kingdom, and with the blessing of the Nameless and our illustrious queen, I am today appointing Princess Searin Talessi to the station of Interim Palace Guard Commander. Here, here!"

The crowd erupted in a barrage of cheers. Clavio produced the small box from his pocket, opening it to reveal the sparrow-shaped pin to the audience. That produced even more cheers. Clavio then moved to pin it onto Searin, realizing that there was nowhere to do so on her armor. Clavio took Searin's wrist and placed the pin in her hand. When he moved in for a hug, he whispered in her ear, "Say something, dear. You look a fright."

Searin's face and arms felt cold. The news of the missing caravan had badly shaken her. She needed to leave this place and find her siblings to ensure they were safe. Instead, she was here, accepting this temporary appointment in front of a crowd of people she didn't care about and who didn't even like her.

She scanned the hall for Zinia, hoping that the sight of the woman would settle her—solidify the cold stone floor beneath her feet. She finally spotted the tall servant pouring ceremonial wine from her silver pitcher into the queen's chalice. She was so close. The two locked eyes. In that cold gaze, Searin noted the same hard resolve the woman had possessed during their spars in the yard.

As Searin remained silent, her uncle took over. "My niece is speechless!" he exclaimed gleefully. The crowd laughed. "In that case, let me say a few words more before we raise a toast. My niece, our princess, is both a capable fighter and a level-headed woman. The only thing sharper than her sword is her acumen. The only thing stronger than her fight is her commitment to our kingdom and its people. She shall do us all proud. Please raise your cups in her honor!"

Searin reached for her chalice but, before she could grab it, Clavio's hand lifted it into the air. A simple mistake of distraction.

After a brief bout of cheers, everyone in the hall raised their cups and drank. Searin searched for another cup but found none. She sighed, not even able to savor this small moment supposedly in her honor. She watched as her mother lifted the chalice to her soured lips. Her eyes then drifted back to Zinia, but the servant woman was pacing away, looking at a tall servant man standing at the back of the hall. Searin looked up at her uncle and realized suddenly that he hadn't moved his cup to his lips.

Something was wrong.

"Stop!" Searin yelled as she lunged toward the queen and slapped the half-empty chalice of wine from her hand. The chalice hit the floor, spraying scarlet across the white marble.

The queen stood. "What are you doing, stupid girl?"

"Stop that woman!" Searin called out, pointing towards Zinia. But no one in the hall made a move. Searin unsheathed Vow and made a break for Zinia just as the woman disappeared into the rear servants' passage.

A woman screamed, "The queen!" Searin turned back to face her mother. Altima clawed at her bulging throat. Her face had turned marble-gray. Clavio reached the queen and caught her just before she collapsed into a spasm. "Someone get a chemist!" Clavio exclaimed.

But no one answered. Instead, the hall filled with the sound of quiet choking as the nobles slowly succumbed to the same purpled, gasping, fate as the queen. The sound of it made Searin's knees buckle.

"What... is... this?" someone managed to call out, only to be drowned out by more strangled cries and the thudding of bodies collapsing.

Just then, a group of guards burst into the hall. No, not guards. They wore white arm bands and their swords were pointed ahead of them, at the pile of collapsed bodies still writhing somewhat but growing evermore still as whatever poison took effect. Searin's last grasp on reality snapped as she realized Zinia was amongst them, also armed, her sword aimed squarely at Searin.

"What have you done?" Searin asked under her breath.

"Drop the sword or die!" another intruder barked at Searin. It was clear now that she was one of the only ones who had managed to avoid the tainted wine. Another young noblewoman who was sobbing over the body of what Searin could only assume had been her husband looked up at a group of approaching false guards. She had barely called out, "Please, don't—" before she was run through with one of their blades.

Searin swung Vow at the nearest man. To his credit, the intruder parried once. He wasn't so lucky the second time, taking a heavy hit directly in the ribs. The man dropped his sword and fell to the floor. Zinia held a hand up to the rest, indicating for them to stay back as she stepped in front of Searin and entered a defensive stance.

Searin's eyes stung with tears, but she could not spare the time to wipe them. "Why?" was all she could ask the woman.

"Because the time has come for Hovardom to be free from your kind," Zinia replied.

The doors to the hall burst open and dozens of armed Blue Scarabs poured in, pointing swords and spears at the traitorous intruders. "Free Kings!" a man's voice called out. Searin glanced back, realizing that it was Velden, the Blue Scarab captain, who spoke. "This ends now. Drop your weapons, and you will be taken alive."

Free Kings? Searin had a hazy recollection of hearing that name. It was the rebel group her father had quelled years ago. How could their numbers have grown so vast without the palace realizing it?

The intruders glanced at one another, unsure of how to respond. A broad-shouldered servant raised a fist in the air. "Brothers, Sisters," he shouted. "The queen is dead, but the princess is still alive! If we must die, let us die for the cause!"

A few Free Kings echoed the cry, "For the cause!" as they all lunged to counter the Blue Scarab soldiers.

"Attack!" Velden ordered, and the Scarabs obeyed. Free King after Free King was cut down. These were not trained fighters, although a few appeared skilled enough to hold their own against the Scarabs.

Searin parried Zinia's sudden attack. The woman had taken advantage of Searin's distractedness to launch a full onslaught. Nothing else that happened in the hall mattered, as the two women exchanged a maddening barrage of blows. Not only had Zinia killed her mother—killed so many people—but she had betrayed Searin's trust. Sparring with Zinia had been the only thing that had brought Searin any joy these last few days. That memory soured around the realization that Zinia had never seen her as anything more than a member of the royal family and that she had been preparing to kill her from the first time they'd met—before that, even.

Swings, parries, and thrusts grew more intense, their dance becoming more intricate, the rhythm more complex. For a moment, Searin felt more connected to the woman than she had ever felt with anyone else.

Zinia's sword sliced Searin's hand. Searin felt the hot blood pour, but she did not slow down or hesitate. Zinia smiled, and it seemed as if she was about to say something when an arrow burrowed cleanly into her eye. The woman fell limply to the floor, blood spraying from her head.

"No!" Searin yelled, kneeling to catch the woman. Zinia's eye had already dulled, and her breathing had stopped.

"Are you all right, princess?" someone asked behind her. Searin turned to face a Blue Scarab soldier who carried a crossbow in hand. Zinia's killer. The Scarab had done what was necessary, but Searin would not thank them.

"Yeah," Searin replied weakly. She gently lowered Zinia's head to the floor and stood. She should have felt something about the carnage she faced, but she was numbed with adrenaline. The nobles had all been killed. Every single Free King had chosen death rather than surrender.

Searin walked away from Zinia's body and towards the table she had, only moments ago, occupied. Clavio still cradled her mother's unsightly body, tears staining his face. "Searin, my girl. I'm so sorry," he cried.

XXXI.

Free

Rovan thought he might vomit. He watched as the *melk* pried apart the dead Blue Scarabs' armor with its beak as easily as one would open a cracked walnut. It then devoured the fruit inside. Rovan removed his gaze from the horrific scene, settling it instead on the terrified young woman shaking in front of him. Sweat dampened her blood-drained brow, her eyes wide in shock.

"What's your name?" Rovan asked her.

The woman's focus remained on the beast for a few moments longer, then slid to the nearby body of her decapitated companion—Rovan was certain she was going to faint. He moved in to catch her, but she managed to stay upright.

"Her name is Yulma," Sesha answered for the woman. At the sound of her name, the woman's focus shifted to the child.

"You know her?" Rovan asked.

"She's a servant. We sleep in the same room."

"I'm fine," Yulma said unconvincingly, answering a question none of them had asked. "What is that thing?" she inquired, nodding her head towards the *melk* but not daring to look back at it.

"She's a *melk*," Sesha said. "She won't hurt us."

Something seemed to fall back into place in Yulma's mind. "I have to go!" she blurted out.

"Go where?" Rovan asked.

"My friend! Zinia... she doesn't know we've been compromised—No! We've been betrayed." Yulma's eyes lingered on the beheaded body, then landed somewhere between Sesha and Rovan. Her face hardened. "I need to warn her before it's too late," she said, turning to leave.

"Yulma, stop!" Rovan said. "I take it you're one of those Free Kings, right?"

Yulma paused and turned to face Rovan, her fists clenched tight. "How would you know that?"

"I drove a wagonload of other Free Kings into the palace for whatever you all have planned for today," Rovan explained. "I needed a way into the palace, and your comrades were desperate enough to ask me for help. One of the men in that wagon was a Blue Scarab in disguise. I recognized him from several years ago, though he did not recognize me. I think whatever you plan to warn this Zinia about, well... I think it's already too late for that."

The young woman shook her head, though she seemed to absorb the truth of Rovan's words. "They brought me and Geren down here," she said. "They killed him. They were going to kill me next."

Rovan took a tentative step towards her. "Listen, Yulma. I am going to take Sesha out of the palace now. You should come with us."

"How do you intend to get us out of here?" Yulma asked.

A good question.

"We can ride her," Sesha suggested.

Rovan and Yulma both faced the child in confusion. Sesha nodded towards the *melk*, who had at last finished devouring the remains of the two Scrabs. Its silver feathers and beak were streaked with crimson gore.

"Ride that thing?" Rovan asked, just to be certain.

"She suggested it," Sesha explained. The girl walked towards the *melk* and ran her small hand through its feathers. "She feels much stronger now that she's had something to eat. She says she will carry us out of here safely."

"How do we know it—*she* won't turn on us?" Rovan asked, surprised to be even considering such an outlandish idea.

Sesha folded her arms and frowned. "She won't hurt us," she said, as if that much was obvious.

The *melk* turned its head towards Rovan, taking him in fully with its bright onyx eye. There was an intelligence in its gaze that was entirely unfitting such a monstrous beast. Rovan sensed expectation from the creature, a wordless taunt. When he nodded, Sesha grinned. The child patted the *melk*'s side, and the beast lowered itself to the ground so that Sesha could climb onto its back. When Sesha still struggled to climb atop, Yulma assisted in hoisting her up. The *melk* stood again and Sesha's head nearly brushed the ceiling.

"See?" the child said, giggling.

On the floor, next to one of the mutilated bodies, lay a still-intact sword. He picked it up and felt its weight in his left hand. *Power* coursed through his arm, making the sword feel more like an extension of himself than a separate object. Rovan retrieved its matching scabbard and transferred it to his belt before sheathing the blade. He was not adept at sword fighting but had learned long ago that merely the sight of one could be an effective deterrent.

Rovan analyzed the cramped hallway that led from this room to the rest of the palace. "I don't know if the *melk* can fit through there," he said. "I wonder how they got it inside in the first place."

"We'll use the stairs," Yulma suggested. "The hallways out there were quiet and empty just a bit ago."

"What are we waiting for?" Sesha called out.

The *melk* lowered its body to permit them to climb on as well. Yulma hesitated before hoisting herself up and then scooting closer to Sesha. She grunted through the movement as if her back pained her. Rovan steeled himself and then followed behind her. There was plenty of room for all three, but Rovan was not sure how steady of a ride it would be, especially without any sort of saddle. The *melk*'s body was too wide to be straddled comfortably and its feathers offered little in the way of a handhold. He would have to hold on by squeezing his thighs. Sesha seemed entirely at ease, leaning forward all the way and hugging the *melk*'s neck.

The motion of the beast rising nearly sent Rovan back to the ground. He grabbed onto Yulma, and she did the same with Sesha. If even one of them fell off the ride, they would all go tumbling down together.

"Let's go!" Sesha exclaimed, and the *melk* rushed back into the dark dungeon and then up the stairs, using eyes that were designed to see even in the pitch black. The prisoner, who now stood outside their cell, shouted at their retreating form. "Yes, yes! Be free my sister! True One, be free!" Rovan was too busy holding on for dear life to hear anything more.

The *melk* bounded up the spiral stairs in just a few heartbeats, reaching the doorway above, and then shattering it as it charged through. Stone and debris dusted their heads and shoulders.

The hallway they were thrust into was deserted, though a commotion could be heard somewhere in the distance. "That way," Yulma indicated. "To the western wing."

Before Rovan could question where Yulma was trying to take them, Sesha exclaimed, "Go!" The *melk* galloped through the hall, its dark claws shredding the rugs that ran its length. Rovan could not see where they were headed from behind Yulma's head, but he could hear the shouts of the people they rushed by. He turned back, realizing they had just passed a cluster of very confused Blue Scarab soldiers.

The *melk* smashed through one large doorway, then another, finally halting within a larger, crowded, hall. The space was littered with dead bodies and the trappings of a feast. Beneath his grip, Rovan felt Yulma let out a choked sob and a shudder. Rovan wondered briefly if she had spotted the woman she had wanted so badly to warn amongst the carnage. To his dismay, a group of armored Blue Scarabs approached the *melk* with their blood-splattered weapons drawn.

"Falma!" a man called out. "What are you doing? Dismount at once!"

"Go!" Sesha called out, and the *melk* turned to face the doors they had just entered. On the other side, a row of Blue Scarab soldiers now blocked their retreat.

From this new angle, Rovan could see the nobleman that was calling out for Sesha to descend from the *melk*. Next to that man stood none other than Captain Velden. Though it had been six years since Rovan had seen the man in Sol Forne, his appearance had hardly changed. Even the plain blue suit he wore was the same as Rovan remembered it. He and the captain locked eyes, and something like recognition sparked in the man's gaze.

"We have to leave!" Rovan exclaimed. "Now!"

Blue Scarabs encircled them. Their barked commands mixed dizzyingly. The *melk* screeched, a sound louder than anything Rovan had ever heard. Everyone in the hall covered their ears, including the Scarabs blocking their path. A wave of nausea and exhaustion overtook Rovan. He tightened his grip on Yulma as the beast charged through the soldiers outside the hall, knocking them aside like twigs. The creature then barreled aimlessly through the halls.

"How do we get out of here?" Rovan shouted.

The beast continued its wild sprint, batting down anyone that dared stand in its path until at last it reached a wide set of double doors. The doors were thick slabs of carved wood and were bolted with iron facets. Rovan's concerns about their sturdiness died in his throat as he braced himself for impact. The *melk* clawed through the doors, shredding them with the ease of a cat clawing through leaves. There must be powerful magic within those claws, Rovan realized—something strong enough to turn even solid stone into little more than parchment beneath their touch.

They found themselves in an open courtyard. A cool rain drizzled lazily atop their heads. Half a dozen soldiers rushed into the yard behind them, pointing their swords and spears at them, and yelling for them to descend from the beast.

Another deafening screech erupted from the *melk* and echoed across the yard. This time, the wave of *life energy* emitted from the beast hit Rovan in the gut like a punch. The guards stepped away in fearful unison. The *melk* took the opportunity to charge at one of the walls that enclosed the yard. "Stop! Stop!" Yulma yelled. But before they could slam directly into the wall, the *melk* leaped upwards. It felt to Rovan as if they were suddenly flying. He opened his eyes, not realizing he had shut them, just in time to see—and feel—the beast's strong-taloned legs meet the wall. The *melk* sunk its claws into the stone and climbed it in two bounds, reaching the parapet in an instant.

Rovan's relief was short-lived. Arrows now fell along with the rain, hitting the stone floor around them. Archers stationed on the adjacent walls fired at them with increasing speed. An arrow struck the *melk* in the shoulder. The creature shrieked as red bloomed among its silver feathers like a ruddy sunset over the sea. Rovan reached for his own shoulder as the beast's pain echoed within him. More arrows whizzed by, coming dangerously close to their heads.

Sesha said something unintelligible to the *melk*, who instantly began running the length of the wall. Rovan and Yulma screamed. "Hold on tight," Sesha called out to them both. And then they were flying once more, weightless against the thin clouds. A thread of sunlight peeked through the cover just then and glittered against the slick rooftops of the city. The sight was dazzling for the few seconds Rovan was able to take it in. Then, they slammed into the nearest roof. The impact sent Rovan's teeth clattering.

The *melk* leaped again to another rooftop, a much shorter distance this time. It continued this pace—running across each roof before leaping to the next—as they made their way south, towards the main gates of the city. Rovan glanced at the streets below as they flew from one tiled roof to another. They were overflowing with armed Blue Scarabs. Rovan had not seen this many of them since the battle at the port of Sol Forne.

The *melk* bounded directly into the street below. It rushed through the nearest gathering of Blue Scarabs, sending them scattering. "Where do we go?" Yulma asked. It was much harder to get their bearings from the ground.

"Do you know how to reach the gate from here?" Rovan exclaimed.

Yulma nodded and began giving Sesha directions, which the girl then relayed to the *melk*.

They squeezed through narrow alleyways and then materialized into an open courtyard, catching a large collection of Scarabs there off-guard. To their credit, the astonished soldiers found their courage and began closing in, weapons drawn. One of them, an extraordinarily tall man, stepped forward and swung his sword hotly at the *melk's* head. The *melk* backed away, then raised itself on its hind legs to avoid the blow.

Rovan only realized he had fallen off the *melk* when he hit the cobblestones. The impact caused him to bite the inside of his cheek, the metallic taste of blood overtaking his mouth. The *melk* stomped on the tall soldier with both its paws, then shredded into the remains with its claws.

"Are you all right?" Yulma called down to him. Sesha and the *melk* had not noticed he had fallen.

Around them, more and more Scarabs were closing in. "Get her out of here. Out of the city!" Rovan yelled.

"What about you?" Yulma asked.

"I will find you!"

Yulma nodded and gripped tighter onto Sesha. The girl's voice rang through the street, urging the *melk* to "Go!"

The beast screeched once more before rushing away, causing many of the soldiers to cover their ears. Rovan braced himself for another wave of dismay. Instead, he found a strange sense of resolve coursing through him. The feeling was akin to that of the essence of *Power* rising up his arm when he held the enchanted sword. Had the *melk* given him this strength on purpose? He would ponder on it later—right now, he needed to escape.

He ran in the opposite direction as the *melk*, taking advantage of the fact that the beast had drawn away all the pursuing soldiers. He did his best to remain hidden in the darkest alleyways, even though he had no idea where he was headed beyond the general sense that he needed to move south—toward the city gates.

Behind him, he could sense that he was being followed. Whoever it was, they were not calling out to him or making much noise at all. He took a right turn and found himself at a dead end. "Shit," he cursed grimly. Rovan pushed and pulled on each door lining the alleyway to no avail. There was no way out—he was trapped.

"Stop right there!" someone called out.

Rovan turned to face the mouth of the alleyway, where two Blue Scarabs stood, swords at the ready. They would not kill him right away—maybe wound him, if he was lucky. Rovan couldn't very well pretend he was just another Vizenian peasant while carrying an enchanted sword. If he was captured, Rovan would be jailed and questioned. He did not know for certain what that would entail, nor did he wish to find out.

"Keep your arms raised and stand still," one of the two Scarabs ordered.

Rovan obeyed. What else was there to do? The two soldiers approached him cautiously, their swords ready to strike should they need to.

One of the Scarabs gripped him by the arm. "Where have your companions gone?" he asked. "Where has that monster taken them?" the other barked at the same time.

So, they'd been following him since he fell from the *melk*. So much for being inconspicuous. "I've got nothing to say to either of you," Rovan said. A momentary inspiration made him add, "But I'm willing to speak directly to Captain Velden."

The two soldiers glanced at one another. "How do you know that name?"

"Because I know the man and can tell you he'll be quite disappointed if he learns I was captured and not brought straight to him." Rovan knew this bluff was a long shot and that, at best, it would only delay his questioning. At worst, he had just made himself seem more valuable as a prisoner.

"What do we do?" one Scarab asked the other.

"We'll take him to the lodge," the other replied. "We can ask the captain about him later."

The two soldiers began tugging him away. One moved to remove the sword at Rovan's belt. "Isn't this one of ours?" he asked in confusion as his hand grazed the pommel.

Something bounced off the armor of the Scarab holding Rovan's arm with a metallic *ting*. The three glanced to the ground in unison at the arrow that had landed there. "What the—?"

Another arrow lodged itself into the man's cheek, its red tip protruding from the side of his neck. The Scarab released Rovan and reached for his face, letting out a strained whine.

Rovan glanced up at the building at the end of the alleyway. Atop it, the figure of a woman reloaded a bow with a fresh arrow. It was too far to make out her face, but that mess of hair was unmistakable. Scintilla shot a third arrow at the other Scarab. The man ducked as it whizzed just above his head, then ran for cover behind another building. The wounded man held his face delicately as if it would fall off if he removed his hands. The side of his neck let out wet pulses of blood in time with his heartbeat.

"Run!" Scintilla yelled from the rooftop, as she notched a fourth arrow.

Rovan bolted out of the alleyway, leaving the wounded Scarab to whimper alone.

"No you don't!" the other Scarab snarled as Rovan ran past him. The soldier grabbed Rovan's arm and shoved him to the ground. He landed heavily, scraping his elbow on the cobblestones.

Rovan quickly unsheathed the sword he had taken from the cell and pointed it up at the Scarab who now loomed over him. The essence of *Power* coursed from the length of the blade down into his arm. Warm needles of pain and pleasure electrified his body.

The Scarab swung his sword, aiming to maim Rovan at the shoulder. Rovan managed to parry and to keep a firm grip on his weapon. The essence of *Power* lent him strength he did not naturally have—or perhaps, it accentuated the little that was already there. Rovan was not entirely certain how it worked. Either way, he felt strong, powerful, and confident enough to rise to his feet and push back against the Scarab's next swing.

The man frowned deeply and readied another blow, but, before it could land, the man was struck from behind with a large plank of wood. The soldier fell forward, knocked cleanly out by the impact. Behind him stood a panting Tieg.

"Let's go!" Tieg yelled, running off into the streets.

Rovan sheathed the sword—the moment he released its pommel, the essence of *Power* left him. He felt weariness overtake him, the pain in his elbow raw and hot. But there was no time to dwell on it. He fled, trusting that Tieg knew where he was leading them. Each time they saw a Blue Scarab or a city guard, they hid as well as they could.

Before long, they had found their way back to the Pleasants district, where the Blue Scarab presence appeared much lighter than near the palace. They paused in front of the inn they had occupied to catch their breath.

Scintilla reached them moments later. "No one is following us, but we must leave the city immediately."

"How did you two know where to find me?" Rovan asked, still incredulous to be seeing them both.

"Just because you ditched us doesn't mean we didn't keep an eye on you," Scintilla huffed.

"And thank the True One we did!" Tieg added.

Rovan lowered his head, ashamed by how he had snuck away that night without so much as a word to either of them. His friends had saved him even after he had abandoned them. He knew he should thank them, but the words felt entirely too small for the gratitude he felt. "I found the girl," he said at last.

"She was the one riding that... thing?" Tieg asked.

"What was that monster?" Scintilla added.

"And where's the enchantress?"

The barrage of questions was dizzying. "Let's get out of the city first, then I'll answer everything," Rovan assured.

"Very well. We have much more to discuss," Scintilla promised darkly.

"Our bundles are packed and waiting in the alleyway behind the inn," Tieg explained.

"Why not keep them inside?" Rovan asked. "The room should still be paid for."

Scintilla and Tieg exchanged a grave look. "We'll explain on the way," Tieg said. "But we're certain that you were set up to fail whatever favor they had asked of you."

"What do you mean?" Rovan asked.

"Those innkeepers," Tieg said. "They're working with the Blue Scarabs."

XXXII.

A Dead Woman

Lyr's hair whipped wildly as the *melk* rushed her and Falma towards the city gates. She blinked tears out of her eyes. Though her body was careening through the streets of Vizen, her mind was still inside the room they had barged into back at the palace.

Among the dead bodies that lined the floor of that hall, Lyr had spotted Saul. The man was unmistakable in his large size, his servants' clothes stained by blood emanating from large gashes at his chest and stomach. She had spotted Alizia's body next, only a few paces away. An arrow to the eye. It would have been instant and painless, Lyr told herself. Another hot tear was wiped instantly away by the wind as they barreled rapidly forward.

Rovan, the man who had helped them escape, had mentioned that Blue Scarabs were hiding amongst the Free Kings infiltrators. How long had the Scarabs known about their plan? The face of every Free King she had met flashed before her eyes, each now seeming a plausible informant.

There was only one person whose fate mattered to her now. Lyr hoped that her mother was safe. Lyr would be presumed dead as far as anyone would know. Her mother would be told she was amongst those lying on the floor of the bloody feast hall Lyr couldn't bear to keep recalling. And the worst part was, it had almost been true.

A line of Blue Scarab soldiers was collected at the gates to turn away anyone who wanted to enter or exit. They entered a triangle formation and lowered their spears preparing to confront the *melk*. Instead, the beast leaped into the air, clearing them easily, and landing, bone-jarringly, several paces away on the other side of the gate. The *melk* raced onwards, not pausing for Lyr to recover either her breath or her grip.

Urstway, the foregate town, was not deserted as the streets of Vizen had been. At the sight of the *melk*, groups of people scattered in every which way, screaming in terror. A group of guards shouted after them, but the *melk* was simply too fast as it sprinted into the edge of the woods beyond the city. There, the *melk* finally halted its run, approaching a tree and clawing at its trunk in what Lyr could only describe as glee. The *melk* raised itself on its hind legs, seemingly forgetting that it held two passengers and causing Lyr to fall back on the soggy ground, Falma on top of her.

"What a ride!" the child giggled.

"That was... something," Lyr said as she stood. Her backside felt worse than it had the morning after she had received the beating from Dregor.

Once the *melk* was satisfied with having shredded the bark from the tree, it rubbed its back on it, its leg spasming in delight.

"I've never seen her so happy," Falma said in awe. "This is where she is meant to be, not inside some enchanted cage."

"I need to go, Falma," Lyr said.

"Sesha," the girl corrected. "My real name is Sesha."

Lyr attempted a smile. "Lyr. That's *my* real name. It's... nice to finally meet you, I guess." Sesha returned the grin. "I need to go back inside the city."

"Are you sure? Those blue guys didn't seem like they were letting people through."

"I'll figure that out," Lyr said. "But I need to go back to make sure that my mother is safe." At those words, the child's smile faded. The girl wasn't tearful, but her sudden frown held a wealth of sorrow. Lyr approached the girl and hugged her tightly. The child hugged her back, sighing into her chest. "I'll be back soon," Lyr assured. "Will you be all right out here on your own?"

Sesha nodded, her head still pressed into Lyr. "I'm not alone."

Lyr released the hug and ran her hand across the child's hair. "Of course, you aren't," she said. "Don't venture too far. But if soldiers come close, hop on her back and flee."

"Flee where?" Sesha asked.

"Away, as far as you can," Lyr said. "But only if they pursue you. Otherwise, I'll try to be back shortly."

Sesha hugged Lyr once more, then sat on the ground to watch as the *melk* rolled back and forth in a puddle of mud. The creature was marvelous, Lyr had to admit—equal parts beautiful and terrifying. She had heard from other Albadonians living in the Pleasants about the legendary creatures and how they were rumored to have returned right before the onset of the great fire. As a child, Lyr had assumed this was little more than colorful storytelling. But now...

Lyr had not realized just how far into the woods the *melk* had taken them. She had to cover quite a distance before returning to the foregate. A large gathering of people had coalesced on the Red Road. They appeared to be complaining to the guards. Lyr caught some of what they were saying and pieced together that the onlookers were accusing the guards of not doing their jobs by refusing to follow the *melk* into the woods. The guards argued in return that their job was to defend the city gate, not to hunt monsters.

A fight between the peasants and the city guard was on the brink of breaking out. No one paid any mind to the young woman who walked out of the thicket. Lyr easily slipped through the fray and headed towards the inner gates. There, a swell of angry peasants pushed against a line of Blue Scarabs that were telling them to turn back. "But there's a monster out there!" "You have to let us in!"

Lyr squeezed to the front then made a break for it through the line of Scarabs. Hands reached for her, but she was faster. The calls of the Scarabs behind her were engulfed by the rush of the crowd—whatever tension had been simmering there, Lyr's escape had just pushed it to a boil.

Lyr continued to run until she was certain no one was following. There were more people out on the streets now, although the Scarab soldiers were commanding anyone they saw to return inside. Like in Urstway, the conversations here centered on the sightings of a strange beast that had galloped through the city streets carrying people on its back. Those who hadn't witnessed it treated these recountings with disbelief.

Lyr rushed past them all, plunging deeper into the city, deeper into the Pleasants. Even here, there was a sense of unease. The omnipresence of Blue Scarab patrols sent its own message that something was occurring. She walked by her home. The thatch roof had collapsed even further within the shoddy hut—it would not be easy to repair.

She continued north to *Chanter's Cove*, the inn where she would find her mother. As she turned the corner, Lyr halted at the sight of Blue Scarabs skittering in and out of the inn. Lyr reminded herself that they couldn't have any way of knowing who she was or what she had done at the palace. She managed a natural gait as she approached the inn, though she could not help the *griffon's* talon she felt squeezing her heart. Had the Blue Scarabs found out that Amya and Filli were also members of the Free Kings? Had they already taken them away for questioning? What about her mother?

A Blue Scarab soldier eyed her passively. Lyr gave her an uncomfortable smile, which the soldier did not reciprocate. The soldier returned her attention to the steaming cup of tea she held. Inside the inn was a scene Lyr would have never imagined in this place: a pair of blue armored soldiers stood in front of the fire, warming their hands, while another three sat at the bar, talking with Filli. A cup of tea steamed gently in front of each of them. The barkeep said something in his deep, loud voice, and the three Scarabs laughed.

An arm gripped Lyr's and suddenly she was being dragged into the kitchen. She spun, preparing to knock a fist into whoever was on the other side of that firm grip but stopped short when she saw tears glittering in Amya's eyes. The woman encircled her in an embrace before Lyr could speak.

"You're alive," the woman choked out.

The disbelief in Amya's tone turned Lyr's guts to ice. This woman had known Lyr and her companions were going to be killed. The reason behind the presence of the Blue

Scarabs at the inn clicked into place. Lyr shoved the woman away with all her strength.

"I'm so sorry, my dear." Tears streamed down the woman's cheeks. "We had no choice but to work with them."

"You betrayed us. You... sent me—us—there to die," Lyr said, her voice choked by rage.

Amya lowered her eyes in shame. "We had lost everything in Pevine. They told us we could have this inn if—"

"I don't want to hear your putrid excuses!" Lyr snapped. "Where is my mother?"

"In the room next door," Amya answered in a thin voice. She held her hands in front of herself as if Lyr would strike her. Lyr considered obliging.

"I need to see her," Lyr said, turning around.

"She can stay here. We will take good care of her," Amya promised.

"I know you will." Lyr turned back and grabbed a fistful of the woman's mousey brown hair. The fear in Amya's eyes only inflamed Lyr further. "You will make my mother as comfortable as a queen from here on out. You wanted to make me a dead woman, and, as far as anyone else will know, you succeeded. I have nothing left to lose which means the only thing keeping me from wringing your throat right now is your usefulness to me as her caretaker."

Amya was barely breathing as the truth of Lyr's threat sunk in. Lyr released her and turned away, no longer able to bear the woman's terrified stare. "I will need coin," Lyr demanded.

Amya nodded cautiously, as if Lyr was a wild animal and moving too quickly might spook her. Amya rushed to the other side of the room, then returned with a small leather pouch, which she handed to Lyr. "Take all of it. Please." The woman's pleading tone begged for atonement she would never receive from Lyr.

Lyr snatched the weighty pouch and placed it in her pocket, then rushed out of the kitchen and back into the main hall of the tavern. On her way to the front door, she caught Filli's startled gaze. It seemed as if the man wanted to call out to her, but he held his tongue. She proceeded out of the inn and passed the disinterested Blue Scarab soldier at the door.

Her body vibrated with unspent violence. Images of Saul, Alizia, and Geren's bloody bodies flooded her mind. Dora's bulging purple face too—the girl she had murdered for no reason. The Free Kings had more than failed—the entire group had been a farce, and Lyr their stupid puppet. They had shown her just enough to whet her appetite for change, given her a new way of conceiving how a city could run—how Hovardom could run. They had exploited her and everyone else's dissatisfaction with their current circumstances, just like they had exploited her father. Lyr felt pathetic, small, insignificant. Had her father also felt this foolish—this used—before he was killed?

Lyr ensured that no one saw her encircling the inn by way of the alleyway at its side. She counted out the windows there until she reached the room her mother occupied. The window was shuttered. Lyr knocked on it softly. A few silent moments went by before it was opened. Her mother stood on the other side. Her gaping stare made her dark eyes huge against her pale, gaunt face. "Lyr?" the woman called out.

At the sound of her own name, Lyr was flooded with more longing than she had ever felt in her life. She reached out her hand, and her mother took it into her cold grasp. Tears filled Lyr's eyes. "Momma, I'm so sorry," she said.

"I prayed to the True One that you would be safe, and I have been heard," the woman said.

Lyr smiled as she reached into her pocket and pulled out the coin pouch, handing it to her mother. "What is this?" the woman asked.

"I must leave Vizen," Lyr explained. "You might hear that I was killed in the course of enacting a coup at the palace." Her mother's eyes flashed with fear, but Lyr pressed on. "It's best if you don't know the details. But I must leave."

"Where will you go?" her mother asked.

"I'm not sure. I will head south, towards Pevine, to start."

"Pevine," the woman echoed with longing. Her fingers brushed the 'NP' branding on her wrist. "And what am I supposed to do with this coin?"

"Use it to fix the roof. Use it for whatever you'd like. Just please, don't become a ghost again."

The woman frowned but nodded. "I'll try," she promised. Then, she returned the pouch to Lyr. "Keep this. I haven't been the mother to you I wish I could have been, but it is enough to know that you are alive. I will be all right here. Go to Pevine. If you look, there will still be folk that uphold the old woodsfolk ways. If the True One places a helper in your path..."

"I won't hesitate to follow," Lyr completed the line.

"I love you, my girl."

Lyr placed the pouch in her pocket, then cupped her mother's hands, kissing them repeatedly. "I will return someday."

"There's nothing for you in this cursed city," the woman said. "Don't turn back. Not for me, or for anyone else." The woman pulled her hands away, then reached to shut the window on instinct before stopping herself. She left it open instead, allowing the gray light to seep in, and herself a view of her daughter as she left her sight.

XXXIII.

Searin

It wasn't until the great feathered beast had galloped away that Searin realized she had stopped breathing. What was that thing? A *reaverlord*? But no, it was too different from the jet-black scaled creature on two legs she'd heard described. This was something else. And someone had let it into the palace to do gods-knew-what. Could the Free Kings rebels really have such beasts at their disposal?

Searin looked to her uncle. Before the monster had crashed into the hall she had been preparing to confront him. Then she'd seen that ursa-like silver nightmare, and she'd heard Clavio call out to those figures that were... well, *riding* the creature.

Realization, swift, and spyglass-clear, washed over Searin for the second time in so few minutes. Her uncle had known not to drink the wine—at this point, that much was obvious. He also had a hand in why that monster was in the palace. Knott was right. Clavio had been playing them all for days. Years, even. Ice crept down Searin's spine as she thought back on her father's suicide—how Clavio had arrived just that morning before the body was found...

Clavio met her gaze. His eyes were dark, strained, and his hair stuck to the sweat on his brow. Searin had never seen the man look so disheveled. It was a show for her benefit, she recognized. Clavio was still pretending to be distraught so Searin wouldn't suspect him. He hadn't yet realized that she was aware of his betrayal.

Searin willed her face into neutrality. The hall itself was teeming with Blue Scarabs, and she could only assume the rest of the palace would be the same. If she tried to kill her uncle now, she might succeed but would be sentencing herself to the same fate. Searin thought of Arisa and Hovard and their missing caravan. What egregious games did Clavio have planned for them? Searin needed to leave the palace. And that meant she'd need to play a game of her own.

Searin buried her face in her hands and began to sob.

Clavio touched her arm. Searin had to halt herself from recoiling in revulsion. "You should go up to your room and rest," he said. "You've suffered such a tragedy. I will have the servants send you a bath."

"Yes," she choked out. Her sobs were only partially an act. Once she had allowed them to start they came fast and bone-shakingly heavy. Searin let them come. Once she was outside this hall, she would have no more time for tears until she had found Arisa and Hovard.

She started walking towards her chambers. Footsteps followed her at a distance—she did not have to turn to know they belonged to Blue Scarabs. They stalked her all the way to the main hall of the palace and up the stairs. Bloody palace guard bodies were scattered across the floor—a good dozen of them. Deep gashes—claw marks, Searin realized—had shredded through carpets, wood, and marble in a path of utter destruction. Another turn and they were in the empty hall outside Searin's chambers.

She gripped Vow, which rested at her hip, and knew what she must do. "*Protect your family,*" her uncle had once made her promise. It was time that she fulfilled that purpose.

She turned as she unsheathed the blade and swiftly entered an attack stance. Her two escorts stopped, reaching for their weapons in surprise. "Allow me to leave and you get to keep your heads," Searin threatened.

"My princess," said one of the soldiers, the lack of hair and eyebrows making her angular face resemble a hairless cat. "We've been commanded not to harm you. It's best if you go inside now—"

"Then don't harm me," Searin cut in with the words followed, a heartbeat later, by the swing of her sword.

The princess lunged at the cat-faced woman, who deftly blocked the attack. The other soldier grabbed Searin's arm tightly, attempting to subdue her without resorting to drawing blood. A huge mistake. Searin elbowed the man in the face. His nose crunched under the weight of the armor. The soldier stumbled back, crying out and holding his bloody nose. Searin could now focus on the other.

The soldier did not waste time, shoving Searin back so that she forfeited her footing. Had there not been a wall behind her, Searin would have tumbled to the floor. She swung Vow wide at the woman's head, more of a distraction than a blow aimed to land. The soldier backed away, so Searin quickly crouched and tripped the woman, the same way Zinia had done to her days before. The bulk of the blue armor sent the woman falling flat on her back and Searin's sword dipped into the slit between the plates at the soldier's shoulder. The woman hissed in pain but stayed down.

Searin took the opportunity to dash away. The soldier whose nose she'd broken grabbed at her as she passed, but he was still dazed from the hit to the face and missed by mere inches.

Searin ran down the stairs into the main hall, then directly into the servants' quarters, hoping that there would be fewer Blue Scarabs there than in the rest of the palace. If she was going to scour the Red Road for the missing caravan, she could not do it on foot. The servants' quarters connected with the external yard, where the stables and kennels were. From there, she would leave on horseback.

As she snuck past the kitchens, Searin could hear the voices of a group of servants being questioned by who she assumed were more Blue Scarabs. There truly was no avoiding them, it seemed. The bodies of several palace guards lay lifeless on the floor. Some of the felled guards wore armbands like Searin had seen on the intruders. They were meant to identify the members of their rebel group, she realized. Searin hastened her pace. Her armor felt cumbersome, and her mind was a desperate drum beat urging her to go faster. A few more strides and she was pushing open the servant's entrance to the stable yard.

Though it was overcast, the diffused sunlight assaulted her eyes after the dimness of the hall. Searin shut the door behind her and ran across the yard towards the stables. She reached the structure just in time to duck behind a stack of hay to avoid being seen by the three Scarab soldiers stationed there. Of course, one of the first things they would have secured at the palace was the means of escape. Three soldiers, though? Searin had every confidence in herself as the better swordswoman, but it would take time to fight back three adversaries, and those were precious minutes Searin could not afford to waste.

Thankfully, the soldiers, for their part, appeared deeply distracted, rapidly exchanging words that, as Searin drew closer, she recognized as descriptions of the same beast that had invaded the hall. Searin's blood chilled as one recalled the beast leaping over the palace wall as if carried by invisible wings. So that thing was loose out there, now? She swallowed.

Looking to her left, Searin saw the gate of one of the stalls within easy reach. She crept towards it and opened it, keeping extra awareness of her movements given that her armor was built more for protection than stealth. Before stepping inside, she said a little prayer that there would even be a horse within the stall. The gods surely had a wicked sense of humor. There was a horse within, and, by some minor miracle, it was already saddled and ready to be mounted. But it was *which* horse it was that made Searin scowl bitterly.

Wick glared down his jet-black snout at her. The stallion had been Clavio's gift to Arisa, and Searin had watched the King's Guard's thwarted attempts at training it with amusement over the last few days. Now it loomed over her with a dismissive snort, a clear-as-day challenge if Searin had ever seen one. She narrowed her eyes.

She stepped swiftly onto one of the slotted planks that made up the side of the stall, using it to boost herself high enough to be even with the waiting saddle. The movement was a noisy one and she had no sooner grabbed the reins before the three soldiers turned to her in alarm. But it was too late for them. Searin kicked into Wick's flanks and the beast exploded forward.

Even with a saddle, it was a feat for Searin to stay upright. Wick barreled towards the three soldiers, paying little to no mind where Searin attempted to steer him. The Scarabs scattered, clearing the path for her and Wick to continue towards the waydoor. While the main gates were used mostly for carriages or mulecarts, the waydoor was a smaller gate that was wide enough to let one or two horses move through in haste.

Searin yanked hard on the reins, pulling Wick into a reluctant halt and turning him somewhat so that her foot could just reach the bottom of the door's iron latch. She kicked it up a few times before it stuck, the entire time frantically aware that the Scarabs were closing in behind her. Once the door was unlatched, she kicked it open. Wick seized upon this newfound freedom without further coaxing. His hooves stomped rapidly on the rain-polished cobbled street. Searin held on for dear life, and set her jaw, praying to the gods that she would not fall.

It had been several years since the last time she had seen the streets of Vizen. Any time she and her family had left by carriage, curtains had concealed them from the view of the city. Searin had always assumed it to be one of her mother's quirks—to avoid the fawning of her subjects—but now she wasn't so sure. The city was a grim sight—cracked walls, broken cobblestones, shabby habitations... Even the recent rains had not washed away what was readily apparent: Vizen was a dying, stagnant, city.

She flew past groups of patrolling Blue Scarabs, and it struck her just how vast their numbers were. She spotted a group apprehending a pair of city guards, tying their hands behind their backs with rope. The guards' eyes were wide in confusion and horror. As she galloped past, a Blue Scarab shouted, "Hey, you!" but Wick was too fast for them to do or say much else.

The city gates were up ahead. Atop the parapets loomed several Scarabs barking orders at guards. A cluster of peasants rushed through the gates, their voices raised in panic. Past the gates, Searin noticed a large wooden structure blocking the path. "Gods, no!" Searin exclaimed. They were raising the drawbridge.

Gripping the reins, she kicked Wick's sides and braced herself for the accelerating gallop. The crowds dispersed at her unyielding approach. As Searin neared the rising lip of the drawbridge, she sent up another prayer that the jump would not spook the horse. Voices called out for her to halt. The clopping of hooves became hollower as the pavement changed from stone to inclining wood. The drawbridge continued to rise as they crested it. Once they reached the end, Wick jumped without hesitation. Searin gritted her teeth and shut her eyes.

The young stallion landed on the other side with surprising grace and resumed his mad dash. Searin opened her eyes and whooped. Wick stopped and snorted angrily, shaking his mane—Searin wasn't sure if the pause was due to the jump or the sound she had involuntarily emitted. She rubbed the horse's neck while making a gentle shushing sound. In turn, the horse turned and snapped his teeth at her.

"Just a bit more," she begged the horse. "Please." Searin flicked the reins gently, and Wick, to his credit, took off at a steady gallop, rushing quickly through Urstway, the forecity.

The recent near-constant rains had rendered the red sediment that comprised the Red Road dark and muddy. Ankle-high puddles splashed underneath the horse's beating hooves. As the woods devoured them, Searin felt adrenaline melt into panic. She looked at the road, a history of wagon and carriage wheels etched upon it. If any had strayed off the path, it should be obvious to her. Captain Velden had said that they passed the first two outposts, so at least she had a lead as to where to begin her search.

It took about half an hour to reach the first outpost. A blue canopy was erected on the side of the Road, encircled by an outcropping of smaller tents. Beneath the canopy was a table at which sat a single Blue Scarab soldier. Another Scarab stood at the other side of the road, his armor glistening in the rain. There were horses hitched near the tents, but they were unmounted. *Good*, Searin thought. By the time the soldiers could be saddled, she'd be around the next bend and out of sight.

"Halt, there!" the drenched soldier called out, as she approached.

Instead of slowing down, she urged Wick to go faster. They galloped through the outpost without so much as a backward glance. The Scarabs there would, no doubt, report the sighting of her to her uncle. That didn't matter now. The only thing that mattered was finding Hovard and Arisa and making sure they were safe.

The words of the cat-faced soldier kept replaying in her mind. "*We've been commanded not to harm you.*" Whatever Clavio was planning involved keeping her alive. Surely, it would be the same for her sister and brother. It must be. It must be.

Her eyes fixated on something ahead, shaking her back into awareness. Several thick lines cut through the mud at the edge of the road—a clear sign of a multi-carriage diversion, and a fresh one at that. Searin battled Wick into a slow trot. They were still a couple of miles from the second outpost that the caravan had supposedly cleared before going missing.

A lie. All of it had been a lie—Clavio pretending to dispatch additional King's Guard, the worry on his face—all of it had been more theater for Searin's benefit. Her face heated as she steered Wick off the Red Road and into the woods following those deep, crimson, furrows.

The woods were all-encompassing. Skeletal trees clawed at the sky, the smell of wet earth blanketing all. After several more minutes of walking, Wick flicked his ears, then halted abruptly, snorting and whinnying skittishly. Searin kicked at Wick's sides, urging him to press on, but the horse moved in circles, refusing to go past the thicket ahead. "Stupid horse," Searin cursed with a frown. Wick answered with a snort.

The snapping of twigs made Searin's heart tense. Someone was nearby. She managed to calm Wick and halt him. Carefully, she dismounted.

Searin crouched and unsheathed Vow. Remaining low and out of sight—though, in her resplendent armor, it was hard to remain inconspicuous—she approached the thicket. Through the rustling greenery, she could faintly hear someone speaking. Then, the smell hit her—sulfur, fire, and blood—dizzying. She reached the edge of the clearing, realizing only then that she was atop a hill. Scattered in the field below were the remains of the royal caravan, horses detached and grazing freely.

There were bodies, too---the Azurat guard and servants. Soldiers came into view from behind one of the carriages—five, Searin counted. Their armor was like nothing Searin had ever seen: dark steel plate surrounded by brown ursa fur. Their fuzzy helmets concealed their heads entirely.

They appeared more beast than man, and, for that, Searin was certain these were warriors from Sazisan. But what were they doing here, so far from the border? How had they plunged so deeply through Hovardom without being caught or noticed?

And what had they done to her sister and brother?

A shiver of fear ran through her, making her saddle-sore legs buckle. She inched forward but slipped in a slick of mud that sent her sliding down the hill on her back. The Sazisani soldiers called out, "Over there!"

Searin was shocked she could understand the man's perfect Hovardian.

One of the soldiers retrieved a steel lance from his back and pointed it at Searin. She prepared herself to dodge the throw. Instead, with a pop, a puff of dark smoke released from the lance, and the earth just ahead of her exploded. Searin shielded her eyes from the debris.

"Load the wand!" one of the soldiers barked.

"It's the princess!" another soldier yelled.

"Shit!"

The soldier returned the 'wand' to his back as two others encircled her. Searin stood, her feet slipping wildly in the mud. "Drop the sword," the nearest soldier said. "We won't hurt you."

"Arisa! Hovard!" Searin called out. "Arisa! Hovard!" She tried once more, but there was no answer. "What have you done to my family?"

"Calm down, princess," the nearest soldier said. His hand hovered over the pommel of his sword.

A startling realization gripped her chest. "How do you know who I am?"

The other soldier ran towards her, sword first. Searin parried the attack and made short work of the soldier, sending his weapon falling into the mud and slicing the man through the shoulder. The man fell to his knees, grunting and gripping his wound tightly. Blood oozed between his fingers, running down his arm.

She would not wait for the other soldier to attack first. She swung Vow at the man's head. The man backed away but slipped in the mud and fell backwards. Searin thrust Vow through the gap in his armor at his neck.

"Stay back!" a voice called out from behind an overturned carriage. At first, Searin had assumed this to be directed at her. Instead, the other remaining soldiers responded by quickly retreating into the woods. The one who had spoken came into view and Searin felt the world come to a lurching halt.

Dregor eyed her ferociously, the tip of his blade already dripping with ruby gore.

"Hovard! Arisa!" Searin called out once more.

"Turn back. Return to the palace. You don't need to be here," the high captain ordered.

Searin wanted to dash toward the traitor and stab Vow through his heart. Instead, she took a few tentative steps forward—even with the fire of battle roaring through her, she knew she must be careful. Slipping in the mud would not do against a swordsman like Dregor.

She neared the man, prepared to pounce into an attack at any moment. He remained still, twirling his sword toyingly. Searin swung Vow. Dregor blocked the attack easily, going from flourish to defense in the blink of an eye. "That was a mistake," he said, then pushed her back with a barrage of attacks the likes of which Searin had never experienced.

She fell back into the mud and kicked at the high captain's legs. Though he was quite sturdy, even he was not immune to the wet slickness of the earth. Dregor fell on top of her, still gripping his sword. This close to the man, Searin could not swing her blade. She set Vow on the ground and attempted to wrestle Dregor's sword away from him. The two rolled in the mud for some time, grunting as each tugged on the sword and swung punches at the other's face. This was going nowhere.

Searin let go of the sword right as the knight tugged on it. The momentum of his pull staggered him back enough for Searin to be able to disengage and roll away toward where Vow lay. She picked up the sword and...

The air was instantly sucked out of her chest as a blast sent her falling back a few paces. Through the ringing in her ears, she heard the muffled voices of the other soldiers arguing. Perhaps that's what reminded Searin that she was still alive. The treetops overhead regained their shape and focus. Searin reached for her stomach—her armor was dented and covered in dark soot. But it had held, as all good Vizenian steel should. Most of her pain was in her back and neck from the rough landing on the ground.

She heard the approaching footsteps of the soldiers. Even as they neared and came into view, vulturing over her, their voices sounded distant. "Gods, you idiot! You could have killed her just now," said one, shoving the other who still held out the smoking lance.

"Yeah, but I didn't."

"Let's tie her up before she stands. Where's her sword?"

One of the men turned away to glance about the area while the other reached into his pack for rope. Searin raised her head. In doing so, she heard something metallic scrape against her shoulder plate. She reached behind her, realizing she had landed on top of Vow. She gripped the sword while the two soldiers were distracted and sliced at the nearest man's calf. The soldier fell to his knees with a scream. Searin stood, ignoring the pain in her back and her strained lungs, and slammed Vow through the man's neck. At full strength, she would have been able to cleanly sever the man's head. Instead, Vow stopped just short, but the intended effect was the same: the man was dead.

The other soldier raised his unarmed hands. "Stop! Princess, please!"

Searin had no time for his pleas. She drove Vow through the soldier's side and the man collapsed into the mud. Dregor watched her do it without even a flinch of sympathy for the downed men. They were lackeys hired by her uncle, then. Perhaps mercenaries or Blue Scarab soldiers, even.

"Where are they?" Searin demanded.

Dregor's eyes darted from her to one of the carriages, then back to her. "You should really come back to Vizen with me. Speak with your uncle."

"I will never call that monster *Uncle* again! What have you done with my sister and brother?" Searin screamed.

The details of the scene around her were beginning to click into place. She counted the carriages—one was missing, and it was not the one Arisa and Hovard had been riding in. It was Reylin's carriage that was unaccounted for. Together—the King's Guard must have put Reilyn and her siblings together in that carriage in order to flee to Rondhill. Yes, that was sensible.

"I was only following orders," Dregor said. "Your uncle—Clavio's orders."

But why dress the attackers up as Sazisani soldiers? Was Clavio aiming to incite rumors of a possible invasion? That would accelerate the calls to resume the war at the Red Coast that Clavio was so fixated on rekindling.

"Where are they?" This time the question was cold venom. Searin held Dregor's gaze and, for the first time, saw the mix of fear and guilt in his eyes. No.

Dregor nodded his head to the leading carriage and Searin felt the ground shift under her as if it would swallow her up. She wished it would. No. They were not in Reylin's carriage, then.

"Nooo!" Searin cried out, desperately, madly. She lunged at Dregor, swinging wildly for any vital points she could. It was all the knight could do to block her advance.

"Did you look at my sister in her eyes when you killed her?" Searin bellowed as she aimed another blow at his head. "Did you think of all the flirting, the kissing, the groping in closets, when you murdered her?"

Dregor seemed ready to say something, perhaps to defend his actions, but his face took on the cold cast of a man resigned to his fate as he parried another volley of frenetic swings from Searin. "It was a means to an end," he gritted out between defensive maneuvers. "I had to get close to her."

"So even that was a lie!" Searin raged. Her muscles were screaming but she had lost control of her body. Her arms moved mechanically with no indication of fatigue. Swing. Step. Swing. Step. Dregor's footing faltered for just a second. But it was enough. Vow's tip dragged across Dregor's dominant arm and dark blood sprouted in its wake. His own sword tumbled to the ground, the muscles and tendons required to hold it now largely severed. He grasped at the wound with his other hand and stumbled back against the nearest carriage, panting. It was over.

"Why?" Compared to her cries seconds before, the word was nearly a whisper.

It took Dregor several more seconds to catch enough breath to answer. "I wish I could tell you it was for some noble belief, or that I hated you and your family for who you were and what you did to me or everyone else, or anything better than the truth. But, if these are to be my last words, let them be honest ones at least." He straightened, and, to his credit, met Searin's gaze with something like shame in his expression.

"Coin. I betrayed your trust, your family's trust, for coin."

Searin spat at the ground near the man's feet as her only response before she raised her sword.

"I know it's more than I deserve to ask but," his breathing was beginning to slow from the blood-loss, "but please, make it quick."

Searin screamed as she thrust Vow through Dregor's neck. Blood spewed through his mouth. His eyes were on the sky as he fell limply to the ground. Searin watched as life fled his body—as the blood pooling at his head and side slowed.

She faced the lead carriage, knowing too well what she would find within. But she needed to see. She limped towards the carriage and placed her hand on the door handle. She wasn't sure if she would cry, wretch, or both.

She pulled the door open. Inside were her siblings, their faces rendered unrecognizable from the wounds caused by that explosive lance. But even so, Arisa was unmistakable in her poise, her hands folded in front of her as if she was relaxed and awaiting her turn to add a quip to a stale conversation. A queen in the making. And Hovard... Little Hovard lay on his sister's lap. Searin reached for one of his perennially bare feet, expecting, hoping, wishing, that they would kick at her. That they would do anything at all. They were cold, just as they had been the night she had spent in his room.

Searin backed away, a tremor running through her body. Sobs overtook her, a strained wail freeing itself from her throat. She looked down at the sword that was in her hand, its blood-stained blade now a mockery of what it had once meant to her. It had been gifted to her by the man who had slain her family. Now, there was no one left for her to protect. Searin regretted every moment she had ever held the blade. She let the sword fall into the mud. Her vow was broken.

She turned away from the sword, the carriage, and what remained of her brother and sister, and headed deeper into the woods.

XXXIV.

Mother and Daughter

Rovan glanced back at the city gate just in time to see an armored rider use the drawbridge as a ramp to jump their horse across the moat. The impact of their landing scattered the crowd as the rider continued at breakneck speed through the foregate town. It was a remarkable sight, but Rovan had endured enough of those for one day.

His two friends hadn't spoken much since they had gathered their belongings from beside the inn and fled the city. Perhaps it was best that way. Guilt burned Rovan's ears. He wouldn't even know where to start with formulating an apology—or saying thanks for that matter.

"So, where's the girl?" Scintilla's voice sliced through their thick silence.

"I... don't know." It pained Rovan to admit it. "I told the two of them to leave the city, and that I would find them somehow."

"Them?" Tieg asked.

"Yulma, a young woman from the palace, is accompanying her," Rovan explained.

"So, you've found the girl in the city just to lose her in the woods. Great." Tieg sounded as weary as Rovan felt.

Something pressed at Rovan's mind like it was fighting to be remembered. He reached into his hood pocket and produced the dull gray runestone of *Guidance* Ashe had given him.

Rovan closed his eyes and focused his awareness onto the stone, shutting out the chatter of people around him, the sound of boots in puddles, and his self-pity regarding his poor treatment of his friends.

At first, he felt nothing but the cool smoothness of the stone resting in his fist. Then, as the seconds became minutes, he felt embarrassment creeping in. Adriel had been half-insane and dying. Why should he have trusted her about having a connection to the Cycle strong enough to do anything at all with a spent runestone? He was about to chuck the blasted pebble onto the roadside when he felt a subtle tug. So subtle he wasn't sure he hadn't imagined it at first.

But no, it was there. A pull not dissimilar to gravity. And Rovan was certain that at the other end of that force would be Sesha.

Rovan opened his eyes. "This way."

Through the foregate town, just before the nearby thicket, was a field where buildings grew sparse. At its far edge, there was a weathered barn. Cautiously, Rovan opened the barn door and slipped inside, followed closely by his reluctant friends. "Rovan, where are you—"

"Sesha," Rovan called out. "It's me. Rovan." When there was no answer, he added, "These are my friends, Tieg and Scintilla."

A pile of hay rose into a looming mound, splinters of straw cascading down to reveal the large shape of the *melk*. Even though he had ridden atop the beast, Rovan could not help but back away at the sight of it. He heard Scintilla and Tieg's sharp inhalations behind him. Sesha appeared a moment later, climbing over the pile. Her wild, dark hair was threaded with golden straw. "You made it!" she marveled.

"I did," Rovan said, and in doing so, he recognized what a feat that had truly been. He allowed himself a moment of relief. "Where's Yulma?"

"Her real name is Lyr. She went back to the city and told us to hide. We were tired, so we came here to rest."

"Are you hungry?" he asked, realizing suddenly that his stomach was twisting itself in emptiness. When was the last time he had eaten?

Sesha nodded emphatically. Rovan reached into his sack and retrieved one of the remaining journeycakes the dwellers at the Womb of the World had provided them and broke off a piece. Sesha took it and ate it voraciously. Rovan did the same.

Scintilla took a seat on a nearby workbench and bit into a piece of goat jerky, while Tieg moved closer to observe the *melk*. "What does it eat?" he asked.

"She feeds on anything that contains great amounts of *life energy*," Sesha said. "Tree sap, black earth, water from a healthy river... blood."

Tieg stepped back. "She's not hungry now, is she?"

Sesha giggled. "She won't eat you. She's tired of eating blood. That's all she's had for months."

"Does she have a name?" Scintilla asked.

Sesha looked up at the beast. "Yes, but it's more like a sound than a name. It can't be said with words. It can only be said with *life energy*. It's like a shriek."

"*Shriek* has a good ring to it," Tieg mused.

The *melk* lolled its head side to side. Sesha smiled. "Shriek. I don't think she minds that name."

"What was she doing in the palace, anyways?" Scintilla asked.

"A man was keeping her imprisoned down there. He was using me to feed her because she wouldn't let anyone else near without attacking. She was so scared and alone before I came. We don't know why she was being imprisoned, but the man always said she would be of great use to the kingdom."

"Who was this man?" Tieg asked.

"I don't know his name. When I first arrived there was a bald old man who gave me instructions. I liked him more. He had a kind smile. Then, about a week ago, he was replaced by another man."

"This bald old man with the kind smile wouldn't happen to have been named Velden, by any chance?" Rovan asked.

"Velden..." Sesha mouthed the name, considering. "Yes, and Captain. That's what the others would call him," she said, nodding.

Rovan's frown deepened. If Velden was involved, this other man the girl spoke of might likely be the Master. Or, at least, whatever poor body was playing host to the Master this time around. When Rovan had met the Master in Sol Forne, he had been a man named Eggar. The djinn, Vaelin, had explained to Rovan that Eggar was nothing more than a puppet achieved through a *Transference* ritual. The real Master was elsewhere. Based on the Blue Scarabs' presence at the palace, it made sense that their leader would be involved in something like this.

Back in Sol Forne, the Master had attempted to take control of a *mer* that lived in the Talmur Sea. It made sense to Rovan that he would try to do the same to a *melk*. "Those men that were hunting the *reaverlord* said that someone in Vizen had paid them to capture the beast. Didn't the enchantress say that *reaverlords* were dragons?"

"Yes..." Scintilla replied, confused by why Rovan would bring that up now.

Could the Master be seeking to imprison one of each of the Ancient Guardians? "*Mer, melk, dragons...* What was the other one?" Rovan asked.

"*Griffons*," Sesha supplied. "But those are long gone."

Rovan was startled by the response. He hadn't meant to voice the question out loud.

"Long gone like the *melk* were?" Tieg asked, rubbing the back of his head.

"You don't think the person Sesha is describing is the same one who hired those errant knights to capture the *reaverlord*, do you?" Scintilla asked.

"Perhaps. But what matters now is that we get her out of here." Rovan faced Sesha. "There's a town to the southeast called Pevine. Your birth mother is there. Her name is Ashe. She hired us to find you and bring her news of you."

Sesha looked up at the *melk*'s dark eye as if seeking the answer to an unspoken question.

"She seems like a good person," Rovan continued. "But you don't have to go anywhere with her if you don't want to. You could stay in Pevine with us. Or I will escort you back to the Womb of the World. You'll be safe, and we'll take care of you no matter what you decide," Rovan promised.

"All right," Sesha agreed.

Scintilla slapped her thighs as she stood from the workbench. "We have something else to discuss." A brief nod was exchanged between her and Tieg.

Rovan's throat tightened. "Can we take this outside?" he asked.

Scintilla and Tieg nodded and stepped out of the barn. Sesha didn't seem bothered by being left in there with the *melk*. In fact, she seemed rather eager to cuddle up to the beast and nap.

Rovan shut the barn door and turned sheepishly to his two friends, prepared for the well-earned lecture he was about to receive. Scintilla started immediately, "We did not travel through the woods, confront a *reaverlord*, sneak into Vizen, and get dragged across those dingy streets to be left behind by you at the last moment."

"This is what I've been wanting to tell you all this time, Rovan," Tieg said. "You're one of the best friends I've ever had, and we've been through so much together, but you've never truly seen me as an equal, have you? To you we're all just... people you need to save."

Rovan sighed. "I was just trying to protect you both. Your safety is my responsibility—"

"Your responsibility?" Tieg scoffed. "I don't remember asking that of you. No, I've only ever asked if I could be your friend. You're the one with some weird complex about being our 'caretaker.'"

Scintilla patted Tieg's arm but her eyes stayed on Rovan. "We worry about you too, you know? You put all this pressure on yourself and say it's for our sake, and we can see how much of a strain it is. But we would never—*never*—leave you behind like that."

Rovan's cheeks burned. He wanted to argue but it was pointless. They were right. He was the one who saw himself as their burdened leader. They had only ever tried to be his friends and instead, he had treated their group like any of his other service duties.

"I... I've been a rotten friend to you both." Rovan's eyesight blurred a bit with unshed tears of shame. "I'm not sure it will make much of a difference to you at this point but... I'm truly sorry for how I've treated you." He couldn't bring himself to meet either of their gazes as the tears spilled over and down his cheeks.

Two sets of warm arms wrapped around him. "Of course, it makes a difference to us to hear you say that, Rovan. I've been waiting to hear it for months now." Tieg ruffled Rovan's hair as he released him.

"Yeah, you idiot. Better late than never," Scintilla teased.

Rovan grinned, but the expression wilted just as quickly as it had bloomed. "You're still leaving, then," Rovan said.

"I'm still leaving, then," Tieg echoed but his grin stayed aimed warmly at Rovan.

Rovan nodded. "Tieg... you know I respect your choice—" Tieg was already rolling his eyes in anticipation of where this was going, but Rovan pressed on, "But... I think you're a fool to leave our group to go back to your family."

Tieg's eyebrows shot up in surprise.

"We all love you, Tieg—I love you. And I wish you'd stay." Rovan felt something inside himself relax for what he realized now was the first time since he had learned Teig was leaving.

"Well, Rovan, thank you for finally sharing your actual thoughts with me," Tieg said. Rovan had expected him to be angry but instead, Tieg seemed... delighted? "I don't expect you to understand why I'm doing this but just know it's important for me that I go back." Tieg wrapped Rovan into another big hug. "I love you too, my friend."

"Will I see you again?" Rovan asked.

"Of course, you will," Scintilla promised, her voice was more strained, tighter, than usual.

Rovan felt like he should say something more, but nothing came to him. Scintilla wrapped her arms around them both, and suddenly his sorrow was too much.

When they released each other from the embrace, Tieg's face was red and blotchy, his eyes misty. "Please take care of yourself. And the others. Never take them or what we've built together for granted, not for a moment."

"I promise," Rovan replied.

The goodbye seemed to last forever, but as soon as it was done, Rovan looked up and Scintilla and Tieg were already headed west. Almost in unison, they reached for each other's hand.

Rovan stood there, watching them go until they vanished behind a curtain of rain. After taking a moment to compose himself, he reentered the barn.

"They left?" Sesha asked.

Rovan nodded and sat on the stool near the pile of hay Sesha and Shriek occupied. "Why?" the girl asked.

"Because... Well, I don't really understand why. But I trust them," Rovan said.

"I think you're a good friend," Sesha said. "I can see how much you care about them."

Rovan smiled at the endearing attempt to cheer him up. "We should leave here soon. We will have to avoid the Red Road, so it will take us some time to reach Pevine."

"We can ride her," Sesha said, pointing at the *melk*.

The creature tilted its head. Rovan felt something pass from it to him, the light caress of assurance. "How's its shoulder?" he asked, remembering that the *melk* had been wounded by an arrow.

Sesha ran her hands over the bloody feathers at the *melk*'s shoulder, revealing pale, unmarred, flesh beneath. "All healed up!"

"Already?"

"She's a fast healer. All it takes is some rest and a steady stream of *life energy*."

"That's good," Rovan said. "Even so, the woods can be dense. It won't be the same as riding through the open city streets."

Sesha smiled. "Have you forgotten that Shriek is a *melk*? The woods of Albadone are her dominion."

They did not linger at the barn for much longer. Rovan poked his head out first, glancing about to ensure that no one was there to be alarmed by the creature. Thankfully, the farmland was deserted. He wagered that most of the farmers and neighboring citizens had gathered at the foregate town to exchange their relative bits and pieces of the day's happenings over a cup of tea or ale. Mulled cider sounded good about now, Rovan thought as he felt the dampness of the rain chill his bones.

He signaled for Sesha and Shriek to exit the barn. Sesha was already astride the beast as they walked out. Shriek lowered herself, belly into the wet earth, so that Rovan could climb on her back. "All good," Rovan said after some adjusting on the *melk*'s wide breadth.

"Which way?" Sesha asked.

Rovan pointed in Pevine's general south-eastern direction. Shriek raised itself on all fours, then charged full speed at Sesha's call of "Go!" Rovan braced himself, clinging onto the child in front of him—he had no idea how she managed to remain so stable.

They wove through the nearby woods at a speed Rovan had never known possible. He gasped as they headed straight for a tree. Shriek turned at just the last moment, snaking around it with a serpentine litheness. Rovan could feel the fluidity of the *melk*'s spine underneath him, bending at unnatural angles to account for the sharp turns. Rovan shut his eyes tightly as the *melk* continued to dodge the trees at unyielding speed and resolved to keep them shut for the remainder of the terrifying trip, opening them only a few times to ensure that they were proceeding in the right direction.

"Is this it?" Sesha asked at the end of an interminable hour.

Rovan opened his eyes, realizing only then that the *melk* had slowed to a walk. He wiped rain and slick strands of hair from his face as he took in the dilapidated wooden barricade encircling Pevine. "It is," he confirmed.

"It's so..." Sesha trailed off.

"Ugly?" Rovan supplied.

"Yeah."

He smiled. The sight of the town filled him with an overwhelming sense of longing. He had not realized a half-ruined town like this would ever feel like home. And it wasn't the place itself, but rather the people in it. The longing he felt outstretched itself across the forest, and beyond the Womb of the World, towards Scintilla and Tieg. Though it was easy to allow his mind to sulk into regret, he decided instead to be thankful for the friendship they shared.

Though they were gone for now, they were welcome to return any time. He hoped they would.

As the *melk* approached the barricade, Rovan hopped off its back, landing ankle-deep into a puddle of mud. *Great.* His thighs were sore from riding the *melk*, making it incredibly difficult to climb out of the thick sludge. The *melk*, too, sank into the earth, almost to her elbows, though she did not seem to mind. As they neared the entrance to the town, the mud became shallower, allowing them to move with more ease.

Rovan glanced at Shriek and noticed she appeared... alarmed. Her head swiveled from side to side and the thick muscles of her body were pulled tight as bow strings. A low hum gurgled in her throat.

"Is it—is she all right?" Rovan turned his concerned gaze to Sesha. The girl too was watching Shriek carefully.

"She knows this place. She's been here before." Sesha's face went pale. "Her family was killed by the actions of these humans. She considers them enemies of the Cycle of Nature and doesn't want me to go inside." Shriek punctuated this last statement with a snort and a stomp of her foot.

Rovan rubbed the back of his neck, eyeing the beast carefully. "I can't speak for what you may have experienced, but the folk I've gotten to know here these last several months aren't like that." He looked at Sesha. "You can stay out here if you'd like but if you choose to come in, it'll have to be without her."

As if she understood his words perfectly, the *melk* aimed a dagger-sharp glare at Rovan. His bowels became water.

Sesha furrowed her brow. "I suppose so."

"Shriek can rest in the nearby woods or find something to eat." When the *melk* did not seem particularly taken by his suggestion, Rovan added, "I will take good care of her, you have my word." That seemed to calm the creature somewhat.

Sesha's mouth twisted, but she seemed to agree. Rovan approached quickly as she slid off the *melk*'s back and caught her before she could land heavily in the mud. Rovan lowered the girl gently onto an area where the earth was more packed. Sesha ran her hand across the *melk*'s shimmering feathers, and the beast groaned worriedly before running off into the nearby woods. The bond the two shared was at once marvelous and strange.

"This way," Rovan beckoned, approaching Pevine's entrance, Sesha following at his flank. Rovan would have preferred a few feet distance, but Sesha insisted on remaining close. Had whatever the *melk* communicated to her scared her so badly?

"What's wrong?" he asked.

"Is... Is she a good person, like you said?" Sesha asked.

"Who?" Rovan said, then immediately realized who the girl was talking about. "Ashe? Yes. She's very nice. She doesn't really speak. Her voice is gone." A strange thing to point out, but the girl would have questions about that—better to prepare her.

"Why is that?" she asked.

"I think it was the fires, long ago. I'm not sure about the details."

"The fires..." Sesha mused. She tugged on her tunic, exposing her clavicle. Rovan had not realized the amount of scarring that was there. But, it wasn't quite scarring in a way he had ever seen before. None of it reached the surface of the flesh, only giving the skin the appearance of scarring without any of the scar itself, as if that was its coloring. "I was burned too," Sesha said.

"You two have something in common then, besides being parent and child," he rambled.

Once again, Sesha neared Rovan, this time brushing against his side. "Are you all right?" he asked.

Sesha shrugged, looking down at the ground. Rovan stopped and faced the girl, realizing what a toll this day must have taken on her. Adriel was the only mother this girl had known. She had been a tyrant of a woman and had attempted to kill Sesha. And now she was dead. The woman had been the only context Sesha had for what it was like to have a mother. It was only natural for her to be anxious about meeting a new one.

"Sesha, you don't have to be afraid. Ashe simply wishes to meet you and know that you are safe. You don't have to live with her. She can be to you whatever you wish for her to be. If you wish her to simply be a friend, like how we are, then that can be it. If you want nothing to do with her after this, that is fine too."

Sesha nodded, raising her head just a little. "Can I... Can I hold your hand?" Sesha's voice was little more than a whisper. It broke Rovan's heart a bit to see the little girl who had been so unshaken by the rest of their adventure suddenly affected by worry.

Rovan's mouth opened soundlessly, but he held back whatever he intended to say. He removed his glove and placed it in his pocket, then reached his hand out towards the girl. Hers was cold and small in his, but it warmed as they walked through Pevine's empty, muddy streets.

The rain was keeping most folk inside. To Rovan's delight, the first person that he spotted was Terreck, puffing on his pipe beneath a newly repaired tavern awning. Trinket sat snoozing at his feet. "Rovan!" Terreck greeted but made no move to approach them lest he disturb the cat's slumber.

Rovan could not help but smile at the long-missed sight of his friend. "Sesha, this is Terreck," he introduced.

"You actually found her!" Terreck marveled.

"You had any doubts?"

"Doubts, never. Reservations, plenty." Terreck winked at Rovan, playfully. "Well, it's a pleasure to meet you Sesha," Terreck greeted with a nod. He paused to give Sesha a moment to speak. When the girl said nothing, Terreck changed the subject. "I take it my sister followed Tieg west."

"Yeah," Rovan said, guilt rising in his chest.

Terreck nodded knowingly. "That's for the best. Somebody needs to take care of that idiot."

"Tieg isn't so bad," Rovan said.

"I'm not talking about Tieg." Terreck took a pull from his pipe and breathed out a cloud of smoke. "They're inside."

It took Rovan a moment to understand who 'they' were, but Sesha seemed to catch the meaning instantly. Her hand tensed within Rovan's. Was there a right way to go about this? Perhaps it was best to speak with the two women first and prime them for meeting the girl. Sesha was strong—stronger than any seven-year-old had any right to be—but she was still only a child.

He faced her. "I can go speak to them first. I can tell them what we've discussed. That you get the final say on things, not them."

Sesha breathed in deeply, then said, "I'm all right. Let's go in."

A very strong child, indeed. Rovan moved towards the door, then faced Terreck. "If you hear any strange sounds outside of town, don't worry. That's just Sesha's *melk*."

Terreck choked on a cloud of smoke, forcing out, "Sesha's what?!" in a cough.

The tavern was emptier than Rovan had expected it to be. There was no sign of Fellen or Iseo or most of the townsfolk. At this time of the early evening, a small crowd was usually here supping. Only one table had people sitting at it. Keith, the barkeep, shared a steaming mug of tea with the two women, Ashe and Alanda, whose backs faced the door. A knot of anticipation formed in Rovan's throat—he could only imagine how the girl must be feeling.

Keith stood, his wide eyes darting between their faces and their feet. Rovan glanced down, realizing they had tracked an enormous quantity of mud onto the clean tavern floor. He would have to make it up to Keith later. A flash of recognition widened Keith's eyes. "Oh, Rovan. I didn't recognize you."

At the sound of his name, the two women stood and faced him. Alanda's eyes moved from Sesha to her companion. Ashe paled at the sight of her daughter. The corners of her mouth pushed inward as she visibly choked back tears. The air in the tavern grew still and tense. Rovan realized that it was up to him to break them all from the stupor they shared.

"I found her," he began, as if the woman could not see that plainly. "This is Sesha. Sesha, that's Ashe. Your birth mother."

The woman and the child remained locked in a strange, quiet, stare. It was then that Rovan noticed the similarities they shared—the same hair, eyes, and identical jawline. If there were any doubts that the two were related, they had vanished.

Alanda placed her hand on Ashe's arm. The woman nearly started, then turned towards the other. Alanda whispered something to Ashe that could have only been, "Go to her," for Ashe began to sheepishly approach them. Sesha, too, cautiously stepped towards the woman, tugging on Rovan's hand. Rovan wondered if he should follow, then opted to allow the two to share this moment. He let go of Sesha's hand, and the girl carried on without him.

Once they stood in front of each other, Ashe knelt to Sesha's level. She pointed at herself and carefully uttered the words, "Ashe. Mother," in her wisp of a voice.

Sesha attempted a smile. She pointed at herself and said, "Sesha."

Ashe nodded with a smile, and mouthed, "I named you."

The two locked eyes and, for a long time, no one spoke, though something, everything, seemed to pass between them. Then, in a gesture louder than any words could ever be, Sesha reached out toward her mother, and Ashe took her daughter's hand.

XXXV.

Vision

Things could have gone worse when all was considered. The plan was messy from the start, but that's what made it effective. A neatly bundled one would have been too suspicious, too obvious. The only person on the outside to finally comprehend what was going on, albeit too late, had been Searin. She was the best of them all, and that's why Clavio had guided her life leading up to this moment so carefully—why he had given her Vow, encouraged her to abdicate her throne, inspired her to pursue becoming high captain of the King's Guard, and, ultimately, why he had taken it all away from her. Her entire life had been one prolonged calculation on his part. It was a shame that she had escaped the palace, but that only proved to Clavio just how necessary she was.

A shame, too, that she had witnessed her brother and sister's demise. That performance was intended to be witnessed only by Lord Reylin and his servants, who had "narrowly escaped" the ordeal and retreated to Rondhill where they dispatched letters to all noble houses about a Sazisani invasion. Clavio had lost every member of his family in the Old World—his *real* family—so he was familiar with the well of grief Searin drew from. Let the girl run out into the world and feel her sorrow. Sooner or later, he would have her back where she belonged.

What really irritated Clavio was that she had killed Ser Dregor, who he had hoped would take over for Captain Velden. The Blue Scarabs needed fresh blood for what was to come. Thankfully, the conclusion of the Free Kings' infiltration had returned a pawn that would act as the perfect substitute for the slain knight—Lieutenant Leano.

Clavio removed his night shift, then stood in front of his large mirror. Deep scars ran up his arms and across his chest, like cracks in dry mud. This body would not last him much longer. He had made use of it for many decades now, only alternating with the one he called Eggar a few times a year to allow this one time to rest. After losing Eggar's body in Sol Forne, he had been forced to remain *Sealed* only to Clavio, which had caused the body great strain.

His *Sealings* were never permanent. He needed a better method, something that lasted. He needed what Calthesya had—a way to keep living forever without limitations. But the enchantress—Mother Adriel, her last vessel—was dead, and her apprentice, Sesha, had been taken from the palace. Though he had at his disposal the best enchantresses in the world, the knowledge they possessed was incomplete. If he was to live forever, he needed Sesha. Rather, he needed the knowledge her mistress had imbued in her.

From his closet, Clavio selected the ceremonial tunic he wore as Thane of Perimat. Now that he was Prime Regent, and sole ruler following the death of the royal family, he would be expected to name a successor. He didn't have an heir—one of the unfortunate side-effects of the *Sealing* was impotence—but his wife did have many eligible nieces and nephews. He would be made to name one of them, and soon. He would have to stall that decision as long as he could. There were more important things on his mind today than succession.

He exited his room and nodded at the two Blue Scarabs that guarded it. The two men followed him down the corridor and into the main hall of the palace. The bubbling sound of mingling nobles would have preceded him before, but now there was only an empty hall. The sound of his boots echoed off the exposed marble floor as if to fill the vacuum of that silence.

Taking a left up the stairs, Clavio ascended the royal tower, but only to the second ring, where the council hall was situated. Clavio entered the hall and took his seat, flanked by his two imposing bodyguards. Already seated were the six ministers of his inner council. Hovering at the other side of the hall was Captain Velden, tolerated yet eyed distrustfully by the seated ministers.

"Thank you all for joining me," Clavio began. "I will get straight to the point. Thanks to Minister Koren's informants, we know that the report by Lord Reylin of a Sazisani invasion has circulated rapidly amongst the surviving nobles. Between a group of foreign invaders murdering the future queen and young prince, and the amount of noble houses who have lost their appointed lords and ladies in the attempted coup by the Free Kings, expectations of swift action on our part are high."

Clavio's gaze traveled across each face at the table as he continued. "We are in a tremendously chaotic time, and I fear that allowing the noble houses to appoint new heads right now would only expose more cracks for our enemies to possibly exploit. Because of this, I will be refusing approval of all new appointments of lords and ladies."

The sound of chairs creaking followed as all ministers but Koren shifted uncomfortably. "But then what is to be done about the houses whose lord and lady were killed during the coup? Who will run their lands?" asked Lord o'Thorpe, the Minister of Labors, rubbing the thick hairs at his chin.

"The same people who will be running all the other lands of Hovardom—the Blue Scarabs." Clavio paused, allowing his words to claim their rightful impact.

"You... you mean to implement a martial takeover?" sputtered Lord Trett, the Minister of Coin. His eyes wandered towards Captain Velden, who had moved across the hall to stand just behind Clavio.

"Yes," Clavio continued drolly, "and all laws, and liberties, except for those dictated by the First Folk in the Old Annals, shall also be suspended as such." The silence that followed was so profound that Clavio imagined he could almost hear the frantic spinning of his ministers' minds as they took in what he was saying. "Temporarily, of course."

"What reason do they have to agree to such terms?" pressed Minister Koren.

"They will have ample reason once they have seen the evidence I have uncovered that the Free King's infiltration of our palace and the slaughter of the nobles was funded by Sazisan all along."

"And what if they still refuse?" Lady Shenna, the Minister of Warcraft, met his eyes unflinchingly. Clavio had always appreciated the woman's fiery temperament.

"Then we will make them understand why this is necessary through... other means." Clavio's grin was catlike. "We will show them exactly what we are up against in this war." He reached his palm out towards the Blue Scarab on his right who handed him the strange Sazisani weapon they had 'recovered' from the site of the attack.

Clavio aimed the wand at a nearby chair and squeezed the trigger. A blast rang through the hall as the seat exploded into shards of wood. A puff of dark smoke lifted into the air around Clavio's head. When it cleared, he could see the faces before him had entirely drained of color.

"Gods' names! What was that?" one of them cursed.

"This is a wand," Clavio explained, holding the hot weapon in front of him. "It is the weapon the Sazisani intend to use to exterminate our people and seize our lands." Clavio took on a more placating tone. "Don't see my use of the Scarabs as a punishment, but as a gift. We are being actively invaded and infiltrated. We are at war. With our guard forces freed from managing towns, we will have more bodies for the front lines at the Red Coast. This is not time for debating and bickering. We must be resolute, and I must hold all the power until this is finished. Until I have led us to the glory that was promised us by the First Folk."

The frozen ministers seemed unsure of how to respond to all they had just learned. Clavio would give them time. They would all eventually bend to the will of the kingdom, just like the nobility of Sol Forne had. But it wasn't enough to heed his words—Clavio needed to taste their allegiance. He stared at each of them expectantly, as if to incept into their minds what they must do next. A timid applause broke out within the hall. Clavio knew it was a farce, a way for the fops before him to remain in his goodwill. But it did feel good to see them grovel when asked.

Clavio concluded the meeting by dismissing those in attendance and approaching Captain Velden. "We need to talk."

The old captain nodded and followed Clavio outside the hall and up the stairs to the fifth ring of the royal tower. By the time they reached the floor, Captain Velden was panting heavily. My, how old the man had grown. If it hadn't been for his sharp wits, Clavio—as Eggar—would have appointed someone younger to command the Blue Scarabs years ago.

"Any word on my niece?" Clavio inquired once the two men were in the room.

"I'm afraid not, sir," Velden said, his arms folded behind his back. "We've recovered her sword and pieces of her armor. But we do not have a good sense of where she went. She could be anywhere in Albadone, or beyond, by now."

"Locating her is the most important task you have," Clavio said, setting the wand on the heap of maps and documents that were scattered across his desk. Servants were not allowed in his office to tidy up, so the place had become rather dusty and disheveled. No one could be trusted near the secrets held within this room. He picked up his old journal, the brown pages nearly falling out of their binding, and thumbed through it delicately. The smell of sea salt still clinging to the old pages brought back ancient memories.

"We will find her," Velden assured.

"Good. No need to retrieve her yet. I just need to know where she is and what she is doing. Any news regarding the child and the *melk*?" Clavio asked, quickly changing the topic.

Velden answered without missing a beat, "The Scarabs followed their trail all the way to the outskirts of Pevine, a small town at the edge of Albadone. One of the men was devoured. The other said the *melk* stalked him through the woods the entire night. He was so delirious with fear when he returned he almost couldn't make his report to me. The child was not sighted with the *melk*, however. It's unclear where she is currently, but we will find her."

First, the errant knights he had hired to capture a *reaver-lord* had failed—or, rather, succeeded in killing the beast—and now, the *melk* he had captured was gone. Gods, but for every one thing that went right for him, two others went wrong.

"And the wretch?" Clavio asked, unable to hide the irritation in his voice.

"The..." Velden drifted off, his face taking on a strangely melancholy cast. "Oh! Yes. Renna... She could still be within the city, but we do not have a solid trail yet."

"Do you understand what we are doing here, Captain?" Clavio pinched the bridge of his nose. A headache pulsed behind his eyes.

"Yes, Master," Velden said, lowering his head.

"Because to me, it seems like you are intent on losing every single one of my assets. I don't care if you have to burn the forest to the ground all over again! Find them all."

"It will be done, Master," Velden said with a fist to his heart.

"Good. I put a lot of trust in you, Velden, because I know you can deliver results. Do not disappoint me again."

"Yes, Master."

Clavio clapped the man on the shoulder. "One last thing before you're dismissed. Now that the takeover has been initiated, it is time we commence the next phase of the war."

"The NPs?" Velden clarified.

Clavio nodded. "Round them up and bring them to the lodge. It's time for them to be deployed."

"Yes, Master." With another salute, Velden left the room.

There was satisfaction in knowing that a plan that had been put into motion decades ago was coming to fruition, warts and all. Clavio had turned the disaster in Albadone from a failure into a way to expedite his mission. It had been difficult to convince the previous king—his 'brother'—to go along with holding captive every chemist and healer who had fled to Vizen from nearby towns and villages. The decision had caused great confusion, but soon their purpose would become abundantly clear.

Still cradling his old journal, Clavio walked to the far side of the office and into the adjacent bedroom. The canopied bed concealed a withered shape within. Two enchantresses were bent over the figure, applying a salve to its scab-gray skin. Clavio dismissed the pair with a wave and forced himself to perform an assessment of his former body. The desiccated remains of his ancient self looked up at him with sightless blue eyes that were still somehow alive, its shriveled, nearly translucent, chest rising and falling with each ragged breath. Clavio sat on the chair across from the bed and opened the journal to where he had last left off his reading, and resumed:

"Though it is the smallest of all the halls contained within the great tower, the top floor is the most impressive. It took me nearly the full day to climb all those stairs, but it was worth it in the end. Four figures in flowing robes of carved white stone glared down at me from the ceiling. And, although they were only statues, I heard their voices in my skull as if they were standing in the room with me.

"I have not shared this encounter with anyone. Though I am their leader, I worry they would think me mad. I've tried to recall exactly what words were spoken, but I cannot

remember a single one. These new gods (as I am now certain that's what they are) spoke to me through impetus itself. Their message to me and my people did not need words.

"These Nameless Gods have gifted us with a new fertile land to be our domain. These pre-built structures belong to us. They have ALWAYS belonged to us, for this is our home by holy mandate and I have been chosen to lead it. Our first city shall be named Vizen, the ancient word for 'vision', for I have been given a vision of a prosperous kingdom to rival any of those of the Old World. A kingdom that will never die."

Clavio glanced up from the page and into the slack, mummified, face of his former self. The vision from that long distant past is what had driven his quest for immortality ever since—had driven him into and out of a carousel of bodies and identities throughout the centuries until he no longer could tell the parts of him that were original from the borrowed bits he had acquired in the process. That is why he enjoyed reading from the old journal. It was like being reminded of a friend he had once been much closer to.

He had seen everyone who had known him wither and die and had met new people to care for and watched them die as well. He had watched so many iterations of loss that the feeling no longer touched him at all. He could no longer care for mortal things as he once had. Now, his only love was the kingdom itself—its vastness, its complexity. Like him, it was something that was more than alive. And, like the old shell of his first form, Claud the Chosen, if the Nameless continued to bless him, it too would never die.

XXXVI.

THE STRANGER

"Stand still!" Lyr chastised.

A tuft of hair fell from Rovan's forehead to tickle his nose. He wiped his face, stifling the sneeze that threatened to erupt.

"I thought you said you had done this before," Rovan complained.

"No, I said I've used scissors before," Lyr corrected. "Sheared some goats once, in the market. But I've never cut a person's hair before."

The woodsfolk had a saying for just about every situation—surely there was one about not antagonizing a person holding sharp objects near your face. Rovan sighed, allowing Lyr to resume whatever she was doing to him. It had been two weeks since his return to Pevine, but his hair had needed a cut for quite some time. The dirty blonde locks had grown to an unruly mop of tangles and points. Whatever mess Lyr made could not be worse than the one he already had—and could easily be corrected by a razor, he thought grimly.

While he was gone, Iseo and Terreck had continued repairing homes. Led by Yona, they had helped complete the roof Rovan had been working on before he left, and two more to boot. It was an impressive feat and one that Iseo would not stop boasting about. Under Terreck's eye, Iseo seemed to have grown stronger and more confident of his place in their group. When they eventually ventured beyond Pevine, Rovan was confident Iseo would ask to travel with them.

Fellen, on the other hand, worried Rovan more than ever. It wasn't his behavior but his health that was concerning. While they had been able to find tasks to occupy the teenager's time, his leg still refused to heal right. Rovan feared the boy would not be able to walk without the use of crutches. Fellen, for his part, had convinced himself and everyone else that it was only a matter of time before he returned to his normal, healthy, self. Behind his words, though, Rovan caught the scent of bravado and, beneath that, fear. His heart ached for the boy.

Lyr had arrived in Pevine three days after Rovan and Sesha. She had been trapped in Vizen after the drawbridge was raised and only managed to escape by bribing her way out. She and a few others who could afford the privilege were smuggled out of the city walls and boated across the moat in the dead of night. She then took the Red Road south, hitching a ride on a mulecart just before the first Blue Scarab outpost. It was a good story that Lyr eagerly shared at the dinner table. Everything else that had happened to her at the royal palace, Lyr kept to herself. Her gratitude that no one pried or asked any further questions was apparent.

"There," Lyr said after a final cut. She ran her hand through Rovan's locks, then brushed away the dusting of hair from his head and shoulders. She glanced about the hall of the tavern in search of something. "Keith, do you have a looking glass?" she called out.

"I believe so," the barkeep called back. The man retreated into the door behind the bar, reemerging a few moments later with a small, circular mirror. He handed the object to Lyr, then stood nearby examining Rovan's hair.

"It's that bad?" Rovan asked the man.

"Hush!" Lyr said, slapping his shoulder. She held the looking glass in front of his face, and Rovan took a long look.

His hair hadn't looked this well-kept in years—not since he was a boy intent on keeping up the pretense of being a noble. Even though he had been rude to her and she had never shared his misguided ambitions, his sister Ensa had cut his hair every week, keeping it neatly trimmed over the ear and well-maintained. Seeing himself like this reinforced that he was no longer that boy. He had chased redemption for so long for all the misdeeds of his youth, ignoring that the only person he needed forgiveness from was himself.

"I have a razor if you want to do away with that beard," Keith said.

"No," Rovan replied. "Thanks, Keith, but I'll keep the beard." While the haircut reminded him of who he had been, the beard would be a reminder of who he was now. Rovan stood from the chair and patted loose strands from his lap. "Thank you, Lyr. It looks wonderful."

Lyr smiled and nodded. "I can do the others too if they'd like," she offered.

"Wouldn't be a bad idea," Terreck said, as he entered the tavern and walked towards them. "Fellen's hair, especially, is starting to look... unruly. Like the mane of a crazed cat." Rain dripped from Terreck's hood as the wet mud from his boots left tracks across the floor. Keith's dismayed eyes darted between the mud, the pooling water, and the pile of hair at Rovan's feet. His toil was truly endless.

"Send him over here, then," Lyr said.

"Will do," Terreck replied. The young man opened his hood and Trinket hopped out. The cat walked under the nearby chair and began to claw at the tufts of hair beneath. "They're back," Terreck said.

"Tieg and Scintilla?" Rovan asked, excitedly.

"No. That person that's been wandering around the area," Terreck said. "I was having a smoke, and I saw them crawl into Yemma's barn when the rain picked up. They're still in there, I think."

Rovan nodded to himself. He had told his friends to keep an eye out for any strangers wandering into town. He knew at some point they would have to contend with the Blue Scarabs that were searching for Sesha and the *melk*. Pevine had been forgotten by the world for several years—its recent efforts to rebuild could attract renewed interest he'd prefer to avoid.

This stranger, however, looked more like a vagabond than anything else. Rovan had spotted them twice before, once outside of town while gathering wood, and once within town, but always from a distance. He had approached the stranger, but they had fled. Rovan did not wish to scare them, only to see if they needed any help or shelter.

"Got anything cooking?" Rovan asked Keith.

"Just the perennial stew," Keith replied.

"Could you fix me a bowl? And I'll need an empty plate as well, please."

Keith nodded and retreated into the kitchen, returning moments later with a bowl full of fragrant potato and onion stew, and a plate. Rovan grabbed the two and used the plate to shield the stew from the rain outside. "Thanks, Keith," he said and headed for the door.

Keith stared at the pile of hair on the floor. "You kids sure like making messes for me to clean."

"Sorry, Keith! I'll sweep it up when I'm back," Lyr assured, sprinting ahead of Rovan to hold the door open for him.

Rovan nodded at her in thanks and exited the tavern, followed by his two friends. The pelting rain never ended. Being wet was now a part of everyday life—Rovan hardly spared it a second thought anymore.

Yemma's barn stood towards the far end of the town. It had once been a warehouse, but now it housed two goats and a few chickens. Yemma, its owner, was very protective of the place, and would not react kindly to a stranger seeking shelter within it. Rovan would have to relocate this stranger. Or perhaps he could convince Yemma to let the stranger stay for a while—the old woman seemed to have a sweet spot for him, especially after all the fencing he had built for her.

There were fewer buildings near the barn, giving the wind passage to whip wildly at their hoods. Rovan had hoped their entrance would be covert and cautious, but a sudden gust had him hugging the bowl to his chest and running for the door. Terreck raced past him and held the door open for Rovan and Lyr to enter, then followed them inside, the door slamming loudly behind them.

"Nameless' arses! What's with that wind?" Terreck exclaimed.

Lyr blotted rain from her face. The wind had removed her hood and whipped her hair into a frenzy. She wrung her drenched locks dry like a rag.

The interior of the dark barn was illuminated briefly by a flash of lightning outside. Two goats roamed freely, approaching them and licking at the water dripping from their clothes. The chickens, on the other hand, were clucking in frustration on the other side of a small wooden enclosure. Their clucking became frenzied each time a roll of thunder sounded.

There was another flash of lightning. Lyr touched Rovan's shoulder and pointed at the far side of the barn. On the floor, behind a stack of hay, was the dark outline of a boot. The shape moved slightly, as if trying to retreat further behind the pile of hay. Rovan did not wish to scare the stranger away if they were in need of shelter and a meal. But he also needed to be sure they did not pose a danger to the people of the town.

"Hello," Rovan greeted pleasantly. "My name is Rovan. Two of my friends are here too." It seemed like a good idea to reveal that to the stranger as a means of gaining their trust. "I brought you something to eat. If you want to stay here, I can speak to the owner of the barn and see if that's alright. Otherwise, Yemma might chase you out with a pitchfork when she finds you." This attempt at levity did nothing to coax a response from the figure.

"There's a tavern in town," Rovan continued. "It has rooms upstairs that are unoccupied. You could stay there if you'd like. It's dry, and Keith brews a great cup of tea. And it also smells a lot less like manure in there." Rovan took a few steps forward. The stranger's leg tensed as if they were preparing to hop up and run.

"Are you hungry?" Rovan asked, attempting a different approach. "I have a bowl of stew here. It has potatoes."

"And onions," Terreck added.

"I'm approaching to hand you the bowl. Then, you can decide if you want to stay here for the night or follow us to the tavern. There's plenty more stew there if you wish." No response came, so Rovan decided to test his luck and moved closer to the pile of hay. One of the goats followed him, continuing to lick the rain from his cloak.

As Rovan circumvented the pile of hay, the stranger stood. With his eyes adjusted to the dark, he could tell she was a woman near his age. Her short dark hair clung wetly to the sides of her face. Her jaw was a severe line. Muscles tensed beneath her soiled clothes. The woman was tall—taller than Rovan—and imposing. She met his eye and Rovan found himself unable to utter a word. He handed her the bowl of stew, which she took. She removed the plate lidding the bowl and took in the stew's savory scent.

"No spoon?" she asked in a trickle of a voice.

Rovan shook his head. "I'm sorry. I didn't think about that."

The woman glanced down at the stew, visibly disappointed, then raised the bowl to her mouth and drank it down in a few steady gulps. When she was done, she wiped her mouth with the back of her arm. Chunks of potato that were too big to drink remained in the bowl.

"There's more at the tavern. And spoons. We have many spoons there." Rovan shook his head. Why had he suddenly turned into a sputtering buffoon?

The woman handed him the bowl, and Rovan was certain she would refuse and ask them to leave. "All right." Her voice was clear and steady.

Rovan found himself grinning. "My name is Rovan."

"You already said that," the woman replied.

"I did, didn't I?"

The woman sighed and wiped the wet hair from her stark face. "I'm Sear—" She halted abruptly, thinking something over in her mind. After a few moments, she said, "Zinia. My name is Zinia."

"Zinia?" Lyr repeated.

The woman turned to Lyr, sizing her up.

"I have a friend named Zinia... had..." Lyr trailed off.

A frown tugged at the sides of Zinia's mouth.

"This way," Rovan said, heading for the door. Something about Lyr had bothered the stranger. Any idiot could tell that the woman had not given them her true name, but it did not matter to him. He was happy enough that she was following him to the tavern—and out of Yemma's barn. Rovan's instincts for character had mostly led him true and they were telling him now that, whatever secret this woman was hiding, posed him and his friends no harm.

They led the stranger within the bustling tavern. Lyr headed behind the bar and retrieved a broom. She hastily began sweeping the pile of Rovan's hair out onto the street.

Rovan led Zinia towards an empty table and invited her to sit down. The woman glanced suspiciously about the tavern, then selected a chair facing the door. Keith was nowhere to be seen, so Rovan headed for the kitchen and poured two bowls of soup before returning to the main hall. His heart jumped in alarm when he saw the empty table where the woman had sat just moments ago.

He was relieved to find her crouching beneath the table, petting Trinket, who displayed his belly pathetically. Rovan set the bowl of stew on the table, and Zinia immediately straightened up, tense and alert.

"There's a spoon there, this time," Rovan pointed out with a half-smile.

Zinia's scowl softened as she stared down at the stew. Taking the spoon in hand, she began eating heartily. Rovan had intended to join the woman, but her guarded demeanor disinvited him. From a separate table, he watched as Zinia ate her food methodically and without stopping. Her eyes were wide and haunted. Rovan had learned to recognize such a look in the eyes of his friends.

Rovan took his spoon and dug in. The stew was a bit bland, but it was warm and there was plenty of it, at least.

※ ※ ※ ※

Two days had passed since Zinia's arrival in Pevine, and she had still not opened up to any of them. The closest they had gotten was when she had asked Terreck some questions about his cat, who showed her more affection than Rovan had ever received from the furball. Besides that, she kept to herself, only appearing within the main hall of the tavern when it was time to eat. Lyr and Fellen had been covering the cost of her meals by doing odd jobs around the tavern. Eventually, Zinia would have to work for her keep. She never inquired about where the food came from—she seemed to expect it to always be there around the same time. What sort of upbringing made one assume such a thing?

Rovan had resumed his construction duties alongside the townsfolk. The rain had taken a break today, so Yona, the town's de facto foreman, had Rovan sitting atop a home laying out bundles of dried straw across the roof.

"Rovan!" a child's voice called out.

On the street below stood two hooded women flanking a little girl. Rovan smiled at the sight. "Well returned, you three!" he greeted. "Give me a moment and I'll be right there." Rovan laid down a small section of straw, then headed down the ladder leaning against the roof. As soon as he reached the ground, Sesha tackled him affectionately. He returned the hug, patting the child's head.

"It's good to see you all," he said, looking at the two women. "What brings you back to Pevine?"

"The Womb of the World is a... strange place," Alanda voiced. "The people there have been asking many questions about Mother Adriel's whereabouts—questions we cannot answer. They've been insistent and downright hostile as of late. We may very well move here, but Sesha—"

"All my things are there!" Sesha interrupted.

Ashe crossed her arms and pointed out west—towards the general direction of the mountain—and then at Pevine, as if to say, "*We can bring your things here.*"

It seemed to Rovan like an argument the three had already had.

"The enchanting bench is too heavy to move!" Sesha complained. "I need it to enchant items, and Shriek can't carry it."

"She insists on remaining an enchantress," Alanda explained to Rovan. She sounded unconvinced by the prospect.

"What else would I do?" Sesha asked. "It's what I've been brought up to be."

At those words, Ashe twisted her mouth. Rovan recognized the regret in the woman's face. "Where is Shriek, anyways?" Rovan changed the subject.

"In the woods, hunting," Alanda said.

Though the *melk* was a terrifying creature to behold, Rovan wished he could see it one more time. It was boyish curiosity, like the need to run a hand over the open flame of a sconce. "We can help you carry your things," Rovan said to the girl. "We can rent out a mulecart in town. I'm sure we could do it in a couple of trips."

Sesha shook her head. "Pevine just doesn't have good enough *life energy* resonance."

"It's always something," Alanda said, sharing a grin with Ashe.

"It's true," Sesha insisted. "You might not feel it, but I do! This town feels sad and asleep. The mountain feels awake, like a song."

Rovan found himself nodding in agreement. "Very well," he said. "So, to what do we owe the pleasure of this visit?"

Sesha reached into the large travel sack hanging from Ashe's shoulder, as Alanda pleaded, "Easy! Easy!" From the sack, she produced a small wooden box and handed it to Rovan.

The box felt weighty in his hands. Items rolled and rattled within. Atop the box's lid was a scuffed and faded carving of a fox, its coloring long gone. "What's this?" he asked.

"It's Mother's... Mother Adriel's things," Sesha said. Her voice had taken on a gray hue.

Rovan opened the box. Within were three smooth stones standing atop a pile of brown envelopes. Though they looked like runestones, their blackness was like no other runestone he had ever seen. Two had the half-moon of *Power* etched onto them, while one had the circle of *Warding*. A fourth stone was there too, though that one was gray and cracked. He could feel *life energy* radiating from them, dangerous like a lick of flame. "What are these?" he asked.

"Mother Adriel wrote about them in some of her more recent notes. They are cursed runestones. Attuning them or releasing their essence is how their curse is unleashed."

"Why would she make these?" Rovan asked.

"She didn't make them," Sesha replied. "I don't think she even knew how. The notes say that someone has been sending them to her through other people. An errant knight gave her one—the gray one there. She opened that one and released the curse. That's how she found out what they did."

Rovan felt suddenly uncomfortable holding this box of cursed runestones. "Who would send these to her? Why would she keep them, if she knew what they did?"

Sesha shrugged. "To study them? I don't know. Maybe you can help me figure that out." She reached into the box and pulled out a few of the old envelopes from beneath the runestones. "Take a look at these."

Ashe took the box from Rovan to free his hands. Rovan thanked the woman and took the envelopes from Sesha. He reached into one and pulled out an old letter. The handwriting was in no language he could read. "What does this say?" he asked.

"I don't know," Sesha said. "I don't speak Elven."

"Elven?" Rovan gasped. "How do you know this is Elven?"

"From the notes. Some of the oldest notes are written in the same language. One time I asked Mother Adriel about them, and she told me it was in Elven. But that's all she would say."

Rovan leafed through the letters, though he could not read them. "So, what do you need from me?"

"You're more well-traveled than anyone else we know," Alanda said. "Do you know anybody who can read these letters?"

"Finding an Elven linguist is not an easy thing to do," he considered. "You would have to go to the Academy of Sol Forne, or to one of the Magstian libraries. Or—"

He halted himself as the thought came to him, obvious and unbidden. "Or you would have to find a native speaker."

"A native speaker?" Alanda asked. "And where would we find that? Last I checked, there aren't any elvenfolk around."

"No," Rovan said. "Not an elvenfolk. But I do know a djinn."

EPILOGUE

CENTURIES AGO...

The ocean was a shimmering orange tongue lapping up the lingering traces of the red setting sun. Distant ships littered the waves like a coalescing of insects. Vaelin could not remember the last time she had seen ships in motion. Those she had been watching for the last few hundred years had been stalled at the port of Llywelyn—the ones the elvenfolk had left behind to weather and rot. But no, the ones she now observed were alive, populated by crews and passengers. Relief bloomed in her heart even as the ache of her Compulsion grew more acute as if it could sense the proximity to new souls.

Ever since the elvenfolk had returned their bodies and minds to the Cycle of Nature in order to right a terrible imbalance caused by their abuse of the enchanting arts, Vaelin had been living with the Remnant in the north. Their small community had aided Vaelin by providing her with a steady source of Contracts until she decided to venture out into the world, seeking the source of her enslavement—the *lucerne*.

Her hunt for the object had gone on for the greater part of a century with nothing to show for it. And the only person in proximity for her to Contract had been Calthesya, the Oath breaker. It was not ideal, but she had to stay alive, or she would render the sacrifice of the elvenfolk pointless.

Striking regular Contracts and placating the Compulsion within her was an essential part of maintaining the Cycle of Nature. Again, this too was a consequence of the elvenfolk's own making, but Vaelin no longer wished to dwell on that. Centuries of enduring the agony of their absence had made resentment too costly a thing to hold onto. The scope of her life had narrowed to the pinpoint of survival. At least, until she had seen those ships on the horizon. And now—

Before the elvenfolk had left, the world was scarred and blighted. Plants had refused to grow, beasts had become savage and bloodthirsty, earthquakes had blistered the land, and the air had thinned. Ferocious summers had made way for uncaring winters. So many had perished. It had taken a great sacrifice—the Great Return—to heal the Cycle of Nature. Even now, three hundred years later, the world was still recovering, though it was showing great signs of improvement. Once again, the Cycle sang to Vaelin with its melodious voice.

"You seem pensive." The croaking sound startled Vaelin. She turned to face the ancient enchantress. The woman leaned heavily on her cane, her withered bones barely capable of carrying her.

"You should not be walking around, Calthesya," Vaelin admonished. "You need your rest."

"BAH!" the old woman spat. "Should I have Contracted you to carry me?"

Vaelin rolled her eyes and winced. The old crone was such a bother. Vaelin reached for Calthesya's arm and held it. Despite her ever-sour attitude, Calthesya leaned into

Vaelin, accepting the support. "I couldn't stay in bed knowing they were coming."

Vaelin nodded. "Do you know who they are?"

"No," the woman replied. "The Cycle has not revealed that much to me. All I know is that they are not from here. I can sense their *life energy*. They are scared. Hungry. Tired. They have traveled a long way to find this place."

"What do you intend to do with them?" Vaelin asked.

"Observe them, at first. Then, if I find any worthy of it, I will teach them Chanter's Tongue and the enchanting arts."

Vaelin was taken aback. "You're not afraid that they will repeat the mistakes of those who came before?"

"I am terrified that they will. That's precisely why I broke the Oath. The Remnant believe the enchanting arts can be buried and hidden away, but I know that the Cycle calls out to people. And I know that there is more value in guidance than in hiding."

"I hope you're right." Vaelin watched as the ship leading the fleet floated closer to the port below. It wouldn't take long for it to dock. She could feel Calthesya's prying eyes on her cheek. "What is it?" Vaelin asked.

"I assume their arrival means our collaboration is close to an end," Calthesya said.

"How do you mean?"

"I know very well how much it strains you to have a single source for Contracts. You must be excited to be able to source them from others."

Indeed, that was exactly what Vaelin had been mulling over. After decades of using Calthesya as her sole Contract, the *life energy* that inundated Vaelin each time had grown staler and staler. Where once she had felt alert and capable of anything upon fulfilling a Contract, the exchanges with Calthesya only left her feeling sluggish and barely suppressed the burning tug of the Compulsion for more than a few hours. If it hadn't been a necessity, she would have stopped ages ago.

"I am," Vaelin answered. "But just like you, I am wary of these newcomers. I will observe them too until I am sure that they are worthy of forging Contracts with me."

Calthesya smirked, her gray skin sagging around the contours of her old skull. "May I ask for a favor when you're amongst them?"

"What is it?" Vaelin asked.

"I need you to watch for youngsters who have a predisposition for hearing the Cycle of Nature. Those who resonate strongly with *life energy*. You will be able to sense them."

Vaelin arched an eyebrow. "You trust my judgment to that extent?"

"Unfortunately, I do. I need apprentices. I need folk to carry on my legacy long after this body is dead."

The ship docked at the port below. A plank was lowered and a small group of people descended. What must they be thinking, finding a fully intact abandoned city on this new continent? Vaelin could only hope that, whoever these people were, they would take good care of this newly healed land. That they would not be like the Elveshari, so taken by advancement that they did not stop and think about what the cost of such progress would be.

"Very well," Vaelin agreed. "I will keep an eye out for any such individuals."

"And if you find anyone exceedingly powerful, bring them to me right away," Calthesya added.

Even from afar, the appearance of these newcomers was unusual. Their skin tones varied but they all shared a warmth, as if each person had swallowed the orange light of a candle's flame.

"What ugly creatures," Calthesya remarked.

Vaelin didn't waste her breath on disagreeing although, in truth, she found their appearance captivating. Calthesya shifted slightly and lost her bearing. Thankfully, Vaelin was there to catch and steady her. "Let's get you back to the cabin before you collapse," Vaelin said.

Before leading the woman away, Vaelin stole another glance at the people crowding onto the docks. She had to hold onto the hope that these people would be better than the elvenfolk. And, truly, they had an advantage. They had Calthesya who, for all her faults, would teach them to respect the Cycle of Nature. And they had Vaelin, who would be there to counsel them every step of the way.

Hope glimmered in her heart. Perhaps this new world could be better. It had to be.

About The Authors

Élan Marché and Christopher Warman met in high school in Oklahoma in 2009. After dating for a decade, they got married in 2020. They currently live in Los Angeles where they work and spend their time watching TV, reading, writing, cooking delicious meals, and generally enjoying each other's company.

www.ingramcontent.com/pod-product-compliance
Lightning Source LLC
LaVergne TN
LVHW041736060526
838201LV00046B/832